TERESA RICHARDS

Evernight Teen ®

www.evernightteen.com

Copyright© 2017

Teresa Richards

ISBN: 978-1-77339-433-6

Cover Artist: Jay Aheer

Editor: Audrey Bobak

TERESA RICHARDS

DEDICATION

For Tyson, Jeremy, Hannah, Callie, and Seth. Thanks for being my greatest fans and for giving me a reason to prove that dreams are worth chasing.

TERESA RICHARDS

TOPAZ REIGN

Teresa Richards

Copyright © 2017

Chapter One

Hardly a Council of War

Lindy

1623—Valstenia
(Southern tip of modern-day Sweden)

The Baltic Sea sparkled below as I clung to the side of a cliff.

Though, perhaps, cliff was too strong of a word. Precipice, maybe. Or overhang. No matter what it was called, clinging was definitely required.

My fingers went numb, my arms shook, and my feet strained to find purchase on the rocky wall.

And I loved every minute of it.

Since my father had died, this was the only place I could go to be alone. To think. To work through the seemingly unsolvable problems I'd been left with. The better cliffs were farther north and to the west, but they were a day's journey away at best. And I couldn't be gone that long.

So I resorted to this … precipice … whenever I needed to think.

It had been a week and a day since my father, King Edvin, had died. In the seven years I'd been home since Maggie defeated the Emerald that had held me bound for four centuries, I'd grown to enjoy life in a castle. I'd bonded with my parents and younger siblings, Carina and Felipe. I'd learned to act like royalty, though I still found myself slipping up after my long years of servitude.

But I had not learned how to be Queen—had certainly not expected I'd be Queen so soon. No one had. And now my Uncle Oliver—or O, as my brother Garon called him—was back, claiming a stolen Topaz posed a dire threat to our kingdom.

I'd wanted to tell him to get in line. Drought posed a threat to our kingdom. A lack of funds posed a threat to our kingdom. Thieves attacking at our borders were a threat to the kingdom. And certainly, I, inexperienced as I was, posed as dire a threat to our kingdom as there ever was.

But with my brother Garon gone and my sister Yelena married to a German baron, I was next in line for the throne. My mother, with her quiet strength, had been a great comfort to me in this new and unexpected role. But it had actually been Borov, my father's most trusted guard, who had best helped me transition to Queen. He nudged when I needed it, supported when I needed it, and corrected—gently—when I needed it. He'd been training me to be Queen since the moment I'd returned, without ever saying anything outright.

A voice floated to me on the breeze. "Queen Shalyndria," it called. Then, more urgently, "Queen Shalyndria, where are you?"

Oh, no. It was Lillian, my handmaid. How had she

found me?

I finished my climb, pulling myself to the top and heaving my body over the ledge. And there, right in front of me, were Lillian's worn shoes—dusty, and with the ties coming undone. She held a horse by the reins.

"Highness, what are you doing?"

I stood.

She sucked in a breath. "What are you *wearing*?"

Well, I couldn't exactly rock climb in a dress. So I'd been doing it in my undergarments—white pantalets and a linen shift top.

Lillian's eyes went wide. "Where are your stays, child? You're positively indecent."

I grabbed my dress from the branch I'd thrown it over, but my stays—early cousins of the corset—were hidden under my bed, where I'd stashed them a few days ago. "Don't tell Mother."

She helped me back into my dress while the wind whipped a lock of her hair free from her cap. "Of course, Your Highness."

I cringed. I could do without everyone calling me that, especially this woman who was twice my age.

"Borov requests your presence in the council room at once."

I glanced at the sun—it was sitting well above the horizon—and my heartbeat ticked up a notch. Waves crashed on the shore below us. "Oh, no. I lost track of the time!"

"The council members are just arriving. Take the horse. I'll walk back."

"We can both ride." I mounted and held my hand out to help her up.

"With respect, Milady, I'll walk."

I huffed. "Lillian, you get on this horse right now." It

wasn't exactly proper for a servant to share my horse. But, really, what was the big deal? I wasn't going to make her hike all the way back up to the castle—it was my fault she'd had to come find me in the first place.

It was a walk I enjoyed. I'd risen before the sun in order to make it. And I'd left myself plenty of time to get back—had I been paying attention to the time.

Lillian eyed the switchbacks leading up to the castle and then sighed. She grabbed my outstretched hand and I helped her onto the horse.

"Good choice." I urged the horse onward, and he carried us back to my family's castle. The closer we got, the steeper the terrain became. Our castle was built into a mountainside, with the front facing the town of Korona, and the back looking out over the sea.

Mare Balticum. It was a sea which was constantly being fought over for control of trade routes. Our position on it made us strong, giving us free access to the trade routes, and the ability to see a seaside attack long before the aggressor got close enough to fire. For this reason, we were rarely attacked from the sea.

We started up the switchback trail that wound up and around the side of the castle, shifting our body weight forward to ease the horse's burden as he climbed.

My mind mirrored the switchbacks, winding back and forth around the knowledge that, like some horrible twist of fate, I was once again responsible for stopping a threat that involved one of Oliver's creations. As soon as we reached the castle, I'd be expected to explain this threat to the members of the council my father had relied on to assist in matters of safety to the kingdom.

A voice inside my head insisted that I should not be the one in charge. That I'd already failed my country once by letting the Emerald live on when I could have stopped it, and that I was going to fail again.

But failure was not an option. I was all my country had.

At least this time my Uncle Oliver was here. He'd been hesitant to tell me much about the Topaz, but if I was going to stop it, I needed to know everything he did.

Today was the day. I had to get him to talk.

The horse clomped across the drawbridge that spanned the chasm separating the front of the castle from the path leading into town. As soon as we entered the front gates, I slid off the horse.

Captain Borov was waiting for me, standing at attention and exuding precisely the right amount of authority—his broad shoulders squared and his features stern, mixed with a trace of submissiveness in the bow of his head. His hair, which had slowly gone gray since my return to Valstenia, only increased his authoritative appearance. He was the most loyal of guards—my father had been right to trust him with his life.

"All the arrangements have been made, Your Highness. Please, come with me." He didn't mention the fact that I'd disappeared on a very important morning, or point out that my hands were dirty.

I stepped into the grand hallway, letting him trail behind me even though I much preferred walking by his side. My proper place as Queen was at the head of any entourage, even a two-person one. Tapestries and ancient weapons hung on the stone walls, adorning the bare spaces from one wooden door to the next.

Borov spoke as we walked. "Madam Hansen was back this morning. Says the royal chickens are still getting into her grain."

"She's only after a new fence, at our expense."

"Still, she must be pacified. She's the largest supplier

of grain in Korona. And then there's King Qadar. He continues to press for a marriage alliance."

I scowled. A faraway king whom I'd never met wanted to marry me, and I couldn't figure out why. Which made me leery.

"I'll give him an answer soon."

"Additionally, the troops in Duke Christoph's territory are due for leave, but we don't have the funds to hire replacements. It appears the tax relief your father instituted was not sustainable."

I stopped walking. "I'm not raising taxes."

"The reserve is drying up, Your Highness. We must act quickly, or we run the risk of the men deserting." The Captain nudged my elbow.

I continued down the corridor. "There has to be another way. We'll find it somehow. Is everyone here for the meeting?"

"Everyone except Duke Christoph, who sends his apologies. He felt it best that he stay and rally his men, given the fact that no replacements are coming. But Oliver is in the council room, along with King Jershon of Trellboro, and the council of five that your father formed to assist in matters of war. And of course, your mother and elder sister."

My head rose sharply. "Yelena is here?"

"Yes, Highness," Borov answered. "Your mother thought Yelena's presence would be a comfort to you. It *is* your first council of war."

"This is hardly a council of war, Captain. My uncle's missing gem is a minor threat to our kingdom's security, nothing more." I said the words, hoping I'd believe them more once they were out of my mouth.

I didn't.

For years, my Uncle Oliver had been referred to

simply as O, while he traveled the country as an elusive and mysterious medicine man. He'd been back at the castle only a few days, and he was still very much a mystery. I didn't know how forthcoming he would be.

"All the same, Highness. It is my job to ever prepare for the worst." Borov halted outside of a heavy, steel-studded door. "Ready?"

I lifted my chin and gave a slight nod. He opened the door.

Nine people stood as I entered the room. My mother and sister smiled. Oliver grimaced. King Jershon, the grizzled old man from the country east of ours, looked like he might fall asleep. But the five council members' faces were tight, their expressions guarded. Tension rolled off their bodies and filled the air.

There was an empty seat where Duke Christoph usually sat.

I glided to my place at the front, my hands clenched by my sides, and reminded myself to keep my eyes up. After four centuries of servitude, my natural tendencies were anything but queenly. I caught my mother's gaze, and her expression was tender—like she was watching me take my first steps.

"Be seated," I commanded, noting that I'd kept my voice from wobbling.

I waited for the group to settle. "There is a threat to Valstenia's security. You have been summoned in the hopes that, together, we may quench this threat peacefully and maintain good relations with all of our neighboring countries." I nodded toward King Jershon of Trellboro, with whom my father had been discussing a merge before his untimely passing. Not that a merge with the tiny Eastern province would have done much good. Trellboro had even less resources than Valstenia did.

I turned to my uncle. "Oliver, would you explain the nature of the threat to our esteemed allies and council members?"

Oliver stood. His movements were stiff, and his expression tight. "Certainly, Highness." He bowed his head slightly, then turned to face the council.

"I am the late King Edvin's younger brother. I am a healer. An alchemist. Some also call me a magician."

One of the council members said, "Is it true you use blood magic?"

There was a collective intake of breath.

Oliver squared his shoulders. "No."

"Please, no questions until he's done talking," I said. "Go on, Uncle. We must know all there is to know."

Oliver continued. "As a youth, I traveled widely, seeking knowledge. I studied physics, chemistry, alchemy, and medicine. I learned all I could of the earth's laws, plants, and minerals. I sat in council with the great thinkers of Europe. I traveled through the Ottoman Empire, and into Asia where I sought spiritual enlightenment at the hands of holy men. Additionally, I consorted with thieves, soothsayers, and harlots."

Murmurs circled the room. My mother's lips came together in a tight line.

Oliver's chin jutted out. "There is much to be learned by knowing all classes and types of people. I have made mistakes, and done things I'm not proud of. But I've done some good as well. Additionally, I made some fantastic discoveries."

He paused.

I leaned forward, watching my uncle closely.

It seemed he was waiting for the very eyes of heaven to be trained on him before he continued. Then slowly, almost reverently, he said, "I have created three artifacts.

Through the use of these artifacts, one can control wealth, beauty, and age."

A collective gasp echoed throughout the room.

"Unholy," I heard someone whisper.

"It's witchcraft," hissed another.

King Jershon's eyelids popped open.

Oliver paid them no mind. "Your Queen was unfortunate enough to learn the negative unforeseen consequences of one of my discoveries, but she has put the threat of wealth to rest." He glanced at me and his features softened. "At great personal sacrifice, I might add."

I looked down at my hands while images of my four hundred years of servitude surfaced in my mind. Watching Calista and Theo lure innocent girls into their cursed inn and being powerless to stop it. Seeing their stolen lives encased in the newly created emeralds I was in charge of harvesting. Those girls had been trapped— some of them for centuries—before Maggie set them free. Did they have lasting memories of the harrowing experience?

I thought of all the time I'd lost with my family. My brother who'd tried to help me and become trapped in time because of it. And Maggie—had she been able to move on from the nightmare she'd endured at my hands?

King Jershon, now fully awake, leaned forward in his chair. "What form does the current threat take?"

Oliver squared his shoulders and looked directly at him. "Beauty."

Chapter Two

Game Plan

Lindy

1623—Valstenia

At the news that we were dealing with a threat of beauty, the tension bled out of the council room. All around me, shoulders slumped, sighs escaped, and bodies leaned back in their chairs. A few council members actually laughed.

I alone remained tense—fully aware that just because the danger wasn't obvious didn't mean it wasn't there.

Oliver said, "The threat comes from a Topaz that grants beauty to its bearer."

A member of the city council voiced the sentiment for everyone but me. "Beauty is hardly a threat."

"Those were precisely my thoughts when I created the gem that grants beauty to its bearer," Oliver said. "But ponder, for a moment, on the power possessed by a beautiful person. A woman, perhaps. Does she not achieve, with relative ease, whatever she seeks? Do men not go out of their way to assist her when perhaps no assistance is required? Could such a woman take advantage of the spell she casts on others and work mischief where they least expect it?" Oliver was breathing hard, his face flushed. "Make no mistake, my friends, one who holds the gift of beauty is a formidable foe."

I sensed there was more to it than that. Something Oliver was keeping back.

My mother, the former Queen Maren, spoke for the first time. "And who now possesses this unnatural gift? I gather you no longer have the cursed Topaz?"

"Sadly, it fell out of my care through … ahm … poor judgment." Oliver cleared his throat. "The woman who now possesses it holds a grudge against the royal family. I believe she plans to seize possession of the crown and take command of Valstenia's armies. But she will be subtle—you will not see her coming until it is too late."

My sister said, "So, what is to be done?" Her tone was steely and her gaze pinned Oliver in place until he squirmed. My sister would have taken to the crown like a thief to an open market.

"Security must be increased," a councilman volunteered.

Another added, "The markets must be purged of riffraff."

The council members began speaking over one another.

"The King's Guard needs new recruits."

"Large cities should prepare for siege by storing food and water."

"Husbandmen must be alerted and given means to protect the kingdom's crops."

My head spun. "In order to destroy this threat, we need to understand it."

"No, Highness, first we must find it," Oliver said.

"We need to understand it before we go looking for it. For example, are there any lasting consequences or side effects from its use? Does it do anything in addition to granting beauty? Did you build in a fail-safe with this gemstone like you did with the Emerald? Is there a path already in place for its destruction?"

Oliver flinched. "Destruction is not necessary,

Highness. All we must do is recover the Topaz—get it out of the wrong hands."

"But what if it falls into the wrong hands again?" councilman number four asked.

"I agree. It's a risk I'm not willing to take," I said. "Not this time. The gem must be destroyed."

Oliver's face went ashen.

I tried to match Yelena's steely glare as I held his gaze. "You came to us for help. This is what we must do."

"But my work—my discoveries—they can do so much good."

I kept my gaze steady. "And also, not. Destruction is the only way to ensure this never happens again."

Oliver took a breath, then hesitated. "Can I speak with you in private?" he finally said.

"Absolutely not," my mother said. "Whatever you have to say can be said in front of the council. We must all understand this threat."

Oliver fidgeted. His gaze darted from my face to my mother's, to Borov's, and back to mine.

He approached my mother and bowed. "The thing is, Queen Mother…" He wrung his hands together. "That is—my sister—for you are my late brother's wife." He cleared his throat.

"Oh, for heaven's sake, please be frank," my mother said.

Oliver's hands dropped to his side. "I don't know how to destroy it."

The room went silent.

My body suddenly felt full of sand—heavy—like I might burst apart and sift through the floorboards.

King Jershon was the first to find his voice. "You expect us to believe that the enlightened, educated wanderer doesn't know how to destroy one of his own creations?"

"I could venture a guess," Oliver said. "That is, I know what I'd do if I wanted to … destroy it." Oliver choked on the word *destroy*. He trailed off, clearly with no intention of sharing his guess anytime soon.

"We'd like to hear your idea now," I said.

"You're missing the point, Highness. Every moment we spend talking is a moment lost searching."

I raised an eyebrow and waited.

We needed him to talk. Had to know everything he knew. How could I get him to talk?

The moments ticked by, faster and faster, matching the heartbeat in my chest. "We will not begin our search until you enlighten us."

Finally, Oliver huffed and pushed a hand through his hair. "Fine. The Topaz was created the same way the Emerald was. I weakened the atomic bonds and introduced a foreign substance that enhanced the original molecular structure."

"What foreign substance?" I pressed.

"A flower that possesses uncanny healing properties. It altered the Topaz so it would 'heal' any perceived inadequacy in the bearer, causing those who see the bearer to see them as perfect and beautiful. There is no built-in way to destroy it, as there was with the Emerald, but once the Topaz is back in our possession, I can remove the plant, which should return the gem to its original, innocuous state."

"You really think you can remove all traces of the flower?" my mother asked. "What if pieces have broken off over time, or disintegrated throughout the gemstone? Won't that make it extremely difficult to remove?"

One of Oliver's eyes twitched and he brought a hand

to his face to stop the tic. "It's still in one piece. And if it's not, for some reason, any number of other substances could be added to counteract the healing effects of the flower. Or, as a last resort, the atomic bonds within the Topaz could be weakened to the point of separation, effectively disintegrating the gem."

There was a beat of silence.

Oliver gazed at the faces in the room. "If there are no more questions, can we please get on with finding it?"

His logic seemed sound. Garon had tried to teach me how to weaken the atomic bonds of a substance, as he'd taught Maggie, but I hadn't caught on as quickly as she had. I'd need some lessons from Oliver.

But first… "Yes, Uncle, we must find it."

"Good. I volunteer to accompany you on a journey to find the Topaz thief and stop her from taking your crown. I believe I know where she's taken refuge."

"If you know where she is, why haven't you gone after her already?" Yelena's glare was like an arrow. Sharp and deadly.

Oliver met Yelena's look with a steely one of his own. "I felt it was my duty to alert the Queen to the threat as soon as I became aware of it. If I were to go after the gemstone alone and fail, the knowledge of its existence and probable whereabouts would die with me. Then, when the threat arrived on your doorstep, you would be completely unprepared."

Nobody moved. Nobody breathed.

They were waiting for me to speak.

Clearly, I'd be safer inside the castle walls. We could send a party of soldiers after the woman, guided by Oliver. The soldiers would be better equipped to fight than I was, if needed.

But was I better suited to address this particular threat

because of my experience with the Emerald? Was there something Oliver wasn't saying—couldn't say under the scrutiny of my mother and Borov—that I should understand implicitly?

Or was there something he'd held back on purpose that I had yet to discover?

Oliver's lips were set in a firm line, his gaze locked on mine.

I looked to Borov, but his expression was unreadable.

My mother was studying me. Her expression was calm, but her hands were clasped a little too tightly.

I squared my shoulders. Regardless of the danger, this was a fight I needed to fight. I would not cower in my castle.

"Yes, we must go after her," I said, keeping my voice even but strong. "Oliver will be my guide. Will anyone else join—?"

Borov stepped forward before I'd finished my request. "I will accompany you, Highness, along with a hundred of my best men."

A hundred? That seemed extreme. All we needed to do was steal back a gemstone.

It was what I'd sent Maggie to do all by herself. Another lifetime ago.

Oliver voiced my concern. "The woman is hiding deep within the forest. Stealth will behoove us, and it will be difficult to achieve with such a large company."

Borov's brow furrowed as he studied Oliver, eyes boring into him.

Oliver didn't flinch.

Finally, Borov said, "Very well. Myself and fifteen of my finest men. You will be our guide, but will remain under constant supervision. I will command the guards. And the Queen will have final say on any decisions to be made."

Oliver nodded. "Naturally."

Borov turned to me. "We leave at dawn. Who would you appoint to reign in your stead?"

"Yelena should have the honor." The throne would have been my sister's place, after all, had she not been married off to a foreigner at such a young age. "My mother will advise her as needed, as she currently does for me."

"Very well." Borov stood and bowed his head. The others in the room followed suit.

I waited the customary ten seconds. It always felt too long, so I had to count in my head to be sure I didn't cut the show of respect short. "Rise," I finally commanded. "You are all dismissed."

The council members filed out.

"Oh, Borov?"

He turned to face me.

"Send a hundred men to Duke Christoph at once."

"We don't have a hundred extra men."

"What about the hundred you offered to send with me?" I smiled, knowing I had him.

Borov's features froze in place. But then his mouth twitched up into the tiniest of grins. "Well played, Your Highness. You are learning quickly. I'll pull them from the Eastern border and send them North at once."

"Thank you."

Two guards escorted my uncle from the room. As he passed me, he said in a low voice, "We must prepare for any possibility. These things are unpredictable." A third guard joined the group and nudged Oliver forward.

A chill ran through me as I watched my uncle leave, surrounded by guards. The unpredictability of O's magic was something I knew of all too well.

Chapter Three

What the What?

Maggie

Present Day—Virginia

Internet stalking took on a whole new meaning the summer after The Emerald Incident. You were supposed to stalk hot guys. Frenemies. Maybe the occasional college recruiter.

Not dead princesses.

But I couldn't help stalking Lindy, even though she'd technically been dead over four hundred years. To me she'd only been gone a few months. She'd saved my family and become my friend, and I would never get to say thank you, or goodbye.

I stalked when I should have been studying. I stalked right before bed. I stalked first thing in the morning. I often didn't realize what I was doing until my computer was already queued up to the history of a little-known country called Valstenia.

But history didn't change. Lindy had lived a good life, and now she was gone. The end.

On a scale of one to crazy, I wasn't sure just how high *'stalking dead princesses'* ranked. It was probably certifiable. *I* was probably certifiable.

Oh well.

"Maggie, you're going to be late for work!" my dad yelled.

My hand hovered over the computer mouse. "Just a sec!"

I also had Lindy to thank for the fact that my dad no longer lived in a grief-induced stupor. Shortly after The Incident, my boyfriend Garon had called, pretending to be the lawyer for a recently deceased—fictional—great aunt, with a handsome inheritance for me and my brother—money we'd actually gotten from selling the emerald Lindy had given me. My dad had been hyper-attentive ever since.

Even though I couldn't get away with much anymore, I wouldn't trade him for the ghost he used to be.

Unfortunately, he'd refused to use any of the money to update my bedroom, or buy me new clothes. He only caught up on the mortgage payments, then put the rest into the bank, insisting it was for us, not him.

As in, it was for college, not for fun. Ugh.

My fingers flew across the keyboard without my permission. I clicked on the link that was my new best friend and went to find my shoes while my computer thought about obeying me. My dad also refused to buy me a laptop. *"Waiting teaches character,"* he said whenever I complained about how slow my old desktop was.

I found my shoes underneath a pile of clean clothes that hadn't quite made it into my drawers yet. The shoes were tan suede ankle boots—with three inch heels—and I hated them. But they went much better than my sneakers with the khaki mini-skirt and starched white shirt I had to wear to my summer job at the Gap. I scowled at the shoes as I worked them on.

When my feet were properly confined, I sat up and glanced at my screen. "Stupid, slow computer! Oh, wait…"

I peered closer.

"Page not found? Really?"

TOPAZ REIGN

Piper said I should stop talking to my computer, but I kinda liked having someone—okay, some*thing*—to yell at whenever I wanted to. It helped me avoid thinking about the fact that Garon had given up his whole life— his destiny, even—to be with me.

I was glad, of course.

Well, at least, the selfish part of me was. But another part of me wondered what I was keeping him from.

"Why couldn't you find the page?" I yelled at my computer. "I've only been on it like a thousand times a day for the past three months!"

I hit refresh.

Page not found.

"Ugh!" I clicked the search box and typed, *Queen Shalyndria Valstenia.* I slid a clip into my hair to pull it away from my face. My bob was too short for the mandated ponytail, but my boss insisted I make some sort of effort to put it back each day. I glossed my lips and did my mascara.

It was really time for a new computer.

"Maggie, I'm leaving *now*!"

"I'm coming, I promise!" My car had refused to start yesterday and was now sitting in the repair shop awaiting a prognosis. So today, I was at the mercy of my dad for a ride to work.

Finally, the page appeared. But the link I'd clicked on months ago was no longer there. The top result used to be a Wiki page listing the details of Valstenia's final years, and the benevolent Queen Shalyndria who had peacefully led her country until it became part of Sweden in the late 1600s. That was the page I'd memorized word for word in the time since I'd last seen Lindy.

But now the top result was a page on Valstenia itself. Holding my breath, I clicked on it and scanned the text.

There was no mention of Lindy—er, Queen Shalyndria—anywhere. My pulse quickened as I re-read the passage. Garon and Lindy's father, King Edvin, was mentioned only briefly. After his death, several names were listed as rulers, but none that I recognized. I kept reading:

"In the late 1600s, Valstenia became part of Denmark…"

Wait, what? Valstenia had become a part of Sweden, not Denmark. A chill slipped down my spine. What was going on?

"Maggie, if you're not in the car in one minute, you're taking the bus to work!"

Eep! I hated the bus. But … I couldn't leave now. All traces of Lindy had vanished overnight. I had to figure out what was going on.

But if I took the bus, I'd be late, and I'd already been late twice in the two weeks since summer had started. There was a huge stack of job applications on my boss's desk in the event that I '*Didn't work out*,' as she'd put it.

I grabbed my phone and ran from the room. The garage door clanged to life below me, and my dad's car started. My ankle turned when I landed on the bottom step, but I grabbed the railing and managed to avoid falling. Stupid, fashionable shoes.

"What took you so long?" My dad said when I hopped in the car. "I'm going to be late for work."

I ducked my head. "Sorry."

"Garon's bringing you home, right?"

"Yeah." My dad was surprisingly cool with me riding around on the back of my boyfriend's motorcycle. I suspected it had to do with Garon's impeccable manners. The seventeenth-century charm had won over my modern-day dad in a single day.

I started to pick at my nail polish but heard my boss's voice purr in my head: *Your hands are a very important piece of your uniform, and they can make or break a first impression. Our customers expect perfection in* every *way.* I slid my hands under my thighs and let the trees blur in my side-vision as our car sped toward the mall.

****

Six hours of folding shirts into perfectly uniform squares did nothing for my nerves. My boss had promised to train me on the registers soon, which would make my job way more exciting, but she kept putting me off. So right now, my entire job consisted of trailing customers around and re-folding the t-shirts, jeans, and sweaters they picked up and discarded at random.

The store was annoyingly neat, which was probably why my room was such a mess these days. A girl could only handle so much neatness.

My worry for Lindy only grew as my hands worked with each piece of fabric. I'd gotten so good at folding that I no longer needed the little square board I'd had to use at the beginning to get the proportions right. While I worked, three possible explanations for Lindy's disappearing page rose to mind.

Theory one: The Internet was under attack by cyber terrorists, who were altering pages at random.

Theory two: I hadn't had enough sleep and a simple typo had led me to the wrong information.

Theory three: Something had gone terribly wrong and Lindy was in trouble. Or, she used to be in trouble. I wasn't sure how to think of it since, either way, it would have happened ages ago. And if she *was* in trouble, or had been in the past, what could I possibly do to help her now?

"Maggie!" My head snapped up.

Corbin, my coworker, eyed me. "You've been folding and unfolding that sweater for fifteen minutes! Better move on before she sees." He jerked his head toward the back where our boss had emerged from her office.

"Oh, thanks."

"Sure." He looked at something behind me and his smile went stale. He nodded toward the store's entrance. "Looks like your ride's here."

I glanced over my shoulder. Garon, with his perfectly messy brown curls and naturally tanned face, stood outside the store. A giant map of the mall, with a Hollister ad at the top, was his backdrop. But Garon looked so much better than the models they had on those things.

I finished folding the shirt I was working on, trying to tame the crazy grin that surfaced whenever I saw him. "See you tomorrow, Corbin."

Corbin waved and then turned his attention to a stack of jeans that had been massacred by a trio of skinny-legged girls. I hurried to the back and clocked out.

A minute later, I was in Garon's arms. The scent of his t-shirt jolted me from the clothes-folding stupor I'd spent the last six hours in. He always smelled like the forest, though I didn't know how he managed it. There must be a forest-scented Tide or something. He'd spent the morning at the kennel where he worked so, really, he should smell like dog, not pine trees.

"Hi." I laced my fingers together behind his back.

He kissed me, and my insides went all warm and syrupy.

He pulled away too soon—it was always too soon when he stopped kissing me—and handed me a smoothie. "Pomegranate Passion," he said.

I eyed the smoothie, debating if I really wanted to stop

kissing him in order to drink it. But Pomegranate Passion was my favorite. And Garon wasn't going anywhere.

I took the smoothie. "You're the best. Want some?"

He shook his head. "How'd it go on the registers today?"

I scowled. "She didn't let me on."

"But she promised," Garon said. "She was going to train you today, right?"

"That's what she said yesterday."

"Lame. I'm sorry." He slid an arm behind my back, navigating me toward the mall exit. "Want to take a drive? We could go to Chesapeake Bay. I don't want to take you home yet."

We pushed through the doors and a wave of summer heat blasted my face. "Actually, you should take me home."

He tensed.

"Don't worry, I just need to show you something in my room."

He quirked an eyebrow. "Oh, really?" We stepped off the curb into the parking lot.

I elbowed him. "Not like that. It's about Lindy."

He stopped walking. "What do you mean?"

A car honked and I pulled him to the side of the road. "I found something. Before I left for work… But it might be nothing. I didn't have time to check it out, and I left my phone in my dad's car when he dropped me off." I stopped walking. "Oh, wait, where's your phone? I'll show you."

"It's dead," Garon said.

He had a cheap phone, with a really crappy battery life. My phone was cheap, too, but at least the battery didn't die every hour without a charge.

"What did you find?" Garon pressed.

"It was really more like what I didn't find." I tugged on his arm. "Just, come on. I really need to show you."

We sped home, Garon leaning into the turns more aggressively than usual.

I prayed my computer was feeling compliant as we headed upstairs. I'd left the page up from this morning and, after a moment of rebellion, my computer woke up and refreshed the text I'd seen earlier.

"I did a search on Valstenia this morning, and this is what came up." I pointed to the computer screen, and read the text out loud. "*In the late 1600s, Denmark became part of Valstenia...* Wait a sec..." I looked closer at the tiny print. "That's not what it said this morning."

Garon rolled the chair closer to the monitor and I settled on his knee. We both scrutinized the screen.

"This morning it said Valstenia became a part of Denmark, not the other way around. I'd thought it was weird because Valstenia actually became part of Sweden."

Garon's forehead creased as he studied the screen. He reached for the mouse, a slight tremor in his hand.

"If Denmark became part of Valstenia, then what happens if we..." He typed into the search box and we waited for a map of Denmark to load.

The search brought up the page we'd just been on—a *history* page, not a current map. He scrolled down to reveal a series of maps at the bottom of the page, showing the gradual takeover of Denmark by Valstenia between the years 1624-1630.

A pit settled in my stomach.

Garon's hand shook harder. He made a fist, flexed his hand. Then searched for a map of Valstenia.

My knees bounced while we waited for the page to load. Finally, a map of Valstenia came up on the screen, and it was ten times larger than the tiny country had ever been. According to this map, the country of Valstenia spanned the southern half of Sweden and continued throughout the whole of Denmark.

And this map was *current*.

Today, this was what the country of Valstenia looked like.

Garon's face drained of color.

The floor tilted beneath me. I grabbed onto the edge of my desk. For grounding. For stability. To make sure my house wasn't crumbling into some dark hole, or portal to another dimension.

Nope. Everything was as it should be.

Except for the map on the screen.

How? Why? What was going on?

Finally, I found words. "The map did *not* look like that this morning."

Garon's voice was husky, like he had something lodged in his throat. "Valstenia's growing."

We fell silent. Silence was the only option.

Finally, Garon said. "My sister would never do this. She loved our homeland, but she'd never go conquer others. She didn't do this."

It didn't need to be said, but I said it anyway. "Then who did?"

Chapter Four

Bye, Bye, Bye

Maggie

Present Day—Virginia

Garon refreshed the map we'd been studying.

Again, Valstenia grew.

In the next refresh, words appeared.

"Valstenian Empire," I read aloud. It now took up all of Denmark, most of Sweden, plus some of Norway.

"This can't be happening." Garon's eyes were wide. His gaze darted around my room, as if an explanation might be hiding under a pile of clothes or old magazines.

He typed his family name—von Thurne—into the search box and read aloud when he found the right page. "*The von Thurne family ruled until 1623, after which the rule changed hands several times. Many are credited with bringing the Valstenian Empire to the glory it enjoys today, and the country now stands as a testament to the power of many working against the one*." Garon banged his fist on my computer desk. "What does that even mean? I have to go back. Find out what's happening—" He caught himself. "What happened."

"I'm coming with you."

"No way, you have a life here. And time travel is dangerous."

"Garon, look how fast this is spreading. Whoever is responsible, they're not going to stop with just Denmark. Assuming this is happening in the 1600s, America is just an idea in a few colonists' minds. They'd be easy prey for whoever is systematically overthrowing Europe. I could wake up tomorrow to find myself in a land where my future doesn't even exist. Please. Let me come with you."

Garon pulled me into a hug. "It's not safe."

That didn't make me feel better. "What about *you*? If you get hurt, I won't even know." My voice was rising in pitch. "What if you never come back?"

"I'll time my return for right after I leave. It'll seem like I'm only gone a moment. Even if this takes years to sort out, you'll never know the difference."

"Years?" I squeaked out.

Garon winced. "Sorry, not the right thing to say. My point is, don't worry. I'll sort it out and be back before you know it."

He pulled out the lighter he always kept in his pocket—his 'escape pod' as he'd called it when I asked about it a few months back. Apparently, when the flame flicked on, it created a surge of energy—a surge he needed in order to time jump. Matches worked too, as did lightning. But the lighter was more reliable.

He gave me a final squeeze, a whisper-light kiss, and then he was gone, with a crack like thunder that rocked the air around me.

I could still feel the pressure of his hand in mine. The warmth that was there one moment and gone the next. I waited for him to return. For him to make good on his word that he'd be back a moment after he left.

But he was not back a moment later.
****

He was not back a day later.

He was not back even a week later.

I could no longer feel his hand in mine.

Every morning, I checked the map of Scandinavia.

Some mornings, the Valstenian Empire was smaller. Other mornings, it had grown. One morning, Denmark was back and I found a reference to Trellboro, the tiny country Lindy had been taken to when her wet-nurse kidnapped her as a baby.

But both Denmark and Trellboro were gone three hours later.

A week-and-a-half after Garon left, a new country appeared. I was home alone—my dad was at work and my brother Tanner was at the local pool where he was a lifeguard—when I saw the new name appear on my computer.

"Boryn," I read out loud. The new country was small, and located at the southern tip of the Valstenian Empire. It looked oddly close to where my mother had grown up, in Sweden.

I typed in another search I'd done a thousand times: *Alette Sparre, Listevia, Sweden.*

My computer thought … and thought … and thought.

Finally, the search engine displayed a list of results. None of the links were familiar, but at the top of the page, Google asked if I'd meant *Alette Sparre, Listev province, Boryn.*

There was that name again—Boryn.

I clicked on the suggestion and a page loaded that was familiar. My breath hitched. I'd seen this one before.

My mother's family had never reached out to us—not before or after she'd died—but I'd done some research and found the home my mother had grown up in. It was in a small town in southern Sweden, where she'd lived her whole life before coming to the U.S. for college. The home was apparently considered a valuable piece of Swedish architectural history, and you could go there for tours—though I had no idea who owned it.

But now the house wasn't in Sweden. It was in Boryn, apparently, even though on the map it was still in the same spot as before.

My gaze wandered to a little sidebar that listed visiting hours and facts about the structure. There were audio tours available in twenty different languages. If you came on a Tuesday, you could have tea in the garden before your tour.

A few years ago, my dad had suggested we visit Sweden—tour the house, see where Mom went to school, those sorts of things. We'd gotten passports and everything. But we'd never actually gone. There was never enough money.

I clicked on a tab that said 'History' and started scrolling through pictures. The earliest picture, at the bottom of the page, was from 1857 and showed a grainy black and white image of a smaller version of the house. I scrolled back up and found some pictures taken in the 1920s, when the house was being renovated and expanded into the mansion it was now.

My gaze caught on one picture, which showed the nearly completed mansion. Five workers were lined up in front of the house, faces serious, thumbs hooked in the pockets of their overalls or behind their suspenders.

But it wasn't the workers I was focused on.

I peered closer. There was a figure in the background headed toward a line of trees, glancing back at the camera. I tried to enlarge it, but that required more brainpower than my computer had, apparently, because nothing happened.

But it didn't matter—I could see well enough.

And I recognized that face.

It was Garon.

At my mother's house, almost a hundred years ago.

My palms went clammy. Was this another change in history? Had this happened since he'd left a week-and-a-half ago? Or had this picture been here all along and I'd just never noticed it?

And—the biggest question of all—*why* had Garon gone to my mother's house?

A few months ago, after we destroyed the Emerald, Garon told me that he'd visited my mother when she was a young woman. He was hoping she'd be able to break the curse because of her noble blood. Could that visit explain the picture?

I studied the image again.

No, this shot had been taken long before my mother was born. But what other explanation could there be?

Footsteps pounded up the stairs and started down the hallway. A second later, my brother Tanner barged into the room, smelling like Banana Boat and chlorine. His hair was messy—like it'd dried in the sun with a little spray sunscreen mixed in.

If I'd had a laptop, I would have snapped it shut.

But my desktop was currently operating in *slower-than-death* mode, and there wasn't much I could do to hide the screen. I tried clicking out of the website displaying the picture, but it was still thinking about enlarging the image like I'd asked it to do thirty seconds ago.

I spun to face Tanner, placing my elbow on the desk and my body in front of the monitor. "Learn to knock."

"Why? You never knock."

"I do so! I could have been changing."

"But you weren't." Tanner ran a hand through his sunscreen-encrusted hair.

I scrutinized him. "Why are you home?"

"My shift's over."

"No, it's not, it's only…" I glanced at the clock on my computer screen. "Oh, crap. Crap, crap, crap! I'm going to be late for work! How did it get so late?"

"Dunno. You must have been having fun."

I whirled into action, digging through the pile of clothes on my bed. "I can't be late! Geez, what am I going to do?"

"I'll give you a ride," Tanner said, his eyes twinkling with a teasing glint.

Tanner didn't have a car. He rode his bike to work. "Unless you got turbo boosters on your Schwinn since I last saw it, I'll be better off taking the bus."

"Now *that* is a great idea," Tanner said. "Turbo boosters, I mean. Not taking the bus."

Why had Garon been at Mom's house in the 1920s? Why, why, why?

I pulled my sneakers off and stuck my feet into my ridiculous work shoes, then twisted a few sections of hair away from my face, anchoring them down with bobby pins. My head felt just as twisty on the inside.

What had he been doing there? Was he stuck in time again?

"Time for you to leave," I said. "I have to change my shirt."

Tanner was peering at the computer screen, his eyebrows pulling together. "What's this?" He pointed at the picture with Garon in it.

"It's a house. Now get out." I put my hands on his chest and shoved.

He didn't budge. Instead he stepped closer to the computer, his mouth hanging open a little. "Is that Mom's house?"

I sighed. "Yeah."

He grabbed the mouse and scrolled up the page to

some of the more recent pictures. The traitorous machine complied.

"I didn't know the house used to be smaller." Tanner eyed me.

I bit my lip.

"You don't have to hide this from me, you know. You're not the only one with mommy abandonment issues." I could tell he was trying to make his tone light—joking. But there was an undercurrent of hurt.

"I know." My voice was quiet.

The clock in the hallway ticked and tocked, marking the silence that stretched between us.

Then Tanner said, "We should go visit."

I stared at him. "What, just pick up and go?"

"Sure. Why not?"

"Because that's crazy. We can't just pick up and go to Sweden!"

His brow furrowed in confusion. "What's sweedin? Mom grew up in Boryn."

Ugh. I did not have the energy for this. History had changed and so Tanner had never heard of Sweden. My ability to remember things other people forgot was really getting old. Garon thought it was some residual effect of being touched by the Emerald's magic.

"Right. Boryn. We can't just go to Boryn."

"Why not?" Tanner said. "I've been saving money all summer and I know you have, too. Let's go. We can tell Dad we need some brother-sister bonding time before I leave for college."

"You can't spend all your college money on a trip to Swe—Boryn. You already had to start over again because of…" I trailed off, realizing my slip too late.

"Seriously, why do you keep saying stuff like that? I never had any money saved up."

Tanner didn't remember what had happened only a few months ago. How my best friend had been captured and Tanner had helped me rescue her. In the process, I'd lost his life savings by leaving it in my hotel room when the cops came after me. But I'd already tried explaining it to him, and he didn't remember. Kept saying I must have had some super lucid dream.

Garon and I were the only ones who remembered what had happened last year. And sometimes, I thought, Piper and Kate did too, even though they never said anything outright. Every now and then one of them would make a comment—about emeralds or spy-bys or broken glass—that made me think they had the memories buried deep inside, just locked away in a place they weren't ready to go yet.

Tanner was still waiting for my answer.

"Sorry, I don't know why I say stuff like that."

"I don't need the money I've saved, Mags. Not really. Dad's got that money from great-aunt…" Tanner paused, scrunching up his nose. "Well, I can't remember her name, but great-aunt somebody who gave us a bunch of money so we could pay for college. I've just been working for fun, really. I mean, what guy wouldn't want to spend his summer watching girls lay out in the sun all day?" He wagged his eyebrows up and down.

"Gross, Tanner."

"Come on, let's go on a trip. Find out what we can about Mom. It'll be fun."

Fun. I didn't know if I could have fun with Garon missing, and history changing, and my boyfriend's past life inexplicably intertwining with mine.

Wait.

What I needed was answers. And what better place to find them than the scene of the crime?

A smile tugged at the corners of my lips. And maybe, in addition to discovering what the heck Garon had been doing at the Sparre house in 1920, visiting Mom's house would tell me something—a bit about my history—that would help me understand my connection to all the craziness of last year. "Okay, let's do it."

Tanner play-punched me in the arm. "Yes! Sibling trip! It'll be sweet, Mags, just wait."

I rubbed my arm, pretending he'd hurt me.

"Okay, I'll leave now. You can get dressed for work."

I glanced at the clock, deflating. "I'll never make it in time. I'm going to get fired anyway, why bother going?"

Tanner grinned. "Don't be a defeatist, you'll totally make it."

"How?"

"I said I'd give you a ride, remember? I have Dad's car."

I punched Tanner for real. "Seriously? You could have told me you had a *car*!"

"I just did." He dodged away as I swung at him again. "But I have to pick up Dad too, so you'd better get ready fast!"

"You are such a turd!" I shouted as he left my room. But I was smiling. Hopefully our passports would still work in this crazy new world where Boryn and Valstenia were countries and Sweden was not. Maybe I'd get some cool stamps to christen my empty passport pages.

Chapter Five

The Flower Seller

Lindy

1623—Valstenia

The castle was stifling. Preparations were underway for us to leave and, even though it was supposed to be a secret, everybody knew. The kitchen staff prepared food for our journey. The stable-hands readied the horses. The armory evaluated our weapons and selected those that would be sufficient to protect us, but not too cumbersome for travel.

Borov was heading to market for some last-minute supplies. I couldn't bear to stay inside, so I decided to accompany him.

Yelena tracked me down just before we left, pulling me into a quiet corner. "Can we talk?"

"Of course." I had a few minutes, at least. "I'm so glad Mother convinced you to come."

"As am I." Her gaze darted to the side as a chambermaid bustled by. She refocused on me. "I hear you've had an offer of marriage."

"Well, that news traveled fast."

"I think you should accept," Yelena said.

I frowned. My sister was fierce in the face of opposition, and she'd had more experience than me, but was a marriage alliance really in our best interest?

She continued, "I know you're in financial trouble."

My blood went cold. "How did you know that?"

"Shalyndria, I know how expensive running a

kingdom is. Valstenia's taxes have been the lowest in the land ever since Father's tax cuts. But it can't be sustainable—it doesn't take inside information to figure that much out. This marriage alliance could be your only chance to retain the goodwill of your people, and obtain the funds necessary to protect them. Qadar is wealthy, and Boryn is a beautiful country. I would jump at such a partnership."

It was no use trying to pretend she wasn't right—she clearly knew what she was talking about. "But there has to be another way to bring in funds. What about King Jershon? He and Father discussed a merge—I could follow through with that instead of accepting Qadar's offer."

"Oh, please. Trellboro is worse off than Valstenia. Qadar's resources put Jershon's to shame."

But that was precisely it. If Valstenia was so pathetic, then why did Qadar want to marry me so badly? We'd never even met. And even if we had, I was under no delusions that he'd be after my charms. What did Valstenia have that Boryn did not?

I couldn't see the answer.

Yelena stepped closer. "If you don't act quickly, Qadar will align himself with someone even stronger."

The air around me went cold. Because the words she hadn't spoken screamed louder than the ones she had: If I didn't accept him, Qadar would align himself with someone stronger—and then they could take Valstenia by force.

Borov strode down the hall toward us. "The preparations are almost complete, Highness. If you're still coming with me to market, we must leave at once."

I smoothed down my dress, which didn't need smoothing down. "Yes, Borov, I'm coming." Then to

Yelena I said, "I'll think about it."

She folded her arms across her chest. "Don't think too long."

****

A traveling cape with the hood pulled forward hid my identity, while my sister's advice whipped my mind into a frenzy. The sea was visible in the distance as we walked, and the air felt cool on my skin. It helped, but it wasn't enough to still my mind.

The town of Korona was a short walk from the castle, and from there it was over a day's ride southwest to Loxgrov, where I'd lived with Calista and Theo in their inn near our family's summer castle.

The path was dusty, with grass growing waist-high on either side. But it was dry and turning brown, tangled like the thoughts in my mind. The sun beat down on my hood and sweat began to trickle down the back of my neck, but I left my hood in place. Better to keep my identity hidden.

The market came into view, with the vivid colors of fresh fruits and vegetables, the scent of just-baked bread, and voices straining to be louder than those of their neighbors. It all wove together to form the comforting fabric of the marketplace.

Being here reminded me of the relief I'd found all those years ago while in captivity to the Emerald, when my only joy came from venturing to market.

Borov kept his distance to avoid drawing attention to me. I wandered from stall to stall, drinking in the cacophony and letting it calm my troubled mind. I noticed a tiny cart on wheels, situated apart from all the others, as if everyone was giving it a wide berth.

It was full of flowers.

Dozens and dozens of them, in unique varieties and

vibrant hues. They reminded me of the flowers Theo used to grow. There were also intricate headpieces and crowns, woven from grass and wildflowers.

I drew closer, spellbound.

As I neared the cart, I noticed another flower painted into the wood at the side of the cart. This one had three layers of ivory-white petals, like the petals of a lily only not quite as large. The petals were rimmed in violet, and tiny violet coils grew from the center where the petals met the stem. The painting was shockingly detailed.

"Flower, miss?" said a voice from behind me.

I turned, and gasped when I saw the speaker. Her face was scarred—melting, it seemed—like a candle lit too long. I stood my ground despite the urge to stagger back in horror.

The woman's skin was puckered in some places and stretched thin in others, like she'd been scalded in a fire. She was a young woman, I realized, not much older than my sister, Yelena. What hair she had was patchy and sparse, and black as coal.

I collected myself. "Hello. I was just looking at your flowers." I tore my gaze from her face and pointed at the painting. "I've never seen one like this before."

"Yes, it's rare for these parts."

"What's it called?"

"Remyallis. They grow on the Baltic shores."

Rem-ee-allis. I repeated the flower name in my head. I tore my eyes away from the painting and examined the other flowers and headpieces. They were enchanting.

The woman busied herself re-arranging the flowers on her cart.

"What's your name?" I asked.

"I am Anka," she said.

"Well, Anka, you're very talented. These headpieces

are stunning. I'll take one for my sis—"

Someone hissed behind us.

I whipped around.

A man, eyes narrowed and face ruddy, glared at us. He spat at the flower seller's feet. "Fula Barn!" he shouted. "Dra at fanders!"

Ugly child. Get out of here.

The woman remained calm, ignoring the man.

He continued to taunt her. "Ful Ankugar! Devil's child. Go back to where you came from!"

The man's voice drew the attention of other market goers. Some stopped what they were doing and stared. Others hurried away as soon as they saw Anka.

Someone in the crowd shouted, "Back to the inferno with you!"

"You don't belong," another hissed.

I stood in open-mouthed silence, horrified that the townspeople could be so cruel. Clearly, this woman had been in some horrible accident. She deserved compassion, not contempt.

The first man spat again and kicked the woman's cart. Several flowers spilled into the street, but she made no move to retrieve them. Instead, she lifted a handle at the back of the cart and, like a lid closing over a treasure chest, part of the cart folded over her flowers, protecting them.

And suddenly I realized: the wheels, the compactness of her booth.

This was a regular occurrence.

The man made a point of stepping on the fallen flowers, grinding them into the cobblestones.

I whirled into action. "Stop! Stop it right now!" I bent to gather the broken blossoms. He'd ruined several of her beautiful headpieces.

"She don't belong," he hissed at me. Then he cocked his head, as if seeing me for the first time.

I gasped. In my haste, my hood had slipped off. I pulled it on and ducked my head, pretending to be absorbed in collecting the flower remains.

He took a step toward me. "And you don't belong either, do you?"

"Uh." I tried to keep my head down, while my eyes raked the crowd for Borov.

The flower seller pushed her cart away without a backward glance. One wheel caught on a cobblestone, causing the cart to shudder and creak, but she didn't stop.

The man stepped closer to me. "You're a royal, aren't you?" He spat again.

A crowd formed around me and I scrambled to my feet, leaving the crushed flowers on the ground. I kept my head down. "Of course not, I'm just a peasant."

He fingered my robes.

I flinched away from him.

"You ain't no peasant."

I glanced down at my traveling cloak—nothing special, but it was clean, and the material was thick and free of wear. I cursed myself—I should have said I was a merchant's daughter.

"Hey, we got a royal here!" he shouted.

I stepped away from him, but a circle had formed around me, blocking any retreat.

"Not just any royal," a woman said, peering at me. "That there's the Queen."

The venom in their voices surprised me. The past few years had been peaceful and, from what my advisors told me, conditions in the villages were better than ever. I'd seen no indication of suffering or unrest in the times I'd traveled to market.

So, why were they angry with me?

"The Queen's a matron," the first man said. "This one's too young."

The woman smacked him upside the head. "Queen Maren stepped down, you git! Her daughter now holds the crown."

The two now had the attention of a large group of people, and the circle of spectators tightened around me. I craned my neck. Where was Borov?

"What's your family been doing with all our money?" the woman said.

Another man joined the fight. "Yeah, don't you have enough already?"

"Keep your hands off our livelihoods!" a woman yelled. She was so thin, her collarbone protruded sharply from beneath her skin. I imagined she'd snap like a twig if someone tugged on her. "Things are bad enough without you thieves taking what don't belong to you."

What were they talking about? Our family had taken nothing from them. My father had lowered taxes, and I'd made no changes. Should I admit I was the Queen and argue my point or would it be better to deny my royal attachments?

I said, "The royal family would never steal from the people."

Even as I said it, I knew if I couldn't figure out another way to pay my soldiers, then I would have to raise taxes. Duke Christoph's men weren't the only ones due for leave.

"Ha!" the twig woman said. "She admits she's the Queen."

A sudden commotion in the square turned the people on their toes.

Horses whinnied. A cry went up from the crowd. I

couldn't tell if the sound was happy or angry. Or fearful.

"Royal soldiers!" someone yelled.

My accusers scattered like roaches from the light, leaving me alone with a square full of crushed flowers.

A royal military company was headed my way. I stayed rooted in place, transfixed by the sight of the company on horseback. They rode as if in triumphal return, but as they drew closer I noted slumped shoulders and tired eyes. The horses' hooves dragged. Even the banner carried by the lead rider was limp and frayed at the edges.

In the midst of the group of soldiers, three men shuffled along, their hands and feet shackled together.

Prisoners. Why did they have prisoners?

"Make way for the soldiers!" I recognized Borov's voice.

Finally!

He was pushing toward the group, from a far end of the marketplace. His eyes were tight as they raked the crowd. Looking for me, I realized.

"Borov!" I called out, heading toward him.

The tightness left his eyes. "My eternal apologies, Highness. I was dealing with some guards who'd stepped out of line. Are you all right?"

"I am. But the people spoke of the royal family robbing them. I don't understand."

"Yes, there were some strange happenings today which we'll need to discuss. But now we must greet the soldiers. Stay close."

"Make way for the royal guard!" Borov shouted again.

The people cleared a path and the company continued toward the castle. When they passed by us, one of them turned and nodded to Borov. He was young—about my age—and he looked … well … he looked a lot like Borov, actually. Fair hair and light eyes. Stocky build.

Did Borov have a son?

I studied Borov from the side as he watched the young man ride past. His eyes shone with obvious pride.

Once the soldiers had passed through the crowd and started on the path to the castle, the marketplace returned to its normal state of semi-controlled chaos. Borov and I trailed behind the soldiers—far enough that we wouldn't choke on the dust kicked up by the horses, but close enough that we'd arrive at the castle shortly after they did.

We fell into step together, and Borov didn't seem to notice that I was walking beside instead of ahead of him, as I should have been. "How long has your son been gone?"

He looked at me, his eyebrows lifting in surprise. "How did you—"

I grinned. "He's an exact replica of you. How long has he been gone?"

"About eight years. Trevin joined when he was fifteen—took an assignment right away."

"Well, I'll be glad to see you reunited."

"His mother passed while he was away. I sent word to him—thought he'd want to come home—but I never received a response."

I remembered Borov's wife passing away. It was shortly after I'd returned.

We walked the rest of the way to the castle in silence.

When we got there, an abnormal amount of people had gathered in the courtyard. Soldiers milled about, even though they should have been heading to the armory to turn in their weapons, and stable hands struggled with feisty horses. The Captain of the guard was conferring quietly with my mother, whose features were pinched with worry.

I joined them. My mother slipped her arm through mine, so we were linked at the elbows.

The Captain nodded to acknowledge my presence, but kept talking, "… great unrest in the provinces, and Boryn's king, Qadar, continues to press for a marriage alliance."

"Captain Ekhert, what has prompted your return?" I said. "You were maintaining our northern borders, were you not?"

"Indeed, we were. The bulk of our army is still in place. But Qadar insisted we bring his proposal to you in person. Then, about a day's journey from home, we were attacked by a group of farmers."

My mother's mouth dropped open. It was not a look I saw on her often. "Farmers?"

"Yes, Your Majesties. Farmers."

"Why would farmers attack a group of trained, royal soldiers?" I said. "Were they armed?"

"Their weapons were crude, to be sure, but they fought with uncanny strength and ability. We were able to capture a few of them, whom we've brought back with us for trial, but the rest fled. The ones we have aren't talking. They're acting like wild animals. Unpredictable. Skittish. And there's something strange in their eyes. I know not what to make of it."

"Thank you, Captain," I said.

The Captain bowed, then strode across the courtyard toward the armory.

"What do you think it means?" I asked my mother.

"I know not." She slid her hand into mine. "But right now, there is a more pressing matter."

I let her pull me toward the throne room. "What could

be more important than a group of feral farmers and a mysterious king who will not relent until I'm his bride?"

My mother glanced back at me. Her face was white— how had I not noticed before—and her eyes tight. "It's your brother."

The only brother I had left was still just a child. "What of Felipe? Is he ill?"

"It's not Felipe," my mother said. "It's Garon. He's come back."

The worry that tugged at her face told me that, despite the fact that she'd missed him as much as I had, his return, today, was not good news.

Chapter Six

Mighty Boryn

Maggie

Present Day—Somewhere over the Atlantic Ocean

The guide book I'd bought to read on the plane was titled *Mighty Boryn: A Country of Wonder and Mystery.* It outlined the history, the customs, and the best ways to get around. It also listed some helpful Borynian phrases. Mostly I practiced *Do you speak English?* and *Where is the bathroom?*

I wished I'd known some Swedish so I could tell how close the languages were. But I couldn't look up any Swedish phrases now, because Google didn't remember what Swedish was. It didn't even remember Swedish Fish—those little red gummy candies. Which was a tragedy in itself, really.

Clearly, Garon hadn't fixed things yet.

But had he at least gotten home safely? Or was he stuck in the 1920s? Or … was it something worse?

I kept my phone around at all times, frantic for a call from Garon's number—or even Dad's, saying Garon had showed up on our front steps and that his motorcycle was in the way.

We were on an overnight flight, but because of the time change, it still felt like the middle of the night when the lights in the cabin came on—too bright—and the stewardess's voice came over the intercom—too loud— saying we were beginning our final descent and to please … blah, blah, blah.

After she made the announcement in English, she repeated it in some other language which was probably Borynian. Seriously, if I was a linguist, this would be so cool.

I rubbed my eyes, trying to squash away the desire to sleep, and pressed the button on my armrest to bring my seat up. I blinked. Wake up, wake up, wake up! We were here. In Mom's country of birth!

My sleep-fog didn't burn off until we'd made it off the airplane, through customs, and to the curb. The morning air was crisp and clear.

My dad had made me download an app for calling while out of the country, to avoid international charges. I checked it for any missed calls or messages.

Nothing.

I sent Dad a quick message letting him know we'd arrived safely.

"Okay, navigator, where to?" Tanner said, hefting his bag onto his back. We'd packed light, and in camping backpacks, so our stuff would be portable.

"Uh, we will definitely get lost if I'm the navigator."

"That's true. Okay, I'll navigate." Tanner pulled up a map of the area on his phone. "Where are we going first? Mom's house or a hotel?"

We exchanged a look and Tanner nodded. "The Sparre house it is."

I read off the address and Tanner typed it in. "It's almost a hundred kilometers away," he said.

"We'll need to catch a train." I pulled out my guidebook and flipped to the chapter about transportation. "The train system is supposedly super easy to use, and pretty cheap, too." I scanned the pages.

"Oh." I turned in a circle, looking for signs to the Metro. "I think we have to go back through the airport." I decided to try a new phrase I'd learned from my guidebook.

I approached an airport employee. "Talar du engelska?" *Do you speak English?*

The woman cocked her head and studied me like I might be crazy.

I repeated the phrase, slower this time. "Ta-laar doo enng-less-ka?"

Finally, her eyes cleared and she said, in a heavy accent, "English? Yes, I know English."

"Oh, good. How do we get to the train station?"

The woman proceeded to give me directions, in broken English that I didn't always understand. We were supposed to go back through the airport, take a shuttle to—what was it, terminal three? Then hop on another shuttle—or maybe a bus—which would take us to Copenhag's central train station. Something like that.

"Tack," I said, another Borynian phrase I'd learned. It meant *thank you.*

I turned to Tanner. "Did you get all that?"

"Not really, but we'll figure it out. Let's go."
****

We found the train—eventually—and got on.

We traveled over a body of water called the Oresun. The sea was like sapphires. The countryside was blanketed in the stunning green of spring, even though we were well into summer. The buildings extending uphill from the water's edge in one of the towns we passed through were each painted a different color—colors more vibrant and beautiful than any I'd ever seen.

I felt like Dorothy when she gets to Oz and, suddenly, there is color. Like I'd been seeing in black and white my entire life until this very moment. I studied each detail, committing the sights to memory.

When we got off the train, in the town of Simrisha where Mom had grown up, I gazed at the sparkling water and the beach stretching out of sight. "We should really make time for the beach while we're here."

Tanner was studying the map on his phone. "We'll need to get a cab to the Sparre house. It's a few miles out from the city—did those guidebooks say anything about hailing cabs?"

"Oh, um…" I scrambled to pull the guidebook out of my backpack. "Probably. But I didn't read the whole thing. We can just ask someone if they know English."

"We're in a smaller city, now. You can't expect everybody to just know English."

I followed Tanner to an ATM. He stuck in his card and punched in his PIN.

"I don't expect everyone to know English," I said. "But tons of Europeans speak it."

"Yeah well, we're not in Europe. We're in Scandinavia."

I shrugged. "Same thing."

"No, it's actually not." Tanner handed me some foreign bills. They looked like play money. "Here, you keep half in case we get separated or something."

I stuffed the cash into my wallet and scoped out the other passengers still milling around the train platform. A man in a business suit was studying a train schedule. He looked well-educated—maybe he'd know English. I walked up to him. "Talar du engelska?"

Tanner pulled me in a different direction.

"Hey, what are you doing?"

"Look," he said, pointing toward the street.

I followed his gaze and saw a yellow car pulling up to the curb, with the word *TAXI* printed in bold black letters along its side. A tiny signpost with a square placard that said *TAXI* stood near the curb, with two people waiting in line beside it.

"Well, couldn't they have made it a bit more obvious?" I huffed, following Tanner to the taxi line. "I mean, honestly!"

"Oh, come on, it's clearly marked. We just didn't look hard enough. Anyway, at least we found it."

We joined the line. I shifted in my Converse and pulled out my guidebook to study more Borynian while we waited.

When it was our turn for a taxi, Tanner showed the driver the address on his phone. The guy nodded and drove us right there, taking us along the coast and turning inland at the very end of our drive. He stopped at the head of what had to be a mile-long driveway. The drive was lined on either side by dozens of swoopy trees, like weeping willows, only with little white and pink blossoms hanging from the branches. At the end of the driveway stood a gorgeous, Victorian-esque house that was like a mansion times a thousand—way bigger than it had seemed in the pictures online.

The ocean sparkled in the distance, an easy walk away.

I gawked. "*This* is where Mom grew up?"

The cabbie said something in Borynian—an explanation of some sort, or an apology maybe—while gesturing to the mouth of the driveway. He seemed reluctant to drive through the gates, even though they stood open as if to welcome visitors.

Tanner paid the cabbie and he drove away, leaving us standing on a patch of gravel at the head of the driveway. White and pink flower blossoms were scattered underfoot, like an exotic welcome mat leading to the grand house before us.

"Can you believe Mom grew up in a mansion and we never even knew? I mean, the pictures hardly do it justice," I said, shouldering my pack and heading toward the house. "Do you think she regretted leaving?"

Tanner tugged on his backpack straps. "I hope not. 'Cause that's when she had us."

I kicked at the flower petals scattered underfoot. They were damp from morning dew that must not have burned off yet, and a few stuck to the toe of my shoe.

"Hey," Tanner said, stopping suddenly. "We used to go for walks like this. When we were little. I'd forgotten until just now."

I cocked my head, trying to remember. But I couldn't.

Tanner continued, "It was just you and me. You used to get wet leaves all over your shoes from kicking everything—like you did with those flower petals just now."

"We must have been really little if I don't remember it—was it before Mom died?"

"Yeah, I think."

"And she didn't go with us? You said it was just you and me."

Tanner cocked his head. "Oh. Well, I guess she must have—we'd have been too young to go out by ourselves. I probably just don't remember."

As we neared the house, more details became apparent. The uber-mansion was white and a few stories tall, with a wrap-around porch spanning the front and extending back along both sides. The yawning porch disappeared from view in the shadows of trees that surrounded the house. There were too many windows to count, each of them with black shutters—some open and some closed.

Off to the right, the land sloped down toward the sea.

To the left were woods. I studied them, trying to figure out exactly where the picture of the construction workers had been taken, and where Garon had been going when he'd been caught in their shot.

Tanner tugged on my arm. "Where are you going?"

Oops, I'd started walking toward the woods.

I changed course. Snooping around in the forest would have to wait. First, we had a house to search.

We walked up the front steps—wide and white-washed to a shabby-chic perfection. The double front doors were wood, and painted a posh black to match the shutters. A sign on the front porch listed the visiting hours and announced that the house was now closed. It would open at 10:00 AM, in just over an hour.

Tanner sat down on the steps to wait, but I went to the front door and knocked.

"What are you doing? They're not open yet."

"Yeah, well, we're not here as tourists, so visiting hours don't apply. This is our family, Tanner."

"Do you really think the family still lives here? It's probably government owned or something."

I shrugged. "Who cares? It's still our mother's home." I made a fist and knocked again, harder this time.

No answer.

Tanner got up and joined me at the door.

We'd never met our grandparents, or been told anything about them. But this was still their house, even if they didn't live here anymore.

Our *grandparents.*

For most kids, *Grandma* was someone they saw all the time—their Nana or their MeeMaw or whatever cutesy name they'd invented. A grandma was supposed to spoil you rotten, buy you stuff, and feed you sugar before bed. A grandma was supposed to read you books and color with you and, when you got older, come to your games and concerts and send you money at Christmas time. And Grandpas were supposed to teach you how to fix stuff, and talk about baseball and Babe Ruth and 'The Good ol' Days.'

These people were connected to us. This home was connected to us. We had a right to be here.

The injustice of being robbed of my grandparents, who'd never bothered to reach out to me after their daughter died, simmered inside me. "Why aren't they answering? This is so rude."

I looked inside the nearest window, but a heavy curtain blocked my view. The blocked window fueled my snooping gene, which I usually tried to keep under control. But this time, I didn't.

I walked to the end of the porch and peeked around the corner. "There has to be another way in, right?"

Chapter Seven

My Brother

Lindy

1623—Valstenia

"Why is Garon back?" I struggled to keep pace with my mother as she swept through the castle corridors. "Is everything okay? Is *he* okay?"

"I don't know."

"You don't know why he's back or you don't know if he's okay?"

"Neither. The servant who brought word only said that Garon required our presence at once." She squeezed my hand, trying to comfort me even though she was clearly rattled. "That was just after the soldiers arrived."

If Garon was really back, then our travel plans would have to wait.

We stumbled into Garon's room—his old room, which had remained unchanged since he left. The physician was bent over him. Yelena, Oliver, and my younger siblings Carina and Felipe stood in a semi-circle at the foot of the bed.

Garon's mouth split into a grin when he saw me. "Lindy. You look older." His voice was weak and his lips were cracked and dry, but his eyes held the same twinkle they always had.

It was really him. I rushed to his bedside, with my mother close behind. "I *am* older. You've been gone seven years. But you look the same, as always." The physician continued his exam, ignoring me and my mother, who now had a hand on Garon's forehead.

"What are you doing here?" I said.

Garon smiled, despite the fact that the doctor was poking at him and our mother fawning over him. "What, you're not glad to see me?"

"Of course I am. But we agreed the risk was too great for you to come back after you left the last time."

"I came to check on you."

There was a beat of silence. Like we were all waiting for the punchline of an ill-timed joke.

"Seriously?" Yelena said. "That's all you have to say?"

The physician finished his exam and stepped away from the bed. Garon propped himself up to a sitting position. "Yes, that's why I came. Is everything all right?"

He wasn't kidding. This was no joke. He'd risked his life in order to *check on us?*

"We're fine, you dope." It was a very un-queenly thing for me to say.

The tension in the room melted.

I pushed further, forgetting I was a queen and becoming just his little sister. "What is wrong with you? You could have died!" I bent and gathered him into an awkward hug, with him on the bed and me standing beside him. "But I've really missed you. Running a kingdom is hard."

My mother settled on the bed next to Garon. "We're happy you've come home, darling. Doctor, how is he?"

"He's half-starved. And dried up like a bone. Needs to get some water in his system."

"Half-starved?" I said. "How did time-travel do that?"

The doctor's gaze shifted. "That's not my area of expertise, Highness."

"No, it's not," Oliver said. "It's mine, as it happens. So let's think through this, shall we? We've been stuck in a fold of time before, but last time it was as mere reflections of ourselves. We didn't age, didn't require sustenance, didn't need to breathe, even."

Whoa. I'd never heard that detail before.

"We did still. Breathe, that is," Oliver clarified. "It felt weird not to. But my point is, we didn't require anything to sustain us. This time, apparently, young Garon retained his corporeal qualities when he got stuck. Did you check the phase of the moon before traveling?"

"Umm," Garon said.

"I suppose not. That's something I've learned since you left—always check the phase of the moon before time traveling." Oliver began pacing, his index finger tapping against his thigh. "And he had no food or water, so…" He held a hand out to indicate Garon's nutrient-starved body on the bed.

My mouth dropped open in horror. My brother had been stuck in time, slowly *starving*? What if he'd starved to death? Where would his body have ended up? Nobody would have even known he was dead.

What had Garon told Maggie about this trip anyway? Was he home for good? Had it not worked out between them?

The physician studied the ground, as if he felt my uncle was gravely lacking in mental capacity, and wondering why we were all taking him seriously.

When Oliver fell silent, the physician said, "Garon will be all right." He addressed my brother. "Young man, the next time you venture into the *woods*"—he emphasized the word, obviously not believing the time-travel story—"I suggest you plan accordingly. It is a fool's errand to begin a journey, on foot, with absolutely no provisions." The doctor picked up his bag. To my mother, he said, "See that he drinks plenty of water, and start him on food slowly—nothing but broth today."

Oliver had stopped pacing and was studying Garon carefully. As soon as the physician left, he said, "Why have you really come?"

Garon's brow knitted. "I really did come to check on things. To make sure you were all okay."

"And why did you believe this to be necessary?" Oliver pressed.

My mother chided him. "Why should he need a reason to come back? Garon belongs here." She'd been against Garon leaving in the first place. And once Oliver told her how dangerous it would be for Garon to treat the past as a casual vacation destination, she'd fought extra hard to keep him from leaving.

"Mother." Garon's voice became serious. "This is not a casual visit."

The room fell silent. We held our collective breaths, hanging on to the quiet like it was the last thing to cling to before being pushed off a cliff.

"I saw something," Garon continued slowly. "In the future. I can't explain it and, now that I see you're all well, I'm even more baffled as to its meaning."

A darkness crawled into my heart. Creeping. Lurking. Waiting. "What did you see?"

"Well, in the future, history is set as if in stone. It can't be changed or unwritten. Right?"

"Right," I said.

His gaze bore into mine before shifting to take in the entire group. Felipe fidgeted and my mother placed a calming hand on his shoulder.

Garon continued. "When Lindy returned home from the future, the history books changed to reflect her as a leader in Valstenia—the last one before Valstenia became a part of Sweden. This is the history that everyone remembers, apart from myself and Maggie. After that change, history remained the same until one morning a week or so ago. At least, it was a week or so for me. Maggie is the one who discovered it."

"How is Maggie?" I said.

Garon's expression softened. "She's well. One morning she was online—er—" He glanced around at the faces in the room and amended, "Searching the historical records. While studying the, uh, historical records, Maggie realized that they'd changed. Over the course of the next day, they continued to change, at an alarming rate. First, history reflected that Valstenia no longer became a part of Sweden at the end of Lindy's rule. Instead, it became part of Denmark. Then, later that day, history changed again to state that Denmark actually became a part of Valstenia, which at that time included a southern portion of Sweden as well. The next day, Valstenia had grown again. It continued to grow until it became so large as to completely overthrow both Denmark and Sweden."

He paused, searching our faces. "Our country then became known as The Valstenian Empire."

My mother's face went slack, as if she'd been slapped.

"Fascinating," Oliver breathed.

Yelena's eyes gleamed with a sort of morbid fascination, like a child watching a slug drying up in the sun.

My own feelings were conflicted. If Garon was to be believed—and I had no reason to doubt him—it could mean our country was doing well. That we'd agreed on some sort of a merger, maybe with King Jershon from my father's council, and we were thriving. That was not a bad thing.

But it could also mean…

Garon finished the thought for me. "I knew something was wrong. Things were changing so fast, I feared someone had usurped the throne and was charging through Scandinavia with the goal of total domination. That's why I had to come back."

The darkness in my heart grew. Given the current climate, this possibility was more likely than a peaceful merger. If I refused King Qadar's marriage offer, would he really try to take my crown by force?

Or was this all to do with the Topaz thief, whom Oliver seemed certain was intent on claiming the throne?

And what of the unrest in the market today? Was someone already making a move against the royal family by turning the townspeople against us? I needed to ask Borov for more details about the disturbance.

Or, what if…

What if…?

My gaze fell on Oliver. He was my father's brother. Did he have a legal claim to the throne? Would he feel he deserved one even if he didn't? He'd been awfully forthcoming with information lately—information he himself had created a need for.

There were just too many options.

"This is positively frightful," my mother said, echoing my own thoughts.

Garon shifted in his bed. "I'm certain of what I saw, Mother. I don't know how or why these things came to pass. I only know that in my future—in your future—they have."

Chapter Eight

Cold Reception

Maggie

Present Day—Boryn

"Maggie." Tanner's voice was a warning.

"Don't worry, I'm not breaking in or anything." I didn't say what I was actually thinking, which was that I probably *could* break in, if I wanted to. This place, for all its splendor, looked about as secure as a dollhouse when compared to the Parker mansion I'd broken into after Kate disappeared. "I just want to scope the place out."

The wrap-around porch seemed to stretch on forever, just as the house itself. We wandered to the right side first, turned a corner, and found a set of double doors—a side entrance.

We knocked on this new set of doors. Waited. Tried again.

Nothing.

We continued past a row of windows and a cluster of flower bushes in desperate need of a trim. Giant blue and purple blossoms hung heavy on the bush, causing the branches to bow and crowd out the walkway. Beyond the bushes, the walkway dead-ended. A tiny wrought-iron table with two ornate chairs stood in the corner, looking more like decorations than something you could actually sit on.

I stopped too fast, causing Tanner to bump into me. "Dead end," I said. "Let's try the other side."

We backtracked to the front of the porch, then

continued on to the other side of the house. This time when we turned the corner, the porch was clear of overgrown shrubbery. And there was a door—a single one, painted red—on our right-hand side. The walkway ended with five steps leading down and into a garden.

We stopped in front of the door and I knocked.

My gaze wandered. Despite this being an ancient— no, historic—house, it'd been remarkably well kept. I guessed they had to keep it up as a tourist attraction, even if it was just a minor one.

I knocked again, harder and longer.

We heard footsteps.

Finally. A sign of life.

Then a voice said something. Something in Borynian that I couldn't understand.

"Do you speak English?" Tanner asked.

There was a pause, then the same voice said in English, "We open in an hour."

"We're not tourists."

Silence.

"We're relatives," I added. "Of the Sparrow—er, Sparre family."

Our mother was born Alette Sparre, but had changed her name to Alette Sparrow when she came to the U.S. Her family was pretty high and mighty in Sweden at the time and I guessed she was trying to avoid drawing attention to herself like the English royals did when they went to college in America.

There was silence on the other side of the door. No footsteps retreating, but also no hint that the person inside had heard. Or cared.

I held my breath. Examined the paint on the door. Unlike the other two doors, this one showed some signs of wear.

Finally, a lock clicked. The door swung open. A woman wearing a crisp black dress and ruffle-y white apron stood before us. "Relatives, you say?" Her English was good, with a light accent.

"Yes," I said.

She narrowed her eyes as she studied us. "Of what sort?"

"Uh…" I faltered. What kind of a question was that? "Of the direct sort."

She pursed her lips and moved to shut the door. "You'll still need to wait for the house to officially open."

My arm shot out to stop the door from closing. "Our mother was Alette Sparre."

The maid froze. Her face drained of color until it almost matched her starchy white apron. "Excuse me," she said, then backed away from the door.

She left it open a crack.

Tanner crossed his arms over his chest to wait.

I pushed the door open and stepped inside.

"What are you doing?" he hissed. "She's going to get someone—she'll be right back."

"Yeah, probably. I'm just making sure."

He groaned, but followed me in. "Barging into the house without an invitation is not the best way to make a good first impression."

"Relax, we'll just wait inside the door. It's not like I'm going to start a treasure hunt or anything." Although … a treasure hunt was not a bad idea. I needed to figure out why Garon had been here. Maybe I could find some old pictures. Or one of those visitors ledgers where guests had to sign in. If Garon had gotten stuck in time, maybe he'd left me a note in something like that.

I realized we were standing in a kitchen. The floors

were a mosaic of black and white tiles. Black countertops gleamed beneath white cabinets, and light filtered in through a window above the double sink. The walls were covered in wallpaper, white with tiny bunches of cherries scattered about—like they'd been spilled from a jar and left where they landed. A small round table—red, with four chairs—stood in the center of the room.

Voices sounded from another room and slow footsteps headed our way. I straightened up. I was possibly about to meet my grandparents for the very first time. Or maybe an aunt or uncle.

Or maybe a cousin! Did I have any cousins? I'd always wanted cousins, but my dad's only sibling—a sister—was single, and I'd given up on her ever having a family.

This place was so fancy. So proper. What if we did something to offend them and they kicked us right out? Maybe coming in uninvited hadn't been the best decision. What if they hated us?

The maid entered the kitchen, followed by an older woman who looked fit enough to run a marathon. The only clue that she was older than forty was her white hair, which was cropped into a pixie cut. She was slender and a bit shorter than me, but moved like she had the muscles of a jungle cat. Honestly, she looked like some sort of sprite.

Was this my grandma?

She came to a stop a little closer than I would have liked, invading my personal space. Up close, I could see some wrinkles I hadn't noticed at first. She looked to be around sixty—maybe older—but she'd obviously kept herself in really good shape. She was probably one of those older women who did Pilates six times a week.

"You couldn't wait for us to open," she said, her

silvery voice laced with disapproval.

"I'm so sorry. Um, ma'am. But we're Alette Sparre's kids and we understand this is her house. We really just wanted to know more about her and her family—well, our family."

The woman pursed her lips.

"Please, we've come a long way. Would you be willing to tell us about our mother? Or show us some pictures? Did you know her? Are you…?" I couldn't finish the question. I hoped she knew what I was asking.

Her eyes softened a touch. "I'm not your grandmother, if that's what you're asking. The Sparre family sold this house a decade ago. Said it was too expensive to keep up. The money from the government helps a bit, but the home is not a popular enough destination to make a real difference. I'll be putting the estate up for sale sometime soon myself."

I felt myself deflate. "Oh."

Beside me, Tanner's shoulders slumped. "Do you know where the family went?" he asked. "After they sold you their house?"

"Well, they mentioned a place in town, but I believe it was more of an interim destination." She swallowed and touched the side of her face, like she was brushing away an invisible hair. "I don't know where they ended up."

My disappointment must have been evident because she added, "But you could try it—the Seaside Inn. The woman who runs it is very good. She might remember something that could help you."

Tanner spoke up. "Could we walk around a bit before we leave?"

The woman hesitated, a touch longer than necessary, and cast a sideways glance at the maid. "We're not open for visitors yet."

"Please?" I begged.

"I'm sorry, but our policy is firm. You'll have to come back during visiting hours. Bea will see you out." The elderly woman turned and left the room.

The housekeeper—had the woman called her bee?— walked to the door and held it open, a silent invitation for us to leave.

Tanner stood.

I couldn't believe they were going to kick us out of our own mother's house without even letting us see it. I debated pushing back, but felt Tanner's hand on my arm.

"Let's go for a walk," he said.

"Fine," I grumbled. He was right—fighting wasn't going to get us anywhere. Best to be compliant and come back in an hour when they couldn't kick us out. Then we could snoop around all we wanted.

Hopefully.

Unless it was one of those tours where they make you stay with the guide the whole time. We'd just have to find a way to work around it. Maybe, if we saw something promising, Tanner could distract the guide while I dug for info.

But then I'd have to let Tanner in on the real reason I'd agreed to come here. How would he react to that?

Bea ushered us out the door. "Thank you for stopping by. We'll see you back soon." The latch clicked behind us.

"We don't really have to go for a walk," Tanner said. "We could just sit on the front steps and wait."

"No, a walk would be nice." I stole a glance at my phone just in case I'd somehow missed a call.

Nothing.

"Where to?" Tanner said.

I eyed the woods where Garon had been heading in

the 1920s picture.

And then Tanner grabbed my arm. "Wait." His fingertips dug into my flesh.

"Ow, geez." I shook him off.

"Sorry, I just…" He cocked his head. "Do you hear that?"

I blinked at him.

He walked back to the red kitchen door, paused, and then continued past it, to a set of steps leading down to the garden.

I followed him, straining to hear whatever he'd heard.

He walked down the porch steps, slowly.

Then, I heard it too.

A clear, sweet soprano. Singing a song I hadn't heard in years. A song that had haunted my dreams ever since…

My heart froze. It froze right there in my chest, while the words of the song scrolled across it.

Tanner's mouth dropped open. Our eyes met. But neither of us spoke. Neither of us could. Speaking would break the spell and, besides, what could possibly be said?

We followed the music, which was coming from the garden we'd glimpsed earlier. A little stone path led from the side of the house and through an open garden gate. We followed it through the gate and into the garden. Past neat little rows of green bunches sprouting from the ground and red tomatoes hanging from the vine.

The chill worked its way from my heart into the rest of my body. Because what I was hearing was not possible.

The music grew louder as we passed row after row of vegetables.

We continued all the way to the back of the garden, where a willow tree stood maybe six feet tall. It was still a baby, its branches just beginning to turn down to create the weeping effect these trees had when they were mature.

As we approached the tree, the singer came into view. She was sitting in a lush patch of grass beneath the willow tree, bent over a spot in the garden that had been dug up. She was working the freshly-turned dirt with a trowel. Beside her, a box held several flower bulbs.

The woman's fingers were slender and long. Dirt clung to her nails and her apron. Her willowy brown hair fell loosely about her shoulders.

I sucked in a breath. I knew this woman's hands, her hair, the way her body moved.

She looked up, startled to see us.

The ice inside me broke. My heart broke along with it. Because the vision before me couldn't possibly be real.

It was my mother.

Chapter Nine

The Arsonist

Lindy

1623—Valstenia

Garon's news that someone was conquering lands in Valstenia's name cast a dark pall over the room and left a silence nobody wanted to fill.

I pulled the crown off my head and held it out to Garon. "This really belongs to you."

He made no move to take it. "Sister."

He said it so gently—so delicately—that it filled me with dread. Whatever he had to say was not something I'd want to hear. I willed him not to say it—to just let the silence stretch.

But he didn't. "I'm not here to stay. Once I get well, I must return."

"You most certainly will not," my mother said firmly. "It was foolish enough that we let you leave once. We can't possibly let you risk your life again for some girl. What spell does she hold over you?"

Garon frowned. "She holds no spell over me. But I chose life in the future and I can't back out of that now. I gave her my word I would return. I must honor it."

I studied him. "So, you're saying you will return merely out of honor? Not that you want to return?"

He stiffened. "I didn't say that. Of course I want to return. But my wants have nothing to do with it."

"Yes, they do," I said.

"You say you must honor your word to this future-girl," my mother said. "But what of your duty to your family? Does that not hold more weight? If the threat you speak of is real, we need you here. And, besides, the danger of going back is too great." She looked to Oliver, a silent plea for corroboration.

"Time travel is dangerous and unpredictable," he said. "Always has been, of course."

"See?" Mother said. "I can't allow you to risk a return to the future. The girl will understand."

Garon pursed his lips but said nothing. I couldn't tell what he was thinking.

Oliver's fingers tapped against his thigh. "There may be another way."

"Please no more talk of time travel," Mother interjected. "The point is moot, as Garon will not be doing any more time traveling. Oliver, I'll thank you to keep your theories, your inventions, and your discoveries to yourself."

Garon let his body sink back into the bed, giving the appearance of defeat. But if I knew him at all, the discussion wasn't over—it was merely on hold. He was letting our mother think she'd won.

Garon would not be traveling back in time.

For now.

Oliver cleared his throat, a sudden tightness in his eyes. His gaze darted between mother and me. "The preparations must nearly be done? For our journey, that is. When will we leave to seek out the Topaz thief?"

Mother rubbed her temples.

"I expect we will leave in the morning," I said.

Oliver bowed, but it seemed stiff. "Very good, Highness. I'll be ready."

****

Everyone had left the room but me, and Garon was

resting. I was sitting by his bed, my mind spinning with the implications of everything I'd learned this afternoon, when Borov came to the door. His face was flushed. "Highness, I need to speak with you."

Something in his tone sent a chill across my skin.

I stepped out so as not to wake Garon.

Borov said, "The royal gardens are burning to the ground."

My jaw went slack.

He continued, "The fire is contained, but the entire garden will be lost."

The city relied heavily on the palace gardens for food. What would this mean for the coming winter?

"We believe this was a deliberate attack on the castle." Borov faltered, as if he wanted to say more but didn't quite know how.

I found my voice. "Is there more?" I prompted.

"It is my personal opinion, Queen Shalyndria, that this attack was meant to send a message." He shifted, his gaze darting to the side. "It was a warning."

"A warning of what? Borov, you may speak frankly. Is this connected to the disturbance you investigated at the market earlier?"

He stepped closer and lowered his voice. "I fear the fire is a warning of things to come. There are whispers in the village of a woman—a witch—who possesses great power. Her beauty is said to surpass that of lilacs in the spring, a star-dusted night sky, and the gleam of the ocean on a clear day. It is said to be surreal." His eyes were thick with the meaning of words left unsaid.

"It is the work of the lost Topaz," I finished for him. "Surely, this witch is the thief?"

"I believe so, yes. My soldiers are searching for her— I sent my son out earlier to make discreet inquiries—but she has eluded us thus far."

"And you believe she is connected to the fire?"

"We have no reason to suspect anyone else."

"But why would a beautiful witch burn the royal gardens? We're missing something, Borov. We don't have the whole story."

I clasped and unclasped my hands together, my fingers twisting around each other and mirroring my thoughts. "This morning, when we were in town, there was a shocking level of animosity toward the crown. I had been led to believe that the royal family enjoyed good relations with the townspeople. But, Borov, has something been done to upset the balance? Have we given the townspeople reason to hate us? Because if we have, we must set it right."

The worry lines in Borov's face became more severe. "I am unaware of anything the royal family has done, but the unrest was clear to me as well. Only a few days ago, a shopkeeper reported some misconduct by one of our market guards. I went to search the merchant out while you were engaged with the flower seller, but was unable to locate him. I made inquiries, of course, but no one knew who I was asking for. Or, if they did, they feigned ignorance."

"Have you looked into it further?"

"I have. But I've found nothing. It's as if the shop-keeper never existed. The guard involved in the complaint is also missing. I know not what to make of it."

"So the accused and the accuser are both missing?"

"Correct."

"And the accused is one of our own. A royal guard?"

"Yes."

Fear in the village. Royal guards acting out. People

disappearing. I could decipher its meaning no more than I could determine what to do. "If the Topaz is nearby, perhaps we don't need to prepare for such a long journey as we'd anticipated."

"Perhaps not. But it's also possible the witch has retreated to the forest—or wherever Oliver suspected her of taking refuge—and we will still have to seek her out. Either way, you should ready yourself for a storm."

****

The storm came sooner than expected.

Trevin, Borov's son, returned before nightfall with news. An old man—a farmer—who'd lived peacefully at his home not two miles from the castle his entire life, had been found scrubbing soot marks from his hands at a stream at the edge of his property. When questioned, the man had openly admitted to setting fire to the castle gardens.

I sat in the throne room, the edges of my sleeves becoming frayed as I picked the threads apart. The arsonist was being brought in for an audience.

Mother stood beside me. Her presence was reassuring, yet she offered no advice. She seemed intent on letting me lead, and making whatever mistakes I may. Borov and Yelena were also in attendance.

The heavy doors at the end of the room swung open, hinges groaning with the weight of the doors. Trevin entered with several other guards and an elderly gentleman whose hands were bound behind his back. This must be the arsonist.

Trevin approached the throne and bowed before me. He looked so much like his father—minus the wear of the extra twenty some-odd years. We hadn't been formally introduced, but now was not the time for pleasantries.

The arsonist's gaze darted from side to side, and his body was restless—like a wild animal that had been caught mid-hunt. I recognized him—he'd supplied the castle with a variety of exotic fruits and vegetables over the years, and had most recently assisted with preparations for my father's funeral.

But there was something wrong about him now. Something in addition to his restlessness.

He came to a stop at the foot of my throne and was forced into a bow. He looked up.

And my blood went cold.

His eyes. They were a pale pink color, like the flesh from one of his foreign guavas. I couldn't remember what color his eyes had been before, but it definitely hadn't been this unnatural pink.

Borov stepped forward. "Anton Moller, you are charged with arson, a crime committed against the crown. How do you answer?"

"Forgive me, Your Majesties." He bowed his head low, this time of his own volition. "I will not hide the truth—I did set that fire. But I had no choice. It was witchcraft, I tell you. I had no choice but to obey."

"Whom were you obeying?" Borov barked.

The man trembled. "'Twas a woman, fairer than blossoms in the spring. With skin soft as rose petals and lips the color of raspberries in summer. She put me under her spell. I had no choice."

I approached the man—slowly, as one would approach a horse in danger of spooking.

"*How* did she bewitch you? Did she use an incantation? Special herbs?"

He shook his head. "She had naught but her voice. It was liquid gold in my ears."

"Where were you when this happened? Do you know

where she went?"

The man got a far-off look in his eyes. "She came to me in the night. A vision of beauty in my dreams. But as the darkness faded into day, so did she."

"She didn't come to you in person?" I pressed. "She was nothing more than a dream?"

"She was no dream—I felt her hand on mine. But she faded like a vision and I've not a hint where she could be." He rubbed his hands together, which were still fire-singed. "But I must find her. When can I go?"

The man kneeling before me was not Anton, the farmer of exotic fruits and vegetables. That man had been a gentle soul—practical, hardworking, and of a sound mind. Also a devoted husband to a wife who'd recently passed. He'd never go on about witchcraft or beg to follow a vision to nowhere.

I glanced at my mother. Her face was the picture of serenity.

How many years had it taken her to perfect this mask of calm that seemed readily available to her no matter which emotion churned beneath the surface?

I refocused on Anton. The law said this man should be punished—he was a traitor to the crown.

But perhaps he could serve another purpose.

I spoke directly to him. "If we let you go, how will you find this woman?"

"I feel a pull," he said, "like a string on my heart—tugging me into the forest. It's drawing me to her, I'm sure of it."

I raised an eyebrow, glancing at Borov.

He gave the tiniest nod.

Good, we were in agreement. "Anton, we will let you go, provided you accept our assistance with your task."

The farmer's unnatural eyes softened and he melted

back into a bow. "Thank you, Your Majesty. You've no idea the pain of the pull."

I addressed everyone in the room. "We leave at once—one party following my Uncle Oliver's lead, as discussed in council earlier—with Yelena at their head."

My sister's head jerked up at this announcement.

I continued. "Another party, under my direction, will accompany Anton. Mother will retain the crown while we are away. Both parties are to report back to the castle in two weeks. Borov, we've been preparing for a single excursion—how long will it take to prepare for a second, simultaneous one?"

"Not long, Highness. I'll see to it."

Yelena pressed her lips together like she was squashing whatever argument sat on the tip of her tongue. She bowed her head and nodded. "As you wish."

Trevin's eyes held a look of approval as he regarded me. And … something else?

I looked away. "You are dismissed. Please see that Anton is kept comfortable, but supervised throughout the night."

I caught Borov's arm as the others left the room and spoke in a low voice. "The men you send with Yelena and Oliver—they are to answer to Yelena, not my uncle."

Borov frowned. "Do you have reason to suspect the two would disagree?"

"Just taking precautions. My uncle's motives seem, at times, unclear."

"Understood. I'll make sure the men know."

When we left the throne room, Garon was waiting just outside the door. He came toward me, moving slowly like he was still weak. But a fire burned in his eyes. "Whatever you're up to, I want in."

"No way. You're not well."

"I'm fine, I promise. I can keep up."

"Keeping up isn't the problem. You need to heal."

"I can heal on horseback just as easily as I can in a bed."

I raised an eyebrow. "I'm no doctor, but I'm pretty sure that's not true. And what if we have to go by foot?"

Garon threw his hands up in the air. "I just missed a few meals. Everyone's acting like I contracted some horrible disease or was mortally wounded in a sword fight. I'm really fine. And, admit it, you want me to come, too."

He was right. I didn't want to say goodbye so soon after his return. Who knew how long it would take to get the Topaz.

And having Garon around would be invaluable as I tried to figure out what to make of the disturbance in the marketplace and whether I should trust Oliver or not. Also, what to do about that pesky marriage alliance offer that could either be the solution to all our problems, or the cause of many more.

I averted my eyes, but wasn't fast enough.

Garon must have seen my expression soften because he grinned and said, "Thanks, sis. I knew you'd see it my way."

I should have argued. I should have insisted that he stay behind and then whirl away in a flurry of un-arguable, authoritative queenliness.

But I couldn't. I just couldn't.

My brother was here, and I needed him.

Garon was coming.

Chapter Ten

No Garden Variety Gardener

Maggie

Present Day—Boryn

I stared at the woman sitting in the garden grass. It couldn't be my mother. My mother was dead. Had been almost my entire life.

But those eyes…

Was I seeing some sort of vision? Was this a long-lost cousin or sister? But … even if it was, why would she be here? The house no longer belonged to the Sparre family.

Tanner fidgeted, his gaze darting between the woman and me. "Mags, are you seeing this?"

"I am." I said it quietly, reverently almost.

I approached the woman, who was staring at us like we might be ghosts. Something about her gaze made me speak gently, as if to a lost child. "Hello, I'm Maggie. This is Tanner."

There was no flicker of recognition in her eyes. No indication, even, that she'd heard me. "Um, do you live here?"

The woman pushed her trowel deep into the dirt, then turned over a pile of earth. She patted it down. Then pushed the trowel back into the same spot, upending the same pile of dirt and patting it back down again. Watching her reminded me of a toddler digging in the sand.

"I had a baby once," the woman finally said, dragging her trowel in circles in the dirt. "She was so beautiful."

She picked up a bulb and squeezed it, then set it back in the bag with the other bulbs and went back to digging in the dirt. "Sometimes when my baby cries, I sing to him."

I quirked an eyebrow up at Tanner.

"But you said your baby was a *she*," Tanner said.

The woman's eyebrows scrunched together. "Yes. She is a she. But there's a he, too."

I stepped closer. "You mean you had two babies?" I said gently.

The woman pursed her lips. "Two babies?"

"Yes, a boy and a girl?" I prompted.

She studied the ground like she'd find the answer there. "Two babies…" She trailed off and began singing the song again.

This time, there was no doubt in my mind. This was the same voice that used to sing me to sleep. This was my mother. My mother was alive—right here before me.

My world rocked. My throat closed up.

What had happened to her?

Tears welled up in my eyes as I listened to her lilting soprano. The words of the song were like ghosts from my past. I felt like Alice being dropped into a Wonderland I'd nearly forgotten. I reached for Tanner's hand— something solid to hold onto. He let me take it and, after only a moment's hesitation, squeezed like he was feeling the same way I was.

My cheeks were suddenly wet with the tears I'd been holding back. Holding back for what felt like an entire lifetime.

When the words to the song faded back into humming, I leaned over and whispered to Tanner, "The family wouldn't have left our mom alone here with strangers, would they?"

"No way."

"So why did those women in the house lie to us?"

"Dunno."

"What do we do? Go back and confront them?"

Tanner squinted, like he was thinking. "No. We should pretend like we don't know anything. Go back through the house as if we're just curious tourists, and look for evidence that they were lying. Then we can confront them."

"Or we confront them now. Finding our mom in the garden is pretty big proof!" I dropped Tanner's hand. "You stay here with Mom, I'll go back to the house—"

A voice rang out from the front of the garden. "Miss Allie, are you in there?" The garden gate banged shut, like someone had just entered.

The humming died in my mom's throat and her gaze darted toward the front of the garden. Her eyes widened. But instead of getting up or trying to hide, she started digging faster. She grabbed a flower bulb and pushed it into the ground, then pressed another one right beside it. Then a third, then a fourth. They were all right on top of each other, rather than spaced out as they should have been planted.

"What do we do?" I hissed.

"Nothing," Tanner said. "Let them find us here. See if they try to deny what we're seeing."

"Miss Allie, you know you're not supposed to leave the house without telling me. It's time to come in, dear." The voice was drawing closer. It sounded like the housekeeper we'd met, earlier. What had the older woman called her? Bea?

Our mother kept pushing bulbs into the soil, like she was trying to bury some sort of evidence before the housekeeper found her.

Or was the woman some sort of nursemaid instead of

the housekeeper I'd assumed she was?

"Alette!" Bea's voice was stern now. "Where are you?"

Mom finished shoving the bulbs into the ground and rose. She wore white linen pants, which were rumpled and grass-stained at the knees. She made no effort to brush herself off before heading toward the voice. "No more!" she yelled. "I want to see my babies."

"Allie, please come inside." Bea came into view. She didn't see us at first—she was too focused on our mother.

"Where are my babies?" Alette screamed. "I want to see them." She stumbled toward Bea, raising the trowel she still held in one hand.

I gasped, realizing she meant to use it as a weapon.

Bea heard my gasp and turned toward me, her eyes widening in surprise when she saw Tanner and I standing in the garden.

In that moment of broken concentration, Alette brought the trowel down on Bea's head, using it like a club rather than a knife. Luckily.

Bea cried out in pain, but I saw no blood.

Tanner rushed forward and grabbed our mother's arm, keeping her from doing any more damage. He worked the trowel out of her grasp and tossed it away into the grass. I bent to pick it up. My fingers curled around the handle.

I rounded on Bea, who was clearly not just a housekeeper. "What's going on?" I yelled, darting forward until I stood inches from her face.

"Whoa, Mags, what are you doing?" Tanner screeched.

I realized I was holding the trowel like a knife—and it was pointed at Bea's throat.

I threw it away, breathing hard. It shot into the ground

like a spear and stayed there, stuck at an angle. "Sorry."

I glared at Bea, no longer holding a garden tool that could be used as a weapon, but shooting daggers at her with my eyes. "What I meant was, this woman looks and sounds just like our mother, and, coincidentally, happens to share her name and lives in the house where she grew up. But you and Ms. Hoity-Toity back there told us the Sparre family no longer lived here or even owned this house. And, oh, one more tiny detail—our mother has been *dead* for twelve years. How do you explain that?"

Bea trembled. "Please, Miss. I've only been employed here a few months. I don't know what's going on, only that the Missus made it very clear that you and your brother weren't to lay eyes on Allie here. I was to take her for a drive while you toured the house, but she wasn't in her room when I went to go get her. The lady of the house is indeed called Sparre. I don't know why she wanted to hide that from you. And I don't know if this woman here"—she gestured to Alette—"is your mother or not. But she hasn't been well since I've been here. She hasn't been well for many, many years, from what I've been told. I'm sorry you had to find out this way."

I took an involuntary step back as I processed her words.

Alette squirmed and managed to break away from Tanner, who looked as shell-shocked as I felt. Alette stumbled on a cobblestone, then regained her balance and rushed toward the house. "Leave me alone!" she screamed. "I just want to see my babies!"

Bea's eyes went wide. "She must have missed her morning medication." She scrambled after Alette.

Tanner and I glanced at each other and, by mutual unspoken agreement, ran after them.

Chapter Eleven

Two Paths Diverge

Lindy

1623—Valstenia

I couldn't decide if Oliver's decision to come to me first, before going after the Topaz thief, made him admirable or foolhardy. True, he'd gained the assistance of the crown in his search, but the time he'd lost might make it impossible to find her.

After several hours of following the same path as Oliver's party, the farmer Anton broke off in a different direction. He veered off the worn path and into a thick section of woods, following an internal pull the rest of us couldn't see or feel. He became agitated when we didn't immediately follow, but the thickness of the foliage presented additional challenges.

Both parties stopped while we discussed our options.

"It will be slow going if we follow him into the woods," Borov said. "We'll have to hack our way through."

"Perhaps we follow the path a bit longer and wait for the woods to thin out?" I suggested.

"They won't," Trevin said. "My men and I have been this way before. The woods stretch on for miles and only get thicker."

"Making it the perfect place to hide," I said.

Trevin nodded. "Exactly."

I squinted into the morning sun. There was no other option—of course we had to follow Anton. He alone felt the pull to the gem. The chances were high that the thief would be hiding in the woods, rather than wherever Oliver had last encountered her. "All right, we follow Anton as planned."

"We'll have to leave the horses," Trevin said.

Borov issued instructions. "Everyone gather as many provisions as you can carry and we'll continue on foot. Trevin, find a safe place to tie the horses, away from the main road. We'll leave one man behind to watch over them."

I found my sister and pulled her away from the others.

"I don't completely trust our uncle," I said. "The fact that he'd have something to gain from me losing the throne makes him suspect."

Yelena scoffed. "Oliver doesn't want the throne! Haven't you heard him say how much he abhors authority and merely wants to be left alone?"

"Of course I have. But it could have been an act—while our father was alive, Oliver never had a shot at the throne. Maybe he never considered it an option until…" I swallowed, not wanting to talk about our father's death. "Well, until it became one."

Yelena was shaking her head. "Oliver's not like that. Plus, what could he possibly have left to hide? He's already admitted to being friends with thieves and harlots."

"I don't know," I said. "I just don't want to be caught unaware."

"Has he done anything worthy of suspicion?"

I cocked my head, thinking through the past few days. "I suppose not. Since his return, he's been compliant and eager to help."

"So what reason do you have to doubt his sincerity? Perhaps his long entrapment with Garon humbled him and inspired him to start anew."

I narrowed my eyes, watching Oliver through the trees. "Perhaps." I placed a hand on her arm. "But you're in charge of his party. Keep a close watch on him."

"Of course." Yelena turned to leave, but then stopped herself. "Have you given any thought to our discussion from before? About the marriage offer?"

I'd pushed King Qadar and his offer to the back of my mind, but the idea had been slowly marinating. And, so far, I didn't like the taste. I just couldn't put my finger on why.

"I have given it some thought. But I'm not ready to make a decision yet."

Yelena's eyes were tight. "Time is of the essence, Sister."

I frowned. "Let's focus on the most immediate crisis first. I'll see you in two weeks' time, back at the castle."
****

"Ack!" I spat out the mouthful of thistles that had just thwacked me in the face.

"Apologies, Your Highness," Trevin said. He was walking just ahead of me, chopping vegetation out of the way and trying to clear the path so I could follow without trouble. The farmer Anton led the way, with Borov at his heels. Trevin and I came next, with Garon and fourteen other soldiers behind me.

The soldiers all held swords, chopping their way through the forest, while the only thing I held was my skirt so I wouldn't trip over it. I needed a sword of my own. Or a machete. And I really needed a pair of twenty-first century workout pants and some running shoes.

But these men were not accustomed to women acting like men. They expected me to act like a lady. Like a queen, actually. And that meant no swords. And no pants.

I slowed to let Garon catch up to me. "If there's one thing I miss about the future, it's comfy pants. And indoor plumbing. I guess that's two things."

Garon pressed his lips together. "Yeah, indoor plumbing. You take it for granted until you don't have it, huh?"

"For sure."

Garon chopped a branch out of the way. "So, how's it been going?" He glanced sideways at me. "Ruling, and all?"

"Honestly, it's kind of a mess. Petty disputes between neighbors, marketplace scuffles, and day-to-day issues that need resolving. And then there's the not-so-petty matters. The safety and well-being of the kingdom. Keeping the citizens happy. And sometimes what will keep them safe also makes them unhappy. There's the ever-present concern of funds and food and armies and making sure we have enough of it all." I ducked under a low-hanging tree limb. "Honestly, I'm not sure I'm cut out for this."

Part of me wanted to ask him to stay. Stay and not go back to the future, ever. If he stayed, we could rule together.

But I wasn't going to do that. Because I cared about my brother, and I cared about Maggie, and they both deserved to be happy. So I said, "But I'll be fine. How were things going for you in the future? How is Maggie?" I stepped over a large rock, then looked at him to gauge his reaction.

"Maggie is good…" he trailed off.

"Good? That's all you've got?"

"Well, she's worried about you. I think she misses you, actually. She suddenly has a really healthy interest in Scandinavian history."

I laughed, and the sound seemed out of place in the middle of the forest. Trevin glanced back, his brow furrowing.

"And do you love living in the future? Do you have a job? What do you do for fun? Please don't tell me you enrolled in high school."

"I enrolled in high school," Garon said with the hint of a teasing grin. "It's fascinating, all the stuff they teach you there."

"Did you take *One-hundred-and-one ways to torture your peers*? Because that's an eye-opening class." I shook my head. "Some of the stuff those kids did to each other would surprise even a medieval torturer."

Garon swept his arm to the side to move a bush out of the way. "Well, that's true." He held the bush aside while I stepped through.

"Okay, so you went to school. What else did you do?" I felt myself relaxing. Dropping my queenly façade and welcoming old mannerisms back.

"I have a job working in a kennel, which I actually really enjoy. And—get this—I bought a motorcycle!"

"What? No way!"

"Yep! It's got a much better personality than any of my horses ever did."

"Wow, okay. So you're having fun, I get it. You don't have to rub it in."

"I'm not trying to rub it in." Garon's eyes darkened. "It's fun and all, but…"

I pushed a tree branch aside and glanced at him. "But?"

His gaze darted to the ground. Then to the sky. "But I missed home." Some of the life drained out of him when he said it. Like he was confessing some heinous crime. "I didn't realize how much I missed it until I got here. But now that I'm here, and you're here, and my family is here, I miss Maggie. I wish I could have both, you know?"

"I do. But, Garon, it's not a sin to miss home."

He hacked at a branch that wasn't really in our way. "I know."

I grew quiet, picking my way through the underbrush. I knew how he felt. I knew far too well. There were definitely things I missed about the future. Air conditioning, for example. Good music. Chocolate cheesecake. Hot water whenever I wanted it. The list was endless, really.

But my home was here. My place was now. I couldn't just change where I was meant to be.

I winced as a branch swung back and caught me in the forehead. "Ouch!"

"I'm so sorry, Your Grace," Trevin said. "The vegetation here is very thick."

I rubbed my forehead. "Garon, you don't happen to have an extra sword handy, do you?"

My brother grinned at me, a lopsided, amused grin. "Nope. And, even if I did, it would not be *proper* to give a lady a sword."

I scowled at him. "Well, I'm not a proper lady, am I? I'm a *modern* lady, and you're the only one here who knows it." On a whim, I raised my voice and said, "Hey, Trevin?"

He glanced back. "Yes?"

"Do you have an extra sword I could borrow?"

He stopped walking and turned to stare at me. Sun filtered through the trees above and cast dappled shadows on his face. "Uh, no." He glanced at Garon, then back to me, like he was trying to figure out some puzzle. Then he said, "But I have a hunting knife." He pulled it from a scabbard by his side and held it out, the hilt facing toward me.

I grinned and took the knife.

"Really?" Garon said.

Trevin shrugged. "Why not? My sword isn't doing a very good job of keeping her from getting hit by stray branches. Why shouldn't she have a means of clearing her own way?" He turned to me and smiled. I noticed for the first time that he had a dimple in one cheek. "The knife won't be as effective as a sword, of course, but it'll be better than nothing. Swipe in one decisive, downward motion." He demonstrated the move with his weaponless hand.

The trees rustled behind me as the first of the soldiers caught up. "What's the holdup?"

"The Queen is taking charge," Trevin said, then winked at me and turned to catch up with Anton and Borov.

"Highness, it's hardly appropriate for you to carry such a weapon," one of the soldiers said.

"I agree," Garon added. There was a gleam in his eye that told me he was teasing. Trying to make me squirm just for the fun of it.

As my big brother, I guessed it was his job. But still.

"Your objections are noted, dear Brother, but in this highly unusual circumstance, you will accept the inappropriateness of my decision." I whacked a tree branch out of my way. "Though, perhaps, our mother needn't know."

Garon grinned and we continued on our way.

The knife wasn't very effective, but made me feel I had at least a small measure of control. It was a nice change.

Suddenly, Trevin was right in front of me. He'd stopped moving.

But my blade hadn't. "Watch out!" I shrieked.

Trevin darted out of the path of my knife just before it sliced into him.

I stared at the knife in horror, my heart trying to jump out of my chest. Maybe I shouldn't be carrying a weapon after all. "I almost killed you!"

A touch of amusement danced in Trevin's eyes. "You didn't almost kill me." He put his hand on mine, tightening my grip on the knife before I could drop it to the forest floor. "It was my fault. I should have given you some warning."

He took a deep breath and bellowed, "Company, halt!"

The men passed the message back.

I peered around Trevin to see what the holdup was, but I couldn't see much. "What's going on?"

"We're at the edge of a ravine," Trevin answered.

"Is there a way across?"

"Not that I can tell. I think my father is waiting to see what Anton does. This is the first time since we left the main road that he's appeared uncertain of where to go."

"May I speak with him?" I asked.

"Of course." Trevin stepped aside and held apart some branches so I could join Anton and Borov at the front of the group.

There was a tiny clearing at the edge of a rocky cliff, where Anton paced. Borov stood watching him.

"Mr. Moller, are you all right?"

Anton brimmed with agitated energy. The pinkish hue in his eyes wavered, like a sunset reflected on the water. "Can't get across," he said, pointing to the ravine ahead. His mousy brown hair hung limply in his face, but he made no attempt to tame it.

My gaze followed where he was pointing. Now that Trevin wasn't blocking my view, I could see there was indeed a ravine—deep and wide. Far below, water gurgled over stones and fallen tree limbs. There was no way we'd be able to get across this.

Anton rocked on the balls of feet, back and forth, back and forth. His eyes were laser-locked on the cliff at the other side. "So close. So close. So close."

Behind me, the trees rustled and Garon joined us, filling the rest of the space in the clearing. One more body and I'd be afraid of getting jostled over the edge.

I placed a hand on Anton's arm.

He flinched away from my touch.

"She's close. So close. Just over the ravine." He nodded to an invisible spot hidden behind the trees on the other side. His body inclined toward it—as if he believed he could fly across the gap and straight to the woman who had bewitched him.

"Perhaps there's a way across. We can follow the ravine until we find a bridge," I suggested, pulling him away from the edge.

"If I have my bearings right," Borov said, "there is a bridge about two miles off. It'll be the one we would have taken had we stuck to the road. It's likely that Oliver's party has already crossed."

Trevin's voice came from behind me, still hidden in the cover of brush. I was glad he didn't try to push through into the clearing. Anton was already too close to the edge. "We should go back the way we came, get the horses, and continue on the road. Traveling beside the ravine is too dangerous."

"Anton, come away from the edge," I urged. "We'll get across, but we must go back the way we've come." I tugged on his elbow, but he jerked away from me, his gaze fixed at a spot on the other side.

He was behaving like an animal—not smart enough to understand that going around would get him where he wanted to go.

"Anton, there is no crossing here," Borov said. "We must retreat." Borov gripped Anton firmly by the arm and pulled him back toward the tree line.

Anton shrieked, and it was the howl of a wild thing.

"Trevin," Borov barked.

Trevin pushed into the clearing, switching places with Garon, and helped his father. The two of them manhandled the squirming, kicking old man back into the forest—back the way we'd come.

I peered across the divide, straining to see something—anything—that might hint at a habitation on the other side. But all I saw was more of the same thick forest we'd already been through.

Garon was waiting for me behind the tree line. Together, we resumed hacking our way through the forest, following Borov and Trevin back to the horses.

"Look out!" The shout came too late. A form barreled into me, knocking me off my feet with great force. It was Anton, and his weight felt nothing like that of a feeble old man. He was a bull and I the red cape.

Except … I didn't seem to be his final target.

He continued past as I flew to the side, my arm swinging around like a whip. The knife Trevin had given me shot out of my hand, and I hit the ground, landing hard on my hip.

"Lindy!" Garon cried out, at the same time that Borov shouted, "Anton!"

Crashing footsteps approached and I scrambled out of the way. Borov barreled past, following Anton.

I leaped up and ran after them, pushing into the clearing just in time to see Anton, stumbling like a feral wolf, run right up to the edge of the ravine and launch himself over the edge.

I screamed as the old man tumbled out of view. My scream echoed in my ears—no, it wasn't an echo—I was screaming and screaming and screaming.

I rushed toward the edge of the ravine. Perhaps he'd grabbed a tree branch. Maybe it wasn't as deep at I'd thought. Could there have been a ledge?

But Borov caught me before I got there. "He's gone, Highness. Don't look."

Trevin went to the edge and peered down, his lips pressing together in a grim line. He met my eyes and gave a tiny shake of his head.

Far below us, water roiled and crashed.

And my limbs went weak.

Anton was dead. The Topaz had claimed its first victim.

Chapter Twelve

Seeing Ghosts

Maggie

Present Day—Boryn

Alette—my mother who was supposed to be dead but was clearly not—stumbled into the house, followed closely by Bea. I didn't hesitate before barging in after them. We followed them through the bright kitchen, down a hallway, and up a flight of stairs. Tanner stayed right behind me.

The older woman we'd seen earlier emerged from a side room while we were running up the stairs. "What in heaven's name is going on?" she shrieked. "Bea, what are you doing? Why is the patient out?"

"Sorry, Ms. Sparre," Bea said, not even bothering to pause in her pursuit. "She's acting up today."

I stopped on the stairs and rounded on the older woman. "You said the Sparre family didn't live here anymore!"

"Yes, well, I lied," she snapped. "Now step aside while I see to the patient."

Tanner planted himself in front of her, blocking her way up. "By *patient* do you mean *our mother*?"

The older woman glared at us through shrewd eyes. I felt the blood pumping through me—each heartbeat ticking by while we waited for her answer.

She pursed her lips. "Yes, I mean your mother." She brushed past us and hurried up the stairs.

My legs turned to jelly. I sank down on the step,

reeling from the shock of hearing this stranger admit—openly—that our mother was alive and, worse, that she'd had no intention of telling us.

Tanner sat down beside me, rubbing his face. There were shadows under his eyes.

How could our mother possibly be alive? After all this time? She'd been dead. For so many years. We'd gone to her funeral…

No, wait … we hadn't. Tanner and I had been too little, according to Dad. We'd stayed home with our aunt.

But Dad had gone. Had there been an open casket? Had he actually seen my mother's body? How could this be within any realm of possibility?

"Do you think Dad knows?" I asked Tanner.

He shook his head. "No way. He couldn't have—wouldn't have—kept this from us for so long."

"But he went to the funeral. And they would have had him identify her body, right?"

"I don't know. I think it was a closed casket—her body would have been pretty mangled up from the car accident."

"Was there even a body? Did Dad bury someone else in our mother's place or was it just an empty casket?"

"I don't know, Mags. But I'm guessing that lady up there"—he nodded up the stairs—"will have some answers."

My body felt like it was going to melt into the floor—energy draining out by the second. But I wanted answers.

I heaved myself up. "Then let's go."

The house was big—like the Parker mansion I'd had to search through after Kate disappeared, but without the sinister vibe. This house was old, charming. Maybe a bit neglected, but not sinister. It actually felt comfortable—like I'd want my own home to feel someday—even though it was massive.

Finding our mother wasn't hard. She was in the second room we reached once we got to the top of the stairs.

Bea and the elderly woman were bent over the bed. Bea had a wet washcloth pressed to Alette's forehead and the elderly woman was...

Wait, was that...?

"Get away from my mother!" I ran to the bed, where the older woman was sticking a needle into my mom's arm.

She finished just before I got there and slid the needle out, popping it into a plastic case full of used needles. Gobs and gobs of them.

I gaped at it, clutching my stomach. "Does she have diabetes or something?"

The woman eyed me. "No."

"What are you giving her, then?"

"It's a mild sedative."

Tanner's clenched his fists. "You *sedated* her? She wasn't trying to hurt anybody."

"The sedative wasn't to protect *you*." The woman glanced at Alette, a wave of tenderness washing over her features. She stroked Alette's hand. "It was to protect *her*."

Bea stepped away from the bed, taking the wet washcloth with her.

"Who are you?" I said, glaring at the older woman. "Who are you, really?"

The woman sighed, stepping away from the bed. "I thought it best to keep you from the truth. For your own good."

"How could it be for our own good to think our mother is dead?" Tanner said.

"That's a long story. Why don't we sit down?" The woman gave Alette's hand a final squeeze and stepped toward the door. "Bea, you'll keep an eye on her?"

"Of course … Madam." Bea curtsied, but the action felt forced. Like she was putting on some sort of show.

Tanner and I followed the elderly woman down the hall and into a cozy sitting room. I didn't see any old pictures on the walls and, now that I knew the truth about this place, the fact that Garon had been here was even more of a mystery.

"Please, sit." The woman pointed to a couch with ornate little claw feet and antique-y floral fabric. There was a piano in the corner—an upright, with a little doily on top that looked like it'd been crocheted by hand. Heavy curtains hung from the windows, blocking out most of the natural light.

The woman turned on a lamp and poured some tea from a pot sitting on a little side-table. She handed us each a cup and settled into a plush armchair.

"My name is Dantzel. I am…" She hesitated, like she was choking on her own words. She swallowed and started again. "I am Alette's mother."

Alette's mother.

My mind went numb. My thoughts came and went in slow motion.

Alette's mother—my grandmother.

I stared at the woman sitting in the chair across from me, waiting for her words to sink in. Waiting for them to make sense.

The scrapbooks we had at home excluded my mother's parents. There were no pictures of them coming for visits or snuggling me as a baby. No Christmas cards or birthday notes. It was like my mother had forgotten about them herself.

Or she'd made a point to exclude them from her life.

The woman, Dantzel, was watching me. Watching Tanner. Keeping her lips pressed together while we processed her announcement.

Tanner spoke first. "You're lying," he said, and his voice was laced with venom.

Dantzel's eyebrows twitched up. "I'm not."

"Well, if you're not lying, then you're a horrible person and I'm not going to sit here and listen to you." He rose quickly, his elbow knocking a lamp on the table beside him.

The lamp wobbled, but stayed put.

Tanner, on the other hand, stalked out of the room.

"Tanner, wait!" My words were lost in the slamming of the door. I flinched. His reaction shocked me almost as much as Dantzel's confession.

It took me a moment to find my voice. "You're not lying," I said, studying her face for any hint of deceit.

She shook her head.

"But you were lying before. Obviously, since you said you weren't our grandmother and now you're saying you are." My voice hitched, betraying the emotions I was holding tightly at bay. "That is what you're saying, isn't it?"

Dantzel nodded. "Yes. I'm your grandmother." She swallowed. "And, just for the record, your brother is right. I *am* a horrible person. I only hope you'll allow me to offer an explanation for my behavior. It doesn't make up for what I've done, but it will, perhaps, help you understand."

I considered. I really wanted to go find Tanner, make sure he was okay. And whatever Dantzel had to say, I wanted Tanner to hear it, too.

But here was this woman—my grandmother, whom

I'd never had the chance to know—sitting beside me and wanting to talk. I couldn't just leave.

"Okay." I tucked my hands under my legs so I wouldn't fidget. "Let's hear it."

"Alette has never been well. As a child, she suffered from terrible migraines, unexplained body aches and pains, and frequent night terrors. Doctors didn't know what to do with her. Could never give us a diagnosis. Had us try pills, therapy, surgery, even. But nothing helped. You can't possibly imagine the agony of watching your child suffer and being powerless to stop the pain."

"No, I guess I can't."

"When Allie decided to go to the United States for college, I was very strongly against it. She'd enjoyed a few months of improved health and took it as a sign that things were changing for her. That she was getting better. I wanted to believe it, but it seemed too good to be true. I knew if she went away I wouldn't be able to keep an eye on her in case her condition worsened. But she's always been stubborn and I could do nothing to change her mind. I agreed to let her go for a semester and then we'd re-evaluate."

"Let me guess—she stayed longer than she was supposed to."

"She met your father. I never understood what she saw in the man."

I bristled, deeply offended by the jab. My dad might not be the handsomest or smartest man alive, but he was a good man and he worked harder than anyone I knew. And he'd loved my mother—there'd never been any question in my mind about that.

Dantzel didn't seem to notice she'd offended me. Her eyes were faraway. "Allie begged for another semester.

Said she'd never felt more alive, never felt more healthy. Mind you, she did not tell me about meeting your dad. Only said she'd made some friends who were helping her. And that she thought the climate was making her feel better."

"What's special about Virginia's climate?"

"Nothing. It wasn't the climate. My Allie was in love, and it made her feel invincible. She married against our wishes. The news that she wouldn't be returning was devastating, and I worried for her long-term health. I sent my husband, Roan, to Virginia to retrieve her, but he came home alone. He told me she was happy and to leave it alone."

"Why didn't you?"

"I did," she scoffed. "At least, I did for a time. And then she got worse. I could tell from her letters, which she wrote every week. They started getting cryptic. More scattered. The most alarming part, however, was the way she spoke of her babies."

"Me and Tanner," I murmured.

She nodded. "Yes. She spoke of you as if you were figments of her imagination, not real, live children. You were just a toddler when it started." She paused, then said quietly, "I worried for your safety."

I stared at my cup of tea, which was going cold.

"I knew if she thought of you as a mere sprite or imaginary plaything, she would not take proper care of you. What would happen, for instance, if she took you to the park and let you wander free while she daydreamed, or became engrossed by the fantasies in her mind while giving you a bath?"

I sucked in a breath.

"You understand, then." Dantzel nodded. "Good. It's true I had never met you, but you and your brother were my only grandbabies. I had to do something."

"Why didn't you tell my dad? He could have kept us safe."

Her eyes softened. "Maggie."

It was the first time she'd said my name and it caught me off-guard. She had my attention.

"I did tell your dad. That was the first thing I did. But he didn't believe there was a problem. Whether he was too in love with Allie to see the truth, or if he just chose to ignore it, I can't be sure. I have to believe that if he thought you were in real danger he would have intervened. But the fact remains that he did not recognize Allie's condition. He couldn't see what I could. I don't blame him. I'm her mother and I'd seen it all before. But you'll understand, then, why I had to take drastic action."

It took a moment for her words to sink in. I gasped when I worked out what she was saying. "You faked it. You faked our mother's death."

She nodded. Just once. But she held her head high, like she wasn't ashamed of what she'd done. "I visited first, to see if I could talk sense into your father. To be sure my suspicions were right. I wasn't about to separate a mother from her babies without good reason. While I was there, I observed Allie engrossed for hours in her scrapbooks, while you and Tanner had free roam of the house. Maggie," she said sternly, "barely two-year-old babies should not have free roam of the house. Just in the few days I was with you, I can't count how many times I took scissors out of your hands, stopped you from choking on Tanner's Legos, or kept you from tumbling down the stairs.

"And Tanner, he was another story. He got into everything—was always climbing on the counter, getting into the medicine cabinet, jumping off the kitchen table. I even saw him put a stepstool on the counter once. When I moved it, he got angry and said he needed it there in order to climb on top of the fridge. He moved so fast." She shuddered. "But the incident that pushed me to action was the day he left the house. Just opened the front door and walked out all by himself, like it was the most natural thing in the world—like it was not the first time he'd done it.

"Allie was working on a page and didn't even hear the front door open. Tanner told you to come with him—said he was going for a walk. He was barely four years old and you were only two. He grabbed your hand and you left the house together, but then you saw a butterfly and wrenched your hand free so you could follow it. You followed it straight into the road. I was there to snatch you back but, if I hadn't been..." She closed her eyes, took a slow breath. "Maggie, there was a car. It would have hit you." She paused, watching me. Giving me time.

I remembered what Tanner had said earlier about him and me going for walks when we were little. Maybe we had, actually, gone by ourselves.

"After that, I knew. I knew if I tried to get Allie to leave she wouldn't. I knew your dad wouldn't get her the help she needed. He told me that Tanner leaving the house must have been a one-time thing and that it wouldn't happen again. He said he'd put a child lock on the front door. But I knew it wouldn't be enough. And I knew if I tried to take Allie away, your dad would intercede. I had no other choice. If your father thought she was gone for good, he wouldn't come looking for her. And you and your brother would be safe." She paused, her hands clasped tightly in her lap.

"I'm not sorry for what I did. I would do it again. But I am sorry for the years you missed with your mother.

And I'm sorry for Allie. She still thinks of you as a baby. Still misses you terribly—" She sniffed. "Well, I guess you heard her asking for her babies, so you know." Dantzel wiped her face, like she was wiping away an invisible tear.

She fell silent. Her shoulders slumped forward and she suddenly looked her age.

It was my turn to say something. I should say something.

But what? I couldn't say it was okay, because it wasn't. I couldn't say I forgave her because I hadn't. Not yet, anyway.

Maybe I would. Someday. But not today.

I opened my mouth and said the only thing I could. "I think I understand."

Dantzel's lower lip trembled. Just for a moment. Then she schooled her features into a mask of strength. But I'd seen through the cracks to the real woman inside. Just for a moment.

"I should go find Tanner." I stood up. Hesitated. Was there a way I could ask her about Garon without sounding crazy?

I have a friend who you might have met, oh, a hundred-or-so years ago. Does the name Garon ring a bell? He knows how to travel through time so he may have been just passing through.

I shook my head. No. I'd dig into the Garon mystery later. Right now, my brother needed me.

I placed my teacup on the platter, eyeing Dantzel. My grandmother. The woman I'd wondered about for so long.

On impulse, I stepped forward and wrapped my arms around her shoulders.

She fumbled with her teacup, jumping like she hadn't

been touched in years.

The hug was quick. And awkward. And it didn't mean I'd forgiven her for what she'd done.

But it was a start.

Chapter Thirteen

Topaz Domino

Lindy

1623—Valstenia

I was shaking.

From the shock of seeing that poor old man fall to his death. From the horror at seeing him so possessed.

What magic did the Topaz hold that could compel a man to throw himself to his death?

I straightened my spine. Took a deep breath. Forced myself to calm down, even though my insides were screaming at the injustice and terror of what I had just witnessed.

One of the soldiers pushed into the clearing. "Borov, sir, Pieter is injured."

Borov's brow furrowed. "Injured, how?"

"A hunting knife, sir. Sliced open his leg." The guard glanced at me, almost like he was trying not to but couldn't help himself.

My mouth fell open as I realized what he was saying. The knife I'd been holding—it had flown out of my hand when Anton crashed into me.

"Oh, no! How bad is it?" I left Garon's side and pushed past the guard who'd brought the news.

Stupid, stupid, stupid! I chanted to myself. They'd been right to not give me a weapon. I had no idea how to use one. And now a soldier was injured because of me.

"It's ... well, it could have been worse, Highness," the soldier said in answer to my question. "The knife sliced through his pant leg and left a deep gash in his calf. But it doesn't appear to have pierced anything vital."

My eyes searched the trees until I saw him. Pieter. He lay on the ground, the dirt beneath him stained with blood. His face was a ghostly white.

Borov rushed to Pieter's side, with Trevin and Garon close behind. I couldn't bring myself to meet Trevin's gaze. What must he think of me now? After taking a chance and trusting me with a weapon I obviously had no business handling.

I should have insisted on some sort of training. Back when I'd first returned to Valstenia, after escaping the Emerald's curse. I should have convinced my father that women should be allowed to handle weapons, and demanded lessons. I should have spent all those years learning to fight, not dangling from rocks by the sea.

How could I keep my people safe with no training? No experience?

I watched as Borov pressed a piece of cloth to the wound.

Pieter grunted in pain.

Another guard stepped forward and handed Borov a sash from off his uniform. Borov started to wrap the wound.

"Wait," Garon cried. "Look!" He pointed off into the forest.

I followed his gaze, but all I saw were more of the same trees, weeds, and shrubs we'd been wading through.

"It's *Achillea millefolium*." He hurried over, kneeled beside a patch of weeds with little white flowers, and pulled several from the ground. "Yarrow," he said, as if that would further explain things.

He brought the plant back and handed it to Borov.

Borov raised an eyebrow, but made no move to take the plant.

Garon kneeled beside Pieter, pulled the roots off the plant and discarded them. Then he rubbed the rest between his hands, mashing the flowers and leaves together. "It'll prevent infection and help him heal faster. But it has to be touching the wound." He looked expectantly at Borov.

Borov glanced at me.

"Garon knows what he's talking about," I said.

Borov shook his head, but unwound the part of the sash that he'd already wrapped around Pieter's leg. Garon arranged the plant so it completely covered the wound.

Pieter flinched, but then seemed to relax.

Borov wrapped the sash up again, pinning the Yarrow to the wound like a poultice. He then held out a flask and tipped some liquid into Pieter's mouth.

"For the pain," Borov murmured.

Pieter choked on it at first, but managed to gurgle some down.

Borov stood and surveyed the group. "We'll return to the horses together. One man will accompany Pieter back to the castle. I will go partway with them to ensure they don't run into trouble, while Trevin leads Queen Shalyndria and the rest of our party to the bridge." He caught Trevin's eye. "Wait for me there, I'll catch up."

Trevin nodded. "Yes, Father." He glanced at me.

I looked away, my face burning.

****

The sun was low in the sky, nearing the end of its descent, when we reached the horses. We parted ways, Borov reminding us to wait for him at the bridge.

Trevin's horse walked a few paces ahead of mine,

leading the way. Garon was behind me, followed by the rest of our party. Trevin had taken his hunting knife back and now had it tucked into a scabbard at his side. I watched it sway under the gentle movements from the horse.

The knife taunted me. *You are no leader,* it said. *You can't protect your people.*

The truth of it chilled me to the core.

Garon brought his horse alongside mine.

I couldn't hold my tongue for long. "I can't do this," I confessed.

"You can't do what, exactly?" Garon said.

"*This.* I can't do *this.*" I swept my arm to the side, indicating my royal dress, the guards, the forest, the kingdom. All of it. "I'm not a leader. And I don't know the first thing about how to win a fight."

"You'll learn," Garon said. "It's going to be fine."

The words sat on the tip of my tongue. *Do you have to go back?*

But I couldn't say it. I couldn't even suggest it. So I said, "Before you go … will you teach me how to fight?"

Garon ducked under a low hanging branch. "Like with a sword?"

"Yes, with a sword. Or a knife, or whatever is best. I can't stand being so dependent and ignorant. If I want to protect my people, now and in the future, I need to learn how to fight."

There was a tightness behind Garon's eyes. "Lindy … I'm leaving as soon as we get back. I'm feeling healthier, and O has given me an earful on his latest time-travel theories—ways I can keep myself safe. Apparently during the time he was lost—after we defeated the Emerald and I couldn't find him—he was doing some time traveling of his own, studying the works of

Maxwell, Planck, Einstein and the like. Analyzing the quantum theory and electromagnetism and other theories he didn't have access to back when we first started tampering with time. He's confident that I can travel back safely to where I want to go."

"If it's so safe, can you come back more?"

"It's not only about the danger of time travel, Lindy. I don't want to keep living two separate lives. I need to pick one and just live it, you know? I spent so much time stuck, and I've been so many different places, I feel like I've never really lived. And if I keep waffling, I never really will."

A lump formed in my throat as he talked. I swallowed it down. "So … you won't have time to teach me, then." It was an observation, not a question.

Garon shook his head. "No, I won't. I'm truly sorry, Lindy."

"I'll teach you," said a voice. It took me a moment to realize it was Trevin.

Heat rushed to my face. Had he been listening this whole time? I stiffened in my saddle.

Trevin shifted on his horse, turning so he could see me, then repeated the offer. "I'll teach you to fight. If your brother can't."

Garon raised an eyebrow, as surprised as I was by Trevin's offer.

I cleared my throat. "Yes, that would be nice. Thank you."

"You're welcome, My Queen." Trevin twitched his heels, urging his horse into a trot. "We'd better speed up if we're going to make the bridge by nightfall."

****

By the time Borov caught up to us, the stars were out and the moon was full, bathing the world in a hazy glow.

We'd had time to prepare a stew, with meat caught and skinned by one of the soldiers, and potatoes from the stash of food we'd brought along with us.

We discussed strategy while Borov ate.

"We should keep moving," I said.

Borov shoveled a chunk of potato into his mouth. "We won't get far without the benefit of light, Highness. We should rest for the night and continue at dawn."

Despite the sense in what he was saying, it didn't feel right to stop. My body rebelled against the very thought of it, itching to carry on, to unravel the mystery that had only become more tangled since Anton's death. "It does seem wise to rest for the night and continue in the morning. But I can't shake the feeling that we shouldn't stop. We are now hours behind the other group. What if they catch up to the thief before us and need our help? If Anton's behavior is any indication, the Topaz possesses power well beyond our understanding."

Borov turned to his son. "Trevin, you know these woods better than I. Can we travel safely with limited light?"

Trevin considered, gazing up at the sky. "The moon is full, but the tree cover is thick in many places along the way, which will block most of the light. However, I do agree with Her Majesty on the need for haste. I, too, have felt a sense of urgency since…" He paused, searching, it seemed, for the right words. "Since the incident."

"We'll need rest at some point," Borov said. "We could still have a great many miles to travel."

"All the more reason not to waste any more time," I said.

"We can travel by firelight," Trevin offered.

I shook my head. "Oliver said stealth would be required. If we are close, we don't want to draw unnecessary attention."

Borov tipped the rest of the stew into his mouth. "But with no light at all, our pace will be exceedingly slow. If we stay and rest, just until first light, we'll quickly make up whatever measly ground we could have traveled in the dark."

"The roads here are good," Trevin said. "They're well-traveled, well-marked. And the horses have walked them before. I believe they'll be able to carry us safely even without the benefit of light."

Borov pressed his lips together, his gaze shifting between me and his son. "You seem decided, Highness."

I fought the urge to squirm under his scrutiny. I'd always listened to Borov's advice. Until now. "I am. We continue."

"Very well," Borov said, rising.

We traveled in silence, letting the night sounds fill our ears. The horses did indeed seem to know where they were going. Trevin led the way with a handful of his men. Borov and Garon rode in front and behind me, with the rest of the soldiers bringing up the rear.

I tried not to look down as my horse clomped over the bridge spanning the ravine poor Anton had lost his life in. If only we'd come this way in the first place. If only we hadn't split up. Then the gentle farmer would still be alive.

But he'd also be possessed with whatever force had held him bound.

I wondered if his binding was similar to the spell the Emerald had cast on me. This Topaz—Oliver had never explained how it worked. But it must include some magical enchantment of the type I'd been under. A real, unbreakable, force.

And what, exactly, had he used to create the Topaz?

Had he included something besides the flower he'd mentioned? Because I knew of no plant that caused mindless obedience.

There were too many unknowns. Why hadn't I questioned Oliver further? The questions I *had* asked now seemed barely sophisticated enough to scratch the surface of what we needed to know. We couldn't fight something we didn't fully understand. I knew that better than anyone.

I nudged my horse to pick up the pace.

"Hey, Garon?" I shifted in my saddle so I could see him.

He urged his horse onward to match the pace of mine.

"Did O ever talk to you about the Topaz?"

"Not at all. He must have made it after he and I split up."

"While he was perfecting his knowledge of time travel?"

"Right. The man was never happy unless he was pushing some boundary or other." He paused, cocking his head to the side. "How much time passed between me leaving and Oliver coming to you for help?"

I thought back. "It was seven years. He came to me right after our father died."

"That's interesting. It only took a few months of our time for me and Maggie to see the changes in history."

The gossamer thread of an idea appeared in my mind. My thoughts swirled, trying to make sense of it. I spoke slowly, waiting for the thread to become something more solid. "You've told me yourself that time is unpredictable, often folding and bending in on itself." The rhythm of the horse walking beneath me was soothing—rocking me to and fro. "Maybe the discrepancies in our timelines don't matter. The fact that you noticed a change means that something changed after Maggie destroyed the Emerald. Do you think Oliver was upset? At losing his first breakthrough creation?"

Garon caught onto my train of thought. "You think he created the Topaz to replace the Emerald, and that its creation was the catalyst that kicked off the changes?"

"Maybe." I paused, thinking. The thread solidified— the creation of the Topaz *had* to have been the first domino. A domino that had fallen the wrong way. And now pieces were falling so fast in a direction I couldn't begin to understand. "We've got to destroy it. Now. Yesterday, in fact. Do you think Oliver left another riddle that will tell us how?"

"I doubt it," Garon said. "And, even if he did, we don't have four centuries to figure it out."

Garon's words filled me with dread. Despite the fact that Oliver had come to me for help, claiming that destroying the Topaz would be as easy as taking out the plant he'd used to create it, something told me it wasn't going to be that easy. And I knew he wasn't happy about destroying another one of his precious creations.

Garon said, "Good thing we know where he is."

Chapter Fourteen

Barefoot in the Orchard

Maggie

Present Day—Boryn

I found Tanner at the far end of the driveway, near the road where the cab had dropped us off earlier. He was punching a tree.

Well, a tree branch, anyway. It was a pliable branch, one that swayed back to him every time he punched it away. The blossoms that had been growing on it were long gone, scattered like dead bugs at his feet.

"What are you doing to that poor tree?"

Tanner whipped around to face me. He stayed in his boxing stance, shuffling from one foot to the other, like he had too much pent-up energy to just stop. His face was red and sweaty. And, a little puffy.

Had he been crying?

Tanner swung around and punched the branch again. The leaves rustled and the branch whipped back toward him. He punched it away. It bounced back. He punched again.

I stepped forward and caught the branch before it swung back toward him.

"Maggie, get out of my way," Tanner said through clenched teeth.

"No, this is stupid. And you're killing the tree."

"I am not." He shuffled on his feet, still in boxing stance, waiting for me to let go of the branch.

My gaze twitched to his fists, which were raw and

swollen. There was a spot of blood on one of his knuckles. "And you're hurting your hands."

He shook his hands out, then clenched them into fists again. "I don't care. Would you rather have me punching that old lady?"

"Tanner, calm down. She explained everything."

He stopped jumping and stood there, gawking at me. "Oh, she explained everything? That's fantastic! I'm so glad she explained how she stole a mother away from her kids and husband, and then faked her own daughter's death! As long as she explained herself. That makes everything A-Okay." Tanner clenched a fist and swung at the tree trunk.

His knuckles collided with a sickening crunch and he cried out in pain.

"Tanner, you idiot!" I screamed, releasing the tree branch and rushing to his side.

He shrugged away. "Back off, Maggie, I'm fine." He tried to flex the fingers of his injured hand, but hissed in pain.

"You're not fine, you big dope. You just punched a freaking tree. That's not like punching drywall, you know."

Tanner cradled his hand and scowled at me. "Yeah, I got that." He was like a wild thing, snarling and hissing and stalking around in front of the tree.

I backed off, giving him some space.

He stalked some more. Snarled some more. Hissed some more. But he didn't try punching the tree again.

Eventually, the frenetic energy drained out of him and he came to a stop, breathing hard and glaring at the tree trunk.

I approached him slowly. "Come on, let's go get some ice."

Tanner cradled his injured hand like it was a hurt bird, but he let me pull him toward the mansion. "I think I'm going to need more than just ice."

****

Finding an orthopedist in Sweden—er, Boryn, or whatever this place was called now—was easier than I'd thought. An x-ray revealed no broken bones, just strained ligaments. We left with instructions to load up on the anti-inflammatories and wear a brace for two weeks.

Going to the doctor gave Tanner some time to cool off, and by the time we got back, he was ready to hear Dantzel out. But after she finished telling him what she'd told me, he only scowled and said, "Where's our grandpa?"

We were sitting around the kitchen table. A plate of shortbread biscuit cookies sat in the center, and Bea was making tea, even though nobody wanted it.

Dantzel looked at her hands. "Roan has been gone twelve years. He had a heart attack shortly after I brought Allie home."

"Oh, I'm sorry," I felt my chest deflate. "I would have liked to meet him."

Dantzel smiled. "He would have wanted to meet you, too."

"So, it's just you and Alette and the housekeeper, then?" Tanner said, stuffing two cookies into his mouth. "In this big old house, all by yourselves?"

Dantzel glanced at Bea, who was pouring tea into three dainty white teacups.

Bea returned the glance. But there was a hint of warning in her eyes.

Dantzel cleared her throat. "Well, there's the groundskeeper, of course. And we have a cleaning crew that comes in once a week. We also have a tour guide who works here, as needed, when things get busy. But lately we've been able to manage the tours by ourselves."

Bea passed out the teacups and Dantzel brought hers to her lips, like she was grateful for the distraction.

"Allie will be waking soon. Please—when you speak with her, don't tell her who you are. It will only confuse her. She loves meeting new people, so I trust you'll be able to get to know her without revealing who you are."

Tanner huffed. "She's our mother. She has a right to know who we are."

Dantzel nodded. "That's true. She does. But it will require some finesse. Please, for Allie's sake, don't tell her. Not just yet."

Tanner scowled. "Fine. But only for Mom. I'm not doing this for you."

"I understand," Dantzel said.

When Mom woke up, Dantzel introduced us as some new friends, then suggested we might like to take a walk.

Mom agreed. We followed her out the kitchen door, through the garden, to an exit that led to the back of the yard. Mom unlatched the garden gate and pushed it open.

I let out a breath of wonder as the open gate revealed an orchard full of fruit trees—pears, apples, and … were those plums? The land sloped down, and beyond the orchard lay the ocean, glittering in the afternoon sun.

"Wow. It's beautiful."

"Yes," my mother echoed. "Beautiful, beautiful, beautiful. Just like a fairy land." She grabbed my arm, then Tanner's on the other side. "Come run with me. We'll be birds."

With a whoop, she started down the center of the orchard. She stopped a moment later to kick off her shoes, leaving them in the grass. "Feel the breeze on your face, friends! This is what it's like to be free."

We ran all the way through the orchard, weaving around the trees and jumping over fallen fruit. Mom's smile was infections. I even saw Tanner grinning as Mom laughed and spun like a little girl, twirling with her arms out to her sides and chasing us around the trees.

When we neared the beach, Mom picked an apple and took a giant bite. The juice from the fruit drippled down the corner of her mouth. She didn't wipe it away. She flopped to the ground and spread her arms out to her sides, chewing while she gazed up at the clouds.

"What do you see in the sky?" she said. "I see a porcupine with no spikes. And a castle."

"Okay, I'll play." I lay down beside her, letting my shoulder touch hers, and gazed up at the clouds. "I see a dragon to go with your castle."

"And flowers. A good castle must have flowers," Mom said.

"Tanner, what do you see?" I said.

Tanner was grinning, still standing, but watching us with a fondness I rarely saw from him. But before he could say anything, Mom stiffened. She sat up.

"Tanner," she murmured.

I clapped a hand over my mouth, realizing my slip too late. I'd said his name.

Mom studied the apple in her hand, but it was like she was looking through it. She tossed it away. It landed in the grass at the base of one of the trees. "My baby's name is Tanner," she said. Then, in a sing-songy voice she added, "Tanner, Tanner, what's the matter?"

I glanced at Tanner, my hands still over my mouth. His face had gone white.

"He's such a good boy, my Tanner. Such a"—she choked back a sob—"good boy." She drew her knees into her chest and hugged them, slowly rocking side to side. "I haven't seen him all day."

She got up quickly and started walking back the way we'd come. "I'm done playing now."

Tanner followed her, looking like he was going to take her by the elbow but then thinking better of it and keeping his hands to himself. I scrambled to my feet and hurried after them.

When we reached the mouth of the orchard, Tanner stooped and picked something up. It was Mom's shoes. He carried them the rest of the way to the house.

The second we stepped into the kitchen, Dantzel fixed me with a glare. "What happened?"

My mother's feet pounded on the stairs as she rushed up them.

"I'm so sorry, it just slipped out," I said.

"*What* just slipped out?" Her tone was like ice.

Tanner set Mom's shoes down just inside the door, like a forgetful child's playthings. "Maggie called me Tanner. It was no big deal."

"But then Mom got all sad and ran back to the house," I added.

Dantzel huffed. "I told you this would happen." She rubbed her temple. "She'll need some time alone."

She gazed at us and, slowly, her expression softened. She reached out, like she was going to touch my cheek.

She didn't. But she said, "You look like her."

"My mom?"

Dantzel nodded, and her shoulders slumped a touch. Like they were tired from being so strong all the time. "You have her nose. And her cheeks."

"Oh." I couldn't think of anything else to say.

"Do you have a place to stay?" Dantzel asked.

"Um." I glanced at Tanner. "Not exactly. We were going to head back into town and find a hotel."

"You may stay here," Dantzel said. "Bea will fix up some rooms."

"Really?" I beamed at Tanner. That would save us money and time and it'd be much easier getting to know Mom if we were right here in the same house. Not to mention I still had some digging to do to solve the mystery of Garon being here during the home's remodel.

"We'll be open tomorrow for public tours, but there is a wing of the house not included in the tour—we'll set you up there. Allie and I stay there as well."

"Perfect." I wondered where the housekeeper stayed, but asking seemed rude somehow. Maybe there was a servants' quarters or something.

"Thank you," Tanner said.

Dantzel nodded curtly. Her mood seemed to swing from ice cold to warm and then back again with absolutely no warning. "You're welcome. I'll be occupied tomorrow, but you may spend some time with Allie. Also, the beach is very nice this time of year and there's a town with some lovely little shops within walking distance. Bea will make some sandwiches shortly for lunch. Dinner is at six. I'll show you to your rooms."

The rooms were modest and minimally decorated. The other rooms in the mansion—the ones that tourists paid money to see—probably had all the good stuff. Maybe Tanner and I should take the official tour tomorrow.

Dantzel led us to our rooms, which were in the same wing as our mother's, but far enough away that it felt like we had a corner of the house to ourselves. Which weird. I'd never had anything to myself other than my ten-by-ten-foot bedroom with the ugly shag carpet and stained, cracked ceiling.

Dantzel paused in the hallway, with Tanner's room on

her left and mine on her right. "Once you're all settled, come to the sitting room where we met earlier. I have something to show you." Then she turned and left, her skirt swishing as she walked.

"Guess we'll have to get *settled* quickly," I teased, knowing my brother needed all of ten seconds to toss his bag on the floor and call it good.

I checked my phone for any missed calls as Tanner disappeared behind his bedroom door.

Still nothing.

"Garon, where are you?" I whispered to the empty room. "And what's your connection to this place?"

Chapter Fifteen

Cottage in the Woods

Lindy

1623—Valstenia

Trevin had been right about the horses knowing the way. They had no trouble navigating the path in the dark. Every now and then, there would be a break in the forest overhead and I'd catch a glimpse of the star-filled night sky. A part of me wished I was back in Virginia, sitting under the water tower at the edge of Calista and Theo's property, without the pressures of ruling a country.

But I kicked the thought out of my head. Sure, life had been simpler when I was the Emerald's captive. But I'd been a captive.

I steadied my thoughts with a deep breath.

Despite the fact that things were more complicated now, freedom was always better than being a slave. I would just have to figure this out.

We hadn't been traveling long when the horses ahead of us slowed. There was a clearing ahead, where the trees thinned out and the moon cast an eerie glow onto a—

My breath caught in my throat.

There was a cottage.

Actually, a better term would be shack. The windows were boarded up—empty of glass—and the roof sagged, like it was tired of standing. There was no hint of light. No sound. No movement whatsoever.

But it was dead of night, so the silence might not mean anything.

Trevin backed his horse up, holding his fingers to his mouth for silence. He indicated for us to retreat.

We fell back into the woods until the cabin was out of sight. Trevin and Borov dismounted, and I followed suit. We formed a tight circle and Trevin whispered, "I saw no evidence that Oliver's party is here, but that doesn't mean they aren't. Or that they haven't already come and gone. If they are here, I don't know what they've done with their horses."

"This can't be the inn Oliver spoke of," I said. "Are we even certain they came this way?"

"Not certain," Trevin said. "But we followed the only clearly marked path through these woods. It is possible that the inn lies somewhere beyond this point."

"Did you see the smoke?" Borov said.

Trevin nodded.

"What smoke?" I asked. The cabin had looked abandoned to me.

"Not more than a wisp," Trevin said. "Coming from a crumbling chimney on the far side."

Borov said, "I will go ahead and survey the area."

"Shouldn't you take some backup?" I said.

Borov shook his head. "Stealth is of the utmost importance. I will not engage. I'm merely observing what we're up against. We'll make a plan when I return."

He tipped his head in a slight bow, then stole off into the forest. Trevin walked down the line and told everyone to dismount, see to the horses, and keep quiet. I took the opportunity to stretch my legs, and then settled down on a fallen log.

But I couldn't just sit. My mind was all jumbled and, it seemed, my body needed to be just as restless.

I stood and paced from one spot to another, weaving around soldiers and horses as the minutes ticked by. The moonlight was scarce—the trees were thick overhead—but in the spots where it did shine through, it was sharp and focused.

A hand caught my elbow. I spun and found myself facing Trevin.

"Highness. If the goal is to avoid detection, pacing is not the best plan."

Shame pricked at my face. "I'm sorry."

"We're all on edge. I don't believe you've drawn any unwanted attention." When he spoke again, there was the hint of a smile in his voice. "Not yet, anyway."

I peered at him in the darkness, trying to make out his expression. Was he teasing me? I honestly couldn't tell.

The moon crept across the sky, making the shadows crawl along the forest floor. The minutes piled up like leaves at my feet.

The forest was silent and still, holding its breath.

I cleared my throat, which had gone impossibly dry—how long had it been since I'd last had a drink? "Borov should have been back by now. Someone should go look for him." I whirled around to give the command.

"Wait!" Trevin caught my arm.

I looked down at his hand.

He released me and stepped back, straightening his spine. "We can't keep sending people over there one by one. We should all go. My father is the best there is—if he had any difficulty, we should assume he encountered trouble and plan accordingly."

"Right." I smoothed an imaginary wrinkle out of my dress. "Of course, you're right."

"We'll split into groups and approach the shack from all sides. That way, if there is someone in there, they'll be divided in their targets. I'll have one or two men hang back to maintain a broader view."

"That sounds good." My voice caught on the last word. I swallowed. "Thank you."

Trevin looked at me, his gaze seeming to pierce the calm I was trying so hard to call up. And I saw something of myself reflected in his eyes.

On impulse, I reached out to him. Caught his arm and held on tight. After a brief hesitation, he put his hand on mine. His skin was rough, but warm. We gave each other strength.

And then he was off, gathering the group and issuing orders in a hushed voice.

I peered in the direction of the shack even though I couldn't see it through the trees. *Borov, come back. Please, come back.*

We kept waiting. Long after everyone was ready to move. Just in case.

But Borov did not come back.
****

The shack was silent as the soldiers approached, and I could detect no movement from within. My hands tightened into fists as I watched from the tree line. Four guards were stationed around the perimeter of the clearing, along with Garon. They were the backup.

I was backup, too, against my wishes.

Trevin insisted I stay with the others, watching from the cover of the trees, while he led the first group in. I supposed he was right to have me stay behind, since I clearly couldn't be trusted with a weapon. But the helplessness was maddening.

Trevin and his soldiers surrounded the shack and crept toward it from their various hiding places.

They were silent. Stealthy. Trained soldiers doing what they did best.

The soldiers reached the shack and Trevin made a

series of hand movements, wordlessly directing his men. They positioned themselves outside the boarded-up windows and beside the doors, with one man remaining farther off to keep an eye on the roof. Everyone had their weapons drawn.

As I studied the scene, a glint near the front door caught my eye. I squinted, trying to make out where the glint was coming from. There was something propped up to the right of the door, leaning against the shack.

Trevin gave the final signal to his men. His soldiers burst through the front door and swarmed into the building.

And I stared at the glinting object, suddenly realizing what it was.

It was a sword. Borov's sword.

And it was bloody.

Chapter Sixteen

Scrapbook Obsession

Maggie

Present Day—Boryn

The bed looked awfully inviting. My eyelids were heavy—that overnight flight was finally catching up to me. But if I slept now I'd be up all night. And our grandmother was waiting to show us something. Hopefully it was something good. Not, like, an antique tapestry woven by some distant relative or something.

I unpacked quickly, throwing my clothes into drawers and then stuffing my bag under the bed. Tanner was waiting in the hallway when I came out. Together, we made our way through the labyrinth of halls, searching for the right room.

When we passed a series of black-and-white framed portraits, I stopped and examined each face. But none looked familiar. If Garon had once been a part of my family's life, he hadn't been notable enough to make the wall.

"Mags, what are you doing?"

"Nothing. Sorry." I was itching for a real snooping session. But I wanted to see what Dantzel had more.

We continued on until we found her.

She was sitting primly on the couch, waiting for us. A large book rested in her lap.

"Is that a scrapbook?" I moved closer. Did my grandmother share the same irrational love of scrapbooking that my mother did?

"Please, sit down," Dantzel said.

I sat.

Tanner stayed standing.

Dantzel sighed. "Your mother made this. I thought you might enjoy looking at it." She ran her thumb along a worn edge of the book, then handed it to me.

I gasped at how much it weighed.

"Allie started scrapbooking when she was seven. The earliest pages are filled with pictures of her toys, the orchard, flowers from the garden, and other such insignificant objects. But it wasn't long before her work became more sophisticated."

Dantzel stood. "I'll leave you two alone. Please let Bea know if you need anything—I have some other matters to attend to." She walked to the door, then paused with one hand on the doorframe. "Hate me all you want. But don't hate your mother. It's not *her* fault she's the way she is."

The way she said it, with a slight emphasis on the word *her*, made it sound like someone else was to blame. But how could that be?

Dantzel left the room, closing the door firmly behind her.

We were alone! And our grandmother was occupied. My inner spy-girl did a little happy-dance.

But … the book. I couldn't just ignore it. This had been my mother's. She'd made it. Inside lay her earliest attempts to capture the world in a way she understood.

Spy-girl would have to wait.

I slid off the couch and settled down cross-legged on the floor, with my back against the couch and the book in my lap. Somehow, it didn't feel right to look at one of my mother's scrapbooks without being on the floor. That was how I'd always looked at them at home, pulling them off the bottom of the bookshelf and thumbing through them in secret so I wouldn't upset Dad.

Tanner settled down beside me.

I lifted the cover and saw the uneven printing—in pink marker—of a child. My breath hitched in my throat. This was the writing of my seven-year-old mother, describing the random smattering of pictures she'd pasted to the page. There were snapshots of toys, flowers, the corner of a rug, an unmade bed. Random things that could only be endearing to a child.

Tears sprang to my eyes. I pressed a finger to the page and traced the uneven lines of her writing, feeling more connected to my mother than ever before.

A crease between Tanner's eyebrows told me he was feeling the same way.

My vision blurred and I had to blink back my emotions. Somehow, these sloppy, unorderly pages felt more real, and more tangible, than the perfectly planned and decorated ones my mother had made when I was little. I turned the pages faster, smiling when my mother had switched her marker color mid-sentence, and when the pictures were so close-up you could hardly tell what they were pictures of.

One page had pictures of the outside of the house, taken from random angles. In the background of one of them was a tiny stretch of woods. I pulled the book closer, examining the picture for any hint of a guy who didn't belong.

There was none.

Soon the kid markers were replaced with professional scrapbooking pens. The pages became more theme-centered. There were different handwriting styles—dot fonts, flowy cursive, and funky block letters. I flipped past a water-themed page where tween Mom had documented a trip to the beach with her friends.

Even though I knew these pictures were more recent than the one I'd seen Garon in, I couldn't help scanning each new page for his face.

But Garon was not there.

There was a birthday party page.

A picnic page.

A few pages about a trip to the zoo.

The book ended, and I'd seen no trace of Garon inside.

I closed the book and stretched my legs out, letting the book rest on my thighs. Tanner and I sat in silence.

Until I said, "Do you think there are any more?"

"Any more what?"

"Scrapbooks."

Tanner shrugged. "Maybe. Why?"

"If there are more then why did Dantzel only bring us one?"

"Okay, maybe there aren't any more," Tanner said.

"There has to be more. Mom loves scrapbooking, and this book ends with her eleventh birthday. There should be stacks and stacks of these." I chewed on my bottom lip.

"Oh, no," Tanner said.

"What?"

"I know that look. Whatever you're thinking, it's a bad idea."

I laughed. "It is not."

"So, you *were* thinking something?"

"Of course I was." I got up and set the scrapbook on a side table. "Let's go check out the house."

"By *check out* do you mean go everywhere you're not supposed to go?"

"Maybe," I said. "Are you in or out?"

Tanner grinned. "In."

We were looking for more than just scrapbooks, of course. But Tanner didn't need to know that.

Now, where would Dantzel keep records from the 1920s?

****

There was a single dresser in the siting room, and before leaving, I pawed through its drawers. They were full of tablecloths.

Tanner eased the door open and we stepped out into the hall. Would Dantzel be upset if she found out we'd gone snooping? What if we called it exploring—would that make it better?

"Finished already?" said a voice from behind us.

I whirled around, my heart jumping into my throat. Crud, I'd forgotten about Bea. Had she been waiting for us to come out?

"Yep," Tanner said smoothly. "I'll just help Maggie find her way back to her room. She's terrible with directions."

"No need," Bea said brightly. "I'll escort you."

Oh, man. How was I supposed to properly snoop with Bea lurking around? "Thanks, but we're really okay on our own."

"Nonsense," Bea said. "It's easy to get turned around if you don't know the place well. Follow me."

Tanner and I exchanged a look. But we were stuck.

We followed Bea, and I made a mental note of every bookshelf and drawer we passed, revising my plan so that it included a little night-snooping.

We'd just reached the main staircase—the house had several staircases, apparently—when the front bell rang. Bea glanced toward it, indecision tugging at the corners of her mouth.

"It's all right, we can take it from here," Tanner said. "It's just down the hall and around the corner, right?"

"Close," Bea said, glancing at the front door like she might try to ignore whoever was there.

The bell rang again, and then the front door opened. "Hello," a sing-songy voice called. "Are you open? Your website said you were but the sign out front says you're closed."

Bea scowled and called down, "Just a moment." Then to us she said, "Take your second right, then turn left and your rooms are about halfway down that hall."

"Got it," I said.

Bea hurried away.

Tanner and I ignored her directions. We took a left and then another left, focusing on putting some distance between us and Bea. We ducked into a room, which appeared to be just another guest room. No bookshelves and no desks. I rifled through the dresser drawers, which were empty except for a spare pillow and an extra blanket.

The next few rooms we poked our heads into were similar.

We passed an antique armoire in the hallway and I pulled the doors open. Inside was a silver platter and a yellowing tea set. Honestly, how many teacups did one home need?

"We need to find a room someone actually lives in," I said. "Or an office or a study or something."

Tanner pulled open the door to a bathroom, which had an impossibly fuzzy pink rug on the black-and-white tiled floor. "If there's a study, that's probably where Dantzel is."

"Oh, right. Good point."

The next door I opened looked promising. Not

messy—the bed was made just as perfectly as all the others—but this room was bigger, and had that lived-in sort of feel to it. On a table beside the bed sat a teacup with the used tea bag still inside.

"Hey, I think this is Dantzel's room," I said. "She's the only one who drinks tea around here."

Tanner glanced to the door, his brow creasing with worry. "She probably wouldn't keep scrapbooks in here. Let's keep looking. There's got to be a room with a bookshelf somewhere."

I was not leaving. If Dantzel was keeping any more secrets, what better place to hide them than in her own personal space? I started pulling drawers open. Yep, this was definitely Dantzel's room. Clothes, jewelry, knick-knacks. These drawers were full of life.

"Maggie, seriously. This is not cool."

"She's still hiding something, Tanner, I can feel it. I need to know what it is."

I felt my pulse in my throat as I pulled open drawer after drawer, trying to search through them without making it obvious I'd been there.

"Are you going to help me or not?" I said.

"Not." Tanner retreated to the door and eased it open. "But I guess I'll keep watch." He peered out into the hallway.

In a drawer of the bedside table, I found a notebook, which I pulled out and rifled through. But the pages were too new—too white—to have anything old enough to help me.

And then my gaze caught on a chest in the corner of the room. "Hey, isn't that a cedar chest?" Kate's mom used to put all of Kate's old dance costumes in a cedar chest to keep the moths away. Cedar chests were for preserving old stuff, right?

I hurried over and tugged on the lid. It didn't budge.

And then I saw the keyhole. "Blast, it's locked. Tanner, help me find the key."

Tanner looked like he was going to stay put. But then he sighed, glanced out into the hallway, and joined me. We pulled open drawer after drawer. Checked the attached bathroom. Looked behind the curtains in the windowsills. Lifted the lid to the jewelry box on the dresser.

No key.

And then Tanner said, "Oh, look."

I followed his gaze. Hanging from a string on one of the bedposts was a tiny bronze key.

"Not a very good hiding place," I said.

"Well, it took us a while to find, so maybe it was. Or maybe there's nothing in the chest that they really care about."

"Why lock it if there's nothing to hide?" I said.

Tanner and I hurried over to the chest. I slid the key into the lock, my fingers trembling. What would we find inside? Old newspaper clippings? Expensive jewelry? Or proof of a time-traveling visitor?

I turned the key.

Nothing happened.

I turned it again, the opposite direction. I wriggled it back and forth. But the key did nothing.

"Here, let me try." Tanner held out a hand.

I dropped the key into it and let him fiddle with the lock.

"Yeah, this isn't the right key," he said.

I huffed, my gaze raking the room for something we'd overlooked. The dressing table caught my eye. It had a little mirror, a hairbrush, and some hairpins sitting in a dish.

I smiled.

The last time I'd tried to pick a lock, it hadn't gone well. I'd ended up with a bloody hand and security guards on my tail. But that had been a freaking national museum. This was an old trunk.

I grabbed a hairpin and twisted it open, trying to remember what my printout on lock picking had said. I inserted the straight end into the lock and felt around for the pins.

"Tanner, give me some light."

He pulled out his phone and shone the flashlight into the lock.

I peered inside. Single lever lock with an upward-releasing latch.

I pushed the hairpin back into the lock, eased the lever to the left, and then pushed it up. The hairpin slid off unsuccessfully.

I tried again. Left, then up.

A cuckoo clock chimed, and my stomach jumped into my throat. My hand jerked, and the hairpin slid off the lever.

Tanner adjusted the light so I could see better.

I stuck the pin back into the lock while the stupid cuckoo bird chirped. The pin caught the lever. I eased it to the side, then gently pressed it up, using both hands to keep myself from shaking.

Click.

The lock popped and the latch flipped up.

"Yes!" Tanner said, pumping a fist into the air. "Where'd you learn how to do that?"

"I broke into a museum once."

Tanner had no idea I was actually telling the truth. Well, sort-of the truth, since the break-in hadn't actually been successful.

I took a deep breath and lifted the trunk's lid, which creaked in protest. We peered inside.

"Blankets?" I squeaked. "Why would they lock up blankets?"

Tanner reached in and moved the blankets aside, revealing a stack of books similar to the one Dantzel had brought us. He smiled. "Nope. More scrapbooks. Just like you wanted."

My heart sighed. The books did not look old at all. Definitely not from the twenties. "Why lock up scrapbooks?"

"Maybe the scrapbooks are Dantzel's greatest treasure." Tanner's voice had a teasing note, but the statement rang true on a certain level.

"We should leave," I said.

Tanner gawked at me like I'd just suggested we jog to the moon. "Really? You were the one who wanted to snoop for more scrapbooks in the first place, and now you're not even going to look at them? What is up with you, Mags?"

What *was* up with me? I'd been so intent on chasing Garon's shadow that I'd totally lost focus on what was important. Our mother was alive. And she was here. And we were being let into her life in a way we'd never dreamed possible. "You're right, I'm being stupid. Let's look at them."

Tanner hefted out two—one for each of us, even though there were several more left in the trunk.

I set one in my lap and began flipping pages. This one showed pictures of Mom during that awkward transition from kid to teen. It looked like, chronologically, it would have come right after the one Dantzel had shown us.

I turned to a page with pictures of Mom in a field of flowers. And then I froze, my hand hanging in mid-air. I frowned at one of the pictures. It showed a woman, standing by herself, the sky a vibrant blue behind her.

"Uh, Tanner?" I stared at the page, a chill crawling across the back of my neck as I peered closer.

"Yeah?"

"Look at this."

He leaned over and I pointed at the picture. I couldn't pull my gaze away from it. "Tell me that's not the same woman we met today. The housekeeper, Bea."

Tanner peered closer. "Yeah, that's her." Tanner jabbed a finger at the page. "Look, Mom even labeled it. It says *My Queen Bea* right there underneath."

Indeed, it did, complete with a tiny, hand-drawn bee buzzing around the caption.

"But…" I spluttered. "*Look* at her!" I pointed to the page. Tanner must see it.

He shrugged. "What?"

"You honestly don't see it?"

"See what? Just tell me what you're getting at, already!"

"She looks exactly the same." It felt like I was pointing out the obvious. "This picture had to have been taken over twenty years ago and when we met her today, she didn't look a day over twenty-five. If that."

Tanner's forehead wrinkled and he grabbed the book away from me. "Maybe it's not her, then. Maybe this is, like, her mom or aunt or something." He snapped his fingers. "Or it could be an older sister!"

"Her sister wouldn't have the same name, you dope."

"Okay, then, her mom. Her mom could have the same name."

I shook my head and pulled the scrapbook back into my lap. "I don't know. It looks *just* like her. But that's impossible, right? The woman we met today would have just been a little girl when this picture was taken."

"Well, how do you know when the picture was taken? Is there a date on it or anything?"

I studied the page again. "No, I guess not. But assuming it was taken the same day as these others, then it would have been taken when Mom was barely a teenager."

"That's a big assumption. This could have been taken later."

"And then spliced into Mom's childhood scrapbook? Why would someone do that?"

Tanner shrugged. "Dunno. But it makes more sense than saying this woman hasn't aged in twenty years."

I said, "Yeah, I guess," even though my mind was screaming *Holy crap, this woman hasn't aged in twenty years!*

Chapter Seventeen

A Drop of Blood

Lindy

1623—Valstenia

Seconds after Trevin and his soldiers swarmed into the building, a soldier burst out and ran toward me. "It's a trap, Your Highness. Run!"

I hesitated, but Garon yanked on my arm. "Let's go!"

I stumbled, following Garon toward the horses.

And then a cry froze my blood, stopping me dead in my tracks.

"Lindy!"

It was Yelena.

Blood rushed to my head, my heart banging inside me like a war drum.

My sister yelled again. "Lindy, get back to the castle, now!"

The sound of metal striking on metal rang through the woods. Inside the tiny shack, a battle had begun. And my sister was in there.

I turned and charged toward the shack.

Garon joined me—Yelena was his sister, too. He reached the building before I did and yanked a loose board off one of the windows, exposing the inside of the shack. I reached him, breathless, my gaze darting around frantically as I struggled to process the scene within.

Soldiers fighting. Swords clanging. Yelena tied up on the floor.

The chaos in the tiny space was lit by a single lantern

hanging from the ceiling in the center of the room.

Oliver sat beside Yelena.

He wasn't tied up. He was sitting there calmly, almost like he was…

Like he was…

My blood turned to ice.

Garon realized it at the same time I did.

"You traitor," Garon yelled, drawing his sword and running toward the front door.

"Garon, no! We need him alive!" I scrambled after him.

Garon didn't listen to me. But just as he reached the door, it swung open and two soldiers emerged, raising their swords against us.

But … these were Trevin's men. My men.

Fighting against us.

I darted away as Garon met both of them. The three became locked in battle.

I ducked into the shack, my head spinning. My gaze jumped around the room.

Several of Trevin's men had turned on him and were now fighting against him. Others appeared to have remained loyal and were fighting alongside him. There was no visible enemy inside the shack—only the men that had entered with Trevin. And Garon was still fighting two men outside.

I stood just inside the threshold, my body frozen in shock, gaping at the scene.

The front door banged open behind me and Borov entered, brandishing his bloody sword. He lifted it. With me in his sights.

A strangled cry escaped my throat as I scrambled backward.

Borov swung his sword.

I dropped to my knees and rolled out of the way. Trevin jumped in front of me and met his father's blade with his own.

My heart was in my throat, pulsing wildly. I scanned the room, searching for an explanation.

"It's the Top—" Yelena started.

Oliver smothered her with his hands, causing the words to die in her throat. "I said shut up! Why can't you do what you're told?"

While Yelena struggled against Oliver's hold, something stirred in the shadows. I noticed a stone fireplace in the corner, with a whisper of smoke rising from a dying ember. There was someone standing beside it. A voice spoke, silvery smooth and sugar-sweet. "That's enough fighting." It was a woman.

Instantly, swords clattered to the floor. Borov threw his down with an eagerness that was unlike him, and the men fighting Trevin did the same.

Had the soldiers who'd attacked Garon outside also stopped or were they still locked in battle?

Trevin kept a grip on his weapon, as did a handful of his men. They stood at the ready, tension rolling off them as they waited for the speaker to reveal herself.

I realized with a start that none of the soldiers who'd come with Oliver were here. I swallowed, fear lining my throat like a thick syrup, and turned my attention to the figure now stepping out of the shadows.

The woman wore a black, hooded cape. When she moved, the darkness moved with her. "That's better," she said, lowering her hood to reveal her face.

I gasped, taking an involuntary step backward. My brain fogged over.

The woman was beautiful. Hair as dark as ravens. Skin like satin. Eyes the brilliant green of spring.

I shook my head, trying to banish the foggy feeling.

Then, for a split second, the fog cleared and her image shifted. I saw not the beautiful woman, but one who was very plain. Ugly, even. She seemed familiar.

Half a breath later, the beauty was there again, back in place as if it'd never left. Had I just seen through some sort of illusion? Or had it been an illusion when the image shifted?

If this woman was indeed the thief of the Topaz, she was clearly using its magic to make herself beautiful. So, the image before me was the false one, while the one I'd just glimpsed must be her true form.

Why had she seemed familiar? I squinted at the woman, willing my eyes to see through the magic once again so I could place the woman beneath the illusion. But no such thing happened.

"There, now, all the rest of you, put down your swords," the woman cooed. "There is no need for violence."

Yelena cried out again, but Oliver's hands were still pressed over her mouth and her words were muffled. The woman glared in their direction and, under her scrutiny, Oliver seemed to shrink into the wall behind him.

Trevin started to lower his sword, then shook his head like he was shaking off the same fog I'd felt. His gaze darted away from the woman and he raised his sword again in earnest.

The woman stepped toward him, catching and holding his gaze. He lowered his weapon, the fight bleeding out of him. Two of the other guards struggled to keep their senses. One eventually lowered his weapon, leaving a single man left holding his sword aloft. His name, I'd learned only recently, was Sedric.

The woman's lip curled as she focused on him. On

anyone else, the expression would have looked ugly, but it only made this woman more beautiful. She walked over to him and placed a hand on his arm. "Drop your sword," she said again.

"No," Sedric said.

I stepped forward, still unable to shake the vision of the beautiful woman before me, but not feeling like she had any control over my body like she seemed to have over the men who'd dropped their weapons. "Release my men," I demanded, tightening my hands into fists so they wouldn't tremble. "And give us the Topaz. We know you have it."

The woman laughed, the sound delicate and musical. Like a chorus of crystal glasses chiming in perfect harmony. "Oh, no, that won't be necessary."

"Of course it's necessary. It belongs to my uncle, though he shouldn't have it either." I glanced at Oliver. "And where are the rest of our soldiers? The ones who arrived with Borov?"

The woman smiled serenely. "We had to kill them, poor dears. The ones who would not be controlled, that is. Borov is a master swordsman, I'm quite pleased he showed no resistance to my charms."

I bristled, my mouth dropping open in horror.

All those men. Young, most of them. With families who loved them and were waiting for their return.

And I'd brought them here.

Guilt pricked at my cheeks. My face. My entire body.

I swallowed a lump, like a maggot in my throat, and steeled myself so my voice would not waver when I spoke. "I demand that you return the Topaz to its rightful owner, for the good of our great country. And that you stand on trial for your crimes against the crown."

The woman laughed. "I have committed no crimes

against the crown."

"Did you not bewitch the farmer, Mr. Anton Moller, to set fire to the royal gardens?"

"Oh, that." She waved dismissive hand. "Yes, of course, but I wasn't committing a crime against the royal family. I was merely testing my powers."

"That old man is now dead. He threw himself into a ravine trying to get back to you."

She tilted her head to one side. "Really. Well, that *is* an interesting bit of news. Quite unexpected, I assure you. But one less mouth for the kingdom to feed, no? Several less, actually, including those adorable soldiers we had to kill." She laughed. "It's a blessing, given the loss of the gardens. If you ask me, the kingdom needs far less people to feed."

Sedric lunged at her with his sword.

And the image before me shifted.

Borov jumped to the woman's defense, knocking Sedric's sword to the floor.

But the illusion was still shaky—like the woman had lost her focus—and for several heartbeats I saw clearly the girl beneath the enchantment. Young, not much older than me. But bitter, like life had aged her unfairly. A disfigured face—scarred as if from a fire.

My brain clicked the image into place.

I'd seen this woman before. That day at the market. It was the flower seller, whom the townspeople had ridiculed and spat at.

And I'd defended her.

She was the thief?

"Anka," I said, watching her reaction carefully. "That's your name, right?"

Borov dropped his sword arm abruptly, as if whatever connection that had compelled him to arms had been severed.

Anka's image shifted and flexed, like she was trying to work the Topaz's magic on me, but I continued to see the homely woman I'd met in the market. She snarled. "How are you seeing through it?"

I opened my mouth, but realized I had no answer.

"I see you, too," Yelena shouted. "Your lies only work on the weak."

At once, Borov raised his sword, again under Anka's power, and turned it on me.

Borov was not weak. So, how was she controlling him, but not Yelena or me or my last remaining soldier?

Sedric grabbed his sword and jumped to my rescue, meeting Borov's blade with his own.

As they sparred, Trevin shook his head like he was coming out of a daze. He fixed his eyes on me and handed me the hunting knife he'd given me earlier. "Don't let go of it this time." Then he joined Sedric in my defense. Again, he was fighting his own father. Another soldier came out of his trance and joined them.

Anka commanded others back in the fight and they obeyed. Soon the battle was going as fiercely as before.

I rushed to Yelena and cut her loose.

Oliver didn't try to stop me. He just sat there, eyes wide, with his back pressed against the wall. "Anka, that's enough," he said.

She ignored him.

Yelena plucked a sword from the ground—probably left by one of the fallen soldiers—and held it high. Despite her bravado, there was a tremor behind her eyes.

Anka stood calmly in the corner of the room, watching the fight. Borov knocked out one of my soldiers. Then he and his group pressed Trevin and Sedric into a corner.

"Just you wait, little *Queen*," Anka said. "It won't be long before I am beloved and you are nothing." She flicked her wrist and Borov disengaged from the fight.

Borov turned to where Yelena and I stood, both of us holding weapons we didn't know how to use. Trevin and Sedric were backed into a corner. The air in the room was thick with tension.

"You may kill her now," Anka said.

Borov didn't hesitate. He strode toward me, raising his sword in a deathblow. His eyes were unfocused and, I realized, resembled the farmer Anton's. Unnatural. Pale pink.

I trembled, raising my knife.

"Wait!" Oliver stepped between me and Borov. "This was not part of the deal. You never said anything about killing her."

My blood went cold. A deal? He'd had a deal with this woman?

Anka raised her hand and Borov froze, his sword hanging over my head.

She smiled, as if she enjoyed dangling death over me. "No, I didn't, did I? But you can't expect me to let her live, surely. How will I take her throne if she lives?"

Oliver seethed. "You need only a drop of her blood to seal the magic."

I froze. Was this blood magic? But Oliver had said he didn't use blood magic. Hadn't he?

Oliver continued, "All you need is a drop. Steal her identity, steal her throne, whatever. Just don't kill her. You may alter her appearance as well, so even if she returns, no one will recognize her."

I shuddered. Medieval methods of altering someone's appearance usually involved some form of torture.

"But what of the witnesses, my dear Oliver?" Anka

cooed. "Are you suggesting I alter everyone's appearance?"

Oliver swallowed, glancing around the shack. His eyes went to the soldiers. To Yelena. Back to me.

His hands twisted together in front of him, around and around.

Then his gaze slipped away from mine. "I'm sorry, Niece. Please forgive me." Then he turned to Anka. "I see that you must kill them. But first you will honor our deal."

My heart pounded in my skull. I was about to die. This woman would take over my kingdom and bring our country to ruin. Garon had been right all along.

Anka smiled, but there was no warmth behind it. "I haven't forgotten. And you did hold up your end of the bargain by bringing her here."

Oliver refused to meet my eyes. Refused to look at any of us. "Stop dancing around it, witch. Where is my daughter?"

The room went still. The silence pressed against my ears.

His … daughter?

I felt my mouth drop open and saw the expression mirrored on Yelena's face.

"Don't worry, Oliver, dear," Anka cooed. "Your daughter is safe. I'll return her home just as I promised. But we must clean up this mess first." She threw a pointed look my way.

Anka fingered a medallion hanging from a cord around her neck. I hadn't noticed it until that moment. A gem was suspended in the center of the medallion. The gem was pale pink.

"Is that the Topaz?" I blurted out.

Anka flinched, like she was surprised I'd seen it.

Maybe it hadn't been visible in her illusion.

Oliver answered my question. "The one and only."

I squinted at it. "But it's pink."

"Topaz comes in many different colors. Pink is one of the rarest." Oliver slipped into scientist mode, his features lighting up with giddy excitement over one of his creations, even though that creation was about to kill me. "This thing of rare beauty is the perfect vessel to hold such unique power."

His expression went somber, like he'd just remembered where we were and what he was about to do. "We only need a drop of your blood so the wearer of the Topaz can take on your resemblance."

"You mean steal my identity? So you can then kill me and crown an imposter who will destroy our country?"

His gaze darted away from mine. "I'm truly sorry. But she has my daughter—I must obey." He sucked in a ragged breath, refusing to meet my gaze. Beads of sweat lined his brow. "I promise your death will be quick."

Oliver walked over to Anka, who held out a glass vial.

He took it and advanced toward me, his motions jerky. When he was close enough that I could speak without Anka hearing, I said, "Uncle, this can't be the only way. I will help you find your daughter. We can get her back without giving Anka what she wants."

He swiped a hand across his brow, wiping away the sweat. He pulled a rubber stopper from the vial, still avoiding my gaze. "Believe me, I've already tried. Anka has her well-hidden. The only way to ensure her safe return is to obey." He pulled out a small knife.

I backed away from him, holding up the knife Trevin had given me. Anka waved a hand and two soldiers were at my side. One disarmed me in a single movement, and the other gripped me by the arms.

Yelena swiped at the nearest one with her sword, slashing into his bicep.

He yelped and several more soldiers advanced. They disarmed Yelena and twisted her arms behind her back. Another soldier replaced the injured one who'd been holding me.

Trevin and Sedric were still backed into a corner, surrounded by Anka's bewitched men. Trevin ducked and lunged at one of them. The soldier dodged away, and another one brought the hilt of his sword down hard at the base of Trevin's skull. He crumpled to the floor.

Sedric's gaze roved around the room, taking in the half-dozen swords pointed at him, the corner he was backed into, and the unconscious Trevin on the ground. He was searching, I imagined, for an escape. But there was none.

"How can you be sure she'll hold up her end of the deal?" I hissed at Oliver. "Once I'm dead and she's Queen she'll have no reason to honor her bargain. She'll probably kill you, too."

Oliver fumbled, almost dropping the vial, but said nothing. He reached for my hand.

I yanked it away.

A soldier grabbed my arm and forced me to comply.

Oliver brought the tip of the knife to my index finger and pressed the blade into my skin.

I hissed at the pain.

A drop of blood emerged, and sat like a bead on the tip of my finger. Then another drop joined the first, then another, and another, until blood spilled off the tip of my finger and ran down the side, like paint dripping from an artist's brush. Yelena's eyes were murderous, shooting venom at Oliver.

I tried to yank my hand away, but the solider had an

iron grip on my arm.

Blood oozed from the wound, painting my finger and then my hand as it ran toward my wrist. Oliver filled the vial.

"You said you only needed a drop." On impulse, I kicked, catching him in the shins.

He winced, but didn't move. Another soldier grabbed my legs from behind and held them still.

Oliver capped the vial, refusing to meet my gaze. He walked over to Anka and handed her the blood with a slight bow.

She snatched it from him, then uncapped the vial and let the blood—my blood—drip onto the Topaz. It fizzed and hissed where it landed on the hard surface of the stone, sending a tiny trail of smoke into the air.

Anka smiled and closed her eyes. The air around her shifted.

I waited for her to take on my image.

And waited some more.

Nothing happened.

She glanced down at her hands and frowned. "Did it work? My hands look the same." She crossed the room in three steps and snatched up my hand, comparing hers to mine. "They're different." She brought her hands to her face, raking her fingers over her features like she was a blind person trying to memorize someone's face. "I feel unchanged."

She rounded on Oliver, who had backed away and now stood beside me. "Did it work?" she yelled at him.

"It … ah … doesn't appear to have."

"Why didn't it work?" she thundered.

He trembled, but stood his ground. "I don't know." His eyes locked on mine for the tiniest fraction of a second. The look felt meaningful, somehow. Was he trying to tell me something?

My legs were pinned together and there were soldiers at both of my sides, but no one was holding my head. In one motion, I turned to the side and bit the hand of the nearest soldier.

He yelped, releasing my arm. I threw my elbow at his face and caught him right in the nose. He rocked back, his hand flying to his now-bloody nose, and kicked the soldier holding my feet.

Suddenly, my legs were free. I turned and kneed the soldier on my left in the groin, then thrust my heel back into the face of the guy still on the ground, so he wouldn't grab my legs again.

Yelena lashed out at her own captors with her feet and elbows. Sedric lunged at Anka's soldiers, some of whom had lowered their weapons to gawk at me.

Anka stalked toward Oliver, fuming. It seemed the more rattled she got, the less control she had over the men. Some of them shook their heads, as Trevin had done earlier, and came out of their stupor.

Borov, however, remained firmly by her side, as if he'd protect her with his dying breath.

Anka grabbed Oliver by the collar.

Terror filled his eyes.

"You're lying," she said. "You know why it didn't work—you just won't tell me. I hope you're happy. Because you'll never see your daughter again."

Suddenly, she had a knife in her hand. She pulled it so fast I didn't even see where it came from. She thrust the knife into Oliver's gut, twisted it, and then kicked him away.

I screamed.

Oliver grunted, fell backward, and collapsed to the floor.

Anka turned to me, her eyes blazing with hatred. "I will still win your crown." She threw the vial with my blood into the stone fireplace, where it shattered. "My beauty is power enough."

With a flurry of skirts, she ran from the shack. Borov and a handful of soldiers trailed after her, reminding me of puppies running after their master. No, more like children following the Pied Piper—under a spell that could kill them.

The rest of the soldiers were either injured or shaking themselves free of her fog. "Go after them," I yelled at Sedric and the few who now seemed lucid. "Try to stop her! Keep our soldiers safe."

I rushed to Oliver and kneeled beside him. His breathing was shallow, his forehead beaded with sweat. His eyes were unfocused. Blood oozed from the knife wound in his gut.

"You're going to be okay," I said, my fingers fluttering over the wound. I had no idea what to do. I couldn't fathom pulling out the knife. Plus, it seemed to be acting as a sort of plug, keeping the blood in.

Garon crashed into the shack, breathing hard after the fight he'd just had outside. His eyes were wild and his sword bloody. "I'm sorry, Lindy. Those men were so strong. They only stopped fighting a moment ago."

Oliver grunted. "I'm a dead man. Find my daughter."

Garon's gaze landed on Oliver and his expression went slack. He dropped his sword to the ground and joined me at Oliver's side.

"We'll find your daughter," I said. "And you'll be okay—you can help us."

Oliver shook his head. A line of red formed at his lips and I realized blood was coming up his throat. "Find my daughter. Her name is Belina." He pressed something into my hands.

I looked down. It was a stick—or a tree branch—maybe four inches long, with little knots along the bark.

"They bloom at summer solstice"—he gurgled. He was drowning in his own blood, but managed to choke out—"what I put in the Topaz."

"Oliver, how do we destroy the Topaz?"

His eyes focused for a single moment. "Find Belina," he said. "Find the Pearl." Then his eyes glossed over and the light faded away.

Chapter Eighteen

Secret Bea

Maggie

Present Day—Boryn

We had to hunt for them, but we found a few more pictures of Bea in our mother's scrapbooks. She never changed, while our mother slowly grew up. In one of the later pictures, Bea was at Alette's high school graduation, gazing at something off to the side while Alette beamed at the camera. Bea had an arm around Alette, almost like a proud mama. Except, by then, they looked like sisters.

"Maybe she's just one of those people who looks young for a really long time," Tanner said. "Like Gwen Stefani."

"Gwen Stefani has a team of makeup artists and personal trainers and vegan chefs whose job it is to keep her looking hot. Real people don't age like that."

"Okay, what about our principal? She looks the same age as her daughter, who just graduated with me."

I looked back at the picture, not sure what to think. What to believe.

"You know there's a pretty easy way to settle this, right?" Tanner said, sticking the scrapbooks back in the trunk. "Just ask her how old she is."

"Women do not appreciate being asked how old they are. And how would you bring it up, anyway? *Grandmother, this brie is perfectly aged. You know, your housekeeper seems perfectly aged as well. How old* is *she?"*

"That's perfect! See, then we'll know."

"No, it's not perfect, Tanner, it's *rude!*"

"Oh, and snooping around Dantzel's bedroom isn't?"

I had no answer for that. "I am not asking how old she is."

"Fine, I'll ask."

"Do you *want* them to kick us out? Right when we're learning more about Mom? We've barely had any time with her."

"They're not going to kick us out for one mildly rude question," Tanner said.

"You mean one *very* rude question."

"You didn't seem too worried about getting kicked out when you were picking that antique lock."

I looked away. "That's different." It was different, right?

"How?"

I searched for an answer that made sense. "We did that in secret."

"You're crazy, Mags." He walked to the door and eased it open, peering out into the hallway. "We're going to be late for dinner."

I put the last scrapbook in the trunk, trying not to recognize the truth behind Tanner's words, and closed the latch. The lock clicked into place. I put the useless key back and surveyed the room to make sure nothing looked messed with. Then I scrambled after him.

As soon as we entered the kitchen, Bea clucked her tongue and herded us through a serving area, where glass-fronted cabinets revealed stacks of china stored within, then on into a large dining room.

I slowed my breathing and put on my most innocent-looking, non-snoopy-person smile. But guilt pricked at my insides.

Our mother and grandmother were already seated around an ornate rectangular table, with Dantzel at the head and Alette in the closest side chair. Dantzel frowned when she saw us. "Heavens, why did you come through the kitchen? The entrance is right there." She pointed toward a large framed opening, through which the bottom of the grand staircase was visible.

Oh. I felt my cheeks flush. We were not used to living in a house you needed a map to get around in.

Dantzel sighed. "I suppose you'll need a tour of the home. There's a group coming in at ten tomorrow morning, but I should be able to fit you in right before."

"We'd love a tour, thank you," Tanner said, his voice sounding unnaturally sweet.

I narrowed my eyes at him.

"Well, sit down then," Dantzel said. "Allie, honey, say hello to our guests."

Our mother was sitting quietly in her chair, hands folded in her lap, with her gaze fixed on some unidentifiable spot. Like she was actually seeing beyond the wallpapered wall. She didn't say hello.

Tanner and I took side-by-side seats directly across from our mother.

She kept staring through us.

I swallowed and unfolded the cloth napkin lying beside my plate.

Dantzel said, "How was your afternoon?"

Bea brought in two plates of food and set them before Dantzel and Alette, then retreated back to the kitchen. Dantzel unfolded Alette's napkin and arranged it on her daughter's lap, then unfolded one and placed it in her own lap. I didn't know how to feel, watching my grandmother care for my mother as if she were a small child. It was touching, yet also made me sharply aware that no one had been there to do that for me.

And a little part of me wanted to be the one taking care of Mom, not this woman I'd only just met.

"We learned some interesting things today," Tanner said, leaving his own napkin untouched on the table.

Bea reappeared, carrying two more plates of food, which she placed in front of me and Tanner.

I jumped in so that Tanner couldn't ask his stupid-rude question. "It was fun seeing mom's scrapbooking skills improve, although I liked the ones she did early-on the best."

Dantzel laughed, spearing a stalk of asparagus with her fork. "No matter how many times I told her no one wanted to see pictures of bedspreads and walls, she was intent on scrapbooking them anyway." She cut the asparagus spear into smaller pieces, rather than stuffing the whole thing in her mouth like I would have done.

"Well, I thought those pages were very endearing." I eyed Tanner, holding my breath. Was he going to do it?

Tanner cut off a big hunk of chicken and shoveled it into his mouth.

Bea left the room and I relaxed.

I took a bite of my own chicken. There was some sort of cream sauce on top, which had a slightly mustardy taste to it. I chewed, trying to figure out what was in the sauce and whether I liked it or not.

Bea came back in with a silver pitcher, condensation beaded on the outside. She poured water for Dantzel, Alette, and me. When she got to Tanner, he looked up at her and said, in a tone that immediately put me on edge, "Why, thank you, Bea."

There was that sugar-sweet voice again.

He continued, "Can I just say how lovely you look?"

Bea finished pouring his drink and raised an eyebrow at him, clearly confused as to where he was going. "Thank you." Her tone was wary.

"Maggie made a comment to me earlier about how young-looking your skin is. I hadn't noticed, so I decided to pay better attention the next time we saw you." He made a show of examining her features.

Oh, I could die.

"I have to say, she was right," he said. "Your skin is flawless. How do you keep yourself looking so young?"

Bea shifted uncomfortably and glanced at Dantzel, who had stopped chewing. "Nothing special, really. Some skin cream..." she trailed off, like she hadn't quite finished the thought. She set the pitcher on a side-table and said, "Alette, dear, shall I help you cut your chicken?"

Bea hurried to her side and began cutting, even though Alette hadn't answered.

Dantzel's eyes were on Tanner, watching him like he held a bomb.

He shoveled another giant bite of food into his mouth, oblivious to the tension he'd just invited to the table.

Or maybe he wasn't oblivious at all and just thought tension would make a nice guest. "Well, there must be something you do," he said around a mouthful of food. "Because you don't look like you've aged a day since those pictures we saw in Mom's scrapbook."

The knife slipped out of Bea's grip, banged against the table, and landed silently on the Oriental rug below.

Dantzel cleared her throat. "Our Bea is quite fortunate to have a naturally young-looking complexion. Trust me, if she had any special beauty secrets, I would have teased them out of her by now." She touched her own wrinkly face and laughed. The laugh sounded hollow.

"Well—" Tanner took a swig of water—was he drawing out the tension on purpose? "The picture I'm talking about was taken over twenty years ago. It had to have been—it was at Mom's high school graduation."

Oh, Tanner, no! Now she would know we were big, fat snoopers.

My face burned with shame. I lashed out with my foot, trying to kick Tanner in the leg, but caught the chair instead.

Dantzel's neck flushed. "Those pictures weren't in the book I gave you."

Bea straightened, giving up on getting Mom to eat. "I wasn't at Alette's graduation." She laughed, like the idea was ludicrous. "I was just a baby then. There must be a picture of my mother in there."

Dantzel jumped on the suggestion. "Yes, of course! Bea's mother used to teach at the high school. She was one of Allie's favorite teachers, in fact. Allie must have taken a picture with her to commemorate the day."

I frowned. Could that explain it?

"Actually, the caption under the picture said it was Bea," Tanner pressed.

"Well, it wasn't," Dantzel snapped, clearly losing her patience with the conversation.

I lashed out with my foot again, this time avoiding the chair leg and getting Tanner in the ankle. Honestly, the guy did not know when to stop.

"I just like to have all the facts, is all," he said, continuing with his meal. He was the only one at the table still eating. Our mother had never even started.

Dantzel folded up her napkin and placed it on the table beside her plate. "Well, young man. There are certain facts that not everyone has a right to know. I suggest you accept that or we will not get along very well." She pushed her chair back and stood. "Bea, will you make sure Allie eats something? I'm going to bed."

Bea nodded. "Yea, ma'am." She fiercely avoided glancing our way as she carried the pitcher from the room. She gave no indication that she planned on coming back, at least while Tanner and I were still in the room.

"Tanner, you are such an idiot!" I said through clenched teeth once we were alone with our mom.

He pointed to my untouched potatoes. "Are you going to eat those?"

"No, but I'm not giving them to you!" I snapped. "I told you not to press it and you ignored me, and now Dantzel knows we snooped in her room, and she's totally pissed at us."

Tanner leaned over me and scooped a forkful of potatoes up from my plate. "Well, at least we learned something."

"No, we didn't."

He chewed thoughtfully. "Yeah. We did. We learned they're hiding something."

Chapter Nineteen

Lay Him to Rest

Lindy

1623—Valstenia

We watched in silence as Oliver's life slipped away.

Garon's features seemed etched in stone, but his hands quavered. Like his emotions were at war. He reached out and gently closed Oliver's eyes.

This man had been Garon's mentor, and the only human interaction he'd had all those years they were trapped together. I wondered if he thought of O primarily as a mentor, an uncle, or a friend. Or was it a combination of all three?

Trevin groaned from the corner where he was still lying after being knocked out by one of the soldiers. I got up and went to him, leaving Garon alone for a quiet moment with our uncle.

Trevin lay on his side, with his head resting at an awkward angle on the dirt floor. He had a nasty bump where he'd been hit, and there was a small cut on his temple. The wound was crusted over with dried blood that had darkened his fair hair. I slid to my knees and lifted his head into my lap, cradling it. He groaned again, but his eyes remained closed.

"Yelena, do you have any water?"

My sister brought over her water skin and handed it to me. "Will you hold this?" I handed her the stick Oliver had given me, then ripped a piece of fabric from one of my petticoats, grateful for the first time that I was wearing a dress and not pants. I tipped some water onto the material, then pressed it gently to Trevin's head, wiping away the blood.

His eyes fluttered open and he looked at me, deeply, like he could see straight into my soul. I felt like I should run and hide. But there was nowhere to go.

Trevin struggled to sit up.

"Shh," I said, pressing the cloth to his forehead.

He pulled away from my touch, grunting as he sat the rest of the way up. "Your Majesty, are you injured?"

"No, but you are. Will you please let me help you?" I held out the damp rag, reaching for his head.

Rather than let me press it to his skin, he took the cloth and did it himself. "You have already helped me. Thank you."

His gaze caught on Oliver and he froze. "What happened?"

"Anka—" I swallowed a lump. "Anka killed him. He's gone."

Trevin's jaw flexed. He bowed his head in a silent show of respect, then got to his feet slowly, testing his balance before he stood all the way up. "And where is the woman now?"

"She fled. But, Trevin—" I put a tentative hand on his arm. "Your father went with her. Of his own accord."

"You mean, he was still under her spell?"

I nodded. "It seemed that way, yes." I hesitated. "Actually, you were under her spell for a bit, too, but then you seemed to snap out of it. What happened?"

He shook his head. "I don't know, really. I remember feeling drawn to her. In a powerful way. But ... there was another pull. A different direction I felt drawn in." He looked away, refusing to meet my gaze. "I suppose that was enough to help me break her spell."

"Hmm. Sedric didn't seem to feel the pull at all. I wonder why?" If I hadn't sent him after Anka with the others, I would have asked him about it.

Garon fingered the edge of Oliver's cloak, and still, I couldn't read his precise emotions. Grief? Detachment? Shock?

Relief?

Garon said, "I bet *he* would have known."

Yelena held up the branch Oliver had given me. "So, what is this thing for?"

I looked to Garon, but he only shook his head. "I don't recognize that."

"He said it was what he put in the Topaz," I said. "I'm assuming he meant this is the branch of whatever flower he used to create the Topaz. Can I see it?"

Yelena passed it to me. There appeared to be nothing special about the stick. It was slender enough that it could have come from a tree or a bush, which didn't help identify it.

"He also said something about a Pearl. When I asked how to defeat the Topaz." I gasped. "Garon, do you think this Pearl is another one of his creations?"

Garon looked up at me, like I'd roused him from some deep sleep. It took a moment for his eyes to clear and comprehension to dawn. "It is. But it's not a new one. I've seen it. And, unlike the others, this one is not horrible."

My fingers trembled. "But the Emerald didn't start out horrible—O meant to use it for good. Could the Pearl be similar? Could finding it make this whole thing worse?"

"We shouldn't waste time looking for Belina," Yelena said. "We need to stop Anka."

"But I promised Oliver we'd find his daughter. Plus, he said we'd need her Pearl in order to defeat Anka."

"He didn't say any of that," Yelena said. "You asked him how to defeat her and all he said was 'Find Belina, find the Pearl.' Those were not instructions. That was him ignoring your question, and begging you to find his daughter."

"That's not true. Telling us to find Belina was his answer to my question." It had been his answer, right? I struggled to think back on our exact exchange but there had been so much happening.

"Maybe finding Belina was both the answer to our predicament, and the final request of a dying man," Trevin suggested.

Garon cocked his head, tapping a finger against his chin. "I don't know where Belina is now, but I might know where she is in the future."

I narrowed my eyes. "What do you mean?"

"There was a place O often went. Well, a time actually. Far in the future—in Maggie's time. He always made me wait in the woods when we stopped there, so I didn't know what he was doing, but now that I know he had a daughter, I'd be willing to bet he was visiting her. If I can find her in the future, maybe she'll have some memories that will help us rescue her now, and stop Anka."

"How could he visit his daughter so far in the future? She'd be dead," Yelena said.

Garon raised an eyebrow. "Not if she still had the Pearl."

It took a moment for his words to sink in.

I sucked in a breath.

O had said he knew how to control beauty, wealth, and age.

If the Topaz controlled beauty, and the Emerald wealth, then the Pearl must control age. Was it like some fountain of youth? A holy grail?

"Oliver told me about the Pearl," Garon said, "but he never told me why he created it. Now that I know there was a daughter, the Pearl makes more sense."

Garon was the only one who knew how to travel to the future—he had to be the one to go looking for Belina. But if he left, there was a chance he wouldn't come back. And I couldn't stop the Topaz alone. I'd been in this position before and I'd completely and utterly failed.

Garon's eyes bore into mine, like he knew I was remembering my failure to defeat the Emerald and his broken promise to come back and help me. "We need to talk to Belina. And since we don't know where she is now, our only option is to find her in the future. With Oliver gone, I'm the only one who knows how to do that."

The lantern flickered overhead as the flame licked up the last of the wax. The light waned.

I didn't like it, but I knew he was right. Garon had to go.

"You need an apprentice," Trevin said to Garon.

My brother's expression hardened. "No, I don't believe I do. The practice of time manipulation is best left untaught. This is one of those discoveries that should have never been made, and the knowledge is going to end with me."

"How will any of this help us defeat Anka?" Yelena said, clearly losing patience with the whole debate.

Garon fixed her with a hard stare. "I believe Oliver meant that Belina and her Pearl could help us defeat Anka."

"Or maybe it's another one of his tricks—meant to occupy us while Anka steals the throne," she fired back.

The room went still.

Yelena was right. We had to consider the possibility.

Everyone looked to me.

Would Oliver really have lied to us on his deathbed? Would he have sent us on a fool's errand by giving us bad information while his daughter was still missing?

My gaze went to my uncle's body, now covered with Garon's cloak. My voice was soft as I said, "Oliver's final moments were spent trying to thwart Anka's plan." I paused, gazing at the faces in the room. "Remember— she didn't get what she wanted, which was my appearance. Oliver was clearly helping us at the end by not telling her how to feed my blood into the Topaz."

"But why would he risk it, with his daughter's life at stake?" Yelena challenged.

Because I'd told him there was another way.

As he was drawing my blood, I'd begged him not to go through with it, promising that we'd help and that there must be another way to get his daughter back. Had he believed me? Had he chosen to find that better way?

Was Oliver dead because of me?

Garon said, "Maybe he came to see that, together, we could defeat Anka. Maybe he'd realized that handing Anka what she wanted wasn't the right thing to do."

I smoothed my skirt down, which was now soiled, torn, and blood-stained. I gripped the fabric in my fists and made my voice as authoritative as I could. "Garon will go find future Belina. Trevin, you and your remaining men will visit nearby villages and ask about this branch." I held up the stick Oliver had given me. "Try to find someone who recognizes it—someone who's heard of a flower or plant that only blooms at summer solstice. Once we know what, exactly, Oliver put in the Topaz, we'll have a better idea of what we can use to counteract its effects if we're not able to remove all traces of it from the Topaz.

"Yelena and I will go back to the castle. My mother is there, along with more soldiers. Since Anka didn't succeed in stealing my identity, she's limited in what she can do. She's clearly unable to control everyone at once and, unless she wants a bloodbath, her next move will have to be subtle. I will initiate the gathering of an army and instruct them to prepare for our next encounter with her."

Yelena frowned, but didn't argue.

Trevin stepped forward. "Your Highness, with my father gone, you're in need of protection. I can't let you travel back through the woods on your own, especially at night. I and two others will accompany you and your sister."

I shook my head. "I need all your remaining men searching for information that will help us destroy the Topaz."

Trevin set his jaw. "With respect, my father would not have left you alone and neither will I."

"Fine. You may accompany Yelena and me while the rest of your men comb the cities. Oliver said this flower blooms at summer solstice, which is in one week's time. We'll meet back here in four days, at which point we will commence our search for present-day Belina, then obtain and destroy the Topaz."

I looked around at those present, made eye contact with everyone to ensure they understood.

One of the soldiers said, "Why not meet back at the castle, Highness?"

"If we find the castle compromised—if Anka is somehow able to get in—meeting back here will be safer." My knees shook, threatening to betray my uncertainty at the plan. But nobody could tell—another benefit of my antiquated skirt. "If any one of the three parties fails to return by the fourth day, the rest of us will wait until dawn of the fifth day, at which point we will proceed without the missing party. Understood?"

Once again, I met everyone's gaze in turn. "Garon, will that be enough time for you?"

He nodded.

I tried to smile at him, but my lower lip trembled. What if he never came back?

"I'll come back," he said, like he'd read my mind.

It was the dead of night, but Anka already had too much of a head start. Yelena and I could not afford to wait until morning.

"Trevin, will you have your men prepare a grave? Yelena and I will start out once we've said goodbye to our uncle. Everyone else may rest here for the night and set out in the morning."

****

Oliver had been the cause of my long imprisonment— the Emerald he'd created had been my captor for four hundred years. And yet, saying goodbye to him was still hard. He'd looked so much like my father, though in personality and temperament they'd been nothing alike. Still, Oliver had been my uncle and, despite his mistakes, he'd been a brilliant man.

Losing him was a tragedy, and I mourned as Trevin's men lowered him into the grave and slowly covered him with earth. The forest seemed to mourn right along with us, the moon hiding its face behind the clouds, and the night creatures keeping silent and still. I slipped my hand into the folds of my dress and fingered the knobs of the branch Oliver had given me.

The man was a puzzle. A brilliant, terrible puzzle. And now he was a light that would shine no more.

Yelena looped an arm through mine. "We've already given Anka too much of a head start."

"Rest in peace, Uncle," I murmured. "We will find your daughter. We will set things right."

Trevin joined us. "I presume you'll be keeping the branch with you?"

My fingers tightened around it, still tucked away in my pocket. Could I entrust this to the men? Having the branch to show people, rather than just describing it, would surely make it easier to find what they were looking for.

"It's all right, Majesty. You should keep it. My men will be splitting up—they wouldn't all be able to have it anyway. However, I'd like for them each to take a close look at it. To feel it, handle it, smell it, even. They need to know exactly what they're looking for."

Relief flooded through me. "Yes, of course they should study it."

I placed the branch in Trevin's outstretched palm. When his fingers closed around it, they closed around mine as well. Just for the tiniest moment. "Don't worry, Your Highness. We will defeat this threat, as we have all others before." Then he dropped my hand and went to his men.

Garon stood apart from the others, watching from afar as we buried his mentor.

I went to my brother. "How are you?"

He swiped a hand across his face, wiping away phantom tears. "As good as can be expected."

"Did you love him?" I said.

Garon glanced at me sideways, considering the question as if he hadn't before. "Yes," he said simply. "I haven't loved many people in my life. And my love for my uncle was turbulent. But sometimes love is that way, you know?"

I nodded. Turbulent. That was exactly what I was feeling over Oliver's death.

Then Garon added, almost as if it was a recent revelation. "Sometimes turbulent love is the best kind."

"I agree," Yelena said, joining us. "How else could I love *you*, Brother?" We fell silent, enjoying the rare moment together, just the three of us.

As all good things do, the moment ended too soon.

Trevin approached and handed me the branch. "The men have all had a look. We should be on our way."

I squeezed Garon's arm. "I trust I'll see you again soon."

"Very soon. Don't worry—I'll beat you back, and when you arrive I'll be bored out of my mind waiting for you."

I laughed. "You'd better be."

I took a shaky breath and one last look at my brother. "Goodbye."

Garon said, "See you in four days."

Chapter Twenty

Blast from the Past

Maggie

Present Day—Boryn

Our grandmother was lying to us. Again. Still.

For the past week, she'd stuck with the story that the woman we'd seen in Alette's scrapbooks was Bea's mother. We hadn't talked about the fact that we'd been in her room. But the knowledge hung between us—a silent, awkward thing that was always there but that nobody would acknowledge. And the only proof of what we'd seen was in our heads, since there was no way I was going snooping again.

But, honestly, I was starting to doubt my own memory.

Yes, the person in the pictures had been a spitting image of Bea. And yes, my mother had decorated one of the pages with hand-drawn bees. But maybe it had just been her drawing bees. Maybe it really had nothing to do with Bea the person. Mom's mental issues called into question her version of reality, along with everything she'd created.

Regardless, we spent as much time with Mom as we could, going for walks through the orchard, helping her pull weeds from the garden, and sitting on the beach watching the ocean ebb and flow.

Today we were hunting for seashells. So far we'd found lots of broken pieces.

Tanner was lying on a blanket where the grass turned

to sand, several yards away from us, with a t-shirt covering his face to shield him from the sun.

Mom and I were walking along the beach. "Will you tell me about Bea?"

A peaceful smile rose to Mom's lips. She wrapped her arms around herself and said, "Bea, so gentle. Bea, so kind. Bees go buzz, buzz, *buzz*." She picked up a shell fragment and pretended to fly it through the air, making a buzzing sound as if it were a bee.

"No, I mean Bea who works at the house. Have you known her a long time?"

"Buzz, buzz, *buzz*." She flew the shell so close to my face that I had to back away.

She giggled.

I sighed.

I picked a broken shell out of our bucket and made mine buzz alongside hers. "Let's go see if Tanner likes bees."

We'd finally been able to tell Mom our names without her getting upset. She still looked sideways at me whenever someone called me Maggie, like she was trying to work out some impossible puzzle. But she hadn't freaked out like she had that first day. Dantzel kept telling her we were only friends, but I think she knew we were more important than that. She just couldn't figure out how.

And I didn't care. I'd watch clouds or count flower petals or buzz seashells with her all day long. We were making up for lost time, even though she didn't understand exactly who I was. Day by day, I felt my heart healing, the ruptured seams slowly stitching back together.

Mom flopped down in the sand and busied herself counting the shell fragments we'd found. She started arranging them in order of size, while I settled down next to Tanner.

I stretched out beside him on the blanket, laying on my stomach. "We need to tell Dad," I whispered.

No reaction.

I pulled the t-shirt off his face and he hissed at me, holding his arm over his eyes. "Mags, the sun."

"Seriously? It's like you're a vampire or something. You're a lifeguard—you're in the sun all the time."

"But usually I have sunglasses! I can't believe I forgot to bring them."

"You're such a drama queen. Just go into town and buy some new ones."

He grimaced. "They won't be the same, and I'm not dropping another hundred dollars on a pair of sunglasses."

"So, you'd rather go all squinty-eyed instead of wearing cheap sunglasses?"

"No, I'd rather wear a t-shirt over my face than go all squinty-eyed or wear cheap sunglasses." He grabbed the t-shirt back from me and plopped it over his eyes.

"Fine. Dork. Did you hear what I said?"

He lowered his voice. "Yeah."

"It's been over a week. He needs to know."

"Yeah, he does." Tanner propped himself up on one elbow, leaving the t-shirt on his head but adjusting it just enough so he could see me. Barely. "But what do we say? How do you tell someone that the love of their life, who's been dead over a decade, is actually still alive?"

"I don't know," I said. "Maybe we don't tell him and we just ask him to come join us? He can find out the same way we did—you almost have to see her to believe it, you know?"

"I guess," Tanner said.

"If I had come out here alone and called you to say Mom was still alive, would you have believed me?"

"Heck no."

"Then why would Dad?"

"I don't—"

An impossibly loud crack cut him off, thundering through the air like a gunshot at point-blank range.

I screamed.

Tanner yanked the shirt off his face and sat up, his eyes wide.

Mom jumped like she'd seen been slapped. She squeezed her eyes shut and pressed her hands over her ears.

"What the heck was that?" I shrieked.

Tanner's eyes were buggy. "It sounded like thunder. Really, *really* close thunder." He searched the sky, which was full of puffy, white, innocent-looking clouds.

A crack of thunder that didn't belong.

I'd heard that before.

Last year in my car, on a hill behind my house. When Garon had disappeared and left me alone with the police closing in. And also, a few weeks ago when he'd disappeared from my bedroom.

I scrambled to my feet and tugged on the corner of the blanket. "Tanner, get off."

"Why?"

"Garon's back, we have to go." I gathered up Mom's seashells and started dumping them into a bucket.

"Garon's … back?" Tanner gawked at me. "Maggie, why would Garon come to Boryn? He thinks you're in Virginia."

I'd told Tanner that Garon had gone home to visit family. I just hadn't told him he'd have to travel through time in order to do it.

My hand froze, holding the last of the seashells we'd gathered. "You're right. He doesn't know I'm here."

But maybe he wasn't here for me. I dumped the last handful of shells into the bucket. "What was that noise, then?"

"Beats me," Tanner said.

"Well, let's go check it out. Maybe Dantzel knows something." I put a hand on Mom's back and gently pulled her hands away from her ears. "It's okay, you're all right. We're going back to the house now. Do you want to carry your shells?"

Mom nodded and I handed her the plastic bucket. Together, we headed back to the house.

"Even if Dantzel does know something about the sound we just heard, what makes you think she'll tell us?" Tanner said.

"I don't know. Maybe she won't. But the sound came from the house—we can at least go check it out."

"I'd say it came from the woods beyond the house," Tanner said, pointing.

My stomach tightened as I followed his gaze. The woods. The same ones I'd seen in the picture of Garon from so long ago. Beyond them was the village Dantzel had told us about.

We let ourselves in through the garden gate and dumped our sandy stuff at the bottom of the porch steps leading up to the red kitchen door. Mom settled down on the top step.

"No, we're going inside," I said, gently tugging on her elbow.

She shrugged away and leaned forward so she was hugging her knees.

"Just leave her," Tanner said. "She's fine."

She rocked gently, then turned her face to the sky. A

serene smile settled on her lips.

"Yeah, okay." I kneeled beside her, took a couple of shells out of the bucket, and lined them up. Mom reached over and adjusted one that was crooked, then selected another and added it to the row.

Tanner was right—she was fine.

I joined my brother, who'd just stepped into the kitchen. I caught a glimpse of the cherry-covered wallpaper, and then Tanner stopped short, blocking my way.

I bumped into him.

"Huh," he said.

"What?"

"You were right," Tanner said.

I pushed around him and stepped into the kitchen.

There, at the little kitchen table, drinking tea and eating biscuits with Dantzel and Bea as if it were the most natural thing in the world, sat Garon.

My stomach knotted up. I grabbed Tanner's arm. I blinked.

And still, Garon was there.

His eyes went impossibly wide when he saw me. He faltered with his teacup and let it clatter back into its saucer. "Maggie! What are you doing here?"

"Oh, you two know each other," Dantzel said. "Fabulous." Her tone made it clear that she did *not* think it was fabulous.

Bea's gaze dropped to the floor. "Oh, dear," she said.

I took a step toward them, not sure I could trust my eyes. Was Garon really sitting here in front of me, in my grandmother's kitchen in Sweden? Er, Boryn? "I'm here because this is my mom's house. What are *you* doing here?"

Garon shook his head, like puzzle pieces were coming

181

together, but that he didn't like the picture they were making. "This is your mother's house? I thought your mother was dead."

"I did, too." I glanced pointedly at Dantzel. "But she wasn't, apparently. We came here to tour our mother's childhood home and, maybe, if we were lucky, meet some distant relatives. But we found our mother, very much alive, and our grandmother here lying about it."

I wanted to run into his arms. To revel in the fact that he was here, right in front of me, and that he was safe. But something in the way he held himself told me he hadn't intended to see me. He hadn't meant for me to know he'd returned.

And that hurt. Maybe worse than the silence of the past few weeks. I narrowed my eyes at him. "Why are *you* here?"

He looked at Bea. My grandmother looked at Bea.

Tanner and I looked at Bea.

Bea fidgeted and avoided looking at anyone.

"Will someone please tell us what's going on?" Tanner exploded. "Why is everyone looking at Bea?"

Finally, *finally*, Bea met my gaze. Then she looked at Tanner and said, "You were right. It was me in those graduation pictures with your mother."

I sucked in a breath.

"I knew it," Tanner said.

Bea continued, as if Tanner hadn't said a word. "I don't age. Haven't for as long as I can remember."

The smile on Tanner's face faded, and I felt my expression match his. Garon's lips formed a grim line. Dantzel alone remained unfazed by Bea's announcement. Our grandmother picked up a biscuit, dipped it in her tea, and took a bite.

Chapter Twenty-One

Combat Training

Lindy

1623—Valstenia

"You'll need to know how to fight," Trevin said.

We'd made good time—stopping only once for water and to rest our horses—but still had a ways to go.

"We have to keep moving," Yelena said.

Trevin stuck his sword in the ground. "I'm not leading you into a possible war zone without attempting to arm you first."

They both looked to me.

Trevin drew a second sword. I hadn't noticed until that very moment, but he had three scabbards hanging from his waist. "From one of our fallen," he said softly. He held it out to me, hilt first. "Highness, taking a few minutes for this could be the difference between a quick death and a fighting chance, if it comes to that."

It was still the dead of night. If Anka had gone straight to the castle after fleeing, she'd be there by now—with a few hours on us. We needed to hurry.

But Trevin was right. We also needed this.

I took the proffered sword. It was lighter than I'd expected.

He pulled anther one and handed it to Yelena. She hesitated, eyeing the weapon like the offer was some sort of trick.

"Go on, take it," he urged.

Her fingers tightened around the hilt and a fire lit up

her eyes.

"You'll need something to block with," Trevin said. He went to the nearest tree, examined it, poked through the underbrush. "Hold on." He moved away, poking through more underbrush.

I eyed Yelena as she hefted the sword. "You've really never held a sword?"

"No. Have you?"

"Well … not a sword, no. I just thought … your husband never taught you?"

Yelena's jaw clenched. "My job is to look good on his arm. That's it. Things don't change just because you're married, little sister."

"Oh." I couldn't keep the disappointment from creeping into my voice.

I'd lost sight of Trevin—presumably he was still poking around in the darkness. I backed away from Yelena and took a few swings with the sword, loving the way the metal sliced through the night air. I actually gasped, it felt so delicious.

My sister laughed and took a few swings of her own. "I feel … powerful."

Soon our blades were both whirring through the air.

"Having fun?" Trevin said, his voice coming from behind me.

I stopped swinging and whirled around to face him, like a kid caught throwing rocks on the playground.

Trevin grinned. "By all means, have fun. Just don't take my head off." He dropped an assortment of bulky forest objects at our feet—a tangle of branches and bark and … was that moss?

"Ideally, you'd each have a shield. Since I only have one, we'll need to get creative with our blocking." He stooped and rifled through his pile, picking up a thick tree limb that had a few small branches poking out along the side. It looked freshly cut.

He measured it against my arm, nodded, then handed it to me. "Hold on to this part here, like a handle"—he adjusted the branch in my grip—"and let's rest this part here." He moved it so my arm fit between several of the smaller branches. With my hand around the part he'd told me to grip, the tree limb stayed steady and, I realized, was like holding a small shield.

Trevin tried a few different options with Yelena until he found another tree limb that fit. "Hold your makeshift shields up like this"—he demonstrated—"as we approach the city. Since we don't have much time, protection is crucial. I'll teach you some defensive moves with your sword, but use them only as a last resort. Your first instinct should be to block and fall back to safety, not attack."

He looked at me. "Stay just behind me, on my shield side to my left. Yelena, you'll stay to Queen Shalyndria's left. We'll move together as a single unit—like one side of a 'V' of birds in flight. With all of our shields up, that will offer you both the most protection. Got it?"

I nodded.

Yelena whipped her sword through the air.

Trevin grinned. "Okay, now on to the fun stuff. We only have time to learn two moves, but in the future, if ever we find ourselves with time to spare, I vow to teach you both more. If you ask me, sword fighting should be mandatory for all Queens-to-be."

A surprised smile stretched across Yelena's face. I felt my expression mirror hers.

If you asked me, Trevin should be in charge of all said classes for future Queens-to-be.

****

The fire-lit turrets of the castle came into view just as night began to lose its hold. It was not yet dawn, but I could sense the darkness giving way. Morning would soon be upon us.

"We need to leave the horses—we'll be stealthier on foot," Trevin said.

We tied the horses to a hitching post in the now-deserted marketplace I'd been to with Borov just a few short days ago. Yelena and I kept our shields up as we moved through the market, walking behind and to the left of Trevin as he'd suggested. Trevin kept his own sword at the ready as we crept through the square, even though there were no obvious threats.

A heap of rubble stood out in the otherwise waste-free marketplace. The heap was human-sized, and covered by empty grain sacks.

Yelena saw it, too. "What is that?"

We drew closer, my stomach twisting in on itself. "Garbage for burning?" I said, trying to convince myself it wasn't a body.

Trevin approached and used the tip of his sword to lift the corner of one of the grain sacks.

I held my breath.

He tossed the sack aside to expose a pile of broken wood.

I exhaled. No body. No blood.

"It's just a pile of rubbish," Yelena said, her voice sounding as relieved as I felt.

"But why wasn't it cleared away?" Trevin said. "The officials who run the marketplace typically keep it rubble-free. They've just thrown grain sacks over it— almost like they were too afraid to touch it, but didn't want to keep looking at it."

"Wait a second…" I stepped closer, my eye catching

on something poking from the bottom of the wood pile.

Trevin held an arm out to stop me. "It could carry disease."

I pushed past him. "If it was diseased, someone would have burned it." I kneeled beside the rubble and pulled at a stem caught beneath a section of wood. The stem was attached to a flower, which came free when I tugged on it. The stem was broken and the petals were crushed and brown, but it was one of the flowers I'd admired at the flower-seller's cart that day in the marketplace.

This was Anka's cart.

She'd been the village scapegoat. A woman so ugly people gave her a wide berth, spit at her in the street, and called her names. I closed my eyes and let the memory of that day come back to me. The memory of her fire-ravaged skin and face. *Devil's Child*, they'd shouted at her.

I turned to Trevin. "The woman—back at the shack—what did she look like to you?"

"Er." Trevin let his sword drop to his side. "Why do you ask?"

"Please, I need to know what you saw."

He poked at the rubble with his sword, avoiding my gaze. "The woman in the cabin was very beautiful."

"That's what I thought. But, Yelena, you saw through her illusion, right? You saw the scars?"

My sister nodded.

Understanding dawned on Trevin's face. "Wait. The woman who owned this cart—the flower seller—*this* is the woman you saw in the cabin? *She* is the bearer of the Topaz?"

"Yes, I'm sure of it."

"The people were afraid of her," Trevin said. "They claimed she practiced witchcraft. They must think her cart is infused with some sort of black magic and didn't want to disturb it."

"If they were so afraid of her, why did they treat her so terribly?"

"People who are afraid lash out in all sorts of different ways," Yelena murmured. And it seemed like she was speaking from experience.

I frowned at her, but she didn't offer anything more.

"I saw how badly the people treated her," I murmured, fingering the broken flower. "I don't blame her for wanting to escape."

"Sister, be wary of compassion. This woman is your enemy." Yelena's eyes held a depth of emotion—a tumultuousness—I'd never before seen from her.

I twirled the flower stem between my fingers. "I just understand what it's like to feel trapped. I don't wish the feeling on anyone."

Trevin covered the cart back up and I stood.

Dawn was breaking.

Chapter Twenty-Two

The Poisoned Pearl

Maggie

Present Day—Boryn

I broke the silence hanging thick like a curtain in the room. "You don't age?" I repeated dumbly.

Bea shook her head.

"So, you're a freak," Tanner said.

I punched him.

"Ow!" He rubbed his arm. "Either she's a freak or she's found the fountain of youth. I'm guessing it's the first."

Bea cocked her head. "I suppose it's a combination of both, actually. I *am* a freak, to be sure. And the fountain of youth isn't a fountain at all. It's a flower."

Wait. What?

This was getting too crazy. My head spun. The room spun. Even the cherries on the kitchen wallpaper spun.

Garon said, "So, the flower he used had magical properties." He said it like the statement solved some mystery he'd been struggling with.

"He, who?" Tanner said.

"O," Garon replied. "Oliver."

"Have you seen him?" I couldn't help asking. "Did you find out why everything is changing? Is Lindy all right?" I bit my lip, knowing now was not the time for those questions, but still desperately wanting the answers.

Garon's eyes took on a softness as he answered me.

This was the way he should have looked at me from the start. "I found them, Maggie. And they're all right, for the moment. Well … everyone except Oliver." He hung his head, as if in prayer. Or … as if in a moment of silence.

My stomach tightened. "Garon, what happened?"

He shook his head, refusing to meet my eye. Refusing to answer me.

He looked at Bea. "I've been to this house with Oliver before, on several occasions over the years. But I never knew who lived here—never understood why Oliver insisted on coming here—until recently. Bea is Oliver's daughter."

This surprise should have shocked me more than it did, but I'd used up my shock quota for the day. The knowledge just rolled into the rest of it, like a drop in an already full bucket. So Bea was Oliver's daughter. Okay, cool. And Garon was sitting here with me in Sweden—no, Boryn—of all places, where he'd probably been passing through back in the 1920s when someone accidentally caught him on film. And, oh, Bea didn't age. Hadn't, apparently, in four hundred years. Wait, I'd known someone like that before and she'd been indentured to an evil, life-sucking Emerald.

I shook my head to clear away the crazy. Lindy was okay. And Bea would be, too.

Bea's eyes were wet. "My father was here?"

Garon nodded. "He came here often. I never knew why, exactly—I didn't know he had a daughter. But now that I know, I imagine he was just checking on you." His face grew serious. "Bea, can you tell me more about the flower?"

Bea swallowed, collecting herself it seemed. "It's called Remyallis. It grows in exactly one place in the world, and when it blooms, it only blooms for a week. Seven days starting at summer solstice. And then the magic goes back to sleep—hibernates—until the next summer solstice. And on, and on."

"So, a person has to, what, eat the flower and then they'll have eternal youth?" Tanner said, one eyebrow quirking up.

"It's not that easy," Bea said. "The flowers have magical properties, but one has to know how to harness them. Or, in our case, one must be brilliantly ignorant."

"Let me guess," I said. "This brilliantly ignorant person was O."

Bea folded her hands in her lap. She nodded once. "But his motives were pure."

"Geez, for all his *pure motives* he sure did some awful stuff," I said. "So, you're being held prisoner to some mystical, magical gem that gives you eternal youth and you need us to destroy it?"

"I never asked you to destroy it," Bea said tartly. "You came here all on your own. It seems to me that Garon is the one asking for favors."

I turned to Garon. "What did you come here for?"

Garon's eyes went wide, like he was begging me to understand. "I don't know. Not exactly. Oliver just told me to find his daughter, Belina." He glanced at Bea. "You *are* Belina, right?"

Bea nodded.

Garon continued, "Since we didn't know where to find Belina in the past, I thought maybe if I found her in the future she'd know how to help. Oliver said we'd need her to defeat the Topaz."

"Seriously?" I squeaked. "There's *another* one?"

"There is," Garon said gently, though his expression hinted at the same exasperation I felt. "I believe the creation of the Topaz is what caused the changes in history."

Dantzel frowned. "What changes in history?"

I turned on her. "Oh, nothing much, just the fact that your country is actually called Sweden, not Boryn, and this strange Boryn place seems to be conquering all of Scandinavia and rewriting history! But it's rewriting everyone's memories, too, so no one knows things are changing except for me."

"*I* know things are changing." Bea's eyes brightened with intensity and focused on me with new interest. "It's happened a few times, that I can recall. I believe Alette remembers as well. It's one of the reasons her mind is broken. She can't make sense of all the changes."

Tanner was staring at me, his mouth gaping open.

Dantzel stared, too, but her mouth was closed. "Close your mouth, Tanner," she snapped. "You look like a fish on a hook."

Bea spoke. "Only those who have been touched by the gemstones' magic will be able to remember. The three stones—Emerald, Topaz, and my Pearl—are linked. The Emerald was created before the others—it was the big sister, so to speak. My father discovered Remyallis's properties after he'd created the Emerald, so there was no trace of the flower in that, but it tainted everything else he did."

"So, how do we defeat the Topaz?" Garon said. "Because right now there's a woman after Lindy's throne and, from what I understand, she's holding … um … *you*"—Garon nodded to Bea—"or, past you, as a hostage."

Bea closed her eyes, like she was harnessing some sort of inner zen. "Yes. I do have that memory. It's a new one. One that's only been added in this latest fold in time." She closed her eyes tighter, little crows' feet appearing at the corners as she focused.

"Anka held me captive by the sea, at an outcropping where the land juts into the ocean. There was a series of rock formations, which formed hidden caves. She held me in one of those, with two ever-changing guards. It is near where Father harvested the Remyallis." She opened her eyes. "You will find me there."

"Thank you," Garon said.

Bea tilted her head. "There is something I have pondered on much. An item that—if it were to be brought back in time—might perhaps save little Allie and so many others in our line who have suffered at the hand of the Remyallis."

"Wait, I thought the flower gave eternal youth," I said. "How does that cause suffering?"

"The flowers are toxic," Dantzel said. Spat, really.

Bea placed a hand on Dantzel's arm, calming her. "My father didn't know. Never knew. We only figured it out recently."

"Figured what out?" Garon said.

Bea hesitated. "The same thing that keeps me young—keeps me alive—also causes insanity. Like a recessive gene, I've passed it down to those I love most. Many of my descendants escaped unfazed, the gene lying dormant inside them, but a few, like Allie, have suffered most acutely."

"Wait, wait, wait," Tanner said. "Our mother is your descendant? I thought you were the maid."

"I am. But I'm also Allie's blood relative. I'm only the maid because I need something to occupy my time." Bea shrugged. "I like to cook."

But, wait … my mind had snagged on something.

If I was related to Bea, and Bea was Oliver's

daughter, and Oliver was Garon's uncle …

I looked at Garon, my mouth dropping open in horror. "Are we related?"

Garon cocked his head, like he'd never considered the possibility.

My body turned to ice.

But then Bea said, "I am not Oliver's biological daughter. That's a story for another day, but—don't worry—you and Garon are not related."

I released the breath I'd been holding. "Oh, man, that totally freaked me out."

"Would you like to see the Pearl?" Bea asked. "My personal fountain of youth?"

Tanner, Garon, and I nodded.

Dantzel looked away.

Bea tugged at a thin, silver chain hanging from her neck. She pulled it out from under her shirt until it was fully visible.

From the necklace dangled a giant Pearl.

I recoiled.

The Pearl was blood-red.

She held it up so we could all see. "Behold the Pearl. Gripped with poison, made potent over time. The Pearl was white when my father first created it, and it saved my life back then. But over the years, slowly, the poison from the flowers took hold. It is now both my life and my curse."

Chapter Twenty-Three

Castle Dawn

Lindy

1623—Valstenia

The castle was still as a winter morning as we advanced toward it. Too early for sunbeams to illuminate the balustrades. Too early for merchants to be out.

Yet *nothing* stirred. No wind in the trees, no birds in the skies.

I swallowed a yawn, commanding myself to stay alert. I couldn't let the lack of sleep cloud my judgement.

We slowed our pace. My gaze crawled across the castle—I examined the towers, the walls, the windows, the alcoves. Everything seemed normal.

Except...

Yelena noticed it the same time I did. "The drawbridge is up."

"I can't recall the last time I saw the drawbridge up," I said.

"In times of peace, the bridge remains lowered, with guards posted at the entrance," Trevin said. And the tightness in his tone mirrored the tightness in my chest.

Had Anka already tried to attack? Or...

"Could there have been hostilities from Boryn? I never responded to the marriage proposal."

"It's a possibility," Trevin said. "Qadar is a young King and his temperament has yet to be tested."

"We should hide," I said. "They'll open the gates for morning food deliveries and we can present ourselves at that time."

"Fall back to the stables, then?" Trevin suggested.

A clanging from within the castle made me jump.

Trevin drew his sword, holding it at the ready, and placed himself ahead of us. Yelena and I angled ourselves behind him, just as he'd instructed us to, and lifted our swords and makeshift shields.

The tell-tale click-clack of the drawbridge rang out. Hinges, stiff with un-use, squealed in complaint as the heavy bridge came down.

"Have they seen us, then?" Yelena said.

"It would seem so," Trevin answered.

I scanned the castle, letting my gaze wander up and around to both sides, searching the windows and ledges for any hint of what was to come.

When the drawbridge came within a few feet of touching down, we saw Borov standing just inside the threshold of the castle.

My throat tightened as I recalled the last time we'd seen him—under Anka's spell. His face was unreadable—it was impossible to discern whether he was free of her or not—whether he was foe or friend.

The drawbridge continued its descent.

Without turning toward us, Trevin said, "Highnesses, you should retreat. Observe from afar and reveal yourselves only when you can be sure of a warm reception."

I stood my ground. This was my castle. My home. My family was in there. If Borov was dangerous, then that meant my mother and siblings were in trouble.

Yelena stood fast beside me.

I gripped my sword tighter. "I'm not leaving my family."

Trevin's jaw tightened, but he kept his eyes on his

father, who stood unmoving and alone on the opposite side of the gulf.

The drawbridge was almost down. One foot away. Half a foot.

It was down.

Nobody moved.

"If he attacks, I'll disable him so you two can slip by," Trevin said. "Find the Queen Mother. I'll search for Anka and join you as soon as I can."

It was as good a plan as we were going to get.

Still, nobody moved.

Then Borov twitched a finger.

Suddenly, arrows split the air, coming from above. One seared the flesh of my upper arm. "The parapets!" I yelled, choking back a cry of pain.

I ducked beneath my tree-branch shield, but it was woefully inadequate. An arrow hit just above my knee. My dress's many layers kept it from penetrating deeply, but my legs buckled.

It was too late to run.

An arrow caught Yelena in the thigh and she fell to the ground, too.

Trevin alone remained standing. He charged the gate.

Soldiers swarmed from the castle.

Trevin struck one down. Then another. And another. His blows were strong and sure. Fierce. Practiced.

But he was grossly outnumbered.

And then soldiers were beside me. My soldiers. Turning on me. Taking me by the arms and hauling me to my feet.

An arrow caught Trevin in the hand and his sword clattered to the ground. Soldiers advanced on him from all sides, one of them knocking the shield out of his uninjured hand.

Borov stepped forward, caught his son by the arms, and secured them behind his back. "You are under arrest, as a traitor to the crown. Queen Anka has ordered your immediate execution."

"No!" I cried out, struggling against my own captor.

Borov turned his attention to me. "Don't worry, he will not be alone."

****

Rough hands pushed me into a cell. "Don't get too comfortable. Wouldn't want you to miss your own execution." The door clanged shut and we were alone.

The cell was damp and cold. I couldn't see. Couldn't free my hands from their bindings. Couldn't tell how many bodies might be sharing the space with me.

And I was so tired.

The spot above my knee where I'd been shot throbbed. One of the soldiers had hastily wrapped it, but it was still bleeding and stung badly.

Yelena had only been grazed, it turned out. Trevin's hand had also been crudely wrapped and probably hurt worse than my knee, but he said nothing about it.

"Highness, hold still." It was Trevin.

I felt hands on my arms. He found my wrists and began fumbling with my bindings.

"Yelena," I said.

Something shifted in the darkness. "I'm here."

I blinked. Varying shades of gray became clear among the black.

Trevin worked on the rope around my wrists, but the knots remained tight. He sighed. "I'm sorry. It won't budge." The darkness solidified before my eyes. Trevin was in front of me.

He tried to loosen Yelena's as well, and then I tried to untie his. But we were tightly bound.

Trevin moved so he was sitting beside me.

The shades of gray became more pronounced until I could just make out two forms—Trevin's and Yelena's—in the darkness.

"I'm so sorry, Your High—"

I cut him off. "Don't. It's not your fault." Despite my best effort, my voice wobbled slightly. How long would it be before Borov made good on his promise to execute us?

"We should have had a better plan," Trevin continued. "I should have gone alone while you hid."

I would have reached out to him if my hands had been free.

He continued, "I shouldn't have—"

"Trevin, stop. I mean it, you did your best." I leaned over, nudging his shoulder with mine. Only, I misjudged the distance between us and leaned too heavily into him. I regained my balance and righted myself quickly.

Yelena spoke up. "What do you think they did with Mother? And Carina and Felipe?"

I shuddered, unable to answer. The question hung there, like a viper in the darkness, torturing us.

My stomach rumbled—we'd been given no food and all our supplies had been taken. We sat in silence, for what felt like the better part of an hour, waiting for … something. My eyelids grew heavy.

And then Yelena said, "I have a confession."

"Okay," I said slowly. "What sort of confession?"

She didn't speak right away.

It was too dark. I couldn't read her expression—had no idea what she might be getting at.

Finally, she took a shaky breath. "I overheard you talking to Borov. About the disturbance in the market place. And I just can't keep quiet any longer."

My throat tightened.

Yelena took another shaky breath, then her words came tumbling out. "It was my husband. He wants Valstenia's ports—control of the trade routes. He's been working with Qadar, trying to secure a marriage alliance with you, and undermining your authority in the meantime so you'll accept. He's had fake guards stationed at the marketplace, collecting taxes in secret, in your name. He figured if he started an uprising and you felt you were losing control, you'd be desperate to accept Qadar's offer."

I felt like I'd been punched in the gut.

So, that was it. It was all about our trade routes. The one thing Valstenia had plenty of—access to the Baltic Sea—and my own sister had been scheming to take it away from me. "Why didn't you tell me sooner?"

There was a long pause. Then she took a deep, stuttering breath. "There was a man—Cohen—a stable hand at my husband's stables. We became … close. I fell in love with him."

She paused. "You have to understand, Lindy, I was miserable. You have no idea what it feels like to have your own husband look through you. My husband found out about me and Cohen, and threatened to kill him if I didn't convince you to marry Qadar." Her breaths had turned into shallow gasps of hysteria. "I'm so sorry," she squeaked.

My mind reeled. If I couldn't trust my own sister, who was there to trust?

"Say something, Lindy," Yelena begged.

"I can't."

It was all I could say. Trevin leaned into me, wordlessly lending me strength.

And we sat there in the darkness, Yelena sniffling as I

tried to figure out how to get myself—and my country—out of the mess we were in.

And I kept coming back to this: there was no way out.

With so many parties fighting for Valstenia, and my funds gone, how could I possibly keep my country from falling apart?

My eyelids were heavy. My body ached. I leaned into Trevin, letting my muscles relax even as my mind whirled in a dark, downward spiral.

The spiral was endless.

Just when I thought I'd reached the bottom—that my heart couldn't fall any further, I felt myself fall some more.

My head rocked forward and then jerked back.

I blinked, my eyes heavy with sleep. I'd been dreaming. Beside me, Trevin was breathing heavily, his head resting on the wall behind us. Yelena was lying on the floor, her chest slowly rising and falling.

What had woken me?

Footsteps, I realized. Descending toward us like a final judgement.

I nudged Trevin. "Wake up," I hissed. "Someone's coming."

Locks slid, the door creaked open.

"Get up," said a voice.

Chapter Twenty-Four

Thumbelina

Maggie

Present Day—Boryn

There was a collective silence, and the world seemed to hold its breath. No one moved. We gazed at the Pearl dangling from Bea's necklace. It was like over-ripe strawberries. As shocking as blood in the snow, but smooth and glassy.

"How much did Oliver tell you about me?" Bea asked.

"Nothing," Garon said. "I was shocked to hear him mention a daughter. As far as I knew, he'd lived alone before I met him—unattached and reclusive. A brilliant wanderer, with a touch of madness. He never mentioned you, or your mother."

"I have no mother. I am a child of the sea, and I came to Oliver on the waves. When I became ill, he saved me with this." Bea fingered the Pearl. "He had no idea it would alter me so."

"What the heck are you talking about?" Tanner said, huffing. "Could you please stop speaking in riddles?"

Bea looked at him. "It's not a riddle. Haven't you ever heard of Thumbelina?"

"Seriously?" I said. "Another fairy tale?"

She met my gaze with one that was calm and unfazed. "Fairy tales are simply tales. Told and re-told, passed down and altered, through generations of retellings." She turned to Garon. "You are right about Oliver being a lonely recluse. He never married, never fell in love—I'm not even sure he wanted to. But when he found me, abandoned on the beach as a babe, sick and in need of refuge, he took me in. He cared for me, nursed me to health, and grew to love me as the daughter he'd never had."

Okay, this was a story I could get on board with. Because it meant I was *not* related to Garon.

Tanner shifted in his chair, eyeing Bea. "Wasn't Thumbelina supposed to be, like, super tiny?"

"I was abnormal—smaller than most children my age—and my bones ill-formed. But I was not, as the tale goes, as small as a thumb." She chuckled, then grew serious. "My health challenges were nevertheless very real. My parents must have thought me an abomination. They left me in a basket by the seashore, where Oliver found me. My body started shutting down soon after that."

"Shutting down?" I said. "What from?"

"I never had an official diagnosis. Father said my growth was stunted. I had deformed hips that caused my thighbones to turn inward, a bent spine, and widespread joint problems that caused extreme pain. He said I screamed every time I moved. He had trouble feeding me because I also had a cleft palate, so mostly I slept and cried, and got ever weaker and smaller. I was just a baby, remember, so I have no memory of this."

Bea took a sip of her tea, then continued. "It was around this time that the Remyallis came into bloom— that's why Father was by the sea in the first place—he'd set up a temporary abode in order to experiment with the flowers. When they bloomed, miraculously, my health improved. The cleft in my palate closed, and it seemed to him that my pain lessened.

"When he realized that my improved health was due

to the flowers, Father harvested all that he could and did what he could to preserve them. He boiled the petals and had me inhale the steam. He dried the stems and crushed them into a poultice, which was slathered on my chest each night before sleep. The treatments actually began to heal my deformed bones. Father tried ingesting some of the flower to see what it would do, but his stomach rejected it so he never gave me any.

"Eventually, when it became apparent that our supply would not last an entire year until the flowers bloomed again, Father used his abilities to imbue a Pearl with the essence of the flowers in the hopes that my body would continue to benefit even after our supply was gone. I started wearing this Pearl on a chain around my neck. And it did its job. Over time, the flowers healed me. Fully and completely."

Bea fell silent. She dipped a cookie in her teacup and took a tiny bite.

We all watched her.

Tanner finally broke the silence. "That's the weirdest story I've ever heard."

I laughed, but the laugh died in my throat at a glare from Dantzel.

"There is nothing funny about Bea's story," she said, her tone icy. "This Pearl, which has unnaturally prolonged her life, has also poisoned my daughter. Your mother."

"Why didn't you just get rid of it?" Garon asked.

Bea set her hands in her lap. "I didn't realize what the Pearl was doing until it was too late. For years, I kept it to remember my father—Oliver, that is—who'd gone off and vanished without a trace."

Garon sat up straighter. "When he was with me, caught in time."

"Yes. I only learned what happened years later when he came to find me. By then, I'd moved on without him. I'd married. Had plans to start a family." Her brow furrowed, like she was puzzling something out. "In this newest thread of time, Anka took me prisoner in the dead of night, leaving my husband behind and throwing a torch on the home." She looked around the room, examining us. "He must have escaped, or you all would not still be here."

She shook her head, like the jumble of memories overlapping from so many different timelines was too overwhelming. Yet still she sat, her hands tucked serenely together in her lap.

It didn't seem right to point out that maybe her husband hadn't escaped and that we were only here because she'd married again.

"At any rate, I kept the Pearl to remember my father. In that timeline, he died of natural causes around the age of fifty. It wasn't for many, many years, that I realized the Pearl was keeping me unnaturally young as well. My husband was almost fifty before we admitted to each other that my continued youthful appearance had to be due to more than just good genes.

"Then, after my husband passed, I couldn't stand the heartache and held to the Pearl that much harder. My children grew and had children. Their children had children. Every other generation or so, one would exhibit symptoms similar to Allie's." She paused. Swallowed, like she was leaving something unsaid. "But I had no reason to believe that the Pearl was harming anyone. It had healed me, after all.

"Dantzel was the first to suspect the Pearl was doing more harm than good. And, with the invention of the Internet, we had all sorts of new information at our fingertips to help solve the riddle."

"But you still have the Pearl." I meant it as an observation, but it came out sounding more like an accusation.

"Yes, I do." For the first time since she'd started talking, she fidgeted. Finally she said, "Death is a scary thing. And I've had a long time to think about it."

"But how can you keep the Pearl around when you know it's hurting my mother?" I said.

"This Pearl is not hurting her. The madness comes from her genes, and I passed those to her long before I knew what I was doing." Her gaze dropped to her hands. Again, she was leaving something unsaid.

Tanner said, "Still, you should have destroyed it just to be sure."

"Maybe." Bea cocked her head at Garon. "But perhaps it can still be of use."

Garon eyed her. "What do you mean?"

"I've been wondering what would happen if this Pearl were taken back in time. Would there then be two Pearls, or would one of them disintegrate? Would they join together? Maybe increase in power? Or would they cancel each other out? More importantly, could taking it back in time somehow undo all the suffering my family has been through?" She took a deep, ragged breath, then pulled the necklace off, over her head. "I'm ready to find out."

Then, suddenly, she gasped. Her fingers flew to her throat and her eyes went wide.

"She's dying!" I lunged for the necklace. "Put it back on."

She swatted my hands away, but put the necklace back on anyway. "I'm not dying," she said, breathing hard. "I've had a memory."

Dantzel sat up straighter. "Another alternate timeline?"

"No." Bea's hand shook, and the Pearl dangling from the necklace chain shook along with it. "Not a new timeline. The end of one."

Dantzel gripped her by the shoulder. "I don't understand, Bea, what are you talking about?"

Bea's eyes were wide. "In the past. There was an execution."

Chapter Twenty-Five

Follow Me

Lindy

1623—Valstenia

A sliver of light entered our cell. A hooded figure grabbed my hands and hauled me to my feet.

"Move," the figure commanded, exiting the cell and grabbing a torch from the wall just outside.

So, it was to be a speedy execution, then. I struggled for breath as my throat threatened to close up. My feet moved, following orders, while the arrow wound in my leg screamed in protest.

My mind went in circles. What about my mother? My siblings? I'd never see them again. And Garon. Would he continue the search for Belina even when I failed to show up at the cottage? Would he stay and fight Anka or would he go back to the future?

I wasn't ready to die. The cords holding my wrists together burned my flesh.

"With haste," the figure said, and there was a touch of panic in the voice.

And … had it been a woman's voice?

We climbed a set of winding, narrow stairs, slick with mildew or rot or something worse.

I realized there was no one behind us. The figure had come alone. Trevin was behind me and Yelena was in front. We could fight back. We could turn around. Wasn't there some secret way out of the castle through the dungeon?

I stopped moving. Trevin bumped into me.

"Yelena," I hissed.

She turned and stopped moving when she saw me.

The figure stopped moving as well. "Please, Your Highness, speed is of the essence. If I am to help you, we must not delay."

Yes, it was definitely a woman.

"Who are you?" I said.

"There's no time, Madam," she said. Then, seeming to reconsider, she pulled back her hood.

It was a servant girl, a youth, not more than fourteen. She looked vaguely familiar.

"I am the daughter of your mother's handmaid. Your mother sent me to get you out. Please, we must hurry." The girl looked close to tears, and there was terror in her eyes.

I hesitated.

"She sent the children away as well," the girl said.

"Carina and Felipe?" Yelena asked.

"Yes. My mother fled with them early this morning, before your return. I am to take you to them." The girl put her hood back in place and continued up the stairs, faster now. "I'm not sure how much time we have."

The girl led us through a series of twists and turns, up one more staircase, then down a half-flight of stairs. She only stopped once, at a fork in the path. She hesitated, like she wasn't sure which way to go, but recovered quickly and continued to the left. "Yes, this is the way. We're almost there."

"Where, exactly?" I said.

"To the wine merchants' entrance—the only entrance Anka hasn't found. It is well concealed to protect the royal winery from pillagers. Your mother gave me very specific instructions."

Soon, natural light came into view and we entered a cavern. Steps to our left led down to a wine cellar, where rows of bottles were stacked along the walls.

The girl scanned the area, frantically, with wide eyes. Her gaze landed on a barrel—tall and narrow—standing beside the entrance to the cellar. She yanked off the lid and pulled out a knife.

"Give me your hands, Highness, I'll cut you free." I turned and she sawed at the ropes. They loosened, then dropped off.

I rubbed my wrists while she worked on Yelena, and then Trevin.

"Arm yourselves," she said, pointing to the barrel where she'd found the knife.

I grabbed a sword from among the weapons inside. When we were all armed and ready, the girl led us to the back of the room, around a bend, and, suddenly, the sky was visible.

Our guide proceeded with caution, her hands gripping the edges of her cloak like she meant to squeeze the very life out of it. She crept toward the opening and poked her head out. "We're clear. Follow me." She slipped out of the opening.

The entrance was no more than a gap in the castle wall, but since one edge was set a few feet farther out from the other, and extended beyond where the inner wall ended, the gap was completely concealed from outside view. Shrubbery grew uninterrupted along the wall, further hiding the secret entrance. The terrain was steep—the entrance was at the back of the castle, on the mountainside—but there was a small path cut into the hill and faint wheel ruts could be seen from the last time a wine cart had been brought this way.

We followed the girl in silence, sticking to the castle

edge and utilizing the shrubbery to stay hidden. My limbs trembled—my body was weak with hunger and lack of sleep. Stabs of pain pulsed from my wound and shot up my thigh.

At one point, our guide dropped to her knees so quickly, I thought she'd tripped.

Then I saw the pair of soldiers.

My heart slammed into my throat and I ducked, praying they hadn't seen us. I was in no condition to fight.

I kept an eye on the soldiers through the shrubbery. Their eyes were glazed over with the same drunken, pinkish hue the soldiers in the cabin had had while under Anka's spell. They walked passed us, as if in some sort of trance.

We waited until they disappeared from view, then continued. We reached the wall to the castle gardens, which was still charred from the fire poor Anton had set under Anka's command.

The girl hopped over the wall and ducked behind it. The land beyond was burned to a barren crisp, but if we stuck to the wall, we'd be concealed from view of the castle.

We hurried away from the castle, keeping our heads low.

And ran right into a group of guards, leaning against the wall and passing a bottle of ale between them.

Our guide jumped, squealing in fright.

The guards froze and, for the tiniest moment, we just stared at each other. Their eyes told me they were bewitched like the others, but apparently that didn't make them immune to the power of a strong drink.

With a cry, they grabbed up their weapons and rushed at us.

"Run," Trevin commanded. "They're drunk, I can handle them."

Yelena and the girl ran.

"I'm not leaving you behind!" I shouted.

"Yes, you are." Trevin pushed me toward the others. "I'll catch up, I promise."

The drunken men rushed toward us, eyes wild and roving. Stumbling every so often in their haste.

"Go! Now!" Trevin yelled.

My gaze darted from Trevin to the advancing men. They were fierce. But definitely drunk.

So I ran, a fresh wave of pain shooting through my leg as I stumbled after Yelena. Away from the castle. Away from Anka. Away from the fight.

But what would I do when I got away? What kind of queen would leave her castle in such a state? How could I possibly stop Anka without weapons or an army?

I pushed the questions aside and focused on getting away. There would be time to come up with a plan once we were safe. Once I'd been reunited with Mother and Carina and Felipe.

The girl stopped moving only once we'd reached the tree-line. Breathing hard, she reached into a fold of her traveling cape and pulled out a letter. "Your mother told me to get you out of the castle and give you this letter once you were safely away."

I took the letter. It was stamped with my mother's wax seal. "Where are my brother and sister?"

"At my mother's house, not two miles off," the girl said. "There'll be food and water." She eyed the bloody spot on my dress, where the arrow had struck me. I felt fresh blood trickling down my leg. "Your wound needs to be properly dressed. Shall we continue?"

I gripped my letter tightly. "Yes, let's get to safety."

"Very well." The girl turned.

"What is your name?" I asked.

"I am Colette."

"Thank you, Colette."

She turned, her eyebrows lifting in surprise. "You're welcome, Highness."

****

Felipe ran out to greet us, but was pulled back by a woman I recognized as my mother's handmaid. "Back inside, child. It's not safe."

She ushered us into the house. Felipe threw his arms around my legs and I hissed in pain. The woman sat me down and unwound my dressing. She examined the wound. "You must have been far enough from the shooter for the arrow to slow down before reaching you—this is not a deep wound. And it looks like it bled out well."

"Is that a good thing?" I said.

"Yes. Less chance of infection if it bleeds well." She pressed a cloth to my flesh and I gasped, my legs going weak at the pain.

Colette tended to Yelena, whom the arrow had only grazed. Carina and Felipe stood, watching with wide, terrified eyes as our wounds were cleaned and rewrapped.

My leg was on fire, but I managed a smile and held out my arms. Felipe ran into them and Carina followed, slowly. "I'm so glad you're both safe," I said, pulling them into a hug.

The two held onto me while I pulled out Mother's letter. I broke the wax seal and unfolded a single sheet of parchment. Yelena moved so she could read over my shoulder.

Dearest Shalyndria,

If you're reading this, then my plan worked and you're safely away from the castle. You can trust Colette and her family, as they have proven their loyalty and bravery this day. By the time you read this, I will have been discovered and it will be too late for me, so I will say only this: I have lived a good, long, life, and I desire the same for you. Do everything you can to stop the woman who has seized your crown, but do not return to the castle until you have collected an army. Rally the countrymen, apply to King Jershon and, if necessary, arm your women and children. Whatever you must do, do it.

Above all, have faith in yourself. You were born to be a leader, and the qualities you need are inside you. You must only learn to recognize them. My love for you and your siblings is beyond compare. Until we meet again, fair daughter...

Yours,
Mother

The parchment shook in my hands. What did she mean, it would be too late for her? Hadn't she already gotten out?

This letter sounded an awful lot like good-bye.

"Please, what did my mother say to you of her plan?" I asked the woman.

"Only that I was to get the children to safety and that Colette would go for you."

"But what of my mother? How was she getting out?"

The woman looked down at her hands. They were weathered, as if from a lifetime of hard work. "Colette, take the little ones outside," her mother ordered. "Stay in back, out of sight."

Carina looked to me with questioning eyes. Felipe clung tighter to my arm. I peeled him off and patted his back. "Go play outside. Stay with your sister."

Colette ushered them out the door.

The woman watched them go, then turned back to me. "Your mother did not tell me her plan."

I studied her. "But you still know, don't you?"

She refused to meet my gaze. "I can guess, Your Highness."

"We have to go back to the castle. We have to get her out," I said, my thoughts spinning wildly.

Colette's mother took hold of my elbow, steadying me. "It's too late. We've had news, just before you arrived. A runner came from the village."

My knees went weak, and I clutched her arm for support. I couldn't bear to ask.

She told me anyway. "There's been an execution. Your mother is dead."

Chapter Twenty-Six

Twisting Time

Maggie

Present Day—Boryn

"An execution?" Garon sat forward in his chair, his eyes tight. "Who?" When Bea didn't answer, he slammed his fist on the table. "Who has been executed?"

I flinched. I'd never heard Garon yell. Never seen him get angry at all, really.

Bea met his gaze and didn't flinch away from it. Gently, she said, "In the memory I just had, I overheard a report from Anka's guards who were holding me captive. I'm sorry … she has killed your sister. Queen Shalyndria is dead."

Dantzel gasped.

My jaw went slack. Icy needles pricked at my heart. "Lindy is dead?"

Bea nodded. "I'm sorry. I can't say when it happened, only that it did. The new memories have just joined my old ones."

Garon was frozen, his face pinched in silent pain.

No one spoke. No one moved.

Garon stood from the table, his chair toppling over behind him with the suddenness of the movement. "I have to leave now. Bea, Oliver said I needed to find you before defeating Anka, but he didn't say why. Is there anything else you can think of that will help? Something you know about the Topaz, maybe?"

"The Topaz is a relatively new creation, something

present only in my most recent string of memories." Bea's lips pursed together as she thought. "I believe its creation led directly to my capture—those memories are also fairly new. In my old timeline, when my father disappeared, my husband and I settled and started a family—" She gasped, her hand flying to her throat.

She clutched the necklace, with the blood-red Pearl dangling from it. "Wearing this Pearl while my baby grew inside me—that must have been what caused the madness."

She turned to me, slowly, and said, "Maggie, I know you care about this as much as I do. Will you go back with Garon and convince me—that is, past me—to give up the Pearl?"

My mouth fell open, but no words came out.

Bea pressed the Pearl into my hand. "If you take this one with you, I know it will convince past me that you're telling the truth. We named our daughter Sarenna. Please, Maggie. I must get rid of the Pearl long before Sarenna is born. If there's any chance of saving her, this is it. And, maybe ... hopefully ... destroying it will also save your mother."

My fingers closed around the Pearl. "Are you saying that your daughter suffered the same way my mother does?"

Bea's eyes were suddenly glassy with unshed tears. She nodded once.

"Then I would be honored to go back and save her."

"Absolutely not," Garon said. "It's too dangerous. Maggie is staying here. Bea, I'll take the Pearl back and I'll make sure your daughter is safe." He held out his hand. "Give me the Pearl, Maggie."

I bristled. Why was he so opposed to taking me back with him? This was my chance to save Mom—to stop the poison from ever affecting her. Of course I was going. My hand closed tightly around the Pearl. "No. Bea gave it to me."

Indecision warred on Garon's features, the pain of his sister's death clearly taking a toll. Finally, his expression softened. "Mags, we've been through this. It's too dangerous for you to go back. I promise, I'll find Bea. I'll tell her about the poison and we'll destroy the Pearl…" He hesitated, like he was leaving something unsaid. "Then I'll come right back."

I don't know why the words sounded off, but they did. I stepped toward him, tentatively. We still hadn't touched since we'd seen each other and I was aching to close the distance between us. "Nothing bad is going to happen. I want to come with you. I need to do this for my family." I grazed his fingers with mine.

He froze, like my touch was a shock—an unexpected, but not entirely unwelcome one.

Then he grabbed my hand. And warmth flooded into me.

His hand around mine felt like it always had.

We felt like we always had.

I didn't know if he was back, or stuck somewhere between the past and the present. But this, right here— this was real.

"If Maggie's going, so am I," Tanner said.

"But what about Mom? Someone still has to tell Dad about her."

Dantzel cleared her throat. "I will contact your father."

I stared at her. "Really." It was more of a challenge than an actual question.

Dantzel met my stare. "Yes, really. You were right, I shouldn't have hidden the truth from Allie's family—

from you. If you'll go back and help Garon destroy the item that poisoned Allie's mind, I will make sure your father knows she's alive and understands where you've gone."

"Assuming you all even notice our absence, right?" I said. "I mean, once we fix everything, we can come back to this very moment. Garon said he could do it, even though he didn't last time." I shot him a pointed look.

He squeezed my hand. "I'm sorry for that. We still could—go back to that moment—after we fix things for good."

But … if Garon had come back when he'd said he would, I never would have found my mom.

Wait … had he just said '*We* still could'?

I grinned. "So, does this mean you'll take me back with you?"

"And me, too?" Tanner added.

Garon's forehead creased with worry. "I meant what I said about it being dangerous, though it's significantly less so now than it was the last time I left."

"Uh, how is that?"

Garon's classic mischievous grin made an appearance. Just for a moment, just a hint of it. But enough that I knew the guy I'd been falling for was still in there somewhere. "O taught me some new tricks."

I didn't even want to know what complicated new time travel tricks O had been thinking up.

"Why do I feel like I'm going to regret this?" Garon said.

Tanner said, "So, I'm coming too, right? That's part of this whole plan you're regretting, right? 'Cause if you're not planning on taking me, you'll have to fight me first. And the last guy I fought was solid as a tree." Tanner laughed at his own joke, nudging me with the hand he'd injured punching an actual tree.

"Fine, you can both come," Garon said. Turning to Bea, he added, "I will do what I can to ensure the Pearl doesn't poison your family. I'll help Maggie find your daughter. But my first priority will be stopping Anka."

Bea said, "If you want to stop Anka, you'll need my help. In the past, that is." She closed her eyes, and continued, "There are so many threads of memories—it's hard to untangle them all—but I believe my Pearl is key. You'll need it to destroy the Topaz."

"I understand," Garon said. His gaze circled the room. "Everyone good?"

Tanner said, "Yep."

I nodded.

"Okay, then. Let's go twist time."

Chapter Twenty-Seven

Life Flight

Lindy

1623—Valstenia

My world crumbled as I processed the words: *There's been an execution. Your mother is dead.* Why hadn't she escaped? She could have, she'd gotten the rest of us out.

Yelena said, "How do you know it was her? Maybe they executed someone else?"

Colette's mother wrung her hands together. "Perhaps I should more fully explain."

Yelena narrowed her eyes. "What is there to explain?"

The woman's gaze slipped back and forth between us. "The report we heard was not, in fact, that they'd executed your mother. The report named Queen Shalyndria as the one who'd been killed."

Yelena's mouth dropped open in horror.

I fought back a wave of nausea as the truth hit me straight in the gut. My voice was barely above a whisper: "Mother took my place."

"No," Yelena gasped.

Colette's mother nodded. "I believe that was your mother's intent. Whether Anka thought she was executing you, or knew it was your mother, remains to be seen. But there was, without question, an execution at the castle this morning—there are eyewitnesses aplenty. The people are being told it was you. And if there was an execution, and it clearly wasn't you, then…" She trailed off, unable to finish the sentence.

Yelena's face had drained of color. I felt similarly empty.

Colette's mother placed a gentle hand on my arm. "I have been with your mother for over two decades. Her love for her children governed everything she did and was her very reason for living. She placed her children above even her country. Who but your mother would have willingly taken your place?"

A sob rocked my body, threatening to break me from the inside out.

"The only thing we can be sure of," she said, "is that when Anka learns you've escaped, if she hasn't already, she will come for you right away. And her search will be relentless. You must leave at once."

It was too much to handle. My mother couldn't be dead. Couldn't have sacrificed herself for me and my siblings.

Yet even as I had the thought, I knew my mother would have done exactly that. Would have done it without the slightest hesitation if she'd thought it would save us. My eyes burned with unshed tears, the shock rendering me incapable of releasing them.

"What of Carina and Felipe?" was all I could say.

"I'll take them north," Yelena said. "Mother has family there, maybe they can help us."

My body was numb, and my head a foggy daze. Could I even trust my sister?

"Lindy." Yelena's tone was gentle. "I know I let you down. But I'm going to do everything I can to win back your trust. I promise, I'll keep the kids safe—far from Anka's reach. And maybe Mother's brother can help us gather soldiers and weapons."

Colette's mother said, "I have prepared supplies for you. Food. A little water. Some crude weapons. You must do as your mother advised and gather an army."

I swallowed. "You're right. Of course."

"We only have two horses," she said. "But you are welcome to them both."

"Please, use them to get Carina and Felipe to safety. I'll draw less attention if I flee on foot." I placed a hand on the woman's arm, my fingers trembling in spite of my effort to still them. "Thank you for your assistance. And for the great service you have rendered to my family. Your kindness will not be forgotten."

The woman bowed. "It has been an honor and a pleasure. Your mother was the kindest woman I've ever known." She turned to Yelena. "The horses are ready. You can leave at once."

"Keep our siblings safe," I said to Yelena.

"I will. I promise. Keep our country safe." She started to leave, then hesitated. She turned and gripped me by the arms, pulling me into a hug. "You are brave, and smart, and so much stronger than you know," she whispered fiercely. "Never forget that."

After a moment's hesitation, I hugged her back. "I hope you're right. For all our sakes, I hope so."

Chapter Twenty-Eight

Time Travel and Tummy Troubles

Maggie

Present Day—Boryn

Tanner, Garon, and I each carried a pack full of supplies as we headed for the woods. My eyes were wet from saying goodbye to Mom, even though she still didn't understand who we were. Dantzel and Bea watched from the front porch as we walked down the long driveway, crossed the narrow country road, and disappeared into the trees.

"So, why the obsession with trees?" I asked.

"That's one of O's time-travel tricks. Apparently, things are less likely to go wrong when you ground yourself to something—like a centuries-old tree—that exists both in the present and in the past."

"I guess that makes sense."

Garon led us to an extra-large, extra-gnarled tree and said, "This is the one I used to get here."

He placed one hand on the tree and, after a moment's hesitation, reached for my hand. A familiar jolt ran through me when we touched. From the way his hand tightened around mine, I knew he'd felt it, too.

Why had he been avoiding touching me?

"Grab your brother's hand," Garon said.

I did.

"Tanner, why don't you put your other hand on the tree, too?" Garon said. "This way we're double-grounded and linked together."

Tanner jerked his hand out of mine. "Wait, you've never done this before?"

Garon huffed. "I've never taken anyone back with me, so technically no. I told you it was dangerous."

"You don't have to come," I said to Tanner.

"That's not what I meant," Tanner said. "I just assumed that he'd done it before."

"Well, he hasn't." I held out my hand, eyebrows raised expectantly. "Are you in or out?"

"Like I'd let you do this alone." Tanner grabbed my hand with a ferocity that said he was freaked out, but trying desperately to hide it. He put his other hand on a knot of the tree, not far from Garon's.

"Okay, both of you hold tight, and keep your eyes on me. I'll do the rest."

Garon gripped my hand tighter, closed his eyes, and furrowed his brow.

I tightened my grip on Tanner, but didn't dare look at him. My eyes were laser-locked on Garon's face.

His features smoothed over and relaxed, then his eyes started twitching beneath his closed eyelids—like the eyes of someone just starting to dream. The twitching increased and I felt sure that his eyelids would fly open any moment and he'd admit defeat.

But then, a tugging sensation started, deep inside me.

Don't look away, I reminded myself.

The tugging in my belly escalated into a dull pain, like a cramp. Was time travel supposed to hurt?

The cramp intensified and became like a knife. Garon's features twisted, like he was feeling it, too.

"Garon," I whimpered.

"Don't look away," Tanner reminded me, his voice choppy, like he was speaking through his own pain.

I fought to keep my eyes open and locked on Garon's

face. And then, my vision blurred, the pain imploded inside me, and the world went black.

I couldn't see, but I still felt Garon's and Tanner's hands in mine. I held on with everything I had. The blackness was gone a second later, and the pain ceased, leaving me with a dull ache in my belly.

My eyes flew open. Oh no, when had I closed them? There was the tree, Garon, Tanner. "Did it work?"

Garon opened his eyes and grinned. "Yep."

I followed his gaze to the tree, which was no longer covered in knots. The bark was younger—not as dry as before—and the trunk was half the width it had been.

Garon took his hand off the tree and Tanner followed suit. I dropped Tanner's hand. I tried to let go of Garon's, but he held on, squeezing tighter.

I looked at him.

He leaned into me and said softly, "I'm sorry I didn't come back sooner. And I'm sorry I was acting weird at your grandmother's house. There are some things I've been struggling with—trying to figure out how to handle—and I didn't feel I could come back until I'd figured it out. But I really am glad you're here." He squeezed my hand, emphasizing his point.

I studied him. What *things* was he trying to figure out?

"Where are we?" Tanner asked, gazing around.

We stood at the edge of a clearing, with a tiny log cabin in the center. Forest stretched around us as far as I could see, in every direction.

"We're exactly where we were before. Four centuries earlier, of course, give or take a few years."

"Cool," Tanner said.

Just then, the cabin door swung open and four soldiers emerged, swords drawn. They converged on us, with the speed and precision of a well-trained army.

One of them held the point of his sword to Garon's throat and spoke in a foreign language. I wondered if it was Swedish or Borynian. Or … did Valstenia have its own language?

Garon answered in English. "I am Garon, son of the late King Edvin and Queen Maren."

The soldier's eyes narrowed and he said something else in his foreign tongue.

"My companions are not from here," Garon answered. "It is for this reason I use the language of the Anglos."

Another soldier said, in English, "Forgive the intrusion, Highness, but we must be sure it's you."

Garon's gaze darted from one man to the next, studying their faces in turn. Then he said, "As we discussed when we were last together, I have gone forward in time, located the daughter of Oliver, and returned with the knowledge of where she is being held captive."

The soldier considered Garon's words, examined his eyes, and then lowered his sword.

"I am Calv," he continued in English. "Welcome back. Come inside and we can discuss our next move." The man's eyes darkened, like a storm cloud was passing through. "The Queen will not be rejoining us."

My stomach tightened. Was it true then? Had Lindy really been killed?

Garon swallowed and I could read in his face the battle going on inside him between wanting and not wanting to hear the news.

Calv offered his report as we followed him to the cabin. Every now and then he stumbled over a word, but his English was pretty good. "Just yesterday we were in a nearby village gathering supplies. While we were there, a rider came through announcing that Queen Shalyndria had been killed. Her mother has supposedly fled the country with the young prince and princess, and a woman who is rumored to possess the beauty of a thousand moons has seized control of the throne. We presume this is the same woman we encountered here at the cabin.

"Surprisingly, there are many who don't see her as a threat, but welcome the newcomer. Those who oppose her are disappearing by the dozens. No one feels safe, and there is mass unrest." Calv glanced sideways at Garon. "Should we not abandon our search for Belina and instead raise an army to defeat this imposter?"

The cabin appeared even more decrepit up close, the wood rotted out and, in some places, completely missing. We followed the soldier inside.

Garon swallowed, choking back his emotion with obvious effort. "I have reason to believe that Belina can help us and that, without her, the cause is already lost."

Calv regarded Garon carefully. "Forgive me for questioning your judgement, but I feel I need to ask. Both for the safety of my men and the citizens of this country." He paused.

Garon nodded for him to continue.

"How will this woman be able to help? The fact remains that your mentor's motives were unclear. From what I can tell, we must focus on the task at hand, which is dethroning the self-appointed queen as quickly as possible."

Another of the soldiers spoke up for the first time. "Regarding our search for information on the tree branch Oliver gave Queen Shalyndria, we found no one who recognized it. There are rumors of a flower that grows by the seaside and blooms only once a year, but we found nobody with firsthand knowledge of the blossom."

A third soldier said, "If we were to follow that lead, it would be akin to chasing ghosts."

Garon said, "I believe that we need Belina in order to defeat Anka. If what you say is true and I am the only one of the royal family left, then I am as close to a king as we've got, and I will not jeopardize our chances of winning by returning to the castle prematurely."

Calv stepped forward. "Hans didn't mean any offense. Of course you may be assured of our assistance."

Tanner adjusted his pack. My gaze flitted between Garon and the soldiers.

"We will leave immediately," Garon said.

Calv bowed. The other three soldiers followed suit, though the one called Hans was clearly not thrilled about it.

****

Garon led us straight to the sea. Like navigating a group through the forest without GPS was the easiest thing in the world. I'd known he traveled a lot in his old life, but I'd never pictured him actually traipsing around the forest on foot.

We avoided the main roads so we wouldn't run into any of Anka's men. After twenty-ish minutes of picking our way through thick brush, I was breathing hard. Another twenty-ish minutes and my feet began to throb.

I was the only one who seemed ready for a rest, but I wasn't about to ask for one. As we walked, I stole glances at Garon, my thoughts whirling uncontrollably. He moved through the trees with an ease and familiarity that made me almost jealous. I'd never moved through anything with such grace.

Garon's life before he came to the future must have been so different from the one I'd always known. Why hadn't I ever tried to imagine it? I'd taken it for granted that the future was better than the past, without ever stopping to wonder if, maybe, it wasn't so cut-and-dry.

Then a thought surfaced—a thought I didn't want to think. But as much as I tried to push it away, it kept coming back.

And the thought was this: *How could I let him give up his home, his family, and a country he clearly loved, just so he could be with me?*

The answer, which I didn't want to accept, but that kept poking at my brain, was that I couldn't. I couldn't let him give this up for me. I never should have. Not to mention the fact that, with Lindy dead, this country needed Garon more than ever. He belonged here, in the past.

The truth hit me with such painful clarity that I stumbled, my toe catching on a tree branch.

Tanner caught my arm before I fell all the way down. "Are you all right, Mags?"

"Yep." I kept walking, pushing myself on even though my lungs screamed for air, my feet ached for a break, and tears threatened behind my eyes.

I couldn't let Garon see what I was feeling. Now was not the time to be weak. Now was the time to fight. I could be strong for Garon, and for Lindy. I could be strong for my mother, who needed me to find Belina and prevent the poisoning of our family line. I could summon my strength for the people I loved.

I just hoped my strength would be enough.

Chapter Twenty-Nine

Join the Cause

Lindy

1623—Valstenia

Trevin hadn't caught up to us like he'd said he would, but I couldn't wait for him at Colette's. What if Anka's men came looking for me? I was too close to the castle. Too easy to find.

But I still hoped Trevin would find me.

I fled through the woods alone, taking a circuitous route back to the cottage to make myself harder to track. Trevin knew the meeting place—hopefully he'd realize that was where I'd gone. My injured leg screamed in protest as I ran, but the bandages remained blood-free, which made me think the wound was on its way to closing.

After putting some distance between myself and the castle, I found a particularly dense patch of bushes and hid myself under them to wait until nightfall. I'd move again when it was dark. I got settled, resting my head on the bundle of supplies Colette's mother had given me. Eventually, my breathing slowed. My eyelids drooped, and my muscles relaxed.

Yes. Sleep.

I let myself drift off.

There were no dreams. Only deep sleep.

And then a shout.

I was awake in a flash. Through the leaves of my hiding place, I saw a group of soldiers—a dozen or so—

hacking their way through the underbrush. They were headed straight for me.

Fear shot through me, my heartbeat rocketing into my skull. I didn't move. Didn't dare breathe. I clenched my hands into fists, fighting the urge to flee. If I left my cover, they'd see me for sure.

The brute who appeared to be in charge yelled commands. "Faster, men. She can't have gone much farther. Rest is for the weak. We stop only when we succeed. Find the girl."

They responded as one, a chorus of ferocity echoing their leader. "Find the girl."

"Find and kill," the leader said.

Then, the echo, "Find and kill."

The venom in their voices made me tremble. I gripped my sword as the men came closer. Their boots went clomping by, mere inches from my hiding spot. The leaves that hid me rustled as the men stomped past, their blades slicing through the brush with a vengeance.

I held my breath until my lungs screamed for air. And then I took it in quick, desperate gulps.

Eventually, the last man passed.

And still I remained, shaking with the horror of being hunted. I waited long after they were gone, not daring to move while it was still light out in case the soldiers had stopped nearby.

At twilight, I crept from my hiding place and fled in the opposite direction the men had gone.

It took me longer than it should have to make it to the cabin in the woods, but I made it. I was days past the agreed-upon rendezvous with Garon and, as expected, my brother was not there.

But neither was Trevin.

The cabin was deserted.

I sat down on a log, resting my head in my hands and feeling more alone than ever before. I'd tried to keep thoughts of my mother at bay while I'd been fleeing through the woods, but they came now, with full force. I tried not to picture her final moments, but my mind wouldn't stop calling up images of her, marching bravely to her death, with her hands tied behind her back.

A strangled cry escaped my throat and I let the tears come, racking my body in great, choking sobs.

When I'd cried myself out, I stood and paced around the clearing. My eyes were puffy and sore.

Okay. I was on my own.

Mother wasn't here to help.

Garon, Yelena, Borov, Trevin. Nobody was coming.

But I couldn't crumble like I'd done as captive to the Emerald. Not this time. I was still alive, and my country needed me.

So, what was I going to do?

I had no idea how to go about finding Belina, but hopefully Garon was working on that. He'd probably returned as planned and taken the soldiers on a quest to find her. It was what we'd agreed upon.

But we still needed an army.

"Okay," I said out loud. Because I needed to hear my voice or I was going to go mad. "Let's go round up an army."

The forest was my only witness.

****

I had to be subtle. I couldn't risk running into Anka's soldiers—or alerting them to my whereabouts—as I recruited soldiers to my cause. But I needed people to know I was still alive. And in order to believe it, there had to be eyewitnesses.

Lots of eyewitnesses.

So I went to the one person I knew I could count on: Duke Christoph. The Duke had good command over his people, unmatched experience in battle and, most importantly, a deep love for his country.

As I traveled, I thought back to the empty seat at our council table when we'd discussed the missing Topaz, and how the Duke had been unable to come due to concerns with his army. Even though we hadn't been able to send as many soldiers as he'd needed, I hoped the hundred I'd sent after our council meeting had been enough. And the Duke's territory was on the northern borders of Valstenia—far enough away that they shouldn't have been affected by Qadar's phony tax collectors.

The sun was going down when I arrived. I stood on a hill overlooking the city, watching from afar as merchants closed up shop and citizens headed home for the night. This town had been fiercely loyal to the crown for decades. I hoped I could count on them just a little while longer.

The snap of a twig sounded in the growing darkness.

I whirled around just as a flock of birds took flight, upsetting the calm of night. I pulled my sword from a sheath hidden within the folds of my dress, my heart matching the beat of the birds' wings as they fled. I edged toward the trees, my gaze darting around in search of the source of the noise.

Maybe it was just a squirrel. Or the forest settling in for the night.

Or … one of Anka's bloodthirsty soldier shells.

I trembled. Had they tracked me somehow? Maybe I should run.

I kept my sword up, taking a step forward. "Who's th—?" My voice cracked. It had been days since I'd spoken to anyone other than myself.

I cleared my throat and tried again, louder this time. Trying to sound brave. "Who's there?"

A rustle, off to my right.

I turned, gripping my sword tightly.

My mouth went dry. My stomach knotted up.

Then, a voice. The sweetest sound I'd ever heard.

It said, "Highness, is that you?"

And Trevin stepped out, sheathing his sword and coming toward me.

I dropped my own sword to the ground and ran to him, forgetting about being strong and independent and brave. Forgetting the fact that I was the Queen and he my guard.

I threw my arms around him, my heart swelling with something that felt like … well … like the sun on a summer morning. Or a new bloom in spring.

It was the feeling of dangling from a cliff high above the ocean, knowing you alone held your fate in your hands. I didn't know what it was, exactly, but I was pretty sure it was more than what a Queen should feel for her guard. And it was more than just relief that I was no longer alone.

But I didn't care.

After the slightest hesitation, Trevin hugged me back.

Suddenly, there were butterflies in my tummy and tingles running along my arms. And, for maybe the first time ever, I felt that feeling—when the world slips away and all you see is the person right in front of you. When, for just a moment, nothing else matters.

Was he feeling it, too? Or was this all in my head?

We stayed like that, for probably longer than we should. And then Trevin pulled away. I couldn't be sure in the darkening light, but I thought his ears were red.

He cleared his throat and stepped back. "I'm glad to see you're well, Highness. How is your knee?"

"Still sore, but feeling better each day. Colette's mother dressed it well. And what about your hand?"

"It's fine." He held it out for me to see. "It was a minor injury at an inopportune time."

I smoothed down my skirt, wishing my stuttering heart could be so easily tamed. "How did you find me?"

"I didn't."

"What do you mean?"

"Well, I couldn't. By the time I reached Colette's after taking care of Anka's guards, you'd already left. I tried following you through the woods, but you did a good job hiding your tracks—I lost your trail less than a mile in." He started talking faster. "So I went to the cabin, but you weren't there either. I waited, but you didn't come. Perhaps you'd already been there—I couldn't tell." He pushed a hand through his hair, leaving it standing on end. "I had no way of knowing where you were."

I put my hand on his arm. "It's okay. It's clear you tried."

"I wasn't done trying. I know Duke Christoph well— served most of my time in his territory—and I came here because I thought he could help me track you down. But now, here you are. I can hardly believe it." His smile lit up his face. It looked like he might hug me again, but then thought better of it.

His eyes were blue. How had I not noticed before? And that dimple was to die for.

Oh, boy. What were the rules about Queens dating their guards?

He patted his hair back down. "So why are *you* here?"

"I came for the Duke's help as well," I said, hoping he couldn't tell that I'd just been admiring his dimple.

"Garon is off searching for Belina—at least I *hope* that's where he is—but even if he finds her, we still need an army before we go against Anka. I came to raise one."

Trevin grinned and his eyes shone with admiration. Which he quickly tried to hide by looking away.

"Well ... should we go into the city?" I said.

Trevin eyed me. "Yes. But first we need to hide your identity."

"What do you mean? We need people to see I'm alive."

"Yes, but only the *right* people. It's true that we're far from the castle, but if Anka has guards down there, or if someone we can't trust sees you first, we risk being captured or cast out as frauds. It's best to hide your identity until we've found people we can trust."

I looked down at myself. I was still wearing the dress I'd been in when we'd first set out with the farmer Anton. It was soiled from my time in prison, bloody from my arrow wound, and the hem was becoming frayed from dragging along the ground. "I wish I had my traveling cloak, then I could at least shroud my face."

Trevin's gaze caught on the hem of my dress. He took a breath, as if to say something, then pursed his lips instead.

I glanced down, trying to figure out what he was looking at. "What is it?"

He stared at my dress, brooding.

I put a hand on my hip. "You can tell me. What are you thinking?"

"It's just..." He looked at my dress again, then glanced away.

"It's just what?"

"I wonder—forgive me, Highness—but, what have you got on under that dress?"

I resisted the urge to laugh at the immediate flush in his face.

"I mean, could the skirt be used as a cloak or veil of some sort?" His blush deepened. "If you have several layers, Highness, perhaps one of them could be repurposed?"

I smiled. "You don't need to keep calling me Highness."

He cocked his head to the side.

My response had taken him off guard.

"Oh," he said.

"My friends just call me Lindy."

"Oh," he said again.

"And, now that you mention it, I do have several layers on and I think you're right about being able to use one of them to our advantage." What I didn't tell him was that I could really take off the entire dress and still be wearing more clothing than most girls in the twentieth century did. My undergarments alone covered more skin than most modern girls covered, ever.

But I couldn't very well ask people to believe that their Queen would come to them wearing nothing but undergarments. So ditching the dress completely was not an option. The question was, which layer to remove?

I grabbed the dirty hem of my dress, lifting the top layer to reveal two layers underneath. "Which one should I take off?"

Trevin blushed again, but then, seeming to refocus on the task at hand, bent to examine them. "The outer layer is filthy, but it does lend credence to your royal claim. Only one of noble birth would have a dress made of such fine material. So that one needs to stay."

He fingered the middle layer, which was a bunched-up fabric meant to give the dress volume. The bottom layer was soft and silky, meant, I supposed, to keep the middle layer from irritating my legs.

But since my undergarments completely covered my legs, that was unnecessary.

"Yeah, the bottom layer's gotta go," I said, before he could suggest it. I lifted the top two layers so I could get at the seam where the bottom layer was attached to the others at the waist. "Here, hold these up."

If he'd been blushing before, it was nothing compared to now.

"Your Highness, I don't think—"

"Oh, come on, it's just a bunch of fabric. I've got plenty more on underneath. And I told you not to call me Highness."

He paused, the tiniest hint of a grin flashing across his face. It was gone a moment later as he went back to being all business.

"All right, *Queen Lindy,* I will hold your skirt up for you."

I started ripping the fabric loose, but it was awkward and hard to get a good angle on it. "Actually, I'll hold the dress up, you rip off the under layer."

Trevin hesitated, a protest probably sitting on the tip of his tongue, but then he handed me the fabric. I gathered it all up in my arms while he tugged at the under skirt. I felt the pull at my waist as the seam gave. Then, with a ripping sound, the fabric came free. He yanked it down and helped me step out of it, then I dropped the outer layers and my dress fell in place around me.

Trevin folded the skirt into a long rectangle and draped it over my head, like the hood of a traveling cloak, so it shrouded my face.

"You're very clever," I said. "This is perfect! The

material is even sort of see-through, if I needed to pull it all the way down like a veil." I demonstrated.

He laughed and pulled it back up so my eyes were uncovered. "Let's save that as a *just-in-case* option. For now, it would be nice if you could see properly. Just keep your head covered enough to avoid drawing attention to yourself until we've found people we can trust."

"Got it." I adjusted the fabric accordingly, letting it drape down over my shoulders like an oversized sort of scarf. I took one end and tossed it over the opposite shoulder to hold the head covering in place. "How do I look?"

I realized I was flirting with him—thinking back on that hug and wanting to be in his arms again, even though I knew I shouldn't.

Trevin stepped back to appraise me, the corners of his mouth twitching up.

"What, is it really that bad?"

Trevin tamed the grin. One of these days, it'd be nice to see him just let loose with it. I bet his smile was even more amazing when it wasn't guarded.

"You look beautiful, Your—" He cleared his throat. "You look beautiful, Queen Lindy. I can't say the same about the head covering, but it'll do the job. Hopefully it won't become something for the ladies to copy at the next ball."

I laughed. "I will try very hard not to become a fashion icon."

"A what?"

"A fashion … oh, never mind. Let's go."

"Got your sword?" he asked.

I patted the weapon hiding in the folds of my dress. "Yep."

We crept into the village, darting between buildings

until we found the village church.

Along the way, I gave myself a stern talking to. I couldn't forget why I'd come here. We needed to raise an army and defeat Anka. I was the Queen, and I needed to act like one.

So, no more flirting with Trevin. The end.

Trevin said. "I'll be right back."

I watched him disappear into the night, then entered the building. I was to wait in hiding while Trevin went through town alerting key citizens of an important meeting to be held in ten minutes at the church.

I ducked into a darkened alcove and wedged myself behind a statue of the Holy Family to wait. The church was silent, lit only by candles and what little moonlight could penetrate the stained glass windows. I wondered where the priest was. My left calf began to cramp. I eased out of my hiding place just long enough to stretch, then tucked myself back behind the statue.

What if no one came? What if they did, but the people didn't recognize me? What if they realized it was me, but didn't care? Or what if Anka's soldiers were in town and discovered us?

Getting the people on our side was crucial. Without the citizens, we had no chance of fighting back. To defeat Anka and retake our country, the commoners would have to unite. And I'd have to inspire them.

The front door creaked. I strained to see to the back of the church where I'd entered a few moments ago. A woman came in, glanced around, hesitated. She made the sign of the cross. Then she lowered herself into the back pew, her gaze dancing around the empty chapel.

She wasn't alone for long. Soon the door creaked again and a man entered, followed by a couple, another man, and, finally, the priest. The group studied each other with guarded eyes. The priest lit some more candles, making it easier to see.

A man entered, more regally dressed than the others. The lines of his face were stern, but his eyes spoke of compassion. There was an air of authority in the way he held himself—shoulders back, chest lifted.

Duke Christoph.

Several more people straggled in and then, finally, Trevin entered. He regarded the people gathered before him.

"Greetings," he said. "I apologize for the late hour and for the clandestine nature of our meeting, but I promise you, it's for good reason. You've all heard the reports, I presume? About the royal execution and subsequent seizure of the throne?"

The Duke said, "Riders came through just yesterday, reporting the death of our young queen and the exodus of the royal family."

"It can't be true," wailed one of the women. "Please tell us it's not true."

Oh, good. Not everyone had been turned against me by Qadar.

Trevin said, "It's not true."

An audible sigh left the group, like they'd exhaled as one. Several people bowed their heads in quick and silent prayers.

"Before I elaborate," Trevin continued, "are any of the soldiers who brought the news still in town?"

A man spoke up. "They are, sir, and staying at my inn. A right nasty bunch they are, I'll tell you that. Fond of the ale, and extra mean when they've taken their fill."

Trevin clenched his jaw. "You say they've only been here since yesterday?"

"That's right."

"Any of them say when they plan to leave?"

"No, sir, but they've paid up for a week. Paid in advance, they did. I thought it was right strange, and told them so to boot, but they paid me no mind."

Trevin bowed slightly. "Thank you. The fact that you have company, and that they seem to be staying for a while, makes it imperative that we maintain the utmost secrecy regarding this meeting. If any of you feel you cannot maintain this secrecy, I invite you to leave now."

The innkeeper fidgeted, then said. "Sir, given the nature of my interaction with these men, I believe it best if I withdraw. I hope you have information that will get them out, and fast, and keep our great country in the right hands, but it's probably best if I don't hear it."

"Very well," Trevin said. "I appreciate your honesty." The man got up to leave and Trevin turned his gaze on the rest of the room. "Anyone else?"

The others stayed put.

"Very well." Trevin waited for the innkeeper to leave, then said, "I am here because, as I said, the news these soldiers are circulating is not true. The truth is that there is a woman, by the name of Anka, who has bewitched a sizable number of the royal army, seized control of the castle, and declared herself the new queen. It is true that most of the royal family has fled, but Queen Shalyndria, the young queen, is not dead."

An unsettled rustle spread through the assembly.

Trevin continued, "Queen Maren, however, wife of the late King Edvin, has been executed by the imposter now sitting on the throne."

The room went suddenly still. Silent as death itself.

"No," breathed the Duke. "Queen Maren was good and kind. A rare gift to her country, and its citizens."

"It is a horrible tragedy," Trevin agreed, his lips set

together in a grim line. "We have come to you this day seeking your assistance in overthrowing the imposter—the murderer—and putting Queen Shalyndria back in place as the rightful queen of Valstenia."

"How can we believe you, sir?" said one of the ladies. "We've been lied to before. What's to stop you from lying now?"

"Nothing but my own conscience, madam," Trevin said. "Fortunately, you don't have to take my word for it, as I've brought someone to corroborate my tale." His gaze swept around the room, his eyes tight.

He didn't know where I was.

I eased myself from behind the statue and stepped into the light.

When Trevin saw me, the tightness bled from his eyes, but his expression stayed neutral. He was a true soldier—an expert if I'd ever seen one.

I continued into the assembly room until I stood beside him. Then I reached up and pulled back my makeshift hood. "I am Queen Shalyndria."

A woman sank to her knees upon seeing me. Another crossed her body as her gaze darted to heaven.

I continued. "Anka, the woman who killed my mother, has sought my life and failed. But she has seized control of the castle and our armies, and placed herself on the throne. I need your assistance if we are to take it back. We need soldiers. We need weapons. And, above all, we need your silence. The imposter must not know of our efforts until we are strong enough to defeat her. If she discovers us prematurely, all is lost."

"Your Grace," Trevin said, his gaze landing on Duke Christoph.

The Duke stood.

"I served under you for a time and know of your

dedication and valor. You are cunning in battle, greatly experienced, and your combat skills are unmatched. Would you consider being our leader?"

Duke Christoph bowed to me. "I would be honored to serve the true and rightful Queen. What must be done?"

"We must build an army," I said. "We must do it quietly, and we must hide them until we are sufficiently strong."

Chapter Thirty

Cliff Slipping

Maggie

1623—Valstenia

The moment Garon suggested we take a break, I tossed my bag to the ground and sank onto a fallen log. I pulled out the water skin Garon had given me and took a long drink.

The others remained standing.

"With all the inventing you and O did"—I stopped to catch my breath—"did you ever try teleportation?"

Garon laughed. "Wow. Teleportation? No, we didn't. But that would be something, wouldn't it?"

"Yep. And it would come in super handy right now."

He leaned down and said softly, just for me, "Well, then I'll get right on that." And his voice was warm, like we were sharing some private joke.

He took a drink from his water skin, then spoke to everyone. "Bea said she was being held captive in a cave system where the land juts into the sea, and that it was near where Oliver harvested the Remyallis flower. There's only one place along this coast that has any peninsula to speak of, so my bet is that it's there. But I've never seen any caves."

I rubbed a cramp out of my left calf.

Tanner said, "Could the caves be hidden? Like by a high tide? Maybe we'll have to wait for low tide in order to access the caves."

Yes! Please let that be the case! Any option that

required waiting was a yes from me. This was only the second break we'd taken in hours and, though I'd rather die than admit it, if we hadn't stopped when we did, I just might have collapsed. These guys were moving at a breakneck pace and my worn-out Converse were hardly up to the task.

Okay, so my muscles weren't up to it, either. And, you know, I hadn't done any cardio for a while either so … yeah. I'd really needed a break.

Anyway, blaming my shoes was easier than admitting I was crap out of shape.

Tanner seemed to be doing fine. All that swimming must translate into the ability to sprint through the woods, while carrying on a mildly amusing and highly annoying one-sided conversation. He'd been talking for miles about the differences between African birds and South American birds and which ones were better suited to their environments. As far as I knew, he hadn't gone bird watching in ages—like maybe since I'd stolen his hunting binoculars for the biggest spy-by fail of all time and failed to replace them—but I guess being in the woods brought out the nature boy in him.

Garon said, "There's no such thing as high tide in the Baltic."

I shielded my eyes from the sun so I could look up at him. "Really?"

"The Baltic is too small to have its own tides, and the opening to the North Sea is too narrow to impact the Baltic."

Tanner said, "How does that affect the marine life?"

I groaned.

"The marine life is unique for sure," Garon said, "but that's more to do with the sea's salinity levels than the tides. The Baltic is fed from both saltwater and freshwater sources."

"Fascinating," Tanner said.

Garon nodded. "It may be these unique qualities that produced the flower which healed Thumbelina."

"You two are such dorks."

Garon grinned at me. "Hey, how are you holding up? We've been going pretty fast."

"Oh, I'm fine." It wasn't technically a lie. I was fine right now—I was sitting on a log.

He squinted at me—like he wasn't sure whether I was lying or not. "The sea will be visible again soon—the forest thins out in another half-mile or so—it'll be all downhill from there."

I stretched my arms over my head, trying to work out a cramp in my side and pass it off as nothing more than a desire to stretch. "Cool."

Tanner said, "I bet there'll be an entirely different set of birds to observe by the sea."

"You are seriously such a nerd."

Garon sat beside me and picked up my hand. "You know, you don't have to act so brave and strong all the time."

I considered his words. I'd always had to be brave and strong. For my family and for my friends. And now I had to pretend I was okay with Garon staying in the 1600s while I went home.

Because with Lindy dead, Garon was King.

Neither of us had broached the subject, but it sat at the forefront of my mind, torturing me.

And I couldn't stay here with him, as tempting as that idea might be. Mom was in the future. I'd missed my childhood with her—I didn't want to miss any more.

So, I did, actually, have to be strong and brave. Now more than ever.

I squeezed his hand. "That's not true, but I appreciate you saying it. It's okay, I can handle it."

One of the soldiers approached. "We should move out. The sooner we find this woman, the better."

Garon dropped my hand, reluctantly it seemed, and stood. "Right. Let's go, then."

I stood and shouldered my pack, which hadn't felt heavy when we'd started, but definitely felt heavy now.

Garon had been leading the way, with Calv and another one of the soldiers. Tanner and I traveled behind them, with Hans and the last one bringing up the rear. But now there was only one soldier behind us.

"Um, where's the other guy?" I asked the soldier who remained. "Hans, I think his name was?"

His expression went blank. At first I thought he didn't understand me. But then he said, in halting English, "I don't know."

I yelled up the line to Garon. "Hey, we're missing someone."

He stopped. "Who's missing?"

I pointed to the lone soldier standing behind Tanner. "There were two of them."

Garon called ahead to Calv, "Where's Hans?"

Calv's brow furrowed. "I don't know. He should be here."

"He went to relieve himself a while ago," the soldier behind Calv said. "Did he ever come back?"

Calv looked up sharply. "When was that?"

"I don't know, at the start of our water break. He should have been back before now, and with time to spare."

"Should we go look for him?" Tanner said, his eyes lighting up like a search-and-rescue trip through the forest would be better than Christmas.

"Curse him," Calv said. "He's gone to raise an army, I'd bet a life on it."

"Raise an army?" I said. "By himself?"

A vein in Calv's forehead bulged. "Well, he won't be by himself for long if he's recruiting an army." He started pacing, his hands going white at the knuckles where he gripped the hilt of his sword. "Hans felt we should gather all the men we could and lay siege on the castle, cutting them off from their supplies long enough to starve the traitors out for a fair fight. It's what we were going to do if you didn't come back." He nodded at Garon.

"The castle has months of supplies stocked up, and ways to get in and out that aren't known to most," Garon said. "Those laying siege will give up or be killed long before they make any noticeable difference."

"What if Hans is found by Anka's men?" the soldier bringing up the rear said. "Will he betray our destination?"

Calv shook his head. "No, I don't believe he would. Hans was a loyal man and loved the Queen dearly. Whatever action he's taken, it was motivated by a deep sense of loyalty to the late young Queen."

"But he could begin assembling an army—men we need on our side—and approach the castle prematurely," Garon said. "He'll get them all killed."

"That is a likely possibility, yes."

"Then we must hurry," Garon said, glancing at me.

I nodded, assuring him I'd be all right. *Hang in there, trusty Converse. Time to step up your game.*

****

When we emerged from the forest, we were at the top of a smallish mountain. The sea below was breathtaking. But we couldn't stop to appreciate it because in order to get to the beach, we basically had to climb down a mountain. I caught glimpses of the sea in between glancing at my feet to make sure I didn't trip.

Dirt and small rocks slid down the mountain with me as I struggled to match Garon's pace. I focused on my feet, willing them not to trip and send me sprawling headfirst down the trail.

After what seemed like forever, the ground evened out and I felt I could safely look up from my feet.

The sea was closer. Much closer.

The ground beneath our feet was now soft and sandy. We walked through a small meadow where an array of wildflowers bloomed in a rainbow of colors. I stopped to stare at them, entranced, while Garon and the soldiers continued.

Tanner prodded me. "Come on, Mags, we're almost there. You can daydream later."

"Oh, so you're allowed to go on and on about birds and marine life, but I can't stop to appreciate the flowers?"

"Yeah, pretty much," Tanner said. "Double standards make the world go 'round."

"Ugh." My calves burned as we walked through the soft ground. Pretty soon the ground turned rocky again and I saw that, rather than taking us straight to the beach, the trail ended in a drop-off. A cliff.

Garon was waiting for us at the top. The soldiers were milling about, taking a water break.

The wind whipped my hair around, and the scent of saltwater burned my nose. "So, how do we get to the beach?"

"There's a narrow path that leads down." Garon handed me a wildflower. It was Tiffany blue. He pointed to the rocky cliff-face at our feet, where several other flowers just like it grew, around the head of a narrow path leading down toward the ocean. "They're growing from a bed of rocks, pushing up through the cracks against all odds."

I took the flower, twirling the stem between my forefinger and thumb.

"Made me think of you," Garon said, glancing at me sideways.

I leaned into him and, for a second, it felt like it always had between us—easy, natural, perfect.

Tanner came up behind us and said, "Is that a man-made path?"

"It is," Garon said. "I don't know who cut it, but my bet would be Oliver."

Calv approached us. "Highness, do you recall the stick your uncle gave Queen Shalyndria on his deathbed? We believe we've found a match."

Garon's eyes lit up. "Really? Show me."

Calv led us to a bush, short and spindly, like a rosebush only with knobs instead of thorns. Tiny buds were just starting to appear.

Garon sucked in a breath. "So this is the Remyallis?"

Calv frowned. "The what?"

"The plant Oliver used to create the Topaz."

"I don't know, Highness. All I know is that this branch here"—Calv pointed one out—"exactly matches the one Queen Shalyndria had us study before we parted ways."

Garon's eyes were bright. "Bea said she was being held captive near where Oliver harvested this plant. We must be close."

Tanner spoke from the edge of the cliff. He was leaning over it, straining to see all the way down. "This path looks a little sketchy."

We joined Tanner at the head. Garon said, "Yes, it does. Let's go."

We picked our way carefully down the cliff, the loose mix of dirt and gravel making the trail precarious. The red Pearl, which still hung from a chain around my neck, thumped against my chest as I walked. I tucked it under my shirt.

I kept as close as possible to the cliff-face on my left. I would have hugged it if I could. I'd never been afraid of heights, but this was taking things to a new level. To my right was nothing but open air—a drop off several hundred yards down to where the sea crashed into the rocks below. And the path was, like, a foot wide.

My limbs felt all tingly—like my body was prepping to pass out. Then, my foot slipped. My heart jumped into my throat and I cried out, my arms flailing.

I had traction back a moment later. I hadn't fallen.

But my body thought I had.

"You okay?" Tanner asked from behind me.

"Yeah." My voice was shaky. My palms sweaty.

Geez, pull yourself together, Maggie. Focus. One foot in front of the other.

I kept my eyes glued to the white tips of my Converse, ignoring the drop-off to my right and keeping my left hand on the cliff-face for a sense of balance.

Down we went, carefully, carefully.

I slipped two other times.

Converse were definitely not made for scaling rocky cliffs.

By the time we reached the beach, my nerves were in shreds and my throat felt like it was on fire. I pulled out my water bottle and chugged. The soldiers stared at me, open mouthed.

I glanced at the bottle—it was one of those disposable

plastic ones that are really bad for the environment and may or may not give you cancer. It had been in my backpack when we came back in time, and this was the first time I'd used it—my water skin was empty.

I guessed I was kind of freaking these guys out.

"Okay, there's the peninsula that juts into the ocean," Garon said, pointing out a land mass to our right. "Belina should be here somewhere. Spread out and look for a cave system."

Tanner pointed at something. "What if we just followed those?"

We followed his gaze. Up ahead, way off to the right, there were footprints in the sand. The footprints clung to the edge of the cliff for a long way—like maybe a football field or two. And then, so far away they could barely be seen, the prints pulled away from the cliff and led to a large clump of rocks nosing farther into the ocean than all the rest.

The ocean waves bashed tirelessly against the rocks, wave after wave spraying into the air and then receding in preparation for another onslaught.

"Good eye," Garon said, clapping Tanner on the shoulder. He turned to the soldiers. "Two of you head in the opposite direction to check things out, just in case the footprints are misleading. If we don't find it before dark, we'll have to wait until tomorrow, and with Hans out there starting an army, tomorrow might be too late. If you don't find anything, come back this way and we'll do the same. We'll either meet back here at the path, or, if the footprints appear to lead somewhere significant, we'll continue and you can catch up to us."

"Yes, sir," Calv said. He and one of the soldiers whose name I hadn't caught peeled off and went in the opposite direction.

The rest of us picked our way over the rocks at the bottom of the cliff until the ground turned to sand. Once we reached the footprints, we saw that it was not one set, but several sets of prints, like multiple people had been coming and going, always sticking to the exact same route.

This had to be the right way.

We walked and walked, but, like a water mirage in the dessert, the rocks up ahead didn't seem to get any closer.

"Holy cow, how far away is it?" I said, my calves burning from walking through the sand.

The soldier who'd remained with us turned to observe me. "Things often look closer than they are when you have an open vista like this. It's actually easier to walk faster, or even jog. Less time for your feet to sink in on each step."

I was *not* going to jog. But I picked up my walking pace. "Hey, what's your name?" I asked the soldier.

"Dieter."

"Well, thanks, Dieter."

Walking faster helped, a little. But my calves were still on fire. I focused on my feet as we picked our way through the sand.

Finally, *finally*, the outcropping of rocks appeared to be getting closer.

"Still no sign of anyone," Garon said, scanning ahead. "Except for the footprints, of course."

"These prints can't be more than a few days old," Dieter said. "There has to be someone here."

We kept on walking.

And walking.

And walking.

And then...

"Wait, is that...?" I put a hand up to shield my eyes

from the afternoon sun, staring at a dot I'd seen on top of one of the rocks. A dot that had just moved. "I think that's a person." I pointed to the rock jutting farthest out into the water—the one that all the waves were breaking on. "Look, on that rock closest to the sea."

I stared some more, my eyes going blurry. I blinked, then looked again. There was a figure—hunched over, or sitting, maybe—on top of the rock.

"I think you're right," Tanner said.

"We must approach with caution," Dieter said. "We don't know if it's a friend or foe."

Keeping our eyes on the figure, we broke away from the footprint path we'd been following. The figure stood. He or she was wearing a cloak that billowed out in the wind.

As we drew closer, more details became clear. The cloak was too big for whoever was underneath it. A belt was wrapped around the figure's waist, which was tiny. And whoever it was hadn't seen us—he or she was staring out at the ocean.

But we were much closer now.

"Maybe it's Grandma," Tanner said.

I stopped walking, causing him to bump into me. "Really? Did you just call her *Grandma*?"

"Well, yeah, technically that's what she is."

"No, she's like a great-great-great-great-something grandma. Don't call her Grandma, it's weird."

"You're weird," he shot back.

"Seriously, Tanner. It's probably not her, but even if it is, don't call her Grandma. It'll freak her out. She's going to be freaked out enough when we tell her we're from the future and that her future self sent us back in time to find her."

"All the more reason to call her Grandma," Tanner

said. "Gotta work the family connection."

I punched him in the shoulder.

"Ow," he said, even though it hadn't hurt him. "Fine, I won't call her Grandma."

"Good."

"Probably."

I looked back up at the rocks, but the figure was no longer there. "Wait, where'd he go?"

Tanner followed my gaze to where the figure had been standing only a moment ago. "How do you know it's a *he*?"

"Whatever. She or he is not there. It's like they just disappeared."

"Will you two please be quiet?" Dieter said, scanning the horizon. "I thought I just heard—"

A dagger whizzed through the air and lodged in his throat, cutting him off with a gurgle. He fell to the sand.

I screamed and whirled in the direction the knife had come from, away from the rocks. Two men were running toward us, swords drawn. One grabbed another dagger from his belt and prepared to throw.

Garon jumped into action, grabbing Dieter's shield and ducking in front of Tanner and me. "Get to cover," he yelled.

The dagger came whizzing past and I ducked, throwing my arms over my head protectively. The knife came so close, I actually heard it.

"The rocks!" Garon said. "Run to the rocks!"

And then, the men were right on top of us. Garon fought them both, meeting one with his sword and blocking the other with his shield.

Tanner yanked at my elbow, pulling me up from the ground. "Come on!"

"We can't just leave him to fight alone."

"Maggie, if either of us tries to help, we will die." Tanner pulled me away from the fight, his fingers digging into my skin. "And you can't keep your promise to Bea if you're dead."

"Get out of here!" Garon yelled at us again.

I turned away from the fight, feeling like the world's biggest coward, and saw that the cloaked figure on the rocks was no longer ignoring us. He'd jumped down and was running toward us, now not a hundred yards away. He had an arrow notched and his bow stretched taught. Aiming our way.

"Tanner, get down!" I pulled him to the sand just as the figure let the arrow fly. It whizzed over our heads and struck one of the men fighting Garon directly between the eyes. The man dropped to his knees and slumped forward.

Garon and the other guy remained locked in battle. Tanner and I watched as the cloaked figure notched another arrow, took aim, and fired.

This one hit the other guy, also right between the eyes.

And, just like that, the fight was over. Garon whirled to face the archer, raising his sword and shield.

The archer notched another arrow and aimed it at me. "Who are you and what do you want?" It was a woman's voice.

And it sounded like…

"Belina?" I asked.

The figure froze, then flicked back her hood to reveal her face.

Tanner was right.

It was Bea.

Chapter Thirty-One

Battle Plan

Lindy

1623—Valstenia

Trevin and Duke Christoph helped me recruit and organize men who were willing to fight. I had no gold to offer them—no promise of wealth or stature—just my commitment that if they helped me retake my crown, I would rule the way my father had, and they would retain the same freedoms they'd enjoyed for decades.

The men who joined us fought for their liberty. They fought to keep their wives and children safe. They fought because they knew that having a tyrant on the throne would lead to suffering and death.

Hopefully, I'd soon find a solution to Valstenia's lack of funds. And then I would reward the men who came to our defense. But until then, all I could offer them was their freedom.

Freedom, as it turned out, was a precious commodity. Our army grew quickly.

"Take them to my family's summer castle—on the Valstenian-Trellborian border," I told Duke Christoph. "Just past the castle, there's a valley with good tree cover that dips toward the land of Trellboro."

This was the valley between my family's summer castle and the inn that had been my home and my prison for so long. In what felt like another life.

In reality, it was now only a few years after I would have become Calista and Theo's prisoner. I'd checked in on them only once, right after the Emerald had been destroyed and I'd been returned to the life I should have had from the start.

Garon had come with me. We'd found that the inn was still there, as were Calista, Theo, and their son, Marsala. But in the absence of the Emerald, they were just ordinary people. No hints of magic surrounding the inn, nothing unsavory about the accommodations, and no wild rumors in town of missing young girls. They'd seemed utterly untouched by magic.

"Highness?" The Duke's voice cut into my thoughts. "Any additional instructions?"

"Sorry." I shook the memories from my head. "Gather additional men along the way, if you can. Organize them into groups and appoint men with experience to act as Generals. Then set up camp and wait for me there."

"Yes, Your Highness," Duke Christoph said.

"Trevin and I will continue recruiting and send any new men your way."

As hesitant as I was to return to the place of my long imprisonment, Trellboro was safe, and far enough from the center of Valstenia to be out of Anka's reach. Plus, relations between our two countries had been especially good since I'd returned.

I'd decided to spare the wet nurse who'd kidnapped me as a baby, because she was the only mother I'd ever known, and I loved her. It had been her husband who'd handed me over to Calista without her knowledge. I'd told my family that a Trellborian woman had found me in the woods as an infant and, not knowing who I was, had saved me and raised me as her own. My father had worked hard, along with King Jershon of Trellboro, to ensure peace between our two countries ever since.

After sending the Duke and our initial army on their

way, Trevin and I traveled from town to town by night, meeting with people in homes and churches, letting them see for themselves that I was alive, and imploring them to join me in dethroning the imposter. Many rose to the cause, retrieving their weapons and reporting for duty.

Soon, Trevin and I joined Duke Christoph in the valley and met with the Generals he'd appointed to discuss our battle plan.

I addressed the men inside of the makeshift tent the Duke had been using as his headquarters. "We must remove the imposter Anka from the throne and retake the castle. To this end, our primary objective must be finding her, capturing her, and confiscating the cursed Topaz so she can no longer use it against us."

"Are there no secret ways in to the castle?" one General asked. "A basement or servants' entrance that could be exploited?"

"When we left, all but one had been discovered by the imposter," Trevin said. "She had them under heavy guard."

"Anka killed my mother instead of me. If she knows I escaped, she will have searched the dungeons and found the exit we used. We can't count on using that one as an entrance."

"Still," Duke Christoph said, "if we attack all known hidden entrances, while simultaneously attacking the front gates, the enemy will be divided. This significantly increases our chance of penetrating the castle's defenses in at least one location, maybe more. Once we breach the castle, it's only a matter of time before the fight is won."

"We must also consider the matter of her mind control," I said.

An uncomfortable silence fell.

"What do you propose, Highness?" the Duke said.

"Since she can only be in one place at a time, attacking in multiple locations at once will increase our chances that some groups will get through without ever encountering her. And for those who do encounter her…" I paused, pursing my lips in thought. "I haven't been able to reach any definite conclusions regarding the power of the Topaz. But I have made some observations. Perhaps, if we examine the evidence together, we might find a solution."

The Duke nodded for me to continue.

"When we faced Anka, it was clear that the Topaz was not giving her the ability to read minds. Nor does it seem she can control a person without first establishing some sort of link. The soldiers in the shack either looked at her, heard her, or touched her before they turned against me. It may be that she has to establish a bond with the victim in order to control them."

"An interesting idea," one of the Generals said.

I continued, "Since she is abnormally beautiful, it's easy for her to do this through sight. Men look at her, fall under her spell, and they're hers. But whether it's through touch, sight, or sound, she has to connect with the person she wants to seize before she has any control. If we train our soldiers to look past her, not directly at her—if they're trained to keep their distance and avoid connecting, they'll have a higher chance of retaining their wits."

The Duke frowned. "Total sensory deprivation would be the only way to guarantee that would work. But, even if we could pull that off, doing so would completely inhibit their ability to fight. If they can't see Anka, they can't see the men they will be expected to fight. If they can't hear Anka, they can't hear each other."

Trevin spoke up. "I believe her control is about more

than just connecting with her victims. I fell under her spell at first, but I was somehow able to fight her off. My father, however, appeared unable to throw off her spell, despite being incredibly strong. There's clearly some factor which allowed me, and a handful of others, to fight her mind control, while preventing my father from doing the same."

Trevin turned to me. "Also you, your sister, and Oliver seemed immune to her illusion. We need to know for sure how the Topaz works—what all these people have in common—before we will be able to effectively fight it."

"Perhaps we send in emissaries," a General suggested. "Groups to collect information. We draw Anka out of the castle by sending a group as a sort of peace offering. Another group would observe from a safe distance how and when Anka uses her mind control."

A vein bulged in the Duke's neck. "So, you're saying we sacrifice an entire group of men?"

"In order to gain knowledge that will help us defeat her, yes," the General answered.

Trevin said, "The men will not die if they come in peace. Anka won't kill good soldiers who can be added to her own forces. She will only manipulate their minds and add them to her collection."

"Precisely," the General said. "Then, once we've defeated her, they will be freed."

I pursed my lips together. "It's too risky."

The General bowed. "With respect, Your Highness, risk is an unavoidable part of the game."

I looked at him, keeping my eyes on him until he met my gaze. "With respect, this is no game."

Just then a soldier burst through the tent entrance, his eyes wide and wild. Voices followed him.

"I told you not to disturb them," a guard said, laying hands on the soldier and pulling him from the tent.

The soldier fell to his knees, not taking his eyes off mine. "She's alive," he said, his voice all wonder and amazement. "Highness, you're alive."

Wait. Was that…?

I squinted at the man. Yes, he was one of my original party—one who'd been with me when the farmer Anton had plunged to his death. One who'd helped bury Oliver.

"Let him go," I said to the guard still trying to haul the wild-eyed soldier out of the tent.

The man, now free, dropped to his knees in a proper bow. "My name is Hans. I told them we should wait for you. I told them we needed to raise an army and come looking for you. But they said you were dead. They were so sure of it."

I walked over to Hans and knelt to his level. "Who said I was dead?"

"Your brother, Garon. And his companions."

I froze. "My brother has companions?"

"Yes, a boy and a girl."

"Was the girl Belina?" I held my breath.

"No. They were on their way to find her—Belina— but … forgive me … I left them. I couldn't go on that fool's errand when I knew there was an imposter and murderer on the throne. I vowed to raise my own army and then, when I heard there was one already, well, I came as fast as I could."

"I appreciate your zeal," I said to Hans. "And I'm glad you've found us."

I stood and faced the others. "We are clearly in need of more information regarding the Topaz and its powers. My brother might have learned something that can help us, and there's a chance that this Belina will know more still. We have to find them. Hans, do you know where they were going? Can you show me?"

Hans nodded. "They were headed for the sea. I can take you."

Chapter Thirty-Two

Hallucinations

Maggie

1623—Valstenia

Belina kept the arrow pointed at me. "How do you know my name? Who sent you?"

Her eyes bore into mine. They were green. Like an emerald.

Suddenly, I wasn't standing on a beach. I was back at the Parker mansion, holding the Emerald in my hands, watching as my blood seeped into it.

My stomach clenched. My palms began to sweat.

No. This was not real.

I pressed a finger to my temple, squashing the vision away like a bad headache and, just like that, I was back on the beach staring into Belina's green eyes.

Okay, that was weird.

Garon dropped his weapon and raised his arms in surrender. "Your father sent us."

Belina narrowed her eyes. "You know my father?"

"Yes," Garon said. "I knew your father very well."

Belina whipped her bow around so it pointed at Garon. Her eyes blazed. "What do you mean, you *knew* him?"

"My name is Garon. Your father was my uncle and mentor. I spent a great many years in his company." He took a hesitant step forward. "A few days ago, the woman Anka, who is responsible for your captivity, killed him. He used his dying words pleading with me to find you."

Her expression remained hard. "You were there, yet you did nothing to save him?"

Garon stepped toward her, his hands still raised. "Anka's blade was quick and sure. No one saw it coming, least of all Oliver."

Belina's gaze flitted from me, to Tanner, and then back to Garon, like she wasn't sure who—or what—to focus on. "Who are your companions?"

"There will be time for introductions. Can you please lower your weapon?" Garon edged forward again. He was getting closer and closer to Belina.

Belina swung her bow back to me. "Who are your companions?" she demanded. Her voice was steely

Garon froze. "This is Maggie and Tanner. They are my friends, and would have been friends of your father as well, if they'd had a chance to know him. I promise, we're here to help you."

Plus, we need her help, I couldn't keep from thinking.

"Prove it," Belina said.

Garon's jaw tensed. He shifted his weight and managed to edge even closer to where Belina was standing. He was almost there. Just a few steps further and he'd be close enough to take her down if needed.

"You are a miracle child," he said. "You came to Oliver on the sea and the flowers gave you life. You became the daughter my uncle never had. You now have a husband and want a daughter of your own. You plan to name her Sarenna." He took another step toward her.

Belina's eyes blazed. "Nobody knows that name, not even my husband."

In a flash, Garon threw himself at Belina, tackling her to the ground.

Her weapon flew to the side.

I scrambled to pick it up.

"I promise, we're friends," Garon said, pinning her arms to the sandy ground, "but I can't have you threatening us. Is there somewhere safe where we can talk?"

Belina struggled against him. "How did you know what I want to name my daughter? I've never told a soul. I don't even know if I can have kids."

"Oh, you can have kids," Garon said. "You can and you will."

The fight bled out of her, like it was sinking into the sand.

"Tanner, Maggie, keep an eye on the cliffs." Garon tied Belina's hands together in front of her, even though she was no longer struggling. "How long before the new guards come?" he asked her.

"Not 'til morning." Her voice was heavy. Like she suddenly carried the weight of a world.

"Good, we have all night to get acquainted—more if we need it. Your father is a master at manipulating time and he taught me well."

Garon was bluffing. At least, I thought he was. He wouldn't risk time traveling again just to get more info out of Belina.

But she didn't know that.

"How do you know about Sarenna?" she demanded.

Garon secured her hands together with a rope, helped her sit up, and then kneeled down across from her. Tanner and I stayed standing behind her, scanning the cliffs for any sign of life.

Garon said, "Since you know your father manipulated time, it will come as no surprise that he taught me, his apprentice, how to as well. It should not be too far of a stretch, then, to accept that my friends here are not from this time. They come from your future and came back, at your particular request, by the way, to help you save your daughter, Sarenna. A daughter which you will have in the near future."

Belina's eyes went all buggy. She looked at Tanner and me with new appreciation.

"Additionally, in the future, you gave us this." Garon nodded at me.

I tugged the necklace with the cherry-red Pearl out from under my shirt.

Belina's mouth dropped open. She tugged at a chain hanging around her own neck and pulled another Pearl from beneath her cloak. The chains and settings matched perfectly. But the Pearl Belina held in her hands was grotesque—white, but shot through with ribbons of blood-red. Wrapped in it, even—like veins around an eyeball.

Or a poisonous snake slowly squeezing its prey.

"Okay," Belina breathed. "I believe you." She reached out to touch my Pearl, one finger caressing the surface. "Why is it red?"

"The flower Oliver healed you with is poisonous. Nature often uses bright colors as a sign of poison—like with frogs and snakes. As you can see in your Pearl, the poison is already starting to take over. Even worse, the poison seems to be affecting your descendants."

Belina's face went slack. She looked to me, then to Tanner.

"Not them," Garon said. "But their mother. And a handful of others along the way. Including your daughter, Sarenna."

Belina struggled for words, her gaze darting between me and Tanner. "You're my ... descendants?"

I smiled and nodded.

Belina's eyes shone. She struggled against the rope that held her hands together and looked at Garon with pleading eyes. "I won't fight, I promise."

Garon pressed his lips together.

"Please?"

He untied her.

She gave me a hug. Then she hugged Tanner.

"Maggie said I wasn't allowed to call you Grandma," Tanner said.

Belina laughed. "Your sister was right. Please don't call me Grandma. But"—she paused—"I'm so glad to meet you. And I'm glad I have a … a family." She turned to Garon. "Is there any way to stop the poison?"

"We hope so. But we'll need your help. We need to know more about how the Pearl was created. And in order to stop Anka, we need to know how and why the Topaz was created, and how the Pearl might help us destroy it. We were hoping you'd have this information."

Belina frowned. "When Father found me, I was a cast-off child, unloved and discarded by those who should have cared for me but didn't because of my deformities. He created the Pearl to heal me."

Garon nodded. "Yes, you've told us that story. Well, future you did. But do you know exactly what Oliver put in the Pearl? How he altered it?"

Belina's face scrunched up in thought. "Well, the flowers, of course. He never mentioned any other ingredient. I was so young when he first made it—all I know is what he's told me since. But…" She pursed her lips. "Father kept a journal. There are several of them still, back at the home where I grew up."

Garon's expression brightened. "Really? How far away is it?"

"Not far. A mile or so south, once you climb back up

the cliffs."

Garon started to get up.

"Don't you want to know about the Topaz?" Belina said.

Garon froze. "Of course. If there's more to tell."

"I don't know much about the Pearl, since I was so young when father created it. But the Topaz—that was only a few years ago." Belina hesitated. "I helped him, in fact."

I sank to my knees in the sand, like it was story time around a campfire. "Really? You helped make it?" Garon still hadn't told me anything about the Topaz. I had no idea what it even did or how it had messed things up so much.

"Yes," Belina said simply. Then, without missing a beat, she lunged for her bow, scooped it up, and whirled around, aiming toward the cliffs.

"Don't shoot!" Garon cried. "They're with us."

That was when I saw the two other soldiers we'd come with, making their way toward us.

Calv's mouth was set in a grim line. The three lifeless bodies were still sprawled on the beach—two were Belina's captors, and the third was Dieter—one of ours.

Calv and the other soldier froze at the sight of Belina's bow.

She lowered her weapon. "You should have told me you had more companions, I nearly killed them."

"Hey," Tanner said, "since you're so good with a bow, why didn't you just kill the guys who were holding you captive and escape?"

"I tried. Many times. But they didn't become careless until they saw you. You all provided a nice distraction, which allowed me time to get my weapon." She glanced at Calv and the other soldier. "Is there anybody else out here I should know about?"

Garon eyed the cliffs. "No, but we should find a less exposed place to talk."

"We can go back to my father's house. His journals are there, and I can tell you about the Topaz once we're safely inside."

Belina extended her hand to help me up from the ground. When I took it, a picture flashed into my mind.

I saw one of those giant leaves, like you see in nature shows about the Amazon—a palm frond or something—covered in dew drops. One of the droplets rolled toward the one next to it, and they joined together. Then that one rolled into another one and joined together again. The water droplet continued rolling around the leaf, soaking up all the drops of dew until there was just one big water droplet sitting in the center of the palm frond—like a Pearl perched on an oyster bed.

"Are you okay?" a voice said.

I shook my head and the vision cleared.

Belina was peering at me, her head cocked to one side.

"Yeah, I'm fine," I said, even though I probably wasn't.

What did it mean that I was suddenly hallucinating? Had time traveling messed up my brain?

****

The house Belina took us to was not so much a house as it was a hideout. Or a tree fort. It was basically just an assortment of animal skins, sewn together and stretched between the trees. Like something Tanner and I would have made out of blankets when we were little. The canvas was anchored to a tree branch above, creating a dome in the center of the space.

Garon pulled the soldiers aside. "Watch the path

leading to the beach and alert me if anybody passes by."

Calv nodded. "Yes, sir."

The inside of the hideout was actually more spacious than I would have guessed. There was an area with a table, a washbasin, and a shelf with two wooden bowls and two tin cups. There were two straw beds, each sitting on the floor, in opposite corners of the space. And, along one "wall" stood a tall bookshelf, crammed with leather-bound books and items that looked like they belonged in a high school science lab.

Belina located a few mismatched chairs and we all sat at the table. "So. The Topaz."

Tanner plopped his elbows on the table and rested his chin in his hands.

Garon glanced at the door.

"A little over a year ago, Father met a woman at the flower patch—the one we passed through at the top of the cliff. This is the patch where the Remyallis flower—the one that healed me—blooms each year at summer solstice. It was the first time we'd ever seen anyone else there. The place is so remote, and we'd tended the flowers for so long on our own, seeing someone there took us by surprise.

"The woman was shrouded in a black cloak, which covered most of her body and hid her face in shadow. She said she sold exotic flowers at market and was looking for new blossoms to add to her collection. Father told her about the different wildflowers that grew at the top of the cliff and offered to help her cut some. The Remyallis was not yet in bloom.

"While they were gathering flowers, the wind picked up, blowing the woman's cloak open. Her hood fell back and my father saw that her face and upper body were covered in scars, like she'd been burned in a fire. Large patches of her hair were missing, replaced by more scars.

"She confessed that she'd been burned as a child in a kitchen fire. She then put her hood back on, and my father didn't press for more details. But the entire time they were together, he was thinking. Wondering if he might be able to help this woman as he'd helped me. Before she left, he told her to come back in two weeks.

"The Remyallis bloomed a week later and he spent the next several days concocting brews, poultices, and powders, using different parts of the precious flowers in an effort to find something that might work for this woman. I assisted my father in this process.

"When she returned, he had her try the treatments, one at a time, over the course of a few days. He was careful to protect the secret of what was actually inside the remedies, only telling her he was a medicine man and thought he'd found something that could help.

"The woman stayed with us during that time. At one point, she mentioned that her parents died in the fire that had disfigured her. I don't know who raised her after that. She spent her days picking wildflowers, twisting them into all sorts of elaborate headpieces to sell at market. She was very talented but, I'm afraid, marketgoers were unwilling—or unable—to see past her skin."

I was sitting so far forward in my seat that my butt was barely in my chair. "So which treatment worked?"

Belina smiled and, for the first time, I saw the same woman I'd met at my grandmother's house.

"It was hard to tell, but I believe it was a combination of the poultice and the steam from a brew, working together to heal her both inside and out. The poultice healed her skin, her scars fading miraculously. The steam, which she breathed in, I believe helped her hair to regrow. She thanked us profusely, crying in gratitude, and then left. She gave me one of her flower headpieces to remember her. We thought we'd never see her again."

Garon leaned forward in his chair, too, his posture matching mine.

"She was back a week later. Her scars had returned and her hair fallen back out. It must have been horrible, experiencing such a miraculous healing only to have it snatched away. She begged us to make her more of the poultice. But, by this time, the flowers were no longer in bloom. All we had left were the ones we'd harvested and dried. The woman begged my father, more fervently than before, to find something—anything—that could help her.

"He told her about the Pearl he'd created to prolong my healing even when the necessary plants weren't in bloom, and said he might be able to do something similar for her. She produced a pink Topaz, which I suspected was stolen, but father didn't challenge her on it. He was entranced by its beauty and thrilled to have such a unique gemstone to work with. He altered the chemical makeup of the Topaz in the same way he'd done with the Pearl and, I believe, with the Emerald before—by weakening the atomic bonds within the gem until it turned to a softened state. He then inserted some of the dried Remyallis, and returned the altered Topaz to its natural solid state."

"Did he put anything else inside the Topaz?" Garon asked.

"No, just the flower petals. But you should know that Remyallis petals, when they're dried and dissolved under the tongue, produce hallucinogenic effects. Fresh petals would have been better—safer—but by then the dried ones were all he had."

"Wait, wait, wait," Tanner said. "So, you're saying that now this lady is on an extended drug trip?"

"Well, actually, it seems that she's become the hallucinogen," Belina said.

It took a moment for her words to sink in. One icy heartbeat. And then another. And then a pit settled in my stomach. "You mean that by wearing the Topaz and having it heal her, she became, like, a living hallucinogen to those around her?"

"Something like that," Belina said. "At least, that's how it seems to me after observing the way her soldiers react to her. Her charms are exciting, intoxicating, mind-altering. And addicting."

Garon held his head in his hands, like he didn't quite believe what he was hearing.

"But my father didn't know that would happen, obviously. He believed only that he was giving her the gift of beauty."

"Is that the last you saw of her?" Garon asked.

"No. Anka came back a short while later, demanding our help in overthrowing the royal family and stealing the crown. She'd figured out that Oliver was the late King Edvin's younger brother—Father must have said something he shouldn't have while she was staying with us—and she knew he'd be able to get inside the castle.

"That's when he realized that helping her had been a terrible mistake. He tried to reason with her. Convince her she didn't need power to be happy. But after a lifetime of oppression because of her appearance, she wanted to be at the top. And, apparently, she'd petitioned the royal family for help at one point, but they'd denied it. She was set on taking them down.

"When reason didn't work, he tried to take the Topaz back by force. But by this time, she'd learned something of her power and had brought along help. Her men detained me and she threatened to kill me unless he agreed to help." Belina paused, breathing hard. "I suppose you know the rest."

Garon said, "Anka thought that if she fed the Topaz some of my sister's blood, then she could take on her appearance. That's how she'd planned on stealing the throne. Oliver lured Lindy to a cabin in the woods just so they could do this."

Belina's brow furrowed. "Are you sure? Feeding blood to the Topaz wouldn't have allowed Anka to look like someone else. At least, I don't think it would have."

"Did he use blood magic when creating the Topaz?" Garon pressed.

Belina rocked back in her chair. "Blood magic is too dark. Father didn't use it."

"I know for a fact that he did," Garon said. "The Emerald was created with a failsafe that required blood magic to unlock it."

"The only thing I ever heard Father say about blood magic was that the price for its use was too great. That it took something from those who used it."

"What did it take?" Tanner said.

"He didn't specify, but one would have to trade something of similar value. Knowledge. Sanity. Health. Something like that. But I don't believe Father used blood magic when creating the Topaz."

"But he could have?" Garon pressed.

Belina said nothing, only looked down at her hands, which were clasped tightly together in her lap.

"What if Oliver lied?" I said. "What if he told Anka she could use blood magic to steal Lindy's appearance, but it wasn't true?"

"Why would he gamble with my sister's life like

that?" Garon said.

"If he was desperate enough, he would have," I said. "The woman had his daughter. Don't you think he would have told her anything in order to get Belina back? If Anka wanted to steal the crown and needed a way to do it, he could have told her there was an easy way to steal Lindy's identity."

"I'm sure my father didn't mean for your sister to get hurt," Belina said.

Outside, an owl hooted in the night.

Garon pressed his lips together, a shadow of pain crossing his face. "Regardless of what O did or did not intend, I suppose the question remains the same: How do we destroy the Topaz?"

We all looked to Belina.

She shrugged. "How do you counteract hallucinogens?"

Garon looked to Tanner, his eyebrows raised.

"Seriously?" Tanner said. "I don't do drugs, man."

"I wasn't implying that you did. But have you ever heard anyone talk about how to counteract the effects of drugs like LSD? That might help us."

I wracked my brain, thinking back to all the 'Don't Do Drugs' assemblies we'd had, but came up blank. "They usually just tell us not to do drugs and then tell scary stories about addicts' messed-up lives."

"Yeah," Tanner agreed. "I've never heard anyone talk about how to counteract the effects of a trip. That's usually not the focus of any drug conversation, no matter who it's coming from."

Garon said, "I still can't figure out why the Topaz affected some people and not others."

"Drugs affect different people in different ways," I said. "Maybe that's why not everyone who sees her has the same reaction to her."

"My father experimented a bit and found that different combinations of the various forms of Remyallis produced different effects, and that those effects differed between him and me. We were the only test subjects he had, but his findings might be of value." Belina walked over to one of the bookshelves and pulled out a leather-bound book. "This is the journal he kept of his experiments with the flower and its different properties."

Calv burst through the flap of animal skin acting as a front door. "Sorry for the intrusion, but there's someone here."

He stepped aside and in walked a girl. Her dress was filthy, and she wore the frumpiest head covering I'd ever seen. But her dark eyes were familiar. She lowered the head covering and I gasped.

Lindy!

She looked older. But it was definitely her.

And she was very much alive.

Chapter Thirty-Three

Reunion of Friends

Lindy

1623—Valstenia

The first thing I saw when I stepped into the tent was my brother, Garon.

All the exhaustion of the past few days fell away as I ran to him. I threw my arms around his neck.

His arms remained limply by his side.

I pulled away.

He was looking at me like I was a ghost. "Everyone said you were d—" His voice broke.

"They were wrong."

His arms slowly regained life and he hugged me back. "If I'd known you were alive, I would have come looking for you."

"Well, I'm glad you didn't. Because then we would have both had to escape from the castle." I took a breath to tell him the awful truth that our mother had sacrificed herself in my place. My gaze darted to the side, not wanting to see his face when I told him our mother was dead.

Wait, was that…?

"Maggie?" I said, disbelief making my voice come out in a very un-queenly squeak. "Garon, you brought Maggie with you?" I stepped toward her and she closed the distance.

We threw our arms around each other at the same time.

"I can't believe you're alive," she said, while I said, "I can't believe you're here."

"Wow, you look so much older," she said, pulling out of the hug and eyeing me.

"Well, it *has* been seven years since I've seen you." I winked. "Gotta have something to show for the time."

Maggie froze. "Wait, it's been seven years? For me it's only been a few months."

"Oh," I stalled. "I guess time travel really messes with things." I turned to my brother. "Hey, does that mean I'm older than you now, since you stayed the same while I've been growing up?"

"I didn't stay the same—I started ageing as soon as I got out of the time loop."

"Yeah, but that was just a month before we destroyed the Emerald. So you've only grown a few months, while I've grown seven years."

Garon glanced over my shoulder and nodded at Trevin, who'd entered just behind me. "Trevin, nice to see you again. How did you find us?"

"Hans was able to bring us to the cliff top, then we tracked your prints here."

A small woman—very petite, and shorter than me by a head—stood from where she'd been sitting and approached Garon. I also recognized Maggie's brother … what was his name?

Garon saved me by introducing them. "Lindy, you remember Maggie's brother, Tanner? And this is Oliver's daughter, Belina."

"I'm so glad my brother found you," I said to Belina.

"She's been telling us about the Topaz," Garon said. "Apparently, it's acting like a hallucinogen because of the dried Remyallis petals Oliver put inside." He held up a leather-bound book. "This is the journal our uncle kept while creating the Topaz—hopefully there's something in here that will help us. But first we have to get the Topaz. And to do that, we need to attack the castle."

Tanner said, "So, really what we need is an army."

I said, "I have an army."

****

We'd been gone less than two days—much shorter than the Duke had anticipated—and now I was back at camp with Garon, Maggie, Tanner, and Belina.

We would start the day-and-a-half journey back to the castle come nightfall, and attack at dawn the next day.

Trevin was giving Maggie and Tanner the crash-course sword-fighting and self-defense class he'd given Yelena and me.

I was sitting with Garon, watching Tanner fumble with his sword, while Maggie was something of a natural.

"You know your plan is flawed," Garon said. "It's entirely too predictable. Attack at dawn. Exploit the hidden entrances. Work your way up from the ground until you find the puppet-master. Anka will pick your men off one by one and you won't even get close to wherever she's hiding."

"I know. I've been trying to think of something else, but there's just … nothing. Direct attack, sneak attack, or try to draw them out. That's all there is, right? We don't have enough resources to draw them out, and a sneak attack is no good because if our men are caught then it's over, just like that. Even if we send in only the soldiers who were able to fight Anka's power back at the cabin, that only gives us three or four men. If they're somehow able to make it close enough to the Topaz—close enough to Anka—without being detected, then three or four men will not be enough. At that point, they'll be sitting in the center of her entire army and Anka will kill them without hesitation.

"The way I see it, the only chance we have is if we create as many distractions as we can and send in as many men as we can. Then we hope that enough of them will be able to resist her charms, or avoid her entirely, long enough to fight back. If the enemy is divided and distracted, we might have a fighting chance."

"There has to be another way," Garon said.

I lifted my chin. "Well, I haven't been able to think of one."

He studied me, and his eyes narrowed. "You know you don't have to do this alone anymore, right? We'll think of something together."

"I need to get used to doing things on my own, now that Mother—" I stopped, realizing my mistake.

His expression went dark. "Now that Mother what?"

I fought back the wave of sadness I'd been holding in ever since I'd found out about my mother's sacrifice. It was time to tell him. He needed to know.

"Anka was going to execute me, but Mother sent a servant girl to help me escape. And then…" I took a deep, stuttering breath, then forced myself to press on. To say the words that needed to be said. "And then Anka executed her instead of me. Mother took my place."

The color drained from my brother's face. He sat like a stone beside me.

I went on. "I don't know if Anka even knew she killed the wrong person, but … I guess she probably did and just killed Mother for helping me escape. Either way, Anka spread word that she'd killed me when really it was our mother. So, once you leave … well, it'll just be me."

Still, my brother sat, unmoving and unreadable.

"Say something," I pleaded.

"I can't," he said, and his face was an ashen mask.

We both sat in silence. At length, Garon put an arm around me. "I can't say anything at all."

Belina found us like that, much later, as the shadows were stretching thin and the day waning. "I have a theory," she said, folding herself up on the grass beside us.

"A theory for what?" Garon asked.

"Why some people seem immune to the effects of the Topaz."

Her words snapped my thoughts back to the present threat.

Belina said, "Hallucinogens affect the pleasure-sensing part of a person's brain, right? Well, I was thinking—what else affects this same part of the brain?"

When neither of us answered, she said simply, "Love."

Garon scoffed. "Love? Really?"

"Yes, really. Hallucinogens attack the brain—change the brain chemicals—but falling in love does this, too. So, being in love, or any degree of love, could, theoretically, protect one's brain from the 'fake high' chemicals of a hallucinogen."

My mouth dropped open.

Belina went on. "I've been talking with your soldiers—the ones who stayed loyal to you during your fight at the shack. One of them is newly married—Sedric, I think his name is. Another has a wife, with a baby on the way. A third has a stack of letters a mile high from a girl he writes to every week. It's plausible that their love protected them from the effects of the Topaz. You also said Trevin seemed able to fight off the effects. From what I've observed of him, he's on his way to being in love, too."

She gave me a pointed look and heat crawled up my neck.

Belina continued. "Any soldiers whose hearts were elsewhere would have been able to fight the Topaz off. Others, who were heartbroken or lonely, would have been easy prey."

Heartbroken or lonely. Like Borov.

Belina paused. "It's just a theory."

And it was a good one. But how had I been protected? I'd only just met Trevin and, even now, saying I loved him would be going a bit far. Maybe my protection had come from some residual effect of the Emerald. And what about Oliver? Was he protected as the creator of the Topaz?

But for everyone else … the love thing kind of made sense.

"Yelena was in love, too," I said softly. "Just not with her husband."

Belina's theory definitely had merit. Had I not seen it sooner because I hadn't been looking hard enough? Or was it because I'd been viewing the problem from the wrong angle?

The cogs in my brain began to turn. And it seemed they were turning in a direction they'd never gone before. Like my world had just spun sideways and I was suddenly seeing things from a different perspective.

Was there another way to attack the castle? One that would require looking at things from a different angle in order to see?

Garon was gawking at me. "You actually believe her? She's saying love makes a person immune. That's crazy."

"So is being able to control someone with a flower," Belina shot back. "Yet here we are."

It was, of course. Crazy. The whole thing was a big, crazy mess.

So, maybe the solution had to be crazy, too.

I pushed myself up from the ground, my thoughts whirling around a new idea. "I need to go run an errand."

Chapter Thirty-Four

An Old Foe

Maggie

1623—Valstenia

I should have taken up sword fighting ages and ages ago. I mean, what a rush. I lunged, and Tanner's sword clattered to the ground.

"Really? Again?" Tanner bent to pick up the sword. "You are scary good at this, Mags."

"I know, isn't it awesome?" I jumped around on the balls of my feet, keeping the blood flowing for our next round. "I've never been good at anything."

"I think you're ready for another opponent," Trevin said. "I'll be right back."

I studied him as he walked away. I couldn't figure out if Lindy liked him or not. Sometimes she acted like she did and other times she seemed to distance herself from him, like she was holding up a wall.

But she should totally go for it—he was strong and handsome, and he doted on her. Although, maybe that was part of his job description, since she was the Queen and all.

Queen Lindy. It was so weird that only a few months ago—in my timeline, anyway—she's been a scared little mouse, prisoner in Calista and Theo's home, and now she was running a kingdom. I wondered how she was handling the transition.

Of course, she'd had longer to get used to the idea than I had.

I gripped the hilt of my sword. It felt perfectly balanced when I held it just right, which was really cool. It was so simple—all you needed was to tweak your grip if something felt off and then, magically, it was right again.

If only life were that simple.

My muscles tensed and I did some practice swings. My blade sliced through the air with precision, the wind whooshing out of the way. I let my body take over, loving the way the blade cut smoothly through the air.

And then I heard a clang.

A shock rocketed up my arm.

My eyes widened and I saw a guy, older than me but not by much, holding his own sword to mine.

Adrenaline coursed through me and I re-focused. "Are you my new partner?"

The guy smiled, and the smile seemed somehow familiar—like from some long-forgotten dream. "Nah, I just like a good fight and you looked like you were having too much fun."

"All right, then. I'm new at this, but don't go easy on me."

"Not a problem," he said, seconds before he lunged.

I met his blow. Our swords clanged, the force of the blow shooting up my arm. Wow. That was harder than Tanner, or even Trevin had ever attacked me.

I circled, my focus narrowing to include only me and my opponent. When he lunged again, I was ready. I dodged out of the way and swiped my sword down. He parried and struck. I met the blow with one of my own.

Our swords clanged, our feet danced, and a crowd grew around us. The rush was unreal. I could live on the exhilaration forever. I felt so alive, so free, so…

My heel caught on something and I fell backward,

landing hard on my butt. My sword flew out of my grip and clattered to the ground. My opponent stepped forward, holding his sword to my throat.

I stared at the blade, breathing heavily. My lungs throbbed. And so did my butt.

Then the blade disappeared and my opponent held out a hand and pulled me from the ground. "Good fight. Watch out for hidden roots next time."

He pointed to the ground and I saw the tree root I'd tripped over.

"When you're fighting you have to have two eyes on the battle, one eye on your surroundings, and one eye on the ground."

"Weird. So you soldiers all have four eyes? Where do you hide the extras?"

His expression went blank, like he wasn't sure if I was serious or not.

I laughed. "I'm kidding. Thanks for the tip. And thanks for the fight."

"You're welcome. No one else will fight me. I'm a Trellborian and I guess they don't fully trust me."

"Wait, you're fighting for someone else's country? Why?"

"I enjoy a good fight. And, truthfully, I'd do anything to get away from my parents. They own that inn, over there"—he pointed off in the distance, but all I could see were trees—"and when the army came through, I asked if I could join." He held out his hand. "I'm Marsala."

I froze, staring at the offered hand. Marsala. I looked at him again—the hair, the eyes, the build.

Oh my freaking gosh, this was Marshall Parker. Older, but definitely him.

"What, are my hands too sweaty or something?" He made a show of acting offended.

"No, I'm sorry." I shook his hand. "You just … you look like someone I used to know."

"Someone devilishly handsome, I hope." He wagged his eyebrows up and down.

Yep. Definitely him.

I felt sick to my stomach. The last time I'd seen him he was trying to sacrifice my friend Piper to the Emerald. That was right after he'd stuck a knife in my gut.

But he clearly had no memory of me. And his eyes held none of the aggression and hostility I remembered from him. He actually seemed … nice.

"Has Lindy seen you yet?" I held my breath.

His face was all confusion. "Lindy?"

"Yeah, the Queen."

"Oh, you mean Queen Shalyndria of Valstenia?"

I nodded.

"I've never met her, no."

"Oh." That was going to be interesting. Hopefully he wouldn't remember her. Hopefully she wouldn't freak out that her nemesis had joined her army in defense of her home and country.

Ugh, this was just too weird.
****
I found Lindy and Garon poring over the journal Belina had given us. I sat down beside Garon, pressing a finger to my temple to squash away the vision of one of those carnivorous fly-eater plant things that had just popped into my head. Ever since that day on the beach, weird pictures kept jumping into my mind. What the heck was wrong with me?

"Found anything yet?" I said, slipping my hand into Garon's. His fingers closed around mine.

"We've learned a lot about how the Topaz works," Lindy said. "And the varied effects it can have on those who come into contact with it, but there is nothing in here that talks about how to counteract the magic. We've talked about weakening the atomic bonds within the Topaz to the point of separation, which would disintegrate the gem, but from what we've read, it doesn't sound like that would actually break the spell. That would only prevent the Topaz from casting a new spell on anyone else."

Yikes, this was tough. "Okay, so, how does it work?"

Garon said, "The Remyallis plant, in powder form, acts as a hallucinogen, which puts the person into a dreamlike state where they see and feel things that aren't real. But, unlike dreaming, where your pulse and body rhythm slow, the hallucinogen causes the blood pressure, heart rate, and body temperature to rise. It can also cause sweating, dry mouth, numbness, and tremors."

"Sounds like a panic attack to me," I said.

"Well, yeah, it is sort of like a panic attack," Garon said.

"Or like being in love," Lindy pointed out.

Garon frowned.

"But those people you saw—the soldiers who were affected by the Topaz—they didn't act panicked, right?" I said.

Lindy answered. "No. They were all precision and devotion. But we didn't see what was going on inside them. Whatever hallucination the Topaz made them see, Anka was somehow controlling it. They saw and felt what she wanted them to see and feel. But from Oliver's notes, it seems clear that no matter what hallucination the victim sees, their base physical reactions will be the same."

"Okay, so what if, instead of trying to take the flower out of the Topaz, you added something calming to the mix?" I said. "Like, what do they put in Xanax?"

"Anti-anxiety drugs are chemically manufactured," Garon said. "We can't get those in the seventeenth century. But there are lots of herbs that have calming properties. Maybe one of those would work."

"We can't operate on *maybes*," Lindy said. Her hands were clenched into fists at her side and there were dark circles under her eyes.

How long had it been since she'd last slept?

Lindy continued, "We have to be certain. Once we get ahold of the Topaz, we may only have one shot at destroying it."

"That's true," Garon said. "But in my experience, waiting to be certain before taking action only guarantees failure. Sometimes you have to jump and figure things out on your way down."

"Sometimes that guarantees death," Lindy said.

"True," Garon said. "But sometimes you find you can fly."

They locked eyes, challenging each other. Lindy looked away first.

"In that case" she said, "I have to go."

We watched her walk away.

Then Garon said, "There's something else we found in the diary." He flipped some pages, searching through the book, then held it out for me to see.

It took me a second, but when I realized what he was showing me, my stomach clenched. There, in the center of the book, were the jagged edges of torn out pages. Several of them, in fact. "Missing pages?" I breathed.

Garon nodded.

"Does Lindy know?"

"She's the one who found it."

We both stared at the torn edges.

"There is clearly more we don't know," Garon said. "And whoever has these pages has the upper hand."

"Anka?" I guessed.

"Well, it may have been Oliver who took them out in order to destroy them. But we should assume it was Anka. And that she knows something we don't."

****

The entire army packed up that night and left on a covert nighttime march, headed for the castle Anka had taken. The Duke split the army into small groups, so they could travel with less chance of drawing attention. The small groups were to make the day-and-a-half journey, then stop two miles from the castle wall to rest until morning. They could stop anywhere they felt safe, as long as they were somewhere along the two-mile perimeter. So, even though the groups were not large, the castle would be completely surrounded. At dawn on the second day, each group had specific instructions about where and when to attack.

Our group completed the march and settled down in clusters to catch a few hours of sleep before dawn. Tanner, Garon, and I leaned up against a tree. Lindy, Trevin, and Belina surrounded another. A bunch of soldiers sprawled out on the ground around us.

Tanner was snoring seconds after we settled down.

Garon reached over and grabbed my hand. I wove my fingers through his and we sat there in silence, staring up at the stars.

Then Garon said, "Do you think great minds come back?"

I glanced at him sideways. "Huh?"

"Do you think that, after a person dies—especially someone who'd been on the verge of a great discovery— do you think that person comes back as someone else in order to finish what they started?"

"You mean like reincarnation?"

"I guess so, yeah."

I frowned, trying to figure out what he was getting at. Then, I realized. "Are you thinking about O?"

"Yeah."

I spoke slowly. "I think that his work will go on, if it's meant to. And whether he's the one doing it, or someone he taught is the one doing it … well, does it really matter? He still made a difference. And that's what counts."

Garon stayed quiet, his brow furrowed. "Maybe you're right. But … you have to admit, it's an intriguing idea. The thought that the same great mind could come back once a century, as a different person, and just pick up where they left off. Maybe all the great mathematicians ever since Archimedes were actually just reincarnations of him."

I laughed. "I think you're a little sleep deprived. And you're forgetting the fact that, sometimes there is more than one brilliant mind alive at the same time."

He nudged me with his thigh. "I'm not saying every great mind is the same person. Just suggesting that, maybe, some of them are. That maybe we'll get a chance to come back again if we have unfinished business at the end of our lives."

"That's an interesting idea," I said, staring up at the stars. "The universe is so mysterious—what do we really know for sure, anyway?"

Tanner grunted. "We know that you're keeping me awake."

Oops.

"Sorry, Tanner," I said. "I thought you were asleep."

Garon squeezed my hand. "Goodnight."

"Goodnight." I squeezed back.

Pretty soon, both Tanner and Garon were sleeping, along with the rest of our group.

But, as tired as I was, my brain wouldn't stop spinning through all the possible scenarios that might play out in the morning. I hadn't been included in any of the war councils, but from what I understood of the plan, it didn't seem like much of one.

And, of course, now I had to ponder the complexities of reincarnation.

And the knots in the tree kept poking my back.

Just when I thought I'd be awake by myself all night, Lindy stood from her spot and picked her way around the sleeping soldiers, carrying some sort of canvas bag. She stopped a few yards away from the men and stood, staring up at the castle, which was illuminated in the moonlight.

I eased myself off the ground and crept over to her side. "So, that's your castle, huh?"

Lindy jumped, letting out a squeak.

I pointed to the castle. "I don't think it's big enough." I was teasing, of course, but Lindy didn't laugh.

"Maggie, you scared me!" Lindy kneeled down and pulled something out of her bag.

A pair of pants, it looked like.

She stepped into the pants, pulling them on over whatever she had on underneath her dress.

Then she pulled out another item of clothing—some sort of tunic. "Help me out of this dress, will you?"

"What are you doing?"

"Just help me, I'll explain in a minute."

I helped her out of the billowy dress, then she pulled the tunic on over some sort of medieval-looking cami she'd had on underneath the dress.

She caught me looking at it and said, "I never thought I'd miss sports bras and yoga pants so much."

I laughed. "Okay, seriously, *what* are you doing?"

Lindy balled up the dress and stuffed it into her bag. "I'm doing something crazy. Trying to tip the battle in our favor."

"By dressing up as a boy?"

"No." She hesitated, then nodded toward the castle towering over us in the moonlight. "Have you ever paid attention to the spires at the top of a castle?"

I followed her gaze, looking up. "I haven't spent much time around castles. So, no."

"They're meant to look majestic, of course—to give the castle a tower-like grandeur. But they have a practical purpose as well."

"Hiding spot for hide-and-go-seek?" I guessed.

"Ha. No. They're ventilation for the fireplaces."

"No way." I squinted at them. It was hard to see all the way to the top in the darkness.

"It's true. There are fireplaces in almost every room throughout the castle, and the ventilation system connects them all at the top." She paused, looking at me with a gleam in her eye. "Which makes them the perfect way to get in. They don't even put guards up there because of the way the castle is situated—with the land sloping so steeply behind it. No one expects an enemy to enter from above."

I gaped at her. "That's because it's, like, a thousand feet off the ground! How would you get an army up there?"

"We don't have to get an entire army up there. Just one person. Me. The army will be down below, fighting their predictable fight, while I will be sneaking in through the fireplaces from above. This way we can do a sneak attack *and* direct attack at the same time. I'll climb the castle wall right now—no one will see me in the dark—and be in place when the first attacks start. I'll find Anka, steal the Topaz, and get out before anyone realizes the fight is already won."

"But if the spires are vents for the fireplaces, aren't they, like, full of fire?" My voice rose in pitch. Her plan was crazy.

"Not in the summer. And, anyway, they don't all vent at once."

"But what if you fall on the way up? You'd die. Like, for *sure*." I looked back at the castle, then let my gaze travel from its base up. And up, and up. All the way up to the tippy top.

"I won't fall. Trust me, I know how to climb."

"So, you've climbed the castle wall before," I challenged.

"Well, not exactly. But remember, I've been back here for seven years. I had to find something to do with my time. My little country has some great rock climbing spots, and, as it turns out, I enjoy dangling from cliffs."

"You're insane. You're crazy. Even if you *did* do it, which I'm not saying you should, you definitely shouldn't do it alone. And there's no freaking way I am climbing up there with you." My knees went weak just at the thought of being so high off the ground. "Let me wake someone up. Maybe a group of you can go."

"No," Lindy said, a hint of panic in her voice. "I'm immune to Anka. She can't work her spell on me. But I can't be sure about anyone else. And I can't risk having someone with me she might be able to turn against me. I've been practicing with my sword, and I'm getting better, but I'm still not great with it. I need to face her alone in order to have a chance. And no one else can know this part of the plan. If Anka turns someone against me who knows I'm sneaking in from above, they'll tell her, and my cover will be blown. You have to swear. Promise me you won't tell anyone."

I waffled. That was a promise I didn't know if I could keep.

"Didn't Garon tell me to jump and figure the rest out on the way down?" Lindy pressed.

He had, of course. Almost in those exact words.

"Well, this is me jumping. Please, Maggie, don't try to stop me. This can work."

I looked back at the sleeping soldiers. Garon and Tanner and the others. What would they do when they woke up and found their Queen missing? What would I say?

But Lindy seemed so sure of herself. So determined. And she was a Queen now. I couldn't stand in her way.

"Okay. I won't tell. But I'm coming with you."

Lindy started to protest.

I cut her off. "Not up the wall. No way could I climb that. But I'm coming with you to the base. In case you run into trouble." I touched the hilt of the sword I'd been given, itching to pull it from its sheath and fight someone.

Lindy's eyes softened and she put a hand on my arm. "Thanks, Maggie. You're a good friend."

Well, I didn't know if a good friend would let someone go scale a zillion-foot wall, but, for better or worse, I was going to let her.

A twig snapped somewhere to our left and we both froze. My gaze darted around the campsite. I examined the sleeping forms of our companions.

Everyone was still sleeping. Nothing stirred.

Lindy peered into the darkness, then said, "We'll have

to hurry if I'm going to make it up there before dawn." She picked up the bag and hefted it over her shoulder. "Let's go."

I glanced back at the group. Everyone was where they should be. I turned and followed Lindy. "What else is in the bag?" I hissed.

"Just some supplies I picked up in town before we left."

Lindy's steps were quick and sure as she led me through the forest. She clearly knew where she was going. Bea's red Pearl bounced against my chest as I speed-hiked, trying to keep up. I tucked the necklace under my shirt to keep it still. Eventually, we reached a path that wound back and forth, steeper and steeper as it climbed to the base of the castle.

But, suddenly, I couldn't see the forest.

I blinked.

All I saw was a blood-red sun sinking into an ocean, tinted pink where the sun touched the water's edge.

Another vision.

I stopped walking. Pressed my forefinger to my temple. Took some deep breaths. Eventually, the vision faded and the forest came back.

Lindy was watching me, her eyebrows quirked up. "Are you okay?"

"Yeah, I've just been having these weird visions."

"Visions?"

"Yeah, like flashes of things. I mostly see them when I'm awake, but I've had a couple of dreams, too. The dreams always start with the Emerald. I see it resting in my hand, and then I see my blood swirling inside of it, becoming one with the gem. Then I see other things coming together—water droplets joining on a leaf, a bird eating a worm, a woman jumping into the ocean, one of those carnivorous flowers closing around a fly. The images don't seem to be connected or make any sense. The only thing I can figure out that they have in common is that something is being ingested or added into or absorbed by something else."

Lindy's shoulders tensed. "When did the dreams start?"

"The day I met Belina on the beach," I said.

She sucked in a breath. "Are you sure?"

"Yes."

She glanced up at the sky, like some clue might be hiding there. "I'd hoped that Belina held the key to destroying the Topaz, but so far she hasn't been able to give us anything concrete. But maybe, inadvertently…"

"What do you mean?" I asked.

"Maybe Belina has given us something without knowing it." Her gaze flicked down to the Pearl resting against my chest. "Were you wearing the Pearl at the time?"

"I haven't taken it off since Bea gave it to me."

"I know the Pearl was created long before the Topaz was. And the Emerald long before that. But I believe all three are still connected. They all had the same creator, after all. And you were touched by the Emerald's magic more than almost anyone—maybe even more than me, since you actually communicated with it. Maybe the Pearl is trying to communicate with you, too."

"About how to destroy the Topaz?"

"Maybe," Lindy said. "I don't know. It's worth considering, for sure. When you get back to camp, tell Garon and Belina about your visions. See if they have any ideas."

I nodded.

There was a rustle in the trees off to our left. An owl

hooted in the darkness and three birds took off in flight.

I grabbed my sword and held it out, defensively. "Birds don't usually fly around at night," I whispered.

Lindy scanned the woods. We listened.

Silence.

"Maybe they were bats," Lindy said. "Let's keep moving."

They hadn't been bats. But I followed anyway, a new urgency in my step. I put my sword back, but kept my hand on the hilt. The trees thinned out until only a few scraggly ones grew, bowed over as they struggled to stay upright on the steep slope at the back of the castle. The moon shone brightly overhead.

Lindy stopped beside one of the trees, this one twisted and knotted. She dropped her bag to the ground and pulled out a crossbow.

"Whoa, what's that for?" I said.

"To set the ropes. You didn't think I was going to free climb, did you?" She put a grappling hook in the crossbow and clicked it into place.

"I don't know what I thought." I scanned the area, my fingers gripping the hilt of my sword. My chest felt too tight. My breathing too shallow.

Lindy took out a coil of thin rope and tied one end to the grappling hook, then placed one foot at the base of the tree and leaned her body back against the tree trunk. She pointed the crossbow up, aimed, fired.

The grappling hook soared through the air. I lost sight of it in the dark.

"Blast, it was short," Lindy said. The line went loose as the hook came back down. She reeled it in, notched it back in the crossbow, and took aim again, higher this time.

Her body tensed up and she took the shot.

A moment later, the hook came tumbling back to the ground. The moon was dipping lower and lower in the sky. We were running out of time. Soon it would be light and Lindy would be spotted while climbing the castle. I shifted my feet, re-balancing myself on the steep slope.

"Maybe if I…" She reeled the rope in, reset the hook, and then climbed up into the tree. She got as high as she could, then fired again. I watched the hook soar up, up, up.

My fingernails pressed into the palms of my hands and I strained to keep my eye on the hook.

It came so close to reaching the top of the wall.

So. Close.

But not close enough. It came tumbling back to the ground.

Lindy swiped a hand across her forehead. She reeled the rope in, reset the crossbow.

"Oh, for heaven's sake," a voice said. "*I'll* do it."

I jumped, nearly losing my footing. I drew my sword and whirled around.

"Put that away, Maggie."

I did not put my sword away. A figure advanced toward us, but I couldn't tell who it was.

Lindy scrambled down from the tree.

"Relax, you two." The figure stepped into the moonlight.

Oh. It was Belina.

"Geez, Belina, you scared me." I tried to put my sword away, but my hands were shaking and I missed the sheath. Clearly, I needed to work on not panicking at the first sign of danger.

"Give me the crossbow. We don't have much time," Belina said.

Lindy's mouth dropped open.

"Come on, I was listening to you and Maggie back at camp. I know all about your plan."

Lindy took a breath. I could almost see the arguments sitting on the tip of her tongue.

"Don't worry," Belina interrupted. "I'm madly in love with my husband. Anka won't be able to control me. And I know you don't want to admit that you need my help, or anyone else's for that matter, but the truth is you could use a skilled fighter up there. I'm coming with you, so don't even bother trying to argue. I was going to follow you up without you knowing, anyway. I'm just not very good at waiting." She held out her hand for the crossbow. "May I?"

Lindy pressed her lips together, but handed it over.

"Thank you." Belina examined the crossbow, made some adjustments, and reset the grappling hook. She braced her back foot against the base of the tree, like Lindy had done, but kept her torso upright.

She took aim.

Fired.

We watched the hook soar through the sky, up and up.

I held my breath.

It went all the way up and disappeared over the wall. Belina tugged gently on the rope until the hook caught at the top and the rope became taut. She smiled. "Got it. Where's your climbing rope?"

Lindy scrambled inside her bag and pulled out a long coil of heavy-duty rope.

"Did you knot it?" Belina asked.

"Every three feet," Lindy replied.

"Good, that'll make it easier to climb."

Working quickly, Lindy tied it to the end of the lighter weight rope attached to the grappling hook at the top. Then she used that like a pulley to thread the heavier rope all the way up to the top.

Belina tugged on it to make sure it was secure.

"How are you both so good at this?" I said.

Belina smiled. "There's not much to do around here if you're a woman who doesn't like to sit still."

Lindy took some weapons out of her bag and tied them around her waist, leaving the bag and whatever else was inside at the base of the tree. Then she looked up at the castle, her eyes hardening with something like resolve.

"Maggie, thanks for your help. Go back to camp. You can tell everyone I'm safe, but nothing else. They can't have any idea of what I'm doing. Make sure they attack at dawn as planned."

I gazed up at the wall Lindy was about to climb, and my stomach churned. Just the thought of being up that high made my palms clammy and my knees weak. "Be safe," I said.

"I will." She gave me a hug. "Now go. You have to get back before everyone wakes up."

I looked once more at her face. Eyes bright. Jaw set. Even in light of the struggles ahead.

She was strong. So much stronger than she'd been as a captive of the Emerald.

I wondered if it was as clear to her as it was to me.

Chapter Thirty-Five

Climb

Lindy

1623—Valstenia

My throat threatened to close up as I watched Maggie disappear into the night. I was actually doing this. I was climbing the castle wall, relying on nothing but my strength, a rope, and a grappling hook.

I was definitely crazy.

How would everyone back at camp react when they found out I was gone?

I thought about Trevin. What if Anka turned him against me? What if he was killed in battle? What if I never saw him again?

And then I wondered: why did I care so much? And was it okay that I cared? I was the Queen, and he my bodyguard's son. I'd managed to stop flirting with him, but that didn't mean I hadn't *thought* about flirting with him on multiple occasions.

I shook the memories from my head and gripped the rope between both hands, wishing I had gloves. I'd forgotten to get some at the shop where I'd bought the rest of my supplies.

I checked the first few knots. They were tight.

I tugged on the rope. It was secure.

"I'll hold the rope steady until you get about half way up, then I'll follow," Belina said.

"Thanks. I'll wait for you at the top." The rope felt rough against the palms of my hands.

I took a few deep breaths, then reached up and grabbed the highest knot I could. I jumped and put my feet on a lower knot, then used my legs to push myself up until I could reach the next knot.

It was like climbing a rope in gym class, back in Virginia, in what seemed like a different lifetime. I hadn't been very good at it back then.

But I was stronger now. And, this time, I had a purpose.

I propelled myself up and up, higher and higher. Letting my muscles work. Letting them breathe.

Ever since I'd returned to Valstenia, I'd found solace in dangling from cliffs. It was where I always went to think. To work out whatever problem was plaguing me. But today there was more at stake than ever before.

Even though I thought Belina might be on the right track with her love theory, I'd felt there was no way the Duke would have taken it seriously and so I hadn't mentioned it to him. I could only imagine how that conversation would have gone.

Sir, let's take a poll of the men and find out which ones are in love. Those who are in love should be the only ones who approach Anka. Their love will protect them.

It was laughable, really. And, anyway, I wasn't certain that was how the Topaz even worked.

No, this approach was better. Have the soldiers attack en masse, while I sneak in and steal the Topaz. And after that…

After that…

Oh, no.

I should have come up with a way to signal the men once I got hold of the Topaz. I'd need to destroy it in order to break the spell, and in order to do that, I'd probably need Garon's help.

No! Why hadn't I thought to work something out with Maggie? She'd be down with the others—I could have signaled for them to retreat once I had the Topaz.

My arms began to burn. I engaged all my muscles so as not to fatigue one muscle group sooner than the rest. I focused on putting one hand above the other, using my legs to propel me upward instead of my arms.

As I rose, the moon fell. Soon, the deep dark of night was turning to gray. I couldn't bear to look up. I didn't want to see how much farther I had to go. I just kept going, forcing my body to obey.

My palms throbbed.

Maybe I wouldn't need to signal retreat. Maybe once Anka lost the Topaz, she'd lose control over the men as well. If that were true, all I needed to do was get the Topaz away from her and the fight would be won.

I felt the rope shift below me. Belina had started up.

I must be halfway.

I ignored my burning muscles. My stinging hands. I pushed all thoughts out of my head and focused on getting to the top.

Up, up, up.

Keep going, I told myself. *You must not fail.*

****

I reached down and helped Belina over the edge just as the morning sun peeked over the horizon. Together, we collapsed against the inner wall in a heap of shaking muscles and red-raw hands.

I'd never been so tired in all my life.

We'd climbed to the top of the castle tower and, as I'd predicted, there were no guards up here. No one had ever even considered that this wall might be breached. It was too high up—the ground at the base too steep—for anyone in their right mind to even try.

But we'd done it.

I let Belina catch her breath as I pulled the rope up and stashed it out of sight. "The first attacks will begin any moment. Once they do, we need to be ready to move."

"What's the plan?" Belina asked, breathing heavily.

"We search floor-by-floor. Once we find Anka, if she's not alone, we'll need to create a distraction to draw her guards out. Then we engage, with the singular purpose of getting the Topaz."

"Then what?"

"We get out. We destroy it. We put our kingdom back together."

Chapter Thirty-Six

A New Pearl

Maggie

1623—Valstenia

When I arrived back at camp after leaving Lindy and Belina, the sky had turned from black to gray. Dawn was on its way, but it was still night. Everyone should have been asleep.

But they weren't.

Duke Christoph was issuing commands. Garon and Trevin stood huddled together, speaking in low voices. Soldiers were readying themselves for battle. Tanner was nibbling on a strip of dried beef.

"What's going on?" I asked, approaching the group. "It's not dawn yet."

"Maggie!" Garon said, his shoulders relaxing. "Where have you been?"

The Duke rounded on me. "Where's the Queen?"

Oh. Right.

"Well, I was sitting by that tree having a hard time going to sleep, when I saw Lindy get up. So I followed her. She's fine, I promise, but I can't tell you where she went."

A vein in the Duke's neck bulged. "Where did she go?" he demanded, advancing toward me.

I shrunk away from him.

"Hey, relax," Garon said, stepping between me and the Duke. "I'm sure Maggie can explain."

Tanner got up and stood by my side.

My voice came out as more of a squeak than an actual voice. "Actually, I can't."

Trevin's jaw flexed. "What do you mean, you can't?"

"I mean, your Queen came up with a plan, which I think might actually work, but she didn't want anyone to know about it because if Anka turns you against her then you'll tell her the plan and ruin Lindy's chances of success." I stared them down. "So, I can't tell you, by command of the Queen."

"Belina is missing, too," Garon said. "Did you see her?"

"Yes. She went with Lindy."

Garon relaxed, but the others still seemed tense.

The Duke said, "I need to know what she's planning. How am I to ensure we don't sabotage her plans unknowingly?"

"You won't. She asked me to make sure the attack goes forward as planned. Don't change anything."

The Duke frowned. "But how can I protect her if I don't know where she is?"

Trevin said, "I'm sure the Queen considered the risks. If this is what she wants, we are bound to obey. Queen Shalyndria is smart. And very brave." He said it with such tenderness, I felt like I was watching a rom-com. Except without the com.

"And Belina is with her," Garon said. "My sister will be fine."

The Duke rubbed his jaw, considering. "Very well. Everyone eat something and be ready to attack at dawn as planned."

I released the breath I didn't realize I'd been holding.

Then, while we ate, I told Garon about my visions. I told him everything I'd told Lindy.

When I finished, he said, "Can I see the Pearl?"

I tugged the necklace out from under my shirt, and he leaned closer to examine it in the hazy morning light. I caught a whiff of his hair and, even though we'd been hiking for days, he still smelled good. Woodsy, and a little bit like a campfire. But good.

"You know," he said, "we've been talking about adding herbs to the Topaz to see if it will counteract the effects of the hallucinogen, but we haven't tried doing that very same thing to the Pearl. If it works on the Pearl, then we'll know it'll work on the Topaz." He looked at me. Our faces were inches apart. "Is it okay with you if I try?"

We hadn't been this close for a while, with everything that had been going on. My heartbeat ticked up a notch. It took me a moment to find my voice. "It's worth a shot." I took the necklace off and handed it to him.

He pulled a handkerchief from his pocket and started unwrapping it. It reminded me of when we'd first met—outside the Natural History museum in DC—and he'd wrapped my bleeding palm with Calendula petals to help it heal faster.

"What is that?" I asked.

"Some herbs I gathered after reading Oliver's notes. Plants that counteract hallucinogens—like anti-anxiety meds. Will you hold it?"

I took the packet from him and arranged the handkerchief so that the assortment of plants rested in my palm.

Garon said, "Do you remember when I taught you how to soften gemstones?"

"Yeah, we were in my car and you drew all those scientific diagrams on my fogged-up windshield."

Garon's lopsided grin appeared. "Well, you have to know the molecular structure of the substance you're trying to manipulate. I didn't have any paper—the windshield was the best option at the time."

"It was very resourceful of you."

His hand closed around the red Pearl. "I've been studying up on Pearl and Topaz, since they're different."

Oh, right. I hadn't even thought of that.

Garon bent his head in concentration. A moment later, the Pearl had been altered into a softened state. Just like he'd taught me to do with the Emerald.

"Let's start with the Kava," he said.

I held the herbs out to him and he plucked a brown root from the bunch. He pushed it into the softened Pearl, then closed his hand around it. Seconds later, the Pearl was back in its hardened state, resting in Garon's palm.

Our heads bent together as we both watched the Pearl. The poison inside swirled, like a red fog trapped in a glass sphere. Then the red turned to pink. The swirling stopped.

"Well, that's closer at least," Garon said. "Let's add some chamomile and ashwagandha seeds."

Tanner joined us and peered over my shoulder.

Garon turned the Pearl soft again, plucked some seeds and flower petals from the handkerchief, and inserted them into the Pearl.

He hardened it.

I held my breath.

The pink in the Pearl swirled again with an influx of creamy white fog. When the colors stopped swirling, the Pearl was cream-colored, with only a handful of pink flecks.

"Almost there. A little passionflower should finish the job."

Trevin and a few of the soldiers joined us as well.

Garon altered the Pearl, plucked some dried purple-y

flower bits from the handkerchief, added them to the Pearl, then changed it back again.

The whole group seemed to hold its breath as we watched. The Pearl went foggy, swirled, and the pink flecks disappeared.

A perfect, creamy-white Pearl rested in Garon's palm.

"Yes!" Tanner exclaimed, pumping a fist into the air.

I laughed, and the sound seemed out of place. "Wow, so that's it?"

Garon nodded. "This Pearl has been healed. Now we just need to find the Topaz and try the same thing."

He made it sound so simple. I hoped it would be.

****

The moment the sun peeked over the horizon, the Duke issued a series of low whistles—the command everyone had been waiting for. The groups stationed closest to us on either side repeated the whistles for the groups beside them. Then the next groups repeated the whistle, and the signal traveled around the circle of groups surrounding the castle. As each group received the command, they broke off to carry out their specific assignment.

But Tanner and I had to stay behind. The Duke said sending us into the fight would prove more of a risk than a benefit.

The plan had been for Lindy to stay with us, along with a few guards to keep the Queen safe. But with Lindy gone, the Duke just left us alone with instructions to watch from afar and signal them if there was any major sign of trouble. Like, if soldiers began pouring out in retreat or if the castle exploded or something. He didn't really specify. He just gave Tanner this ram's horn thing and said if he blew into it, the call could be heard for miles.

So Tanner and I sat on a fallen log while the morning sun rose. My knee jiggled up and down as I thought of all the soldiers risking their lives inside the castle. *Garon* risking his life inside the castle. And Lindy and Belina sneaking down from above.

I was itching to use my sword for real. "Ugh, this is the worst. What's the point of being good with a sword when I'm stuck outside?"

"Mags, you do realize you've never been in a real fight, right? It takes years of practice to become a master swordfighter."

"How would you know?"

Tanner hesitated. "Well, it's just a guess. But I'm pretty sure I'm right."

I gazed up at the castle. "You know, once the first wave of soldiers has attacked, the defenses will probably be down."

"Oh, no. Maggie, no. No snooping. Not this time."

"Why not?"

"They need us out here, just in case."

"Just in case, what? The Duke only gave you that stupid horn to make it seem like we had a purpose." I stood up. "I'm going in."

Tanner's eyes went wide. "Seriously, don't."

"Tanner, I'm not asking for permission. I'm going. The question is, are you coming with me?"

Tanner stood up. "I'm bigger than you, Mags."

"Yeah, well I'm better than you with a sword." I touched the handle.

"Are you really threatening to fight me so you can then fight your way into the castle?"

"No. I'm threatening to fight you if you don't let me sneak into the castle to try and help my friends. Seriously, Tanner, come with me. We'll be super stealthy. No one will see us, I promise."

"Something tells me that's not a promise you can keep." Tanner's half-smile told me I had him, even though he was still struggling with the idea. He'd never admit it out loud, but I knew he craved adventure just as much as I did.

I grinned. "Follow me. Stay close."

Then, in what would likely prove to be a splendid show of either valor or stupidity, the two of us crept toward the castle.

Chapter Thirty-Seven

Find Her

Lindy

1623—Valstenia

"If you were a crazy megalomaniac where would you go?" I asked Belina.

She glanced at me sideways. "Huh?"

"Never mind, let's check the throne room. That's the most obvious place of power." I led the way down a flight of stairs, trying to move quickly but cautiously.

From far below, the sound of a fight drifted up. Metal on metal as sword met sword. Soldiers shouting their battle cries.

We approached the throne room

"Shouldn't there be guards outside?" Belina said.

"Not if they've all been called to defend the front gates. But be ready for a fight, just in case."

Belina notched an arrow in her bow and pulled it taut. I drew my sword.

I flung the door open and we stepped in.

My gaze darted to the right, then to the left. I whirled around, expecting an attack from behind. But there was nothing. I took in the rest of the room—empty throne, empty hall.

The room was deserted.

I felt myself deflate, the pent-up adrenaline having nowhere to go. I did a few swings, letting my sword slice through the air. "I was certain she'd be in here."

Belina said, "Do you think she's out with her

soldiers?"

"Maybe. That *would* be the best way for her to use her mind control. But I suppose anything's possible." I swung my sword through the air again, then walked over to the thrones and searched behind them, checking behind a large tapestry. "This room is definitely empty."

A clanging noise from below made me jump. The floor rattled.

Belina's eyes widened. "What was that?"

"Sounds like the drawbridge being lowered."

"But is it being lowered by us or by them?" Belina said.

I shook my head, not wanting to think about who might be losing. "Either way, everyone's probably at the front gate, which is why there are no soldiers up here."

I made my way back to Belina and noticed the Pearl hanging from her neck.

I did a double take.

It was milky-white—pristine. Not a trace of the poison I'd seen snaking through it only yesterday. "Hey." I pointed at it. "What happened to your Pearl?"

Belina looked down. And her eyes went huge. She grabbed the Pearl. Held it up to the light, examining it from all different angles. "I've no idea. Only this morning, it was—"

She was cut off by the door banging open. A company of soldiers filed into the room, heading for a door at the opposite end.

They had pink eyes.

"Hurry, men," their leader said. "We're needed at the front gates."

Belina notched an arrow.

The men saw us and froze.

The man who'd been issuing commands spluttered.

"What are you doing here?"

Belina aimed her arrow at the man's head. "Where's Anka?"

The man snapped his mouth shut.

I stepped forward, placing a hand on Belina's arm and addressing the men. "We don't want to hurt you. The woman called Anka has brainwashed you. I am your rightful Queen."

The men shuffled, their stares shifting from Belina, to me, and then back to their leader. A few of them rubbed their eyes and started blinking.

The leader's brow furrowed. He drew his sword. "Anka is our Queen. The imposter must die."

He advanced toward me, and several of his men followed suit. But some of them stayed put, shaking their heads like they were waking up from a dream.

Belina took aim and let an arrow fly. The leader fell to the floor, an arrow stuck squarely between his eyes.

She notched another arrow. Took aim.

"Belina, wait!"

"This is a battle, people are going to get hurt."

"Some of them are fighting off the spell."

The ones who weren't, however, were still advancing on us. I gripped my sword in my hand, trying to remember the moves Trevin had taught me.

Belina let another arrow fly, this one catching a man in the throat.

"Don't kill them!" I yelled. "These are our country men. Fathers, husbands, sons. They're acting under a spell. Just disable them."

Belina grimaced. "Fine." She shot another arrow, this time hitting a man in the knee. He crumpled to the ground.

Belina fired arrow after arrow until the men got too

close and she had to draw her sword.

We faced them together.

A soldier raised his arm to strike. He was young—not quite twenty, I guessed. I met his sword with mine. The shock of the blow rocketed up my arm.

He swung again and I blocked. Soon we were locked in a fight. I moved how Trevin had taught me. Swung and blocked and held my ground.

But there were lots of men and only two of us.

The men who weren't fighting looked like they might finally be coming out of their fog. They stood there, shaking their heads and rubbing their eyes. When they saw Belina and I locked in battle, several of them joined the fight, attacking our attackers from the rear.

My gaze skipped around the room, searching for anything that could give us the upper hand. Anything we could use.

And then I saw the tapestry hanging behind the thrones at the front of the room. It was thick. And heavy.

Hmm.

I angled my back toward the tapestry and started backing up, step by step. Belina mirrored me, maybe without even realizing it. The fight moved ever closer to the front of the room until we were just in front of the tapestry. From this close, it towered over all our heads, the height of several men.

I spotted the rope used to hang the tapestry, rigged up like a pulley. Just a bit farther. I shifted to my right. Sidestepped. Lunged at my opponent, and then whirled around, swinging my sword with all the strength I had at the rope that held the tapestry.

My blade sliced through the rope.

The loose end whipped into the air and the tapestry fell.

I launched myself to the side, throwing Belina out of the way as the heavy material came down on our opponents.

I grabbed Belina's hand and pulled her up. "Run! The tapestry won't stop them for very long."

Two of the men bringing up the rear had jumped out of the way and hadn't gone down with the rest.

But their eyes had cleared. These men were on our side.

"Highness, we'll finish this," one of them said. "Go find Anka and get your crown back."

The other one said, "She's hiding in the nursery on the fourth floor."

"Thank you," I said to the men, not stopping to ask why she was in the nursery, of all places.

Then Belina and I ran from the room.

****

There was only one nursery in the castle, and it was the very one I'd been taken from as a baby. No one had used it in years. The closer we got, the more I wondered what Anka was doing there. If any room was the antithesis of power and might, it was the one where babies were rocked gently to sleep.

We exited the stairwell and turned right. "The nursery is set apart from the rest of the bedrooms, to keep the babies from waking the household."

We hurried down a hall, rounded a bend, and skidded to a halt.

Two guards were standing outside the nursery door. Before they could react, Belina had shot arrows in both of their throats.

I knew she had to, but still I cried inside.

And then we heard it: Whimpering. Like from a child.

I frowned. All of the children had gotten out of the

castle.

So, who was crying?

As we approached the nursery, the whimpering got louder. We drew our weapons. I placed a hand on the door, holding Belina's gaze, sending her the silent message to be ready for anything. I willed my stuttering heart to be still.

Then I turned the knob and stepped into the room, sword raised. Belina followed closely behind.

Nothing jumped out at us. In fact, the room looked empty.

I searched for the source of the noise, and my gaze caught on a mostly-bald head on the far side of the room.

There, standing beside one of the beds and facing away from us, was Anka, in her true, deformed form. She was focused on something in the bed.

A person, I realized, lying still.

It didn't seem like Anka had heard us enter. Belina and I glanced at each other, then silently crept forward.

Who was in the bed?

And then Anka said, without turning around, "You're too late. I have already won."

I froze. Was she talking to us or the person in the bed?

She glanced back. "Yes, I mean you, little Queen."

A shiver ran down my spine.

Belina broke away from me and started creeping around the edge of the room.

I took a deep breath and said, "You haven't won. The front gates have been breached, and your soldiers are falling back."

I didn't know if it was true. But I hoped it was.

Anka swiveled to face us. "I have won because the people call me their Queen, and they no longer want you, an entitled royal, telling them what to do."

"How do you know what the people want? You've brainwashed them. They're under a magical spell—that's not reality."

Anka's chin jutted out. "Reality is whatever people believe to be true."

Belina was halfway around the room. Had Anka really not seen her? Or did she just not care that someone was sneaking up on her?

"Who was crying?" I said.

Anka glanced back at the bed. "Why don't you come and see?"

Part of my brain was screaming that we should just kill her now and be done with it. She'd murdered my mother.

But I said, "Belina told me about the accident. How you lost your parents. We know you blame the royal family for all the suffering you've endured. But this is not the answer."

Anka's spine stiffened, just a smidge.

Belina was almost to the bed.

My fingers tightened around the hilt of my sword.

Anka smiled. "Oh, I think this is the perfect answer. And, like I said before, you're too late. Once the magic has been sealed, there is nothing you can do to stop me."

What did she mean, *Once the magic has been sealed*? Nobody had ever said anything about sealing magic.

Belina reached the bed. And stood there, gawking down at it. "Is that…?"

"It is," Anka said, finally looking at Belina. "Little Queen," she said to me, "you really should see this."

I advanced, my palms sweating. The person lying on the bed came into view.

And my heart went icy cold.

It was Yelena.

No! Had Anka's men intercepted Yelena and my siblings? Where were Carina and Felipe? My stomach lurched.

Yelena's eyes were closed, and she was whimpering like a child having a bad dream. And sitting beside Yelena, nestled into the bedsheets, sat the Topaz.

Wait … was it …?

It looked liquid-y. Like a lump of strawberry Jell-O.

Had Oliver taught Anka how to soften gemstones? What was going on?

Almost like she'd read my mind, Anka pulled a bundle of papers from the folds of her cloak and waved them in the air.

The missing pages from Oliver's diary!

"Blood magic is fascinating stuff," Anka said, pulling out a knife. "All we need now is your sister's blood."

Chapter Thirty-Eight

Storm the Castle

Maggie

1623—Valstenia

"What's the plan?" Tanner hissed as he followed me through the brush.

"Last night Lindy and I passed a back entrance to the castle. She said it leads to the kitchen. One of the groups should have taken out the guards there by now—we'll just slip in and start searching the castle for Anka. Easy-peasy."

Tanner rolled his eyes, but followed me until we reached the tiny path that broke away from the switchbacks. We took it, stopping at the last spot of tree cover. I pointed out a door standing open at the back of the castle. "That's it."

I frowned. There was something on the ground near the door. Was that…?

"It's a body," Tanner said grimly. "See the arm lying on the ground?"

I did. The arm was all that could be seen. Whether it was still attached to a body hidden just inside the door, or … not attached…

I swallowed. *Be strong, Maggie.*

"Yeah, I see it." We waited a few minutes, watching the entrance, but nothing stirred. No soldiers emerged, no voices cried out. There were no signs of life, even, let alone an ongoing fight.

"I say we just go in," Tanner said. "Waiting here is

stupid."

Part of me wanted to turn and run away. Where, I didn't know. It wasn't like I could time travel back home by myself...

My throat went dry.

Oh, no.

What if Garon didn't make it out alive? Tanner and I would be stuck here forever. Why hadn't I thought of that sooner?

I heard myself saying, "You're right, let's go in." My heart was in my throat, my pulse thumping wildly, but I launched myself into the clearing. Behind me, loose rocks scattered as Tanner followed. I kept my head low, expecting arrows or soldiers or something to come flying at us at any moment.

But none came.

We crossed the clearing and made it to the entrance.

Nothing could have prepared me for the scene that lay beyond the door.

I stopped, my hand flying up to cover my mouth. Tanner gripped my arm, his face going white.

The arm we'd seen from outside was still attached to a body, but the head was bent at an unnatural angle, the eyes open and lifeless. Blood oozed from a gash in the man's chest. My gaze skimmed over the man and landed on the next man, who lay in a similar state. And then on to the next. And the next.

The entire entryway was filled with fallen soldiers, their bodies broken and their eyes vacant.

"Are these our men?" I asked, my voice squeaky.

"I hope not," Tanner said.

Carefully, we picked our way over the fallen men.

We passed through the entryway and into the kitchen, where more men had fallen. From the kitchen, we made our way into the grand hallway.

Still no signs of life.

The castle was a labyrinth. Now that we were inside, I had no idea which way to go. We went left, our feet tapping against the stone floor despite our best efforts to keep quiet. And then there was a clanging sound from overhead.

Tanner froze. "Is that the drawbridge, maybe?"

"I don't know."

The hallway ended and we turned down another. Tanner was ahead of me. Suddenly, he whirled around and we collided. "Turn back," he hissed, grabbing me by the shoulders and spinning me around.

The footfalls of dozens of soldiers came toward us, sounding like they were running through the halls.

Tanner's eyes were wild, frantic.

"Over there, under the bench!" I shoved him toward a giant wooden bench sitting along one wall.

We slid underneath it, Tanner pushing me in first, just before the group of soldiers turned down our hall. I made myself as small as I could, pressing my body to the stone wall and pulling Tanner further under the bench as the men marched past.

"The front gates have been breached," one man said. "Fall back, but keep the enemy from ascending. We must protect the Queen!"

A chorus of voices, almost as if they were responding without thought, said, "Long live Queen Anka."

The soldiers filed past, then the hallway went silent.

I whispered, "Did you hear what those soldiers said? To not let the enemy ascend? That must mean Anka is on one of the upper floors."

"Yep. Let's find the stairs." Tanner peeked out from under the bench. "All clear."

We slid out from our hiding spot and darted through the now-empty hallway, in the opposite direction the soldiers had gone. We turned down another hall and went around a bend, searching for some stairs.

"There," I said, spotting a narrow opening that looked promising. We ran toward it and found a set of narrow steps leading up. They twisted around and around, so much so that I felt dizzy by the time we reached the top.

Shouts in the upper level made us retreat and wait in the stairwell until things went quiet. Then we searched the floor, which consisted of a large dining hall, a dance hall, and a few smaller rooms—like conference rooms or whatever the medieval equivalent was.

"No more dead bodies," Tanner said. "The fight must be contained to the first floor."

"Good news for us," I said. And good news for Lindy and Belina.

We went up another floor and searched it quickly. It was mostly bedrooms—all empty. We headed for the stairwell again—how many floors were there before it was just turrets and towers?

Tanner paused on the bottom step.

I bumped into him. "What?"

"Shh." He put a finger to his lips.

I listened. At first there was nothing. Then, a moment later, I heard it too.

Voices. Muffled, but close.

We went back into the hallway. I cocked my head, listening.

"This way." I darted to the right, rounded a corner, and found a hallway we hadn't seen before. At the end was a single door. Two guards lay dead at the threshold, with arrows to their throats.

I swallowed, my mouth going dry.

Tanner and I locked eyes. Pulled out our swords.

We walked toward the door, and the voices became clearer.

"Little Queen, you really should come see this," a woman said from behind the door. There was a pause. Then the same voice said, "Blood magic is fascinating stuff. All we need now is your sister's blood."

"Where are Carina and Felipe?" It was Lindy's voice. Only it was wobbly.

"Maybe lost, maybe in the belly of a wolf. There are just so many possibilities." The voice cackled. "Now let's get on with it. Qadar wants me now, not you. And he's anxious to finalize our deal."

My fingers tightened around the hilt of my sword. I took a deep breath, then yanked the door open. Tanner and I swept in.

Lindy and Belina were there. And also a woman, disfigured beyond anything I'd ever seen, but grinning like a psychopath. She was leaning over an occupied bed on the far side of the room.

Lindy turned and saw us. "Maggie! What are you doing here?"

"We came to help." Only … it didn't look like they needed help. The disfigured woman—Anka, I presumed—was alone, except for whoever was lying comatose on the bed. And now it was four against one.

Belina ignored us and spoke to Anka. "My father never used blood magic. You're lying."

Anka's grin only widened. "Hello," she said to Tanner. "You're just in time."

Tanner narrowed his eyes.

Then she twitched her fingers at him and, immediately, my brother raised his sword and turned toward Lindy.

My heart rocketed into my throat as I realized what was happening.

Lindy realized it too. "She's controlling him!" she yelled.

Tanner's eyes were wild, flipping between horror and hatred. From blue to pink and back again. With one hand, he reached down and grabbed the ram's horn the Duke had given him. Bicep trembling, he brought it up to his lips and blew.

The sound reverberated throughout the castle.

Then, the horn clattered to the ground and Tanner's eyes went vacant. In the blink before he went completely pink-eyed, his expression screamed at me that he'd lost control of his body. Then his lips twisted into a snarl and he advanced on Lindy and Belina.

"Tanner, stop!" I threw myself in his path, blocking his first blow with my sword. Tanner raised his sword again, and again I met it with my own.

My knees went weak. I'd wanted a fight, but not with my own brother!

Chapter Thirty-Nine

Come Together

Lindy

1623—Valstenia

Maggie met her brother blow for blow, edging her way around the room so as not to get backed into a corner. Her movements were more precise than Tanner's, more focused, but I could tell she was holding back.

Obviously. She didn't want to hurt her brother.

Tanner, on the other hand, seemed to have given in completely to Anka's power, and was fighting his sister with a ferocity I'd never before seen in him. His movements were sloppy. But he was strong—stronger than Maggie. I watched in horror as Maggie backed toward an upended doll's cradle, which was lying on the floor.

"Maggie, watch out!" I yelled.

But I was a second too late. Maggie tripped over the wood and tumbled backward, the sword flying out of her hand. Tanner stalked toward her, raising his arm in preparation to deliver a deathblow.

Maggie scrambled backward, trying frantically to get to her feet.

Belina pulled out her sword and darted forward, meeting Tanner's sword with her own as it came down.

"Don't kill him!" Maggie screamed, jumping to her feet. "Please, don't kill him!"

The glint of a knife caught my eye. I jerked my attention back to Anka.

She was positioning Yelena's arm so it was right beside the softened Topaz. And she held the knife ready to slice my sister's arm open and infuse her blood into the gem.

I knew nothing about blood magic, but surely this was it. Belina had said that using blood magic came with a price. But who would pay it? Anka or my sister?

The missing diary pages were sitting on the bed where Anka must have left them. I snatched them up.

Anka barely blinked. "Go ahead, I don't need them anymore. Once your sister's blood map enters the gem, the changes will be permanent, and so will my new soldiers' loyalty. I will look like your sister forever, and the spell will be unbreakable." She brandished the knife. "Blood magic seals all other magic."

I lunged for her. "Stay away from my sister!"

The knife clattered out of her hand as I knocked her to the ground. On the other side of the room, Belina and Maggie were locked in battle with Tanner.

Anka squirmed away from me. For such a bony human, she was surprisingly strong. She grabbed a heavy candlestick off a table and launched it at me.

I ducked. The candlestick flew over my head and clanged against the stone wall. Anka's gaze darted behind me to Yelena's sleeping form. She lunged to the side, trying to get around me.

I blocked her.

She darted to the other side.

I mirrored, holding her back.

Then, the door swung open and someone burst into the room.

It was Garon. "I heard the ram's horn," he said breathlessly. "What's going on?" His eyes went wide as he took in Belina and Maggie fighting Tanner.

Anka smiled. "Another visitor. Now we can have some real fun."

"Garon, get out!" I yelled. "Before she claims you, too."

It was too late. My brother was already gazing at Anka.

Metal clanged on metal as the fight with Tanner continued. Maggie and Belina were being backed into a corner.

Garon cocked his head to one side as he stared at Anka. Then he narrowed his eyes, sprang forward, and grabbed Tanner from behind.

"No!" Anka said.

Tanner's sword clattered to the floor as Garon wrestled him to the ground.

"Garon?" I yelled.

He looked up at me. His eyes were dark brown, as they'd always been. "I'm fine. She can't control me."

My chest expanded. His feelings for Maggie must be stronger than I'd thought. Belina's love theory was gaining traction in my mind.

With Tanner on the ground, Belina and Maggie lowered their weapons, breathing hard. Garon held Tanner down with one knee, pressing his face into the floor as he secured Tanner's arms behind his back.

I rounded on Anka. Belina and Maggie joined me. "You are greatly outnumbered, Anka. Free my sister from whatever spell she's under."

Anka lifted her chin in defiance.

I advanced toward her. "You will return my sister, and my kingdom, or I will send you to join my uncle in death."

Anka's gaze darted to the bed, where my sister and the softened Topaz still lay. Yet still, she said nothing.

"Wait, Lindy, don't kill her," Maggie said.

I glanced at her. Was she crazy? Anka deserved to die. The law required it, in fact. Treason was not a crime to be forgiven—it was one deserving of a swift and fatal punishment.

"This woman has committed treason," I said.

"But to have her death on your head?" Maggie said. "That has to weigh on a person, you know?"

Of course I knew. Every decision weighed on me— that was part of being a ruler. Part of my burden.

But ... perhaps I didn't have to kill her now, in front of everyone.

Anka dodged to the side again, trying to get around us. I mirrored her, keeping myself between her and the bed where my sister lay. Beside me, Maggie and Belina both had their swords drawn and pointed at Anka.

"I think I know how to destroy the Topaz," Garon said, still struggling to subdue Tanner, who was kicking and squirming. "Before this morning's attack, Maggie and I healed the Pearl. I should be able to do the same thing to the Topaz."

I remembered how Belina's Pearl had suddenly been poison-free this morning. "Whatever you did to Maggie's Pearl altered Belina's as well."

"Really?" Maggie said. "But this Pearl is a later version of Belina's. Changing it shouldn't affect the original, right?"

Garon adjusted his grip on Tanner's arms, fighting to keep him down. "Only if time is strictly linear. But if you think of time as being more like an ocean than a stretch of land, then changes made to one would affect the other, no matter which one came first. In a body of water, it doesn't matter which droplet was added first. Once they join together, they become one and change affects the whole thing equally."

Belina said, "But whatever you did, it didn't actually destroy the Pearl." She held up the Pearl hanging from her necklace. "You just removed the poison. And the Topaz isn't poisoned."

That silenced everyone.

And then an earsplitting shriek racked the air. It came from Maggie.

She was gripping her head in her hands, the tendons in her arms strained and her eyes squeezed shut.

"Is it another vision?" I put a hand on her arm, but she jerked away from me, holding her head between her hands and breathing hard. The Pearl bounced around on its chain, still hanging from her neck.

I pulled her hands away from her head and tugged the necklace off. Once it was gone, she relaxed. Her eyelids fluttered open.

"What did you see?" I said softly.

She took a shaky breath. "An emerald-colored eel. In a pond. It swallowed the Topaz, and then the Pearl."

I remembered the other visions she'd shared with me, and what they all had in common. "That must be the key, then—things coming together."

My mind spun as I reasoned it out. If the function of the Pearl was to restore what was lost, like with Belina's health when she was young, and her youth as she aged, then, essentially, the Pearl healed decay.

And the Topaz was decayed. Ravaged by drugs. It caused hallucinations, making people see things that were never actually there.

If we were to combine the two stones, the Pearl would heal the decay in the Topaz, returning it to what it actually was: just a Topaz, free from the effects of the hallucinogenic plant.

Would that work?

"Garon, can you soften Maggie's Pearl?"

He was still holding Tanner down with one knee, but he nodded. I hurried over and handed him the Pearl. A moment later, he gave it back to me, now soft.

I closed my fingers around it.

And then...

It happened so fast.

Anka ducked, picked up the knife she'd dropped earlier, and swiped it at Belina's calves, slicing through her pants and into the flesh beneath.

Belina screamed as her legs buckled. She fell to the ground.

Anka twirled and went for Maggie next. Maggie jumped back, narrowly avoiding the blade. Anka dodged around her and headed for Yelena.

On the floor, Tanner thrashed against Garon and managed to get one of his arms free. He swung a leg around and hooked it around Garon's leg. The two became locked in a wrestling match.

I ran across the room, the softened Pearl clenched in my fist. All I had to do was make it to the bed before Anka. But she was much closer, with Maggie running after her.

I pumped my legs. Launched myself over the fallen toy cradle.

Anka reached the bed and stretched out her arm, with the knife gripped tightly in one hand, toward Yelena.

Maggie was close behind.

My lungs were burning. My pulse racing. But I was almost there.

Anka pressed the knife into the soft flesh of my sister's arm. A bead of blood appeared, and then grew.

Maggie grabbed Anka from behind, threw her to the

floor, and then scrambled toward the bed.

Yelena's blood started streaming down her arm and toward the Topaz, like a poisonous snake down a milky white branch.

Anka grabbed Maggie's legs and yanked her away from the bed, just as Maggie snatched the Topaz from its perch. Maggie fell to her knees, but held the gemstone out to me as I closed the gap between us. I lifted my hand, with the Pearl still safely cupped inside. All I needed to do was get them together.

And then, a bony hand knocked into Maggie's from below. The Topaz flew up in an arc, and the same bony hand snatched it out of the air.

I sucked in a breath, but stepped in front of the bed. Anka may have the Topaz, but she was not going to get my sister's blood. We stood there, staring at each other, Anka's eyes fixed on Yelena's blood-stained arm and mine fixed on the softened gemstone she held.

Anka's gaze darted around the room, no doubt trying to see a way around me. Then she narrowed her eyes and turned on Maggie, kicking her in the gut. Maggie, who was still on her knees, doubled over. Anka dropped her elbow into the base of Maggie's skull, and Maggie slumped over, out cold.

"I *will* get what I want," Anka said, whipping out her knife and holding it to Maggie's throat.

My nerves were stretched tight—my muscles, tendons, joints—all felt ready to pop.

"It doesn't really matter whose blood map I use to seal the magic," Anka continued, gazing at Maggie. "True, this one is no royal. But she's pretty enough. Her appearance will do just fine. My soldiers will still bow to my every command." Anka pressed the flat edge of her knife to Maggie's skin.

"Stop!" I yelled, stepping toward her.

"I wouldn't come any closer," Anka said, twisting the knife around so the point was at Maggie's throat.

I froze.

"I'll kill her," Anka said.

Garon was still fighting Tanner, but his dark eyes went murderous. Garon scrambled to his feet and ran toward Anka, leaving Tanner on the ground. Only he didn't get very far—Tanner grabbed him from behind and pulled him back into the fight.

I stared Anka down, not daring to move any closer. A single twitch of her wrist and Maggie would be dead. I barely dared breathe. "What do you want?" I said evenly.

"Naturally, I'd prefer your blood to hers."

"And what makes you think I'd give you my blood when you'll only kill me and my friends the moment I do?"

Anka pursed her lips. "Okay, I'm willing to negotiate. If you give me your blood, with a promise to leave and never come back, I will let you and your pathetic companions go free."

"Don't do it, Lindy," Garon said.

I rounded on him. "You want her to kill Maggie?" My head spun. Circling. Trying to see a way out.

But there was none.

Belina and Yelena were bleeding. Maggie was unconscious. Garon had his hands full with Tanner. And Anka was millimeters away from slitting Maggie's throat. There was nothing left to do.

Except, maybe if I could get a little closer…

I tightened my fingers around the Pearl still in my hand and said, "I accept your offer."

Anka's face split into a grin. "There, now, smart girl."

Anka let go of Maggie, letting her slump to the

ground. "Come here, little Queen. Slowly, now."

I stepped forward.

"Wait," Anka commanded, her eyes narrowing. "The Pearl. You've still got it."

My blood went cold.

"Put it down," she said. "Right there on the floor beside you."

No, I couldn't put it down. If I did, how would I get the two stones together?

Anka turned the knife back to Maggie. "I can still kill her."

I sank to the ground, my body suddenly weighing a thousand pounds. My hand opened and I set the Pearl on the floor, even as my head screamed at me to find another way.

But I couldn't see one.

"Now, roll it away," Anka commanded.

I did. Then I rose. I lifted my chin and stared at Anka, my expression set in stone.

Anka smiled, still holding the knife to Maggie's throat. "That is good. Now come here."

I had no choice. I couldn't just let her kill Maggie. My feet felt like marble as they shuffled forward, closing the distance between us.

Once I was within reach, Anka pointed her knife at me. "On your knees." She set the Topaz on the floor between us.

The Topaz was right there. So close.

If only I still had the Pearl. I searched for it, moving only my eyes. But I couldn't see where it had gone after I'd rolled it away.

Anka pressed her knife into the soft part of my inner arm.

I hissed as the tip seared into my flesh. Anka pressed

harder, shooting pain up and down my arm. My blood flowed.

Anka's claw-like fingers dug into my arm as she twisted it into position over the Topaz. She began chanting, the words sounding garbled and wrong. Like a language that should never be uttered.

Suddenly, I felt icy cold. I started to shiver.

And something nudged my thigh.

The pain seemed to be seeping into my brain like a thick fog. It was hard to think. But I looked down to see what had touched me.

I blinked.

It was the Pearl.

My blood ran down my arm.

The Topaz sat below, ready and waiting.

Through the fog, I registered Belina, on her hands and knees, with a trail of blood stretched out behind her. She must have crawled to wherever the Pearl had ended up and rolled it back to me, realizing I needed it for whatever I had planned.

My free hand shot out. I grabbed the Pearl just as the first drop of blood spilled over the edge of my arm.

"You can have my blood," I said to Anka through gritted teeth. "But you cannot have my crown."

In a single movement, I cupped my free hand, with the Pearl inside, over the Topaz. The two gems sank into each other, and the Pearl and the Topaz became one.

Like two water droplets coming together. Just like in Maggie's visions.

I snatched the joined gems off the floor before my blood could penetrate the surface. An explosion of color occurred as the Pearl's pure white broke into a spectrum of colors inside the Topaz.

Anka shrieked. "What have you done?" Her eyes were

thunderous. Gray, like storm clouds on a rainy day. And just as turbulent.

Tanner stopped fighting and sat like a shell, staring off into space.

I twisted my bloody arm free of her, scrambled to my feet, and ran to Garon.

"You horrible, rotten girl," Anka said, jumping up and running after me. "You've ruined everything."

"Garon, change it back!" I yelled.

I reached him, handed him the gemstone, and whirled to face Anka, who was charging toward us with her knife raised. I grabbed someone's sword form the ground and met Anka while Garon bent his head over the gems. His eyelids fluttered.

Anka screamed and lunged at me.

I swung my sword, trying to knock the knife out of her hands. But I missed, catching only air. Anka swung her knife at my stomach. I jumped back, arching away from her. She lunged, trying to stab me in the gut. Then the arm. Then the leg.

Still, Garon worked on the gem.

Why was it taking so long?

Garon muttered something about the molecular structure being different, then tried again.

Anka swiped and caught me in the forearm. Her blade burned as it sliced into my skin. I yelped and swung with my sword, finally knocking the knife out of her hand. It clattered to the floor.

The room went deathly still.

Garon opened his eyes and looked up. He uncurled his fingers to reveal a hardened gemstone sitting in his palm.

As we watched, all the colors bled from the stone, leaving it gray and empty. Then, like a puff of smoke, it disappeared.

The Pearl around Belina's neck did the same.

For a single heartbeat, no one moved. Silence reigned.

Then, like a thunderbolt, a shock wave rocked the castle, knocking me to my feet. Maggie groaned and rolled over. Belina cried out in pain. Tanner swayed.

But the gemstones were gone.

My lungs expanded, and a lightness filled my entire body.

Tanner shook his head, like he was shaking off a fog, then his eyes widened as he took in the scene. "Oh, no, did she get me? What did she make me do?"

Garon helped him up.

And then Anka screamed.

And screamed.

And … starting shrinking.

I rocked back on my heels. "What's happening?"

Garon's eyes were tight. "The Pearl is restoring what was lost."

Anka screamed like her skin was on fire. And she kept shrinking, like a horrifyingly real version of the Wicked Witch of the West after they throw water on her. Anka was going to shrink right into the floor, leaving only a steaming pile of clothes crumpled on the ground.

But she stopped two-thirds of the way there, huddled in a ball and shaking.

Hesitantly, I picked my way toward the shaking form. "Are you all right?"

The form moved, then a little head appeared—that of a child. She turned her face up to me and I stepped back in shock. Wide, youthful eyes searched mine. A face full of delicate features, flawless skin, and thick, auburn hair. Sitting before me, huddled on the floor under clothing now much too big for her, sat a child. Maybe four years old, if that.

Was this Anka?

The child's chin trembled as she took in her surroundings. "Where am I?"

It took me a moment to find my voice. "You're in the castle."

Her eyes went wide. "Where's my mum?"

I looked away, then forced myself to look her in the eyes. They were stormy gray, just like the thunderclouds I'd seen in Anka's eyes before. "What's your name, child?"

"Ankalette." Her gaze darted between my face and the others in the room.

All eyes were trained on her.

"Where's my mum?" Her lower lip trembled.

Anka's parents were probably still dead—killed in the fire that had scarred her all those years ago. I doubted even Oliver's magic could bring them back from that.

What was the most gentle thing I could do right now? This was no longer Anka the villain. This was an innocent child, all traces of the villain—and what had made her one—gone.

The Pearl had restored to her what was lost—her childhood. Her innocence.

I put a hand on her shoulder. "There was an accident. Your mother is gone. But you are safe now."

The child clearly had no memory of what had just transpired. She'd been wiped clean. Taken back to a time before she'd been broken and maimed.

A commotion in the hallway outside the nursery stole my attention. I looked up just as Trevin, Duke Christoph, and several men entered the room. The Duke's eyes went impossibly wide as he took in the scene. "Tend to the wounded," he said to his soldiers.

Trevin ran to me. "We came as soon as we could. Are

you okay? What happened?"

I looked at Ankalette. Trevin followed my gaze and did a double take.

Ankalette looked from me, to Garon, and to the soldiers who'd just entered the room. Her gaze fell on the upturned cradle, where a doll had fallen to the floor and now lay with her limbs at awkward angles.

Then the child broke down in tears, wailing for her lost mother.

I kneeled by her side, trying to comfort her. But inside I was crying for my own lost mother, for my broken kingdom, and for all the death and heartache that this child had caused.

Chapter Forty

Letting Go

Maggie

1623—Valstenia

Three days after the whole gem-destroying thing in the nursery, Lindy and I stood together in one of the castle turrets, overlooking her kingdom. On one side, the terrain was green for miles. On the other, the sea sparkled below.

Lindy was filling in the gaps for me of what had happened, since I hadn't been allowed in the meeting where all the important people discussed everything.

They'd discussed the matter of Tanner and me heading home.

And whether Garon should go with us or not.

I really wanted her to start there, but also, I didn't. She started from the beginning, and I let her.

"After taking my siblings north," Lindy said, "Yelena went to King Jershon of Trellboro for help. They came with an army and joined the fight just after our own forces breached the front gate. But she'd traveled ahead of them, and Anka's men found her in the woods outside the castle. That's how Anka captured her."

"So is blood magic really a thing, then? If Anka had succeeded in getting Yelena's blood into the Topaz, would it really have been the end?"

Lindy nodded. "It appears so, yes. Anka spoke of a blood map, which is really just DNA. Once the DNA bonds to the molecules inside the gem, the spell can't be undone."

"So, the missing diary pages described how to do it?"

"Yes. The research was from years and years ago, back when Oliver had just learned how to alter gemstones. He used blood magic when he created the Emerald, but he was apparently unaware that its use required a price."

"So, how did he find out?"

"I can't be sure, but I found two references in his journals to someone called Sonya. One was a love poem. Then, later, after he swore off blood magic, he mentioned his sorrow at letting her down. Belina said the price for using blood magic would be something big—like knowledge, sanity, or health. But what if using blood magic actually cost him his capacity for romantic love? That would explain why he didn't seem fazed by the Topaz. And that must have been when he decided the price was too great for using blood magic."

"Yikes," I breathed. But my mind had just spun off in another direction. At the word *love*.

Lindy continued. "Garon and Belina never knew about the blood magic, but everything was still there in Oliver's journals. Anka must have gone back to his hideout and found it after she captured Belina."

Love. Did I dare mention the rumor I'd heard about Lindy and a certain someone? I almost did. But instead I said, "What's going to happen to little Anka?"

"Borov is going to take her. He always wanted a daughter."

"He's the guard who turned on you at the cottage, right? Trevin's dad?"

Lindy frowned. "He's been heartbroken ever since his wife died. It wasn't his fault."

"I know." I turned my face up to the sun. I didn't

know what was going to happen between me and Garon—how we could possibly make our love work—but the warmth of the sun on my face almost made me believe everything was going to be okay. Almost.

"Has Belina left yet?" Lindy asked.

I nodded. "This morning. She seemed in good spirits, even without the Pearl. And she hasn't felt any differently since it was destroyed. She still seems healthy and everything." I glanced sideways at Lindy, unable to hold my tongue any longer. "So. You and Trevin, huh?"

Lindy's face flushed. "You heard about that?"

"For such a big castle, news travels surprisingly fast."

"It was just a kiss."

"A kiss that rocked you to the core." I poked her in the side. "Come on, admit it. You've been grinning for days."

She blushed harder. "All right, fine. It was more than just a kiss. It was life-defining. Trevin is everything I never knew I wanted, and everything I never thought to look for."

"So, who made the first move?"

A tiny smile tugged at the corners of her mouth. "It was after one of the council meetings. Trevin and I were walking alone—I was flirting with him, I'll admit—and suddenly he pulled me into an alcove and kissed me. It was so unexpected but also so completely right, you know?" She sighed, wrapping her arms around herself. "After that, whenever there was a moment to steal, we took it. We kissed in the armory, behind the tapestry in the throne room, and on the staircase in the north tower heading to the roof. And, um, again on the roof." Her smile deepened. "That was a good one."

I melted inside—thrilled for this friend of mine who deserved happiness maybe more than anyone I knew. But also sad for myself and the uncertainty of my own situation. Would Garon stay here or would he come back with me? And which one did I want him to choose?

I made my voice teasing. "And now you're going to live happily ever after with Trevin, in your giant castle by the sparkly blue sea."

Lindy grinned. "Well. I hope so. But first I have to work on some policy changes."

I laughed. "Good for you. Hey, did you figure out what to do about the kingdom's finances?"

"As a matter of fact, I do have an idea about that. See, the reason Qadar wanted to marry me was so he could have access to our beaches. Our trade routes. But what if, instead of giving away that asset, I open Valstenia's beaches and charge other countries to access them? Our location on the coast is our greatest asset—why not monetize it?"

"That's a great idea!"

Lindy grinned. "There are still a lot of details we need to figure out, but I think it could work. Ooh, and Marsala agreed to be an ambassador between Valstenia and Trellboro."

I laughed. "I can't believe you didn't freak out when you saw him. You really trust him?"

"He's different now. And everyone deserves a second chance, right?"

"I guess so."

"My mother believed in second chances." Lindy gazed out at the sea, her fingers clasped together in front of her. "I'm going to pick up the pieces of my broken kingdom and build something great. In her honor." She paused. "I'm glad I got to see you again, if only for a little while."

My stomach clenched. This was it—my moment of

truth. I couldn't put it off any longer. "What did the council decide about Garon?" I held my breath.

She spoke slowly. "Everyone has a different opinion, of course. But ultimately, we decided that the decision lies with him. He needs to decide whether he'll stay or go back. And I can tell he's really struggling with it."

"You want him to stay here." I let it sit, then said, "Don't you?"

"Of course I do. He's my brother. But I also want him to be happy. Back in the nursery, when Anka was trying to control him, he didn't even flinch. It's like he was untouchable. You know what that means, right?"

"That he loves me?"

Lindy nodded.

I said the thought I'd been thinking ever since he'd come back the first time. The thought that had been buried deep inside me but that I'd been too scared to put into actual words. "Sometimes loving someone is not enough." The statement hung between us, filling up the silence.

Then I added, "What if there's something Garon is meant to do—here, in the time he was born in—that he won't be able to do if he comes back with me? I can't take him away from that."

Lindy frowned. "You should go talk to him."

I swallowed the lump that had formed in my throat. I didn't have to talk to him to know what the right thing to do was. Garon belonged here, in the past. In *my* past. It wasn't right of me to let him give up his destiny. I had to let him go.

I fidgeted, tugging a thread loose from my sleeve. "He belongs here. He should stay." The words were out of my mouth before I could take them back.

And then, I didn't want to take them back. As painful

as it would be to say goodbye to him, I knew it would be okay. *I* would be okay.

****

Garon and I went for a walk and found a fallen log to sit on in the woods beyond the castle walls. It reminded me of the place we'd sat, behind my school, when he came back after we'd destroyed the Emerald.

He held both of my hands in his. "Maggie, I've decided to come back with you. To live in the future. I choose you."

My heart trembled. My body ached. I couldn't believe what I was about to say. My eyes were wet before I'd even started speaking. "Garon, you can't." I squeezed his hands, choking down a sob. "This is where you belong. You have a place here—a path. Your destiny is here. I can't take you away from that."

Garon's expression went slack, like he's just been slapped. "How do you know my destiny is here? Whoever said that?"

"You were born here. Fate doesn't make mistakes. You and I were never meant to be together."

He gripped my hands tighter, almost fiercely. "But we *were* meant to meet. You can't deny that. And why would Fate arrange that only to rip us apart later?"

"I don't know." I bit my lip. I did feel like my time with him had changed me. And for the better. I was stronger and more confident than I'd ever been. "Maybe we were meant to meet. Meant to change each other, even. But now—"

My throat threatened to close up. I swallowed, put a hand on his arm, and continued. "But now, I feel like it's time to say goodbye." I looked into his eyes. "And I think, deep down, you know it, too."

Part of me was hoping he'd disagree. Or try to prove I

was wrong. Or ask me to stay here even though my mom was waiting for me in the future. Or something.

But his expression slowly crumpled. "I know." His eyes shone with emotion. He reached for my hands, and held them between his own. "I'm not sorry for coming back for you. I'd do it again, and I wouldn't change one single thing about the months we spent together. But I am sorry for the pain. I wish I could somehow erase it."

"I don't. The pain means we had something good. Something worth having. I'd do it again, too."

We sat there, on a log in the forest. Not speaking. Not moving. Just being together. For as long as we could.

And the moments ticked painfully on.

****

Lindy, Trevin, and even Yelena came to see us off. Trevin stood closer to Lindy than I'd seen him stand before. And Lindy's cheeks flushed when he put a hand on the small of her back.

I gave Lindy a hug. "I'll never forget you."

"Neither will I," she said. "You have been a true friend. Good luck, Maggie. I wish you every happiness in the world."

Garon led us back to the tree, by the cabin in the woods, where we'd arrived. We went forward in time, cracking back into existence into what was hopefully now rightly called Sweden.

Tanner said, "Garon, I'll miss you, man," and gave him one of those half hugs that guys do. He started walking toward the house. "I'll let you two say goodbye."

My body felt like lead. My breath came in short, icy gasps.

Garon wrapped his arms around me. He held on for a long time.

And I held on back.

I breathed him in, committing his rugged scent, his thick hair, the feel of his body beside mine, everything, to memory. I never wanted to forget what this felt like.

Garon was my first love, and no amount of time could ever change that.

I couldn't tell how long we stood like that, savoring our final moments together.

And then he pulled away and kissed me. One final, soul-wrenching kiss. "Goodbye, Maggie," he whispered in my ear, his breath hot on my skin.

And then he backed away. Put a hand on the tree.

He was gone before I could call him back. Before I could scream out that we were making the biggest mistake of our lives.

A single tear rolled down my cheek. And then another. And another.

My heart crumpled up and I swear I actually heard it crying out in pain.

So this is what it felt like. To have a breaking heart.

I let the pain wash over me. And fill me up. I committed it to memory. Then I tucked it away as a gentle reminder of the good times we'd had.

I wiped my eyes. Took a few deep breaths.

And a few breaths more.

I swiped a hand across my face.

Then I went to find Tanner. He was waiting for me by the front gate, kicking a rock around.

He put an arm around my shoulder, silently offering comfort, as we walked together toward our grandmother's house.

My eyes felt puffy.

But I needed to pay attention. This was it. The test. Had we managed to change anything? Would our mother be better or had it all been for nothing?

We approached the house. Dantzel was sitting on the front porch, sipping a cup of lemonade. Her expression was stern, as it had been when we'd first met her.

My heart sank. If Mom was better, shouldn't our grandma be happier?

And then the front door banged open and our mother stepped through. She wore a blue and white polka-dot dress and red heels. She had an apron on. Her eyes were clear, intelligent, able.

Hope fluttered to life inside me. "Mom?"

My mom smiled. "Did you two have a nice walk?"

I looked at Tanner, whose mouth had dropped open.

"Close your mouth, darling, you look like a goldfish," Mom said. She stood on the top step of the porch—waiting, it seemed, for us to come inside. "Maggie, what's wrong? Did you get something stuck in your eye?"

My feet were frozen to the ground. It was her. It was really her. My mother, not only alive, but *well*. Healthy. Not crazy.

Mom laughed. "That walk must have really worn you two out. Where did you go that you don't even have the energy to climb a few stairs?"

She came to us, grabbed us both by the arms, and made a show of pulling us inside. Her heels clacked on the wooden steps. "Go and wash up, Yvette made crab cakes for dinner." She glanced at Dantzel. "You too, Mom. Come inside, you hate cold crab cakes."

She turned back to us. "I wish your father were here—he loves crab cakes."

"Wait, where's Dad?" Tanner said, a note of panic in his voice.

Her brow furrowed. "He had to stay home, remember?

Important business meetings. But he loves Yvette's crab cakes—they're the same ones she made the night he met my parents."

I felt my mouth drop open.

Mom put a hand to my forehead. "Are you feeling okay?"

I found my voice. "Yeah. Yeah, I'm okay." Then I threw my arms around her and squeezed hard. Tanner joined me, folding us both into a bear hug.

Mom laughed. "I usually have to beg and beg for hugs from you, and now that I'm covered in pie crust you both decide to attack me?"

I pulled away. "Sorry, Mom. We're just … happy to see you." I glanced sideways at Tanner, who wore a goofy grin.

"Yeah." His grin widened. "What she said."

"Okay, well, if you're sure you're feeling all right, I'll just go finish up the pies." She glanced at Dantzel. "Mom, come inside, you'll catch a chill."

Dantzel—Grandma—sat on a rocker on the porch. I approached, hesitantly. "Hi, Grandma." Then, just to see if she'd give any hint of remembering, I said, "We're back."

"Oh, good. Just in time for dinner. How was your walk?"

I glanced at Tanner and said in a low voice, "I think after dinner we need to look through Mom's scrapbooks."

It seemed that we'd missed some very important years.

But, I sensed, we had some very good ones ahead of us.

Epilogue

Maggie

Present Day—Virginia
First day of Junior Year

School was buzzing with the news of a new breakthrough in Spatial Relocation Technology. Everyone called it SRT, but really, at its core, it was teleportation. I couldn't figure out why they didn't just call it that. Over the summer, some science journal had published an article that had apparently been decades in the making, and today a follow-up article had been published, stating that the mainstream use of SRT was expected to occur sometime in the next five years.

Spatial relocation research had apparently been a big thing for a while now, and everybody had heard of it.

Except for Tanner and me.

And it wasn't because we hadn't been paying attention or had been out of the loop. It was because SRT hadn't been a thing before we'd jumped through time. Our little jaunt to the past seemed to have caused some big changes.

SRT was the biggest one.

But not the best.

The best change was the fact that we had our mom back. Our home—which no longer had peeling paint or faded curtains or carpet that belonged in 1973—now contained mountains of scrapbooks that offered all the proof we'd ever need that destroying the Pearl had changed things for good. There were pictures of us with Mom throughout our whole life. Birthdays, holidays, school events. She was there for all of them. And our Swedish Grandparents, Dantzel and Roan, were even in some of them.

The worst change, of course, was the fact that Garon was no longer in my life.

But I'd done some stalking-slash-research on Valstenia and the boy who would always would be my first love. And I'd learned one very important thing: the father of the SRT movement—the man who'd come up with the very earliest theories that were at SRT's core—had been a Valstenian prince.

Named Sir Garon von Thurne.

My Garon.

He'd freaking invented teleportation. At least, the earliest, crudest theories and drawings which had led to its invention, had been his.

And, if I remembered correctly, teleportation had been my idea. I'd suggested it to him while we were hiking to the beach to find Belina.

Once the teleportation technology went mainstream, it would completely revolutionize everything. With the ability to teleport, or spatially relocate, or whatever, no one would need cars. Or airplanes. Or trains. There'd be no more rush hour traffic. No more wasted time running from one place to the next.

SRT was expected to change the world in unprecedented ways.

And leaving Garon in the past had clearly done that. I couldn't believe I'd almost let him come back with me—he'd obviously been meant for so much more.

But now, even months later, the pain of losing him was still there. Not as raw as it had been. But still there.

I learned that after Garon died, someone called Anton Meijer picked up his research. And then a man named

Gustov Freidman. And after that, Carlyle Nessinger. From there, SRT became a movement, drawing more and more attention and more and more brilliant minds.

The warning bell jolted me from my thoughts. All around me lockers banged shut, and kids hurried to their classrooms. I had AP Physics first. Starting the day off with a bang this year.

Piper and Kate had saved me a seat, and I slid into it just before the late bell.

"I am totally going to fail this class," Piper said. "I can't believe you guys made me take it with you."

"You're going to be fine," Kate said. "This is better than taking regular Physics with all the slackers."

Piper scowled. "I would have fit right in."

The teacher started class by showing us the video clip that had been all over social media this morning: the SRT breakthrough announcement. When it finished, he said, "Does anyone know the name of the theorem at the heart of these advancements?"

A hand shot up. It belonged to a guy sitting near the front of the room. A guy I'd never seen before. But, even from behind, he seemed sort of familiar.

"Who is that?" I whispered to Piper.

She frowned. "You mean Grant?" She pointed to the guy with his hand up.

"Yeah, is he new?"

She squinted at me. "Umm, are you okay? We've known Grant since, like, third grade."

I froze, racking my brain, trying to figure out if I'd just forgotten this mystery boy or if this was another change courtesy of my romp through time.

Kate leaned over. "Remember our epic spy-by fail that ended in a marshmallow war with a group of boys?"

My mouth dropped open. Nope, I definitely did not

remember that.

Kate continued, "That was at his house."

Yikes. Okay, there were apparently some more changes I needed to get caught up on.

The teacher called on Grant and he answered a question which I no longer remembered. "The theory of spatial awareness and time-space relativity."

A chill crept across my skin.

Because his voice seemed so familiar. Almost like ... almost like...

No. It couldn't be.

Garon had stayed where he belonged this time, and because of it, teleportation was an actual real thing. That couldn't be him sitting there in the front of class.

Could it?

I willed him to turn around. My leg bounced under my desk chair as I stared a hole into the back of his head. Grant's hair was a little different than Garon's. Less curly. A lighter brown. But about the same length. And just as mussy.

Turn around, turn around, turn around.

But he didn't. And I didn't hear a single word the rest of class.

As soon as the bell rang, I jumped out of my seat and practically ran to the front of class, tripping over someone's backpack strap and nearly face-planting into the nearest desk.

I caught myself. Looked up into Grant's face.

And...

It wasn't Garon.

My heart went cold and I immediately felt like an idiot.

Of course it wasn't Garon.

"Are you okay?" Grant said, his forehead wrinkling in

concern.

My face warmed. "Yeah."

Part of me wanted to run away. Kick myself in the pants for even allowing myself to think this might be my Garon.

But ... I was curious, too. This guy was obviously here because of something I'd changed in the past. Why?

"How did you know that stuff?" I said. "About Garon von Thurne's theory?"

His face lit up and an easy smile appeared.

Again, it seemed so familiar.

"I just love his work," he said. "I've been following the spatial relocation research for something like ten years now, ever since I saw a display in a science museum when I was a kid. I got really into it, and traced the research back to its founders." He paused, looking at me with new interest. "You must be a die-hard fan, too, if you know von Thurne's work."

A die-hard. "Yeah, you could say that."

Piper and Kate came over, carrying my book bag, which I'd left on the floor by my desk.

"Maggie, you coming?" Kate said.

I took the bag from her. "I'll catch up."

She gave me a weird look, then shrugged, and the two of them left the room.

I looked at Grant. He wasn't Garon. But his warm brown eyes held the same tenderness. His face held the same excitement I'd seen so many times on Garon.

"Your name is Maggie?" he said.

"Yeah."

"I've always liked that name. Did you know that one of von Thurne's earliest drawings was labeled *Maggie's ride*?"

I gaped at him. "Seriously?"

"Yeah." He pulled out his phone and started typing something into the search box. A moment later he held it out so I could see the screen. "There's a copy of that on display in the SRT wing of Chicago's science museum."

I peered at the screen. On it was a drawing—no, a diagram—with a labyrinth of overlapping circles and lines. Calculations were scribbled off to one side, and at the bottom were scrawled the words *Maggie's ride.*

All the air left me in a whoosh.

"Cool, huh?" Grant ran a hand through his hair.

Just like Garon used to do.

I looked at him. Seriously, who *was* this guy?

Students started filing in for the next class.

"I guess we should leave, huh?" he said.

"Yeah." I swallowed. "I'm headed to English. How about you?"

"Trig," he said. "They're the same way—want to walk together?"

"Sure."

We left the room. As we were walking down the hall, Grant said, "Do you think great minds come back?"

I froze, my heart stuttering to a halt. Again. I looked at him. "What did you just say?"

He repeated the question, even though I'd heard him the first time. "Do you think great minds come back?"

"What do you mean?" I asked warily, suddenly feeling like gravity was shifting around me.

"I mean, I've always wondered if great minds come back over and over until they get it right. Take the evolution of physics, for example. There was Galileo, Newton, Dalton, and Planck, each alive during a different century. And over a thousand years before any of them, there was Archimedes. What if they were all the same person— Archimedes—just coming back over and over to finish what he started?"

I'd gone weak at the knees. Because I'd had this conversation before. Leaning against a tree under a starlit sky sometime in the 1600s. This couldn't be a coincidence. My voice was soft as I said, "You mean like reincarnation?"

He grinned. "Exactly!"

I spoke slowly. "So you believe that, when a person dies, he or she comes back again as another person?" My throat had gone impossibly dry. I swallowed, the air scraping me on its way down.

"Well, why not?"

I didn't have a good answer for that, or for whether reincarnation was a real thing or not. But I did want to know what he thought about... "So, when that happens, does the person keep all their memories from their past lives?"

He laughed. "Of course not. Do *you* remember all your past lives?"

"Oh, so now you think *I've* had past lives?"

"Again, why not? Maybe you were a medieval warrior princess. Maybe you got into swordfights for fun."

"And I suppose you were the father of SRT?" I challenged.

Grant pushed a hand through his hair. "Man, wouldn't that be cool?"

"Have you ever thought about time travel?" I said. "Like how one would do it?"

Grant shook his head. "Time travel's impossible. That one's a no brainer."

A slow smile crept across my face. "Yeah, I guess it probably is."

Deep inside me, my heart began to thaw. And the pain of losing Garon washed away. Because he was here, right beside me, right now. This was him, I was sure of it. This boy so impassioned and lighthearted and kind. I saw it in his eyes, and in the way he carried himself. I heard it in his words.

The universe had brought us together again, in its own unpredictable, complex way, giving us a second chance.

Grant might not remember our history, but that was okay.

Because I remembered.

And that was enough.

The End

TERESA RICHARDS

Evernight Teen ®

www.evernightteen.com

CPSIA information can be obtained
at www.ICGtesting.com
Printed in the USA
LVOW07s0755241117
557396LV00001B/28/P